# FORBIDDEN FLING WITH THE PRINCESS

AMY ANDREWS

# ONE NIGHT TO ROYAL BABY

JC HARROWAY

MILLS & BOON

First published in Great Britain 2025
by Mills & Boon, an imprint of HarperCollins*Publishers* Ltd,
1 London Bridge Street, London, SE1 9GF

www.harpercollins.co.uk

HarperCollins*Publishers* Macken House, 39/40 Mayor Street Upper,
Dublin 1, D01 C9W8, Ireland

ISBN: 978-0-263-32514-0

08/25

This book contains FSC™ certified paper
and other controlled sources to ensure responsible forest management.

For more information visit www.harpercollins.co.uk/green.

Printed and Bound in the UK using 100% Renewable Electricity
at CPI Group (UK) Ltd, Croydon, CR0 4YY

# FORBIDDEN FLING WITH THE PRINCESS

## AMY ANDREWS

MILLS & BOON

To Clare and Jo. It's been an absolute blast spending time in a fictitious Mediterranean kingdom with you both. Let's do it for real, some time!

# CHAPTER ONE

FOR THE FIRST time in five years, Edmund Butler had nowhere to go and nothing to do. No pager to rule his life. And he was making the most of it on a Seychelles beach where the sun was hot and the beers were cold. There was peace. Serenity. Sand so white it hurt his eyes. Water so clear it could have come from an ancient Scottish burn.

He needed this. He *really* needed this.

As he reached for his second of the four beer bottles in the bucket, he became aware of the distant thump of rotor blades but he paid them no heed. Joy flights ran regularly across the various islands of the archipelago.

Cracking the top, Ed took three long swallows then pulled the lever on his deckchair until he was fully reclined. The chair had been conveniently placed on the sand beneath the fronds of a gently swaying palm on a deserted stretch of beach, although given the tiny exclusive island only ever hosted two dozen people, everywhere was pretty much deserted.

Shutting his eyes behind his Polaroid sunglasses, he let out a deep, contented exhale and tuned into the gentle swish of the tide as it lapped at the beach. The steady *thump, thump, thump* got louder however, obliterating the mellow ebb and flow of the ocean and Ed briefly considered stripping off his board shorts and giving the occupants a real show. He didn't, but it made him smile as he waited lazily for the chopper to *buzz* off.

Unfortunately, it did not.

It got so loud he actually raised his head to discover it was coming in to land on the spit of sand at the far end of the beach. Intrigued, he levered himself upright and idly watched as the surface of the water rippled violently beneath the downwash. There was a glossiness to the chopper that reeked of wealth with its sleek indigo fuselage, dark tinted windows and no identifying logos. It certainly wasn't like any of the commercial ones he'd seen doing scenic flights the past few days.

Maybe it was a private hire? A celebrity?

Moments later, the skids kissed terra firma, kicking up a cloud of white sand. The engine cut immediately, reducing the powdery veil and the level of noise, but the whine of the rotors as they slowed still reached him on the breeze.

With the blades not yet come to a standstill, the side door suddenly opened. Out stepped a brawny guy in dark fatigues. He had a military-style haircut, aviator sunglasses, black boots and an equally black gun holstered at his hip.

Private security? Yep, probably a celebrity.

The guy turned and offered his hand to a second occupant who took it as *she* exited barefoot, in a flurry of honey-brown curls and liquid silver fabric whipped around from the rotor draught. Ed caught a glimpse of bare bronzed arms as the woman lifted one hand to her hair and the other to her skirt that was threatening to go full Marilyn as she was ushered out from under the blades. The fluttery fabric, which seemed as though it would be more at home on a Parisian catwalk than on a beach, was perilously close to taking off.

Finally, as the couple moved far enough from the chopper, the mystery woman shook her head, her hair bouncing back into place to reveal her face. She was very *movie star* in a pair of large, impossibly cool sunglasses, her lips popping in a vibrant shade of red, her mouth as full and lush as the curves beneath the silvery silk that dazzled like tin foil in the sunshine.

The high halter neckline of her dress exposed her shoulders and clung to her full breasts. Belted loosely at the waist, the generous fabric in the skirt moved like liquid metal in the light tropical breeze, outlining the generous proportions of her hips and thighs and fluttering behind her like the tail of a kite.

Statuesque with a coppery complexion, everything about her screamed *celebrity*. Not that she was familiar to Ed, but that didn't mean much given he wasn't one for gossip magazines or tabloid dross. She certainly moved in that way that people with means and money always moved, like recognition was not only expected but foregone.

Ed took another sip of his beer as she was escorted, he assumed, to the resort reception, which meant she'd have to pass by his chair. With her armed protection by her side, it was quite the show but, whoever she was, she'd probably come here to *not* be ogled by strangers. The resort was the ultimate in discreet relaxation and he wasn't about to spoil that vibe so he lowered the back of the chair again, stretched his legs out and shut his eyes.

The last thing he expected was for her to approach him. 'Ah-*hem*.'

Ed's eyes flicked open in surprise to find the woman and her security guard looking down on him. Well, *she* was looking down at him, the guy in black was standing at a discreet distance scanning the nearby tree line and ocean as if he was expecting an imminent attack. Their approach had been ninja-like.

The sand, he supposed.

She was even more gorgeous up close, her smooth caramel complexion unblemished, her red lips screaming *look at me*, curves somehow more tempting stationary than when they'd been moving.

Or maybe that was just because they were in easier reach.

'I'm sorry to interrupt your relaxation,' she apologised, a slight accent to her polished English, 'but you are Edmund Butler, yes? Dr Edmund Butler?'

Ed was pleased that his sunglasses hid his surprise. There were parts of this world where he was very well known. Considered a rock star, even, his services in high demand. But not here on this island in the middle of the Indian Ocean where he was just Ed from London.

'Yes,' he confirmed warily as he reached for the handle of his deckchair and levered himself upright, placing his half consumed beer bottle in the bucket of ice.

The action caused her to straighten and take a step back. 'Perfect.' She nodded, relieved, and held out her hand. 'My name is Princess Xiomara de la Rosa of Castilona and I need your help.'

Ed's surprise morphed to suspicion. Ignoring her hand, he looked to the left and right, wondering where the cameras might be, because surely, he was being pranked right now? He was involved in a longstanding game of *gotcha* with a bunch of his old med school buddies. It had been growing more elaborate over the years as their pay cheques had expanded but this was next level.

A *princess* of some place he'd never heard of, and therefore probably didn't exist, had landed in a helicopter asking for *his help*? Like Princess goddamn Leia?

'Okay, funny.' He nodded and let out a fake *ha-ha* laugh. 'Did Julian send you?' Dr Julian Bosworth was a grown-ass endocrinologist at the cutting edge of pancreatic research but still acted like he was on freshers' week at Cambridge.

He was also a massive *Star Wars* fan.

She gave a somewhat pained smile as her hand dropped. 'I'm sorry, I don't know any Julian and I understand this is unusual—'

'It's Thacks, isn't it?' Ed interrupted, pulling off his glasses, staring at the tree line behind him now with even more scrutiny than the guy in fatigues. 'You can come out Thacker, joke's over.'

Harry Thacker had perhaps been the smartest of the lot of them, choosing to go into dermatology, where there was no on-call and no weekends and no shortage of people willing to pay boatloads of money to keep their skin looking young. And he had a garage full of fancy motor vehicles to prove it. He'd been hatching something ever since Ed had set up that fake email about his brand-new high-end imported sports car being lost overboard somewhere in the English Channel.

'I can assure you, Dr Butler, this is no joke and I am who I say I am.'

She turned to her bodyguard and spoke to him in what sounded like Spanish. He stepped forward, delving into the left pocket of his shirt, extracting what looked like a passport, and handed it to her before returning to his previous position. She held it out to Ed who, bemused, accepted it, noting immediately the bold gold letters pronouncing it to be a *Diplomatic Passport*.

Okay, it looked *real*, but in this day and age this kind of thing could be easily faked to be realistic enough for someone who wasn't trained in forgery detection. Xiomara Maria Fernanda de la Rosa—*sheesh*, what a mouthful. His gaze was drawn to the photograph, which was her but also wasn't. Her curls were pulled ruthlessly back into a sleek topknot with not one hair out of place, the neckline of her shirt hugged her throat and her lipstick was a demure shade of pink.

And then there was her hundred-yard stare peeping out from those green eyes that seemed very poised and *regal* and maybe even a little sad.

'Nice try,' he said, handing it back. 'But I set up an entire fake website and account for a car company in two hours. I'm not that gullible.'

Her red mouth tightening, she too removed her sunglasses to reveal barely concealed impatience glowing in the golden flecks of her green eyes. 'Why don't you Google me?' she suggested with an imperial air that was painstakingly polite, leaving Ed in little doubt that even suggesting it was beneath her. She folded her arms. 'I'll wait.'

Ed blinked. Whoever this woman was, she was a very good actress. Thacks had done well.

Realising this wasn't going to be over until he did so, Ed grabbed his phone that was sitting on the tray next to his bucket of beer and Googled *the Princess*. The first image in the search was an official portrait of the royal house of de la Rosa with the woman standing in front of him staring, poised and elegant—a *tiara* on her head—at the camera. The caption beneath informed him it was from earlier in the year at the coronation of King Octavio of Castilona, which was apparently a small island kingdom off the coast of Spain.

There were pages and pages of images. Some formal— perfect royal smile outlined in varying shades of pink as she performed some duty or other. Some clearly taken by paparazzi—gritty, grainy, distant. *Waaay* less formal, including one in an electric-blue one-piece, standing ankle-deep in an ocean somewhere, her hair a mass of careless waves springing around her head.

All of them proved that she was indeed who she said she was.

Ed glanced up from his phone to find her passively waiting his response. 'Okay.' He tossed his phone on the recliner. 'You're a princess. Apologies.'

Xiomara waved her hand dismissively in a way he assumed she waved to crowds from her gold-encrusted horse-drawn coach. 'It's fine. Shall we start again? My name is Xiomara de la Rosa. I'm very pleased to make your acquaintance, Dr Butler.'

She presented her hand again, not in a *let's shake* way but in a very *papal* here-is-my-ring way. Ed sure as hell hoped she didn't expect him to kiss it. He wasn't opposed to kissing this stunning woman, but her hand would not be the first choice of where to put his lips.

Swinging his legs around, he pushed into a standing position, which saw the guy behind her tense, his hand automatically hovering over his holstered weapon. Ignoring him as much as it was possible to ignore a clearly ex-military guy *and a princess* on a beach in the Seychelles, he encased her hand in his, giving it a brisk shake before withdrawing. The guard relaxed his stance and went back to surveilling the surroundings.

'I'm sorry, have we met before?'

Ed had met a lot of people throughout his career, both in the UK and around the world. He'd even met royalty. But he was pretty sure he'd have remembered a European princess and, in particular, *her*. But why else would she come looking for *him*?

And, more importantly, how in the hell had she known *where* he was?

'No.' She shook her head. 'We are unacquainted. But I have a problem and you are the solution. My cousin, the King...his wife is pregnant with twins and the latest scan shows major issues and I would like you to accompany me to Castilona to advise and treat.'

If Ed hadn't already established Xiomara was the real deal, he'd definitely be thinking he was being pranked right now. His brain—usually able to juggle myriad complex tasks including in utero foetal surgery—was blanking out. There were so many questions crowding around up there, he plucked the first one he could latch on to.

'How did you know I was here?'

Maybe not the most important question of the many but he was on *holiday*. For two blissful weeks. His first one in five years. Then he was going to Africa as part of an NGO to train doctors in foetal medicine. And the only people who knew his current location were his parents, his close friends, his PA and a few people within the NGO.

She lifted a bare shoulder in a dismissive shrug. 'My cousin is a *king*. We have our ways.'

Ed's gaze flicked to the hired muscle, struck by how absurd it all seemed. He couldn't help but feel as if he'd landed in the middle of a James Bond film, what with a princess landing in a helicopter and a foreign nation knowing his exact whereabouts.

But the absurdity quickly morphed to irritability and then to affront.

This *wasn't* a movie. This was his life. His *real* life. And he was a private citizen. So whatever was going on with the King's twins and no matter how much he might have very much enjoyed her company in another set of circumstances, Princess Xiomara and her *ways* could get back on that helicopter and fly home.

'I'm sorry but I deal in a very specialized area of foetal medicine.' It was his turn for strained politeness. As much as he wanted to tell her to kiss his ass, she *was* royalty and he *was* British. And even if his humble roots chafed at the concept of unelected hereditary rule there was no need to be rude. 'I could certainly recommend someone for your cousin and his wife.'

His attempt at being reductive to her royal pedigree was a tad petty but *he was on holiday.*

'Dr Edmund Butler,' she said, those golden specks in her eyes flashing again. 'Fellow of the Royal College of Obstetricians and Gynaecologists, head of the Intrauterine Surgical Alliance, chair of the World Symposium of Foetal Surgery, founder of the Foetal Surgical Research Institute, author of over seven-hundred peer reviewed journal articles that have been cited over fifty thousand times, the leading expert on endoscopic laser surgery for Twin-to-Twin Transfusion Syndrome.' She folded her arms. 'You are exactly who I need.'

Well, okay then. She'd done her research.

'I have all the details in a file in the helicopter but, briefly, Queen Phoebe is twenty-two weeks pregnant with twins. A routine ultrasound has just identified stage one TTTS.'

Despite the fact he was *on a beach, under a palm tree, in his board shorts, on his first holiday in five years,* Ed's brain clicked over. Stage one could just require close monitoring or could quickly evolve into a situation that required immediate action. The scan results would help but performing his own ultrasound would be the best way for him to get a feel for this particular scenario.

Wait. *No.* He was on holiday, *damn it.*

'Well, as you can see—' he gestured around '—I'm currently on holiday. But I can put you in touch with three other top foetal surgeons, all who are colleagues of mine in London and excellent at their jobs. I'm sure any one of them would be more than happy to advise and or treat as required.'

Ed's earlier Googling had informed him Xiomara was twenty-seven, but if he thought her relative youth would make her easily cowed, he was wrong. Her poised royal vibes were more than a match for his hard-earned leading expert persona. Although he supposed it was difficult to look like the leading expert in *anything* dressed in nothing but a pair of floral board shorts.

'But *you* are the best, yes?'

'Yes.' Ed saw little point in denying what was established fact.

'Then it is only you I want.'

Her chin jutted determinedly and Ed was left in no doubt Princess Xiomara was unused to being denied. Which was too bad for her because he was starting to get really ticked off. A state which had been exacerbated by the crazy lurch in his pulse at her *it is only you I want*. In a more...romantic setting he might have appreciated her direct language, but right now he resented that his traitorous body was all *team curvy princess*.

'Unfortunately, I am currently unavailable. Something I could have just as easily conveyed over the phone, along with my recommendations. Given you know my whereabouts, I assume you also have my number.'

A slight smile flitted briefly across her red mouth in a silent kind of *touché*. 'I didn't want you to tell me no.'

'I'm telling you no, now.'

Another chin jut as she glanced disparagingly at the bucket of beers. 'You don't appear to be doing anything very much at the moment.'

'That *is* the point of a holiday.'

'Drinking beer at ten in the morning?'

Okay, he was done with this now. Given his almost perpetual on-call state, Ed rarely consumed alcohol so if he wanted to drink beer all day, every day whilst *on vacation*, he was going to do exactly that and not be shamed by a posh little miss who'd probably never worked a day in her life.

'Listen, lady—'

'Actually,' she interrupted, that red mouth of hers twitching almost imperceptibly, 'it's Your Royal Highness.'

Ed lifted an eyebrow. Yeah, he wasn't going to call her that. And yet, despite his irritation, he was impressed with her arrogance. Up until this point, he didn't think he'd ever met anyone more conceited than a specialty surgeon but she'd definitely blown that out of the water.

'*Xiomara*,' he conceded. She might have a royal pedigree but his medical pedigree was not to be sneezed at, nor was *he* easily intimidated. 'I'm afraid you've wasted your time here today.'

Clearly not deterred by his dismissal, she continued. 'We will, of course, ensure you are adequately compensated.'

Ed shot her a sardonic smile. 'I don't need your money. I have plenty of my own.'

Okay, he didn't have *princess* money, but he commanded a high-end salary, owned an apartment in Kensington, drove an expensive car and had made wise investments. Not bad for a kid who'd grown up being home schooled in whatever hotspot his humanitarian aid worker parents were in at the time.

'One hundred thousand pounds.'

Ed blinked. *What the...?* Was she joking right now? Her calm expression, the way she held his gaze without batting an eyelid, told him she was serious. He shook his head. 'No.'

Without skipping a beat, she increased the offer. 'Two hundred thousand pounds.'

Folding his arms, Ed stared her down. 'No.'

'Three hundred thousand pounds.'

'No.'

'Four hundred thousand pounds.'

'*Xiomara.*' He gave an exasperated shake of his head, trying to decide whether to be annoyed or, frankly, a little turned on by a woman splashing around cash to get her own way. To get *him* to do her bidding.

'You want more?'

'You could offer me a million pounds and the answer would still be no. You invade my privacy, you shatter my peace and quiet, you disregard the fact I'm on holiday and then you arrogantly assume I can be bought? The answer is *no.*'

She raised one thick, perfectly coiffed eyebrow. 'So you will see the twins die because you're annoyed at my methods?'

'Just as well there are several other specialists who can help you.'

'Five hundred thousand.'

Ed laughed then. What else could he do? It was comically ridiculous. 'You cannot be serious right now?'

'Look at my face, Dr Butler.' Her features morphed from quietly determined to bullishly resolute. 'You think I do not take the lives of my cousin's unborn twins and future sovereigns of my country seriously?'

'Clearly, when there are very viable alternatives, you do not.'

'The King and Queen of Castilona deserve the best and that is what they will get. Seven hundred and fifty thousand pounds.'

He sighed. 'No.'

Pressing her lips flat, she regarded him for a long moment. Ed wasn't sure how she managed to look down her nose at him when he had her by a few inches, but somehow, she did.

'One million pounds donated to your Foetal Surgical Research Institute.'

Ed had opened his mouth to tell Xiomara no again but, after a stunned beat, clicked it shut. Well...*crap*. That kind of money bought a lot of research potential to an organisation who relied on charitable donations to do their valuable work.

Princess Xiomara de la Rosa of Castilona had found his Achilles heel.

# CHAPTER TWO

XIOMARA TOOK IN the coral reefs fringing the island as it grew smaller and smaller below them, the rotor noise above almost non-existent thanks to the superb soundproofing inside the luxuriously appointed helicopter. The Indian Ocean sparkled like a jewel, the clear waters forming a demarcation between the warmer shallows and the sapphire layers of the deep.

Opposite her in a plush white leather seat sat Xavier Torres, wearing earphones with an angled mouthpiece to communicate with the cockpit. Castilonian by birth, his mother a cook in the royal kitchens, Xavier had spent time away in the military before a roadside explosion had affected his sight in one eye, precipitating his return. He'd been part of the royal family protection detail ever since and assigned to her for the last three years. Mostly he kept her shielded from the paparazzi but, as per royal protocols, he accompanied her wherever she was on business for the monarchy.

Beside her on a white leather bench seat sat a bare-chested, barefoot, board-short wearing world-renowned expert in fetoscopic photocoagulation surgery for Twin-to-Twin Transfusion Syndrome.

*Mission accomplished.*

Xiomara had been underestimated her entire life. As a female in a monarchy dominated by a male succession line, she had been raised to be a *princess*. Despite being well educated, articulate and capable, she'd been reduced to hostess duties—cutting pretty ribbons, making pretty speeches and looking pretty in official family photographs.

Her father, Mauricio, had ruled Castilona as Regent for almost a decade, stepping in for his young nephew, Octavio, who'd only been nine when his parents—King Miguel and Queen Eleanora—had died in a car accident. Mauricio, Miguel's twin and younger by two minutes, was a cruel and bitter man who had been a distant father with high standards and low morals.

He had only ever seen Xiomara as a chess piece to move around a board, expecting her to be seen and rarely heard. His to show off when it suited, and to neglect when it did not. If her mother had not intervened on several occasions, she would already be married to a man of his choosing and producing royal babies. Royal *boy* babies to secure the line *should something happen to Octavio* who, constitutionally, hadn't been able to rule until he turned twenty-eight.

Every time her father had said that, it had put an itch up her spine.

Thankfully, Octavio had come of age—unharmed—recently and finally ascended the throne. Xiomara had been thrilled for her cousin, not least because her father's power over him, the country *and herself* had been broken. But mostly because, like his father Miguel, Octavio was a good, smart, honourable man that Mauricio's poison had never managed to undermine.

Xiomara and Tavi, as she affectionately called him, had always been close and to see him sitting on the throne where he should rightfully have been a long time ago, were it not for archaic constitutional clauses, gave her such joy.

For him and Castilona.

Seeing him meet then fall in love with Phoebe and their

excitement over her pregnancy had been an utter delight. So, when this devastating news about the babies had come to light, she'd been determined to fix it for them.

To prove her mettle. To prove, once and for all, she should never again be underestimated merely because she'd been born a girl.

Within two hours, she'd identified the exact doctor they needed for the royal babies and Tavi, who had been dealing with not only his own emotions and an anxious Phoebe but also ever-present matters of state, had entrusted *her* to go get him.

Finally being given something worthwhile to do and with the full force of the de la Rosa name on her side, Xiomara had gone full steam ahead.

Of course, the man in question hadn't made it easy. Not finding him nor getting him to agree.

She couldn't remember the last person—her father excepted—who had not automatically acquiesced to her, so his *no* had been quite a revelation. But had also, rather strangely, intrigued her. She'd *liked* that he hadn't gone all obsequious when she'd introduced herself. That he hadn't known—*nor particularly cared*—who she was.

She'd *liked* that he hadn't felt cowed by her status and folded to her demands.

Edmund Butler had challenged her. Had pushed her. And Xiomara had been there for it. She'd felt truly alive in those moments they'd verbally sparred. And the way he'd said *yes* when she'd asked him if he was the best. No demurring, no false modesty, no self-deprecating dismissal of his prowess. Just *yes*. All deep and sure. Some might even have said conceited.

Arrogant. Egotistical.

But she'd read all about him and Edmund Butler's ego

was writing cheques his body could definitely cash. In *every* sense of the word. Barely dressed on a Seychelles beach he'd been a sight to behold. His broad shoulders and magnificent chest—sporting a ladder of puckered abs and a smattering of hair in all the right places—had taken up every inch of her peripheral vision, sparking a very inconvenient frisson of awareness.

A frisson that was still vibrating through her body.

Perhaps that had been why it had taken her so long to figure out that she'd been offering him the wrong incentive. Money did talk, of course, but not quite the way she'd expected. She'd been so heady with their back and forth and his overwhelming physicality, it had taken her some time to realise she was dangling the wrong carrot.

Having investigated him extensively in the last two days, she should have known the way to flip Edmund Butler was through the Institute. She'd watched a TED talk he'd given where he'd spoken about his brainchild and its work with authority and passion in that deep English baritone. From there she'd fallen down an internet rabbit hole where she'd discovered fascinating papers and case studies and a wealth of vital data from the Institute that had thrust it to the forefront of foetal medicine research.

But that took money. Lots of money.

She had no idea if the Castilonian coffers could cover the eye-watering amount she'd thrown at him but Tavi had told her to do whatever she needed to do and that was what she'd done. It *hadn't* been a test, she knew that—Tavi wasn't her father—but she'd taken it on board as one and if she had to pay the sum out of her own substantial bank account, she would.

And she'd done it. Dr Edmund Butler was *in the helicopter,* currently thumbing through the folder of material she'd brought with her—scans, reports, blood results, maternal history notes. And for the first time in forty-eight hours, since the ultrasound performed at the Clínica San Carlos had confirmed there was a serious issue with the babies, Xiomara was breathing easy.

Sure, from her research into the condition she knew there was still a way to go, but with *the* Edmund Butler finally agreeing to accompany her to Castilona, Xiomara knew they were one step closer to ensuring that Tavi and Phoebe's babies would be okay.

'Well, Dr Butler?' she asked when he finally shut the file.

'Ed,' he insisted, looking up for the first time since he'd strapped in and opened the folder. 'Let me at least feel like I'm still on holiday for a little longer.'

Xiomara wasn't sure she could call this guy *Ed*. It seemed so…inadequate. So…*ordinary*. When what he did, what he was going to do for Tavi and Phoebe's babies, was *extra*ordinary.

Not something she ever pictured an *Ed* doing.

For sure, he was doing his best to be that guy. Lying under a palm tree, drinking beer at ten in the morning, his tousled russet hair and scruffy face so different from the perfectly groomed, cleanly shaven man she'd watched give that fascinating, witty TED talk. But even in holiday mode, dressed for a day lazing on the beach, there was a rangy kind of vitality to him that told her he rarely relaxed.

So yeah, an Ed he was not. Ed*mund*—maybe.

'Well, Ed*mund*?'

A brief sardonic smile touched his mouth but he didn't protest further. He clearly wasn't about to split hairs over *her* choice of name for him, given how he'd pointedly refused to use her title.

'I'll need to do another ultrasound as soon as possible upon landing.'

Xiomara nodded, admiring his businesslike pragmatism. He could still be bitching about his interrupted holiday plans but from the second he'd accepted her proposal he'd morphed from beach bum to internationally renowned foetal medicine specialist. He hadn't even batted an eyelid when she'd told him someone had already been to his room, packed his bag and was transporting it to the helicopter. He'd just nodded, as if he'd been impressed by her efficiency.

'We'll head straight to the clinic when we arrive on Castilona.' She consulted her watch. 'We touch down at the international airport here very soon. The jet is fuelled and ready to go and it's a ten-hour flight home.'

Glancing up, Xiomara found him watching her with eyes the colour of her father's most expensive cognac. Eyes a woman could drown in if she had a mind to.

'That puts us on the ground in Castilona at eight in the morning,' she continued. 'They'll be there waiting for us.'

'Good.' He nodded as if he'd expected nothing less. 'This…clinic. Is it any good?'

Xiomara tried not to feel any affront on behalf of her country at the dubiousness in his voice. He was asking a perfectly logical, very professional question. It was a *good* thing. But that didn't stop a stiffness straightening her spine or the frost in her voice. 'Clínica San Carlos is exceptionally well appointed, with the latest in ultrasound technology and a fully appointed operating suite.'

He seemed satisfied with her answer. 'Is it possible to have the images emailed to me?'

'Of course.' Xiomara immediately messaged the clinic's radiologist, her fingers flying over the keyboard of her phone as she asked, 'What can you tell from the notes? It's not…too late?'

Reading that the condition could be fatal for one or both twins without treatment had been sobering but Xiomara had been reassured by the research that they'd caught it early. Still, given that the man beside her had written a lot of the papers she'd read, it would be good to hear it straight from the horse's mouth.

Or *stallion*, in his case.

'From the last report, Phoebe is in stage one. The amniotic fluid parameters are still normal and the donor twin's bladder is still visible so I normally wouldn't intervene at this point, just monitor. There's a fifty-fifty chance that the condition will resolve by itself.'

Xiomara was encouraged by his calm, analytical approach. He was neither laissez faire nor panicked, oozing professionalism and confidence, which put her immediately at ease. 'That's encouraging,' she murmured, placing her phone in her lap.

Another brisk nod. 'The condition most often develops slowly enough that there is time to consider the best course of treatment. But—' his gaze locked with hers, his eyes earnest above the cut of his cheekbones '—things *can* progress quickly, so the… Queen will need to be closely monitored.'

'Of course.' Xiomara doubted that Tavi would let Phoebe out of his sight. Her phone vibrated and she read the message. 'What is your best email, please?' she asked, not bothering to look up from the screen.

Xiomara tapped it in as he relayed it and within a minute she was reading a response. 'Okay… The images should be with you by the time we land.'

'Thank you.'

Placing her phone back in her lap, she picked up the conversation again. 'So…what happens if it's progressed and requires further intervention?'

'We'll transfer Phoebe to London. I doubt your clinic—as well appointed as it may be—has a fetoscopic laser set up?'

Xiomara smiled sweetly at the sarcasm. 'Not a lot of call for it, no.'

The chopper veered to the right a little and he turned his head to take in the view out of the window as the buildings and runway of the international airport came into view. Xiomara took advantage of his distraction to inspect his profile. His unshaven face did nothing to hide the square-ness of his jaw and the jut of his chin. The sensuous half curve of his mouth was just as fascinating as the hollow beneath his prominent cheekbone. A pulse thudded at the side of his neck and, for a ridiculous second, she wondered what it might be like to be the woman who was allowed to lean in and nuzzle him there, feel the flow of his life force on her lips.

What would he smell like there? The sea and sunshine? Like he did now. Or did he usually wear cologne? Something light and woodsy or rich and spicy?

'*Dos minutos, Princesa*,' Xavier said, his hand temporarily closing around the foam tip of the microphone attached to his headset.

Startled by the voice, Xiomara dragged her gaze away from Edmund and smiled her thanks at Xavier, who'd she forgotten was there. Sure, he was very good at being able to melt into the background—despite his size—but security was difficult to ignore, no matter how unobtrusive.

Until today.

The only man she'd been aware of since she'd set foot on that beach was the shirtless one beside her and she didn't even want to think about what that might mean.

'Two minutes,' she repeated in English for Edmund.

Which couldn't come quickly enough. At least on the private jet, they wouldn't be in such close confines.

And he wouldn't be half naked.

Five hours later, Xiomara emerged from the private sleeping quarters of the jet, phone in hand, feeling refreshed. She hadn't thought she'd sleep between her anxiety over the situation with the royal babies and the disturbing presence of Edmund Butler—both on her plane *and* in her head—but she'd been asleep seconds after her head hit the pillow.

She supposed that was a consequence of very little sleep this past forty-eight hours and the overwhelming relief of having achieved what she'd set out to do.

Said achievement was sitting at a square table big enough to accommodate eight large comfortable chairs, two on each side. It was the place where royal business was usually conducted mid-flight and, despite his jeans and T-shirt, Edmund looked thoroughly at home, clearly engrossed in whatever was on the screen of a laptop as he tapped away, a cup and saucer near his elbow.

He'd changed into more appropriate clothing once they'd touched down at the airport but if Xiomara had thought it would eliminate the bolt of heat she felt every time he looked her way she'd been sorely mistaken. The denim was soft and worn, hugging his quads and ass like they'd been personally tailored to his measurements. And his graphite-grey T-shirt sat snug across the flat of his abs and taut at the seams of his shoulders.

Xavier, spotting her entrance, stood and greeted her. He was occupying one of the half dozen single armchairs on the opposite side of the aircraft, which could be configured in any number of arrangements.

'Your Royal Highness.' Henri, the flight steward, smiled at her and gave a slight bow. 'I hope you are well rested. Lunch will be served shortly. Can I get you a drink in the meantime?'

Xiomara was aware of Edmund looking over his shoulder at her as she smiled at Henri. 'Coffee, please.'

It was only then that she met his gaze. Their eyes locked as he silently acknowledged her presence and another bolt found its mark, deep and low. 'Would you like a top-up?' she asked, forcing her legs to move towards him.

'Please,' he said with a nod, his eyes moving to Henri. 'Thank you.'

Trying to act nonchalant, Xiomara slid into the chair opposite Edmund, pleased that the distance of the table was between them as she placed her phone down. He shut the lid of the laptop and Xiomara shook her head. 'Please, don't let me interrupt you.' She waved her hand. 'Continue.'

His lips twitched. 'Why, thank you, *Princess*.'

He didn't open his laptop again but he did chuckle and Xiomara realised that had probably sounded like she'd just issued some royal decree. She winced internally—why did this man have her tied in knots? Why was it that she could hold her own with dozens of foreign dignitaries on any given day that would cause the most self-assured person to blanch but in front of this man, despite her outward appearance, she felt completely out of her depth?

Henri approached with their coffees, giving Xiomara a reprieve, a chance to collect herself, and she felt much better equipped to make small talk as he withdrew.

'You changed,' he said.

It was a brief statement of fact but there was nothing brief about the impact of it on her body as his gaze dropped to her shirt then flicked up to her hair, which she'd pulled back into a high ponytail, before returning to her face. His eyes brushed her mouth and she momentarily wished she hadn't switched out the red lipstick for a more sedate shade of pink.

'You're observant.' For someone who'd been photographed *a lot*, Xiomara had, too often, felt invisible in her life.

He shrugged. 'You made quite a statement on the beach.'

Xiomara didn't think that was meant to be a compliment but the fact she'd had an impact on him caused a spike in her pulse. She'd chosen her outfit carefully, applied a thick layer of red lipstick, because she'd *wanted* to make a statement. The man had impressed her—was there anything wrong with wanting to also impress? She couldn't dazzle him with her occupational credentials but at twenty-seven and a paparazzi favourite, Xiomara knew how to get a man's attention.

'Yoga pants are much more comfy to fly in.' Xiomara had been groomed to be a fashion plate and it was fun to have a closet full of amazing designer clothes but, in private, she was an oversized T-shirt, flip-flops and messy-hair-don't-care kinda girl.

'I will take your word for it,' he said with a slight smile. 'I trust you slept well?'

'Thank you, yes.'

He raised an eyebrow. 'Must be nice to have your own bedroom in the sky.'

It was on the tip of her tongue to invite him into said room for a personal tour so she picked up her cup and took a sip of coffee, swallowing down the urge. If he'd been another man who was causing her this level of sexual titillation, she probably would have. There were, after all, five hours left of the flight and she could think of no better way to pass the time than finding out just how good Edmund Butler was with anatomy.

Also, no place more private—no paparazzi up here.

But the last thing she wanted to do was muddy the waters between them. She needed Edmund for one thing and one thing only. Nothing else was important.

'I'm very lucky,' she conceded.

Her father had always considered wealth and privilege as his due. Her mother, who had mostly raised Xiomara, had taught her the meaning of humility. Thankfully, Mauricio had decided to leave Castilona upon Octavio's ascension, choosing to exile himself in Saudi Arabia. Her mother, Mira, had decided not to leave with him and their divorce was pending.

'Have you flown on a private jet before?'

'Once or twice.' He nodded. 'Short trips for work-related things. Quite different to having one at your constant disposal, I imagine.'

Xiomara couldn't help but think he was judging her right now and that rankled, but she needed to keep her eyes on the prize. 'Royalty does have its privileges.'

'So…this is what a Princess of Castilona does?' He gestured around the interior. 'Flies around in private jets being an…emissary?'

Yeah, okay, he was definitely judging her now. But he was also challenging her again, like he had on the beach and maybe, in lieu of any horizontal action, it would have to do.

'Sometimes.'

'Isn't it chafing being at your cousin's beck and call?'

Folding her arms, Xiomara eyed him. 'No. My cousin *is also my King.* So, when he sends me to get you, I get you. Which is something I'd have thought you, *as a British citizen*, would appreciate.'

'Nah.' He shook his head. 'I'm not much of a fan of unelected figureheads.'

Xiomara blinked. Well, that she hadn't expected. She'd

seen pictures of him with different members of the British Royal Family at functions and she'd read several of his research papers that had been funded by various royal trusts. 'You are not a monarchist?'

He chuckled and it puffed whorls of warm air currents in her direction, brushing against her skin, tightening her nipples to achy points. 'Not all Brits are monarchists, Xiomara.'

She supposed not and yet it was easy to believe, looking at picture after picture of him schmoozing with society and aristocracy types, arriving in fancy cars and wearing fancy suits, that he was one of them. Despite knowing his roots to be much humbler.

'Is that because you grew up poor?'

There was a pause as his amber eyes lit with surprise before another chuckle oozed its way across the table. 'I wasn't poor,' he said, his mouth still curved in a generous smile. 'I mean we didn't—' he looked around the interior of the jet '—have our own private plane, but I never wanted for anything. I just *grew up* in poor places.'

'Because your parents worked in the humanitarian sector?'

'Well done, Princess,' he said sardonically, performing a slow clap. 'What else do you know about me?'

He seemed both irritated and intrigued that she'd checked out his background but if he thought she was going to apologise for doing so, then he was going to be severely disappointed. Tavi and Phoebe were *royalty*. Castilona might be largely unknown but that didn't mean she could be laissez faire about their safety.

Folding her arms, Xiomara met his gaze. He was going to be sorry he'd asked.

'You're thirty-four years old, born in Papua New Guinea, the eldest of three children. Your parents are doctors and for the first twelve years of your life you travelled as a family from one crisis spot to the next. You attended international schools or were home tutored during this time of your life. Your parents took the family back to the UK in time for you to commence high school. You attended a local comprehensive school in London before receiving a full scholarship to Cambridge to study medicine. After qualifying you specialized in Obstetrics and Gynaecology with a particular interest in fetoscopic techniques. You have three nieces and two nephews. You were engaged briefly ten years ago but have never married and have no dependants. In two weeks you are travelling to Africa for your regular NGO stint.'

Xiomara finally drew breath, their eyes still locked. 'Did I miss anything?'

'Only all the juicy bits in between, but that's—' he lifted a shoulder in a shrug as a small smile lifted the corner of his mouth '—fairly comprehensive.'

It was, although, he was right, had there been more time she would have commissioned a much more detailed report into his background, including information about his ex-fiancée. But it still wouldn't have told her the things she'd found to be the *most* interesting. For example, how thoroughly mesmerizing he was in a pair of floral boardies. How his laugh was warm and deep and welcoming. How the online videos didn't do the smooth baritone of his cultured English accent justice.

And now, of course, those were the intriguing *juicy bits* she suddenly wanted to know *all* about.

'I'm afraid you have me at a disadvantage, Xiomara. Perhaps you can fill me in on what I need to know about you?'

A laugh spilled from her mouth unchecked. The truth was, he didn't need to know anything about her. She was born to be inconsequential. To be in the background. 'I am a princess in a system that privileges male succession. I am…ornamental.' She picked up her cup in salute. 'That is all you need to know about me.'

Xiomara had no idea where that had come from. The truth was, until meeting him, she'd never really questioned her place in life and who she was outside of the de la Rosa dynasty. She'd railed against it from time to time for sure, but had largely accepted it. What little girl didn't grow up harbouring a secret fantasy of being a princess in a palace at some point?

Then this amazingly accomplished guy had come along and in a hot minute had shone a light on her *lack* of accomplishments. Her lack of individual purpose. Her lack of individual *ambition*.

He regarded her for long moments, his amber eyes probing. 'Poor little rich girl, huh?'

Plenty of people back home would have rushed to assure her that her life was full of purpose. That there were many important ways she could represent Castilona and lead a rich and fulfilling life. But not Edmund. There was clearly going to be no sympathy from a guy who must have grown up an eyewitness to enormous poverty and hardship.

But actually, it felt good that he wasn't up for indulging her pity party. That he was neither invested in—or paid to—kiss princess ass.

She gave a grudging smile from behind the lip of her cup. 'Something like that.'

He eased back in his chair, still holding her gaze. 'You possess an enormous amount of privilege,' he said slowly, as if he was choosing his words carefully. 'I'm sure you could do whatever you set your mind to.'

His bald statement made Xiomara itch all over. She suddenly felt inadequate and passive in her own life. Which made her irritable. At herself, but also at this man she'd known for all of a few hours judging her. It was okay for him; he'd had the kind of freedom she'd never had.

She glanced across at Xavier. A gilded cage was still a cage. 'It's not quite as easy as that.'

'Nothing worthwhile ever is, Xio.'

Her breath hitched at the easy way *Xio* had slipped from his lips. And just like that her irritation melted away in a warm spotlight of intimacy. He wasn't judging her; he was challenging her. Gently. As if he wanted her to succeed.

And he'd called her Xio. She'd been called it before, of course, but not since her father had become Regent and the shortened name hadn't been considered *royal* enough. And not in the way Edmund had said it.

'Apologies.' He grimaced as he shook his head, his brow furrowing. 'That was very familiar of me. It just…slipped out.'

'No, it's okay.' She shook her head. 'I like it.' Even more so because it had *just slipped out.*

He nodded slowly, a smile hovering on his full lips. 'Xio it is then.'

Everything warmed at the illicit promise of his words until her phone buzzed on the table, startling her back to the here and now. Her pulse was an unsteady echo through her head as she glanced at the screen flashing her cousin's name. *Tavi.* 'I'm sorry, I have to take this.'

'Of course.'

Xiomara stood and crossed to the other end of the plane for some privacy but, as she listened to her cousin, she couldn't help but watch Edmund, his head bowed over his laptop. He'd called her *Xio.* Soft and low. As if they had a secret.

As if they were already lovers…

# CHAPTER THREE

SIX HOURS LATER, Edmund was standing in the radiology department of the exceptionally well appointed and clearly very exclusive Clínica San Carlos. The royal jet had touched down less than an hour before and Xavier had whisked both him and the Princess—who had insisted on accompanying him—to the clinic, where they awaited the royal couple.

It was hard to believe twelve hours ago he'd been on a tropical beach in the middle of the Indian Ocean, with barely a building or a soul to be seen. And now here he was, in a small Mediterranean island kingdom boasting an array of expensive yachts in the harbour, hillside vineyards and row upon row of white-washed buildings, their terracotta rooftops a warm, welcoming ochre as they'd made their descent.

On their way to the clinic from the airport they'd passed winding cobblestone lanes where pedestrians dodged mopeds and colour was everywhere. Vibrant splashes of pink and purple bougainvillea had been trained to grow around doorways and across overhead trellises, dappling the light in charming sun-filled alleys. Fat yellow lemons and red geraniums sat in pots on windowsills and terraces.

And then there was the royal palace, which he was looking at now through the window. Wrought iron gates with gilt spikes were guarded by uniformed men with shiny gold buttons. Beyond he could see a large gravelled forecourt dominated by an ornate fountain and then the pale stone walls of the building itself, which was more classically hand-some than lavish.

Columns and arches defined the edifice with small balco-nies in between displaying more vibrant hues from flower boxes alive with pinks and reds, yellows and purples. And the pièce de résistance was the spectacular central dome, drawing the eye upward.

He shook his head—how was this his life?

The only thing he'd ever wanted to be was a doctor and that, like his parents, had been the driving force all his adult life, but he'd never pictured it taking him to places like *this*. He'd assumed he'd follow family tradition into the NGO sphere, and he did spend time every year training doctors in developing countries, but it was funny how life events could lead a person down roads and side alleys they'd never planned on taking.

Like this one to Castilona.

Ed had been to a lot of fancy places in the world but this was a revelation. Despite the fact he'd had his vacation in-terrupted, he wasn't sad to be here. Only sad that he prob-ably wouldn't be here long enough to really explore, and he made a mental note to come back some time.

The door behind him opened and he turned to find a woman entering, followed closely by Xiomara, who had changed yet again. A strappy purple sundress showed off her golden skin as her hair bounced loosely around her head. Her lips were shiny with some kind of pinky gloss, which was nowhere near as bold as the red look from the beach but just as fascinating.

'Good morning, Dr Butler,' the newcomer said, smiling as she crossed the distance between them at a brisk clip. She was petite, fine-featured and smartly dressed in a pinstriped pants suit. Her dark hair was worn back in a sleek chignon and her handshake was as businesslike and professional as the rest of her.

'I'm Dr Lola García,' she said, introducing herself as she held out her hand. 'Director of Clínica San Carlos.'

Like Xiomara, she spoke perfect English with the merest hint of an accent and was an exceptionally striking woman. Attractive, confident, clearly career orientated. And yet he had to force himself to concentrate on her as they shook hands and not let his attention stray to the other woman hovering near the door. A woman who'd practically parachuted into his life, snagging his attention from the get-go.

For someone whose only career aspiration was *princess* and who was, by her own admission, ornamental, Xiomara had completely confounded him.

'The King and Queen's vehicle has just pulled into the entrance portico,' Xiomara informed him. 'I'll go meet them. We won't be long.'

Ed acknowledged Xiomara's statement with a nod but forced himself to keep his gaze firmly trained on the clinic director. 'Please call me Ed,' he said as Xiomara departed. 'Nice to meet you. It's an amazing set-up you have here.'

He turned around, gesturing with his hand at the state-of-the-art equipment. Frankly, he wouldn't have been surprised to find exactly what he needed to perform the fetoscopic procedure on Queen Phoebe.

'Yes, we are very fortunate to have government support as well as some amazing patrons to keep our doors open.'

'It looks quite exclusive.' The building wasn't anywhere near as grand as the palace but it was hewn from the same pale stone and the frescos decorating the walls in the entrance foyer had reeked of wealth.

'It is. We do a lot of plastic surgery here and many of our

clients come from around the world to have procedures done away from prying eyes. But we are just as proud of our public wards that provide free treatment to our population as well as our commitment to community health provision in the form of community clinics and other programmes.'

Ed nodded as Lola's eyes sparked with the kind of ferocity and zeal he'd often seen in the NGO sector. She was clearly passionate about her work, which increased her attractiveness even further, and yet it wasn't Lola's voice occupying space inside his brain.

'I'd love a tour after the ultrasound,' he suggested in an effort to concentrate his focus.

'I can definitely arrange that.' She smiled. 'Now—' Lola tipped her head towards the sonogram. 'You've seen the images from two days ago, yes? You know where everything is at?'

'Thank you, yes.'

'I've organized for one of the nurses from the department to be in the room in case you need a hand or need to know where something is.'

'Thank you,' he said again.

As if the nurse had been summoned, she knocked then entered, dressed in brightly patterned scrubs. Close on her heels, a tall man in an expensive suit who looked several years younger than Ed, entered. He had a bronzed complexion and a swathe of dark hair—the archetypal hot young royal made famous by celebrity magazines. He was holding the hand of a blonde woman who looked pale and tired and was clearly very pregnant, a T-shirt stretched over her belly.

King Octavio and Queen Phoebe, he presumed.

Neither of them looked particularly regal right now, despite the quick curtsey Lola had bestowed. There was a presence about the King, in the way he held himself, that told Ed he was used to sweeping into a room and having everyone's attention. But not today. Today he looked just like any other man whose pregnant wife was experiencing difficulties.

Not a *king.* Not *royal.* Just a husband and a father.

'Dr Butler.' He thrust his hand out as he neared, his voice also only lightly accented. 'Octavio de la Rosa. We appreciate you interrupting your holiday to be here.'

Ed's gaze slid to Xiomara as he shook the King's hand. She'd entered the room behind the royal couple and had stayed there. He'd seen a different side to her since landing in Castilona, the one she'd hinted at on the plane. Stepping out of that helicopter she'd been in the driver's seat, but here she'd taken a definite back seat, seemingly fine with being in her cousin's shadow, actively trying to fade into the bland medical background.

Like some kind of chameleon. Like she could make herself invisible. But *he* saw her.

'Your cousin can be very persuasive,' Ed said. 'You should put her to work at the UN.'

Octavio gave a hint of a smile. 'I may just do that.'

Ed was pretty sure Xiomara had blushed but then Octavio was gesturing to the woman beside him and his gaze shifted back to the royal couple. 'May I introduce you to my wife. Her Majesty, Queen Phoebe.'

'Oh, please.' The blonde waved away the title with a slender hand, which she then thrust at him to be shaken. 'Just call me Phoebe. Not quite used to all the pomp and ceremony just yet.'

Despite the fact she didn't look Mediterranean, Ed was surprised to hear a twang to her voice. He'd assumed she was English but her accent said Australian? Or maybe New Zealand? He bowed slightly over their clasped hands. 'As you wish.' He smiled at her then, noting how drawn she seemed around her eyes and he reminded himself that, according to her notes, she was only twenty-four. 'How are you doing?'

She let out a heavy breath. 'Okay. I guess.'

Ed nodded. He'd been through this many times with many couples. It was a stressful and worrying time and no less for these two just because they happened to be minor European royalty. And he wouldn't treat them any differently to any other couple. They needed him to be knowledgeable and decisive and give them the best possible outcome—two live babies.

They were looking to *him* for that. They had put themselves and the lives of their unborn babies in his hands and everything he did from this moment forward was about that.

He smiled reassuringly. 'Well, how about we just get right to it so we can see what's happening with the babies and can make a plan?'

'Oh, yes.' She smiled but it was wobbly. 'A plan sounds good.'

Ed asked Phoebe a bunch of pregnancy-related questions as he fired up the sonograph, mostly to distract her because he already knew the answers from her chart. Her husband helped her onto the examination couch and the nurse busied herself getting the Queen settled as Edmund adjusted some settings.

'Do you want the lights out, Dr Butler?' the nurse asked.

'Yes, please,' he said as he grabbed the gel that had been sitting in its heated cradle and turned to Phoebe, who was lying slightly reclined, her shirt pulled up to expose her belly.

Octavio stood on the opposite side of the bed, holding his wife's hand, kissing it lightly and smiling at her confidently as the room darkened. 'Everything's going to be okay, *querida*,' he assured. But there was a tightness around his eyes betraying his own deep concern.

'Okay,' Ed said, his face lit by the light from the screen. 'Let's take a look. Bit of goop.'

He squirted the warmed gel onto the royal belly and used the transducer to distribute it where it was needed. There was always a brief moment before the image appeared on the screen when a litany of worst case scenarios flashed through his mind. Sometimes he had to give parents devastating news and that was the last thing he wanted to do today.

A sliver of light brightened the room and he glanced up from Phoebe's abdomen to find Xiomara slipping out of the door, only to have Phoebe call her back and reach out her other hand. 'Please stay,' she asked. 'I have two of these and I need all the hand holding I can get.' Phoebe glanced at Ed. 'Is it okay if Xiomara stands at the head of the bed? She won't be in your way.'

Ed's eyes met Xiomara's across the dark room and held. He had no doubt the determined young woman who had plucked him off a Seychelles island knew how *not* to be in the way. But, intentional or not, Xiomara de la Rosa was definitely *in his way*, be it at the end of the bed or far across the room.

Every cell in his body was humming right now as she stared at him and he could feel the corresponding hum pulsing off her. As if they were two tuning forks seeking out their perfect *concert A*. Here, not here, she hummed to him. She was in his head. In his thoughts. And tonight, when he slept, she'd probably be in his dreams.

Ed couldn't quite believe anyone could have that impact in less than twenty-four hours, but here they were.

'Of course,' he murmured, dragging his gaze back to Phoebe. 'There's plenty of room.'

The door clicked shut, extinguishing the slice of light, and Ed busied himself looking at the screen as Xiomara rounded the bed and took up position, putting herself within reaching distance and smack bang in his peripheral vision. Phoebe lifted her arm above her head and Xiomara slipped her hand into Phoebe's with a reassuring smile.

'Okay, then,' Ed said. 'We're all set.'

Returning his gaze to the screen, he manipulated the wand through the gel with one hand while clicking a button with the other to project the picture he could see on his screen onto the larger screen hanging on the wall behind him at the foot of the bed, where everyone's eyes were currently glued. The babies filled the screen, squiggling and kicking around, and Phoebe's soft, '*Oh,*' got lost on a strangled kind of sob.

'What do you know about TTTS?' he asked, directing his question at both Phoebe and Octavio.

'Lola has filled us in and we've been doing some online research,' Octavio murmured, his gaze locked on the screen. 'She did urge us not to but we needed to know everything we could.'

Ed nodded. He too advised his patients not to Dr Google anything but he understood, when all of mankind's knowledge was available at the tap of a key, how tempting that was. And knowledge was, after all, power. The problem was, he had no idea if his patients were finding good information or stuff that was misguided, misleading or just plain wrong.

And then there were the pictures. There were some gruesome images out there which often weren't helpful in emotionally fraught situations.

'To be honest, though,' the King continued, 'it's all been a lot to take in so perhaps if you could go over things again?'

'Of course.' Ed's gaze skimmed Xiomara as it flicked to the sonograph screen, her presence flaring brightly on his internal radar as he tapped some buttons.

'As you know, TTTS occurs when twins are monochorionic, that is, they share a placenta. See—' Ed manipulated the transducer to get the view he wanted, bringing the placenta up on the screen. 'Like that.'

He held the wand in place for a moment or two before continuing.

'Sometimes, in about ten to fifteen percent of twin pregnancies, there is an unequal sharing of blood between the two babies due to blood vessel connections on the surface of the placenta so one twin gets too much blood and the other doesn't get enough.'

'Which means there's too much amniotic fluid and urine for one of the babies, right?' Octavio said.

'Right. Normally, when we ultrasound twins, we give each twin a number—twin one and twin two—but in TTTS we talk about the donor twin, who is the one receiving too little blood, and the recipient twin, who is the one receiving too much blood. Here—' Ed took a few moments to get the best view again '—is the recipient twin. You can see that black bubble? That's the rather large bladder.'

Ed half turned to point to it on the large wall screen behind. 'And here—' more angling of the wand brought up the second baby '—is the donor twin. Whose bladder is still visible.' He again twisted and pointed to the much smaller bubble of fluid.

'And that's a good thing, right?' Phoebe asked.

'Yes.' No urine would have been a major concern. But Ed could see there was a change from the last scan and the computer measurements were already diagnosing a degree of polyhydramnios, or excess amniotic fluid, within the recipient twin's sac. They were still within technical normal limits but the *trend* was a concern.

Once again, his eyes fell on Xiomara, who was watching him closely. Could she tell just by looking at him that he was worried? The way *he* could sense *she* was?

'But,' he said, returning his attention to the royal couple, 'I think the numbers are moving in the wrong direction.'

A shaky indrawn breath spilled from Phoebe's lips. Octavio's throat bobbed as he lifted his wife's hand to his chest, clasping it tight.

'I want to stress,' Ed said, 'the measurements are still all within the normal range, and you are still in stage one, but they're now at the upper limits of the range.' Ed didn't believe in telling patients bad news without offering them solutions and options. 'It would be my advice to have fetoscopic laser ablation, where we insert a small scope into the uterus with a laser attached, allowing us to destroy the problem vessels. It takes about forty-five minutes and if everything can be organised quickly on this end, I can perform it in London first thing tomorrow.'

'Yes.' Phoebe nodded briskly, sniffling. She glanced at Octavio. 'We'll be able to arrange the jet and security quickly, yes?'

'Yes,' he agreed without hesitation. 'I will organize it and make arrangements to stay at the consulate in Belgravia as soon as we are done here.'

'Good.' Ed nodded. He was pleased that the royal couple were keen to move forward with speed and had the wealth and privilege to do so.

He noticed Phoebe's grip on Xiomara's hand was still quite fierce and he glanced at the woman at the head of the bed. Their eyes met and she mouthed, 'Thank you,' at him, her gaze bright with relief and admiration.

Ed's chest tightened. In his career, he'd received just about every medical accolade there was to be had. And they were great, of course, but it was always the relief and gratitude of patients that meant the most.

Xiomara looking at him as if he'd hung the moon was a whole other thing.

He'd never been one to brag about his accomplishments to impress others—*women* included—instead, he let his success do the talking and, frankly, he was too busy to indulge in ego stroking exercises. But he'd be lying if he didn't admit that impressing the Princess felt pretty damn good.

And he hadn't even done anything yet.

Three hours later, Ed found himself back on the de la Rosa private jet. An emotionally exhausted Phoebe was resting in the bedroom with Octavio by her side. She was bearing up well and trying to stay positive but Ed could see through her façade to a woman who still held very understandable fears for her babies. Octavio had admitted to undertaking online research so Ed figured they'd found a host of stuff there that could give even the most stoic couple nightmares.

It was only natural that either parent would find it hard to relax until after the lasering had been performed and deemed a success.

Even the procedure itself was a lot for people to grasp. Messing around inside the womb, the amniotic sac of an unborn baby, still somehow seemed like something from science fiction. Not a procedure that had been performed and perfected over the past thirty years on tens of thousands of babies. He could only hope that his experience in this area had help allay some anxieties.

The pilot came over the sound system to announce they were on their way to cruising altitude, that the weather was looking good and they should be touching down at London City Airport in around ninety minutes. Having made all the arrangements for tomorrow's procedure before departing Castilona, all there was for Ed to do was sit back and enjoy the view of the bobbing boats and terracotta rooftops growing smaller and smaller as the plane steadily lifted.

'It's just as pretty from the air, isn't it?'

Ed smiled to himself at the husky edge to the slightly accented English before turning away from the window to find her taking the seat opposite him in what was her fourth outfit since they'd met—red capri pants and an oversized green button-down shirt. He hadn't been surprised to find Xiomara would be accompanying the royal couple. She seemed very close to her cousin and his wife, and it was only natural that Phoebe wanted to have as much support as she could get.

He'd also been secretly pleased. The thought of flying away and never seeing her again had made his blood itch in a way that was both scintillating and disturbing. Sitting opposite her as they stared at each other, their attraction *humming* away, only confirmed it. He wanted her. Deeply, wholly, shamelessly.

He wanted her like he'd never wanted another woman.

But there was also something very *virgin princess in a tower* about her that made him wary. When he'd first met her, there'd been nothing demure about her at all as she'd bartered for his services like she'd grown up in a Turkish bazaar. And then they'd arrived in Castilona and she'd morphed into that person she'd told him about on the plane—ornamental.

The dichotomy both intrigued and confused him. Part of

him wanted to storm the walls and climb the tower to rescue that woman that had whisked him away in a helicopter, and yet the other part of him could see that the door wasn't locked. She was *choosing* to stay.

As if the tower was as much a construct of her mind as it was made of bricks and mortar.

Ed had no idea what that meant, only that it probably wasn't wise to find out. She was, after all, a princess who did…*princessy* stuff about a million miles away from his world. But in twenty-four hours she'd completely blindsided him and he knew if he didn't get to sink his hand into her hair and kiss her soon he might just go mad.

'It is,' he said, his gaze drifting over that amazing halo of curly hair, the arch of a cheekbone, the curve of her bottom lip, the graceful line of her throat, the swell of her cleavage nicely framed by the V-neck of the shirt. 'I will have to return one day to explore it more.'

Ed hadn't meant anything sexual—not consciously anyway—by his comment but he could tell by the slight up-tilt of her mouth and the amused lift of her eyebrow that she'd taken it that way. 'Please do let us know should you ever return. You are welcome to stay at the palace as our special guest at any time.'

Ed chuckled. *Please do let us know.* Looked like a pin-up girl, spoke like a princess. 'I was thinking more like a moped and a tent.'

She laughed then. '*You* know how to pitch a tent?'

It was Ed's turn to lift an eyebrow. Had she deliberately used that phrase? Her English was certainly good enough to grasp innuendo so was she…flirting with him? With three black-booted security guards, a steward and two other palace staff within hearing distance?

*Not* very virgin-princess-in-a-tower.

Nor was the way she'd crossed her leg, a sparkly flip-flop dangling off her equally sparkly toes. Maybe the combined palpable relief of everyone on board at being on the way to London was loosening her up a little.

'I've pitched lots of tents in my life,' he parried. 'Only way to travel.'

'This from the man I found at an exclusive resort in the Seychelles?'

'Well.' He lifted a shoulder. 'It's been a long time since I've had a proper holiday and I'm about to spend four weeks visiting places that aren't known for their indoor plumbing. What is money for if not to treat oneself every now and then?'

She didn't answer the question, just tilted her head and asked, 'Why so long?'

'Life has been completely hectic. Between patients and research and getting the Institute up and running and travelling to symposiums and conferences and guest lecturing and doing some NGO work, I looked up and suddenly it's been five years.'

He'd thrived on his schedule though, the professional drive he always felt pushing him ever onwards. But his family and friends had been begging him to take a break or risk burning himself out so he'd finally agreed to stop their nagging.

'And then a princess from a faraway land jumps out of a helicopter and takes that away from you too.'

She said it in an utterly self-deprecating way, leaving Ed completely charmed. He smiled. 'A princess in a silver dress.'

He was pretty sure that dress would be the last thing he thought about as he left this world.

Her cheeks pinked up as her gaze moved to the window,

staring out of it as if there was something extra fascinating about the endless blue nothing.

'What about you?' he asked. 'I don't suppose Princess Xiomara of the royal house de la Rosa has ever camped out anywhere.'

Returning her attention to him, her expression turned affronted in the most aristocratic of ways, her pink cheeks changing from embarrassed to indignant. 'I've camped before. I can rough it.'

Ed threw back his head and laughed, ignoring her indignant, imperious expression.

'What?' she demanded.

'That—' he gestured to her clothes '—is the fourth outfit I've seen you in and I've only known you twenty-four hours.'

'You seemed to be obsessed with the clothes I wear, Edmund.'

Not as obsessed as he was at seeing her out of them… But, *nope*. Do *not* go there! Time to get the conversation back on track, Ed*mund*. 'So…when is the best time to visit Castilona?'

She smiled as if she knew very well what he was doing, but thankfully she took the bait. 'Any time during summer, but in two weeks the Fiesta del Vino de Verano begins and goes on for the entire month of August.'

Ed narrowed his eyes as he tried to translate from his school-boy Spanish. 'Sounds like there's wine in there somewhere?'

'You are correct. Festival of the summer wine.'

'My kind of festival.'

She tilted her head to the side, another smile hovering on her mouth. 'I thought British men liked beer?'

'I like beer well enough, but for savouring? Can't beat a glass of wine.'

'Well, you should definitely visit during August. All the cafés and restaurants feature the local vintages, every cellar door on the island puts on speciality menus, shops and houses and piazzas are decorated in grapes and vines and it all culminates on the last Sunday of the month with the ritual grape crushing in the *Plaza Centrale,* which is full of half barrels where locals and tourists alike can jump in and stomp grapes with their feet.'

'Sounds like fun.'

She nodded. 'It is.' Their gazes locked and held for a long moment and he wasn't sure if she *wanted* to convey that she was up for some fun but she most certainly *was* and the hum between them pulsed like a living entity, swirling and tugging.

'Your Royal Highness?' the steward interrupted, completely oblivious to the crackle between them, although God knew how. The air currents were so charged it surely had to be a hazard having them both on this aircraft. 'Queen Phoebe is asking for you.'

'Thank you.' She bestowed a demure smile on the steward as she unbuckled. 'Will you excuse me, Dr Butler?' she asked, all prim and polite and virgin princess, as if she hadn't just communicated all kinds of possibilities with those endlessly fascinating green eyes.

Ed nodded just as politely. 'Of course… *Xio.*' Two could play at that game.

He didn't miss the slight falter in her step as she walked away.

# CHAPTER FOUR

'OKAY, PHOEBE, WE'RE all set,' Ed announced from behind his mask.

He'd performed another ultrasound this morning when the royal couple had presented themselves at the hospital after a night in their apartment situated within the grounds of the Castilonian consulate in Belgravia. It had confirmed that the TTTS had progressed to stage two, with the donor twin's bladder having no visible urine, and the decision to go ahead and ablate was the correct one.

'How are you guys doing back there?' He peeped over the drape that had been erected between the head of the bed and Phoebe's bared, draped abdomen.

'Hmm, good,' Phoebe murmured sleepily. 'Nervous but whatever you gave me has helped.'

Grace Adams, the anesthetist, had administered some light sedation along with placing an epidural. The procedure was minimally invasive and not felt by mother or babies, but it was important Phoebe stayed still throughout and that she was the most relaxed she could possibly be given the high anxiety of the situation.

Being gowned and gloved in an operating theatre, beneath the overhead lights, surrounded by people dressed exactly as he was and a host of medical equipment he knew inside out was second nature to Ed. This was where he felt most at home. He knew what had to be done and he was good at his job. Standing here, about to wipe some prep over Phoebe's exposed belly, he did so with the supreme confidence of a man who was the best in his field.

But he was always cognizant of how different it was on the other side of that drape.

'We give good drugs here,' Grace said, a smile in her voice as she patted Phoebe's shoulder.

Ed glanced at Octavio who, even in scrubs, paper hat and a mask managed to look regal. 'How you doing?'

He nodded but there was a tightness around his eyes. 'I'll be better when it's all over.'

'And that's my cue,' Ed said good-naturedly. 'All right, let's begin.'

The rhythm of the theatre took over as Ed's focus narrowed. There was the blip of Phoebe's heart rate on the monitor but otherwise it was just the low murmur of necessary instructions and discussion as instruments were asked for and Ed's colleague positioned the ultrasound transducer, which would guide the entry of the fetoscope into the recipient twin's amniotic sac.

'Okay, I'm putting the scope in now.'

Ed usually narrated throughout any procedure where the patient was awake, to keep them informed and help ease anxiety. An operating theatre was a highly medicalized environment which could be overwhelming to lay people already stressed enough.

Puncturing the skin, Ed manoeuvred the instrument under the guidance of the ultrasound. The fetoscope was long and flexible, less than four millimeters in diameter but packed with technology. Within the slender package there was a camera, a suction tube and the laser.

'And we're in,' he said as the watery world of the royal

babies came to life on the screen at the foot of the operating table.

Ed took a second as he usually did to just marvel at the miracle of it all. It was a sight few ever got to see, the gentle float of a foetus inside the womb, tiny but perfectly formed. Toes and fingers, nose and lips and a network of spindly looking vessels visible beneath the translucent skin.

'Just navigating to the placenta now.'

Manipulating the scope from the outside, Ed watched the screen as the smooth ruddy landscape of the placenta came into view. More functional than attractive, it was nonetheless a marvel of evolution, its tributaries of red and blue supplying everything a baby needed to grow and develop.

'Okay, found the cord insertion site—we'll spend some time now mapping the surface,' Ed informed them. 'We identify all the vessels connecting the twins first, then we seal them off with the laser.'

Ed and the team worked in tandem, methodically pinpointing where he'd need to treat. Given the narrow field of vision afforded by the scope, this was often the longest part of the procedure but they had to be thorough.

Satisfied that they'd found the problematic connections, Ed prepared to progress to the next stage. 'Right, now on to the *Star Wars* part,' he joked. 'All good your end, Grace?'

Grace eyed the monitor and the steady blip of Phoebe's pulse. 'Yep, all good.'

For the next ten minutes, Ed systematically ablated each of the vessels he'd noted on his reconnaissance, the laser flaring bright on the screen as it obliterated each interconnected pathway.

After checking and rechecking that they'd got them all, he announced, 'We're done.'

'It's all good? You're happy with it?' Phoebe asked, still sounding a little spacey but clearly needing the reassurance.

'Very happy,' Ed said with the confidence of having performed the procedure countless times. 'As we discussed earlier, I'm just going to reduce some of the amniotic fluid from around this little one and then we're done.'

Excess amniotic fluid increased the chances of premature membrane rupture and pre-term birth and he was here to give the babies the best possible outcomes. Twins were often born slightly premature anyway but the object here was to ensure the babies got as far advanced in their gestation as possible before making their entries into the world.

'It's good, *querida,* it's good,' Ed heard Octavio murmur to his wife.

Fifteen minutes later, Phoebe was being wheeled back to her room accompanied by her husband as Ed de-gowned, tossing it into a bag, the frigid climes of the OR fresh on his skin.

'So, are you going back to the Seychelles?' Grace asked as she removed her mask and disposed of it in the bin.

'Nah, think I'll stick around now I'm back.'

He should return, he knew. He still had nine days booked and paid for. But the de la Rosas would be staying on in London for the next week as a precaution and considering how much money they were donating to the Institute, the least he could do was stick around and be on hand in case any complications arose.

Not that he was expecting any but, as with any procedure, there were risks, which he'd already discussed thoroughly with Octavio and Phoebe.

He could certainly do the follow-up ultrasounds. They didn't need to be performed by him—a sonographer could easily do them—but he knew Phoebe and Octavio would appreciate him taking a personal hand in their case. He didn't think for a moment that they thought their donation bought them special treatment but, given that he was still on vacation and he had no patient load or anything else on his plate, he was happy to give them the gold star treatment.

And yes, okay, the fact he might get to see more of Xiomara wasn't exactly a hardship. He assumed that as long as the royal couple were in London, she'd be in London too, which opened up a lot of possibilities.

'Staycation, huh?'

'Yup.' Sure. Why not?

He lived in one of the world's most popular tourist spots, why not noodle around his own city? Or take one of the many easy daytrips that could be had from the nation's capital.

Maybe even invite a certain princess along for the ride?

Xiomara's chest gave a funny little leap at the knock on the door. She was sitting in the chair next to Phoebe's bed. Phoebe hadn't stopped smiling since they'd arrived back at the luxuriously appointed private suite. Neither had Tavi. It was such a relief seeing the weight lifted from their shoulders. It had only been four days since the terrible ultrasound result but it had felt like a month.

Not that it mattered now because everything was going to be okay and that was all thanks to Edmund Butler, who was standing on the other side of the door.

Xiomara knew it was him.

She could *feel* it in that way she'd been aware of him since setting foot on the Seychelles, a storm in her belly as chaotic as the sand that had blown around her from the helicopter rotors.

'I'll get it,' she said, leaping up, waving Tavi back into his seat.

Xiomara forced herself to cross the room sedately like a princess who'd undertaken years of deportment and posture lessons. Not a giddy teenager giving into the demands of her tripping pulse.

Drawing in a steadying breath she opened the door, but it whooshed out of her as Edmund loomed there, taking up all the space in a set of scrubs.

Hell, it took all of her fortitude not to swoon in a heap at his feet.

*Dios!* A man should not look that good in what were essentially blue pyjamas. Even if they did hug him to perfection.

'*Xio,*' he greeted as his gaze roved over her face and hair and neck and, God help her, lower.

She'd dressed this morning in her favourite form-fitting, V-neck pink T-shirt with a glittery tiara stamped across the front, teaming it with a flowy, layered skirt of soft tulle that hid a multitude of sins and flirted with her ankles. For comfort, she'd told herself. Nothing stiff or formal or fancy for a long day sitting in the hospital keeping Phoebe company.

But in truth, she'd worn it for him, this man who seemed to have such a preoccupation with her clothes. Because she'd wanted him to look at her as he was now, his gaze brushing her neck and the swell of her breasts that were spilling out of satiny demi-cups to form a pillowy cleavage. She'd wanted to see his amber eyes darkening to a predatory tawny.

She'd wanted him to look at her as if she wasn't some pretty, unattainable, untouchable princess on a pedestal but as if she was a woman who knew her own power. A woman who craved his touch.

She might be a little younger than him but she was no virgin.

And in those long beats she totally forgot herself and their surroundings. And that two of the palace security detail were witnessing this mutual display of ogling that violated all kinds of royal protocols. Commoners should never look upon a royal princess with such unbridled lust. And a princess should definitely not be wondering how easy it was to get a man out of a pair of scrubs.

Were there snaps on those trousers or a drawstring?

Suddenly breathless at the direction of her thoughts and stunning lack of royal decorum, Xiomara gave herself a mental shake. *Do not mentally undress world-famous doctor with the King and Queen of Castilona mere metres away.*

'Dr Butler,' she murmured, clearing her throat as she stepped aside. 'Do come in.'

He grinned at her then, filthy and wicked, as if he could read every one of the dirty thoughts behind her demure royal façade and was going to take great pleasure in making her say each one of them out loud to him when he finally got her into his bed.

Because Xiomara knew, without a shadow of a doubt, that was exactly where this was heading.

'Thank you, *Princess*.'

His voice was low as pitch and as he brushed past her, the sleeve of his scrubs whispering over her décolletage. Xiomara's belly flipped and muscles deep inside squeezed tight.

'Ed.' Tavi rose and met the doctor halfway, reaching out his hand to shake it.

Xiomara watched as the man she regarded most in the world—her beloved cousin, her monarch—also violated royal protocol and pulled the good doctor into a brief, hard bearhug then apologised for it as he let go.

'Sorry,' he said, clearly surprised and possibly a little embarrassed at his spontaneity. 'I didn't plan on doing that.'

Edmund laughed and gave the royal shoulder a brief squeeze of reassurance. 'It's fine,' he dismissed. 'Happens all the time.'

'You're lucky I'm not up to standing yet or you'd have one from me, too,' Phoebe chimed in.

Another laugh from Edmund as he switched his attention to Phoebe. 'How are you feeling?'

'Good. Relieved. Happy.' She held out her hand. 'Thank you again.'

Ed took three paces to the bed and took her outstretched hand, enfolding it in both of his, patting it absently. 'Happy to oblige.'

'You've been a godsend,' she said. 'We're so lucky Xiomara was able to locate you. I don't know what I'd do without her.'

Xiomara held her breath as Edmund glanced across at her, those tawny eyes roving over her again as if they were the only people in the room. His gaze touched *everywhere,* igniting a series of sparks beneath her skin and when it lingered briefly on the glittery tiara stamped across her breasts her nipples hardened shamelessly.

'You are indeed,' he murmured. Then he turned back to Phoebe, looking from her to Tavi and back to her again. 'Do either of you have any questions?'

'What time in the morning will you do the ultrasound?' Phoebe asked, diving straight in.

'I'm normally doing rounds by seven-thirty, but I could come earlier if you'd like?'

'Oh, no.' She shook her head. 'You've been too kind already. Whenever you'd normally get here is perfectly fine.'

Ed chuckled then and Xiomara felt it from across the

room like a subterranean kind of rumble working up through her toes and her calves and her thighs, setting up camp right between her legs. A man's laugh should not have such a potent effect on a woman's body.

This sexual attraction was fast veering out of control.

'How about I get here at six? I know you'll be anxious until you can actually see the procedure has worked and I don't mind.'

Phoebe pulled her bottom lip between her teeth and Xiomara could see she was clearly torn between needing confirmation the procedure was a success and being demanding or unreasonable. 'We've already asked so much of you.'

Another laugh. 'I'm pretty sure I can get my ass out of bed a little earlier tomorrow for a million-pound donation.'

Tavi hadn't batted an eyelid when Xiomara had informed him what she'd offered. She'd shown her cousin the information she'd gathered on the Institute and he'd been thoroughly impressed by Edmund's brainchild.

'Given the circles we move in,' Tavi said, 'I don't think it'll be the last money finding its way into the Institute's coffers.'

'Thank you.' Ed inclined his head slightly. 'That's very generous. Research doesn't come cheap.'

'It does not,' the monarch agreed.

'Okay, so, six it is.' Ed smiled at the couple. 'As discussed, if all is well with the ultrasound—' a sudden crease in Phoebe's forehead caused him to falter '—which I'm fully expecting it to be,' he reassured with a smile, 'you can return to your lodgings in Belgravia. I'll do a follow-up ultrasound on day two and day three as well. Then another at day seven. You can return to Castilona after that and continue with weekly ultrasounds there. And of course I will be at the end of a phone at all times if you need me.'

Phoebe smiled gratefully, the crease between her eyes ironed out. 'Thank you.'

He nodded. 'Get some rest. You look like you have some catching up to do.'

'She does,' Tavi said, dropping a kiss on the back of his wife's hand.

'You do too, Tavi,' Xiomara said.

Her cousin had been keeping up a stoic façade, bolstering Phoebe and taking all her fears and anxieties onto his big shoulders. But she knew him too well, could see beyond the veneer to how exhausted he was from worry and lack of sleep.

Xiomara swore he'd sprouted grey hairs overnight.

'I will,' he said. 'I just have a few things that need my attention today then I can relax.'

A round table situated near the window in the suite had a sheaf of papers and a laptop set up and ready to go. Tavi had been neglecting matters of state but royal business didn't stop for anything. Now, however, with Phoebe's procedure done and things looking good, he would be able to tackle the backlog. Especially with Xiomara here to keep Phoebe company.

'What are your plans for the day?' Phoebe enquired. 'I'm very conscious we've interrupted your holiday, and we're so sorry for that.'

'Do you know,' Edmund said, a smile playing on his mouth, 'I have a Netflix account I barely ever use and I've never watched *The Crown*. I hear it's quite good.'

Tavi and Phoebe laughed. 'Back when I was plain old Phoebe James from New Zealand, I adored it. Loved all the glitz and glamour,' she confessed. 'Had I known back then I was going to be a *queen* one day, I might have taken some notes.'

'I guess that's a bit of a head spin?'

Phoebe bugged her eyes. 'You have no idea. But—' she smiled at Tavi as her hand slid on her pregnant belly '—I wouldn't want to be anywhere else.'

Xiomara envied Phoebe. She understood it was a strange new world to be thrust into as an adult but to have had all those years of being a normal person sounded like bliss to her.

'Right, well.' Edmund straightened. 'I'll leave you to rest and I'll see you both bright and early tomorrow morning.' Glancing at Tavi, he said, 'You have my number if you have any concerns.'

Tavi stood and shook hands again. 'Thank you, yes.'

Completely absorbed in the fact Edmund was about to walk out of the room and how very much she didn't want him to, it took Xiomara a beat or two to realise that the door had opened abruptly and that Xavier had entered, an expression of urgency on his face.

'Apologies, Your Majesties, Your Royal Highness,' he said with a bow. Then he spoke quietly to Tavi in Spanish. Tavi muttered a curse under his breath that didn't need any interpretation.

Curse words had the same cadence in any language.

'What?' Phoebe asked, her eyes widening as she looked from her husband to the bodyguard who had crossed to the windows and was pulling the curtains closed.

'There's some paparazzi outside the main entrance,' Xiomara translated for Phoebe, her stomach sinking.

'Oh.' Phoebe sighed. 'How on earth did they know about this?'

Who knew how the vultures ever found out these things? Whilst some people courted that kind of attention, Xiomara never had. Neither had Tavi. But it always seemed to find them. Royal fever always ran hot with the paparazzi, and with Tavi and Phoebe's snap wedding and now the twins, it had stepped up a notch, bringing with it the inevitable conjecture—would Princess Xiomara be next?

Tabloid interest in her had always been strong, especially during the years of her father's regency. Speculation about any man she was ever seen with seemed to get more and more intense and pictures of Xiomara—with or without a man—could go for a pretty penny. Which made it difficult to keep her private life private. She was largely left alone on Castilona but in Europe there was always some pap or other on her tail.

Tavi sighed. 'I guess we'll have to make a statement.'

Advised by the department of royal protocol, Tavi and Phoebe hadn't released any information about their trip to London, hoping to keep their private details private. It was a difficult line to walk, Xiomara knew, working out what was up for public consumption and what was not. As the monarchs of Castilona, a lot of their life was not their own—that was just a fact.

But Tavi had wanted to give them some breathing space should the news in London not be good. Had it been a different outcome today, he'd wanted to be able to process that with Phoebe without the entire world wanting a piece of them. With paps at the door, however, things could easily get out of hand. Speculation would mount and soon grow rife if they didn't try to control the message.

'Can we wait till after the ultrasound tomorrow?' Phoebe asked, worrying her bottom lip. She was new to the tabloid circus and already not a fan.

'Of course, *querida*.' Tavi smiled at her. 'I'll speak with my office about it and get them to work on some language.'

Phoebe nodded as Xavier addressed Edmund. 'Dr Butler, we can accompany you out the back entrance if you like?'

'Oh…' He frowned. 'No, it's fine,' he dismissed. 'I doubt the paparazzi are going to be interested in me and my car's out front.'

Xavier inclined his head. 'As you wish.'

He departed the room and, with another quick goodbye, Ed followed. Xiomara tracked his progress—she couldn't not—his scrubs pulling taut around his quads with each long stride. Pausing at the door, his gaze slid briefly to her, lingering on her mouth. It was the merest of seconds but Xiomara's breath hitched, the air in her lungs suddenly turning to liquid heat.

Then he was gone, the door clicking shut behind him, leaving Xiomara to contemplate how many more hours she'd have to wait before she could politely dismiss herself and go to him.

# CHAPTER FIVE

SEVEN HOURS. IT took Xiomara seven hours to extricate herself from the hospital. She didn't mind—not *much*, anyway. Tavi's work took longer than expected and as she and Phoebe had become fast friends this year, keeping her company while her husband worked was easy enough.

But she was buzzing now as she stepped out of the lift on Edmund's floor, flanked by her royal protection. Buzzing with pent-up energy from being cooped up in a room all day. Buzzing from the bare-knuckle ride through London traffic to lose the paps that had been waiting at the back entrance with their ridiculous telephoto lenses and mopeds. Buzzing with banked desire, the embers smouldering away deep inside her belly, waiting to roar to life once again.

Buzzing for *him*. For Edmund.

She had no idea how he would feel about her turning up on his doorstep and for a horrible moment she was gripped with uncertainty. What if this was all one-sided and she was so in lust she'd been misreading his signals? What if he flirted with every woman who crossed his path? What if right at this very moment he was Netflix *and chilling* with another woman?

Had switching out her pink gloss for red lipstick in the car been a mistake?

Her steps faltered but it was too late, they were at his door and Xavier was knocking and it was opening and there he stood, a T-shirt hugging the contours of his chest, shorts that hit just above his knee moulding the lean musculature of his legs, his feet bare. She was beginning to realise this man looked good in anything.

She had no doubt he'd look just as good in nothing.

His eyes widened a little in surprise but then they took a turn over her body that was possibly more pornographic than it had been earlier in the day, roving everywhere, hot and restless and thorough, lingering on the tiara stamped across her breasts, leaving Xiomara in little doubt she *had not* misread his signals.

'Princess,' he murmured as his gaze returned to her face. 'I don't recall giving you my address.'

His voice was low but brimming with an indulgent kind of humour, curving his lips, drawing her gaze to them like moth to flame. 'You didn't.' She raised her eyes to meet his. 'May I come in?' For she would surely die if she didn't kiss him in the next minute.

His gaze flicked to the two men standing behind her. 'Will they be staying? Should I put out snacks?'

Xiomara smiled at his easy humour. It would have been fair for Edmund to be annoyed at her invasion of his privacy. As well as arriving unannounced on his doorstep with two guys—the confirmed presence of the paparazzi had dictated more manpower—who regarded him as a potential threat to their protectee. The fact that he wasn't, that he was almost amused by it, cranked up his sex appeal another notch.

'They just need to check out your apartment then they'll leave.'

'Do you mind, Dr Butler?' Xavier asked.

Edmund didn't say anything for a beat, he just held her gaze before sliding his hand up the doorframe, anchoring his fingers over the top and stepping aside. Carlos stayed behind in the corridor as Xavier entered the apartment and there they stood, him and her, just looking at each other, gazes locked, as a beefy guy in black moved around behind Edmund and another stood sentinel behind her.

But her security might as well not have been there for all Xiomara noticed, her world narrowed down to the man directly in front of her, staring at her with heat and intent, every deliciously wicked thought going through his head right there in his amber eyes for her to see. Any temporary doubts she might have had about a one-sided desire completely obliterated.

He wanted her. As much as she wanted him.

Her pulse tripped like crazy, a tiny hammer at her temples and throat. Her nipples poked hard as diamonds against the confines of her bra. An ache, hot and needy, flared between her legs and it was all Xiomara could do to not squeeze her thighs together.

'All clear,' Xavier announced as he exited the apartment. 'Call us when you're ready to come home later.'

His gaze still locked on her, Edmund said, 'She'll be staying here tonight.'

Xavier didn't miss a beat. 'Call us if you go out.' It wasn't his role to judge Xiomara's actions, just to ensure she was adequately protected and his absolute discretion went without saying.

Amber eyes darkened to tawny. 'We're not going anywhere.'

Xiomara did squeeze her thighs together then as a surge of heat cranked up the ache. The possessiveness of those two statements was absolute. He hadn't asked, he hadn't suggested. Royal princess or not, she was staying the night and they were going nowhere. The squeeze only worsened the situation however and she almost moaned at the deliciously torturous sensation rolling through her pelvic floor.

'Your Royal Highness,' Xavier said as he and Carlos departed.

Xiomara barely registered their departure, her eyes only on Edmund as his hand dropped from the door and he took a step back. Every cell in her body quivering in a state of supreme excitability, Xiomara took a step forward, crossing the threshold. 'I'm sorry,' she said, her voice husky and as quivery as everything else. 'I should have checked you were okay with this.'

He retreated another step, allowing her to advance, but as soon as she cleared the doorway he reached for her, snagging her waist with one hand as he batted the door shut with the other.

'What took you so bloody long?' he growled.

Caging her hips with his hands, he walked her two paces to the wall and pinned her there with one big thigh between her legs and all ten fingers thrusting into her hair as his mouth crashed down on hers.

*Dios,* yes.

Xiomara's heart rate spiked as her senses exploded with the smell and the taste and the feel of him coming at her from every direction. The heat of his mouth, the rub of his chest against the hard, tight points of her nipples, the urgent press of his thigh causing the most insane friction at the apex of her thighs. The hot, insistent probe of his tongue had her clutching at his shirt, causing the strap from her handbag to slide off her shoulder and fall to the floor.

Not that she noticed as she opened to him, whimpering into his mouth, ploughing her hand into his hair as the kiss deepened. The sound of his harsh breath roared like a stadium in her head and the timbre of his low groan ruffled the hairs on her nape and all she could think was—*yes*.

*This.*

She'd been thinking about *this* all day. Hell, she'd been thinking about it since the moment she'd spotted him through a haze of white sand on that beach. And it had already exceeded her expectations. Edmund Butler didn't kiss her like she was a princess. Like he was trying to impress her or win her favour. Like she was special.

He kissed her like she was a woman.

Everything felt hot, her blood itched and her lungs were on fire and she never wanted it to end. His hand slid to her ass, lifting her leg, pressing her inner thigh to the outside of his hip, jamming his leg in higher and harder, angling everything just right, leveraging that space between her legs like he and he alone knew exactly how to conquer it.

Moving restlessly against the thick bulk of his quad, Xiomara gasped as muscles deep and low shuddered at the action and she knew she'd die if he wasn't inside her soon.

'Edmund…' she panted against his mouth, her hands sliding to his belly and the snap of his shorts as the need to touch him consumed her. 'Please. I need you…right now…'

Which turned out to be the wrong thing to say as he dragged his mouth from hers, his tawny gaze suddenly cloudy like he was coming out of a daze. 'Jesus, *Xio*.' He groaned as he pressed his forehead to hers, their ragged breathing intermingling. 'I don't usually jump on women the second they walk through my door.' He pulled away slightly to look into her eyes. 'We should slow down.'

Xiomara's brain wasn't exactly in an analytical space right now so she had to force herself to concentrate on his words as her fingers stilled at his fly. Slow down?

She *did not* want to slow down.

If this was some kind of courtship, she wouldn't be starting like this. She *didn't* do this. She'd want to date and get to know him more. Make out a little. Build to this moment. But this wasn't that. Because in one week she'd go back to Castilona and royal life and he'd be heading to Africa to do his thing. This was a moment snatched out of time. A bubble of opportunity.

And she'd be foolish not to take what was on offer.

Sure, the man fascinated her and she liked him very much but it wasn't like they could ever be a thing. He had an amazing career. People who needed and depended on him and his skills and talents. He was driven, she knew that about him as sure as she knew the sun would rise in the east tomorrow. Why would he give that up to be her glorified handbag as she undertook her royal duties?

*This* was all they could have.

'No.' Xiomara hooked her leg around the back of his thigh. 'I came here for this.'

He chuckled. 'Xiomara Maria Fernanda de la Rosa, I'm shocked.'

*Pfft.* As if. 'You don't like direct?'

'I like direct very much.' To demonstrate his appreciation, he hitched her higher against the wall, his thigh grinding into all the heat and wet between her legs. 'Tell me how you want it.'

'Here.' Xiomara was proud of how strong her voice sounded when the grind of his thigh was scrambling her brain and melting her insides, inching her closer to orgasm. 'Against this wall.'

One black eyebrow winged upwards. 'Wouldn't the royal Princess prefer a bed?'

'No.' Too many men treated her like a princess. 'I don't need a feather bed or a gilt frame.' Her fingers made short work of his fly, dragging it down. 'I don't need pampering or pretty words.'

Locking her eyes on his, she slid her hand inside, brushing against the long, hard length of him through the barrier of his underwear. The loud suck of his breath was as dizzying as the steady, intimate rub of his thigh.

'Just you and me and this.'

Reaching inside his underwear, Xiomara freed his erection, pressing her mouth to his as she wrapped her hand around his girth, his deep, guttural grunt sweet on her tongue.

He didn't need any more direction after that, his hand smoothing up her torso, taking her shirt up as well. Up, up, all the way up until he was breaking the kiss and her hold on him to pull it over her head, exposing the demi-cup of champagne-coloured satin that lifted and presented her breasts, the mocha of her areolas peeping out from under the darker lace trim.

'Bloody hell,' he whispered, staring at them like they were the holy grail of mammary glands. 'Is it disrespectful of me to say *great tits*, Princess?'

Xiomara supposed it was, but she liked the way he disrespected her, how he looked at her like he couldn't get enough and he didn't wait for an answer anyway, his hands lowering to peel down the cups, his head lowering to tongue the swell of her cleavage.

She whimpered as the hot, wet heat of his mouth closed over an achingly taut nipple, her back arching as the scruff of his whiskers scraped in all the *good* ways. Twisting a hand into the hair at his nape, Xiomara held him there as her other hand returned to his shorts, grasping him firmly again, revelling in the thick, blunt heaviness of him. He grunted at the play of her fingers as he pulled the other nipple into his mouth, swirling his tongue around it, then sucking hard, shooting a flaming arrow of desire straight to the point where she was now shamelessly rutting against his thigh.

She didn't need evidence to know she was wet and ready for him, she could feel the slipperiness between her legs, smell the heady odour of her arousal. Nor did she have to be an expert to know that things were escalating quickly, sparks firing behind her belly button and the base of her spine, nerve-endings fluttering in anticipation. Unless she wanted to experience her first orgasm with this man by dry humping him all the way to the end, he needed to be inside her—now.

Massaging him from root to tip with one hand, Xiomara groped in her skirt pocket for the condom she'd stashed there before she'd left the hospital. 'Edmund,' she panted as she plucked it out, the galloping need to have him inside her becoming a fury in her brain.

'*Mmm?*' he murmured as he nuzzled his way up to her throat, his tongue swiping the shallow dip at the juncture of her collarbones.

'Condom,' she muttered, thrusting it at him.

Tearing his mouth from the side of her neck, Edmund obliged, his fingers apparently trembling as much as hers as he fumbled with the foil packet, cursing under his breath. 'Hell.' He gave a self-deprecating laugh. 'I'm shaking.'

Xiomara smiled, pleased at the note of disbelief in his voice, as if he wasn't used to being this kind of shook-up. She liked that he seemed out of his depth. 'Me too.'

Their gazes met then and despite the rapid-fire of her pulse and the erratic timbre of her breathing and the desperate signals from her body, they found a couple of beats of stillness for him to tear the packet open and toss it on the ground. Xiomara smiled triumphantly as he brandished the condom before reaching between their bodies and sheathing himself with stunning efficiency.

Sliding his hands to her hips then, he rucked up her long flowy skirt inch by inch, gathering the fabric at her sides as he went back to work on her neck, nuzzling her from the fast flutter of her carotid pulse to the angle of her jaw. Cool air, blissful on her heated skin, swirled around every inch of her exposed legs as more and more was slowly revealed, and when his fingers finally came into contact with the bare, dimpled flesh of her upper thigh he muttered, '*Yes,*' in her ear.

Then, as his hands slid around to her butt, they stilled. Pulling away slightly, his gaze snared hers, a wicked smile spreading across his face. 'Princess, are you *commando* under there?'

Xiomara smiled. She'd removed her underwear in the bathroom, shoving it in her handbag at the same time she'd stashed the condom in her pocket. 'I thought it might be quicker.'

'Good thinking,' he muttered.

He kissed her then, hard and deep, and after urging her to lock both legs around his waist, the blunt thickness of him notched at her entrance and then—blissfully, thankfully, surely—he thrust inside her with one flex of his hips, rocking her head against the wall and causing her to cry out and clutch at his shoulders.

'You okay?' he asked on a pant, his forehead pressed to her temple, puffs of his breathing disturbing the curls at her hairline.

*Okay?* Xiomara was better than okay. Her eyes shuttered at the influx of pleasure, stars popping behind her lids as the tight glove of her fluttered around him, precariously close to rippling out of control.

'Uh-huh,' she muttered, trying to catch the breath she'd lost to the mastery of his possession.

Xiomara had been with men before. And it had been fun and light and flirty. She'd had good lovers and rarely been disappointed in an experience but *this* was next level. She'd never been *had* like this. So totally and completely. As if he'd branded her with his mind as well as his body.

This was…*consummation*. And she hadn't even climaxed yet.

He groaned, deep and rumbly, his heated breath brushing her skin. 'You feel *good*.'

Xiomara gave a half laugh. *He* felt good. So good she was sure he'd have her there in one more thrust, which would be kinda embarrassing. Wasn't it supposed to be men who had issues with finishing too soon?

'I have to warn you,' she said as she prised her pleasure-heavy eyelids open. 'This isn't going to take long.'

He laughed, puffing more warm breath at her forehead. 'I've thought about doing this every waking and sleeping moment for the last four days. I won't be far behind you.'

And then he withdrew and entered again in one steady movement, causing Xiomara to cry out again and clutch him to her, one hand on his shoulder, the other buried in the hair at his nape, his chest smooshed against hers as he withdrew and thrust again.

And again.

And one more time as the flutters became ripples and the ripples became contractions, pulsing through her pelvic floor, shooting sparks up her spine and along every nerve-ending in her body. She cried out as the pleasure rocketed from zero to one hundred in a wave of pure bright incandescence.

'*Yes, yes, yes*,' he muttered, his breath hot at her neck,

his big hands clutching the backs of her thighs, spreading her, angling her as he rocked himself in and out, the friction and motion pulling in all the right places. Every gasp from her dragged a corresponding groan from his throat as her walls clamped tight around him, their hearts slamming together in unison.

'*Dios*,' she moaned as everything started to break apart, the contractions taking over, engulfing her in light and sparks. '*Edmund*!'

She didn't know why she called his name with such desperation but she suddenly felt like she was falling and he was the only one who could catch her. The only one she wanted to catch her. And he did, he had her safe in his big hands, anchoring her to the wall, anchoring her to him.

'It's okay, I got you. I got you. Let go, *Xio*. Let it all out.'

Until that moment, Xiomara hadn't realised she had been holding it in. But his sexy, urgent rumblings had flipped some kind of switch undoing all that reserve and aloofness she'd needed to navigate royal life every second of the day. Every last pretention and hangup slipped away as she gave in to the pleasure rolling through her in deep, clenching waves. All of her ingrained reserve and polite formality dissolving as she gave herself up to the moment, letting the princess façade slip, crying out at the pleasure seeping into every cell in her body.

Something she'd never done before, some part of her always aware of the role she was playing. She'd worn her royal skin like a cloak, even being intimate with a man. Because that was what they expected. They wanted the princess.

But not this man. Edmund Butler didn't give a damn about her royal pedigree. She could be herself. She could be *Xio*. She could just be a woman.

'Edmund,' she said again, deep and low on a long exhaled moan, revelling in the hedonism of her complete surrender.

'Xio…' he said, his shoulders quaking, his quads shaking as he thrust and thrust. 'God… *Xio*…you feel…so good.' A strangled kind of noise, somewhere between a gasp and a groan, spilled from his throat as his hips jerked to an abrupt halt for several long beats before he cried out in release.

Xiomara's pulse tripped at the guttural sound, so rich and unbridled as his thrusts resumed, disjointed and jerky. '*Yes,*' she moaned, turning her head and capturing his mouth. 'Yes, yes,' she said against his lips, licking in to him, kissing him deep and wet, swallowing his pleasure as he let go and lost himself inside her and she coasted through the misty remnants of her own pleasure.

Coasting and coasting until he was spent and so was she, but he was holding her there still, pinned by his big, hot, trembling body to the wall as if he couldn't move. Or didn't want to.

She certainly couldn't. And didn't. She never wanted to leave this spot.

She just wanted to wallow in the weight of his chest and the span of his shoulders and the hard bang of his heart shaking his ribcage—and hers.

Eventually, when the hot, husky raggedness of his breathing had settled and Xiomara didn't feel like her heart was going to explode, he stirred, pulling his head from the crook of her neck. His eyes roved over her face, which must look an absolute fright, her hair tossed about, her red lipstick completely kissed off.

'Now can I take you to a bed?' he asked, his voice gravelly, humour lighting his slumbrous amber gaze as it settled on hers.

Xiomara grinned. 'I think you're going to have to. I don't think I'll be able to walk.'

'Good.' He kissed her, brief and hard. 'Hold on.'

Not bothering to disentangle himself, he strode with her still attached to his person as if she weighed nothing, his big hands spanning the crease where her thighs met her ass and holding on tight. Xiomara clung to him, clutching the solid block of his shoulders, clamping her thighs tight around his hips, not wanting to break their intimate connection.

'I'm impressed you can carry me like this,' she admitted as he strode through a doorway. Xiomara knew she was no lightweight.

'You should be more impressed I'm actually capable of standing after that orgasm.'

She laughed. 'I'm impressed with that, too.'

He kissed her as he lowered her to his mattress in a flurry of skirts. 'Let me clean up,' he whispered, dropping a kiss on her nose. 'Don't go anywhere.'

Considering her legs still felt as weak and useless as wet noodles, Xiomara wasn't any kind of flight risk. She shivered as he withdrew then watched idly, too blissed-out to move as he headed for what she assumed was the en suite bathroom. From this angle, he appeared to be fully dressed although she knew he'd look less so from the front.

Still, she doubted he'd look as dishevelled as she was, spread on the bed, her bra cups pulled down, her skirt rucked up, her hair a springy tousled mess. She was utterly wrecked. Very different from the put-together princess image she always tried so hard to project.

The toilet flushed and, vaguely, Xiomara thought she should put herself to rights but her eyes drifted shut. Dopamine had her in its grip and she was happy to float along in the slipstream.

'God, you look beautiful.'

Xiomara smiled as her eyes drifted open. She was absolutely sure she did not—ravished maybe, not beautiful. But she could feel his eyes brushing over her body, lingering on her nipples, which hardened wantonly, and the note of absolute appreciation in his voice had her forgetting about her own inner critic.

Levering herself up, the flats of her forearms bent behind to support her, she opened her mouth to tell him flattery would get him *everywhere,* but the words lodged in her throat. He was naked, wearing nothing but a smile as he lounged in the en suite doorway, and there was no power on earth that could have stopped Xiomara's eyes from taking the tour.

Dark hair on his arms and legs and a light smattering on his chest emphasized his masculinity and Xiomara was helpless not to follow the line of hair that narrowed as it travelled down his abs, arrowing south until it became a thin trail from his belly button, bisecting the V of muscle between his hips, feathering out again as it got lost in the thatch of hair between his legs.

With the condom gone she could see *all* of him, his size big enough to widen her eyes as she inspected the part of his anatomy that had possessed her so thoroughly, hitting her in all the right places. Even in the aftermath he was impressively hung and butterflies fluttered in her belly as she thought about how good he might taste. What he might do if she rose from the bed right now, sank down on her knees before him and took him in her mouth.

His smile disappeared as his amber eyes heated to tawny. '*Xio,* I don't know what you're thinking right now—' He pushed off the doorway and prowled slowly in her direction. 'But your nipples just went hard as pennies.'

He was right—they had. Shamelessly sitting up and begging for more, almost painful in their tightness. Without thinking about it, she pressed the flats of her palms to them, trying to ease the tingle of arousal.

How could she want him again so soon? Wasn't she completely spent five minutes ago? And yet desire stirred in her belly again.

'If you think that's helping,' he said with that amused tone in his voice she was coming to know so well, 'you're wrong.'

Their gazes met and held as he loomed over her now and suddenly the press of her palms was more erotic than soothing and the urge to arch her back rode her like the devil. Her breath tumbled from her lungs as she slowly squeezed her breasts, the hitch in his breath enormously gratifying.

'Tease,' he muttered, his gaze moving from her eyes to the play of her hands as she replaced her palms with her fingertips, brushing them across the erect tips of her nipples.

Xiomara smiled as her own gaze drifted, focusing on the thickening between his legs. 'Why are you all the way up there?' she asked.

'I have no idea,' he muttered as he planted a knee beside her and lowered himself down.

# CHAPTER SIX

EDMUND STIRRED RELUCTANTLY the next morning, wrapped around Xiomara. Her warm back and bottom were snuggled into his front, his legs cocooned hers and his face was buried in her lush mop of curly hair. She smelled like jasmine and vanilla and something much earthier that spoke of their fevered sexual antics and he wondered why he was awake at five-thirty when he hadn't gone to sleep until after three.

Sure, his raging morning wood—not helped by the press of lush ass cheeks—was one reason, the early summer light poking in around the edge of the fancy blinds was another. Then he remembered the third.

The ultrasound.

He groaned internally. The last thing he wanted was to get out of this warm bed and leave this warm woman he was nowhere near finished with yet. But Phoebe and Octavio were giving the Institute one million pounds and for that they got extra special service. He might not know Phoebe very well but he knew women in this situation and, queen or not, she'd probably already be awake, counting down the minutes until he arrived.

He'd promised to be there at six and he wouldn't let them down just because he couldn't control his libido for a couple of hours.

Inhaling a clean hit of jasmine and vanilla, he gently tried to ease his arm out from under her neck. Xiomara had also had a late night and there was no point in them both being awake. He could make it to the hospital and back again within an hour and just slide in behind and wake her in a much more pleasant way.

'Mmm.' She grabbed his arm as he tried to extract it. 'Good morning.'

Edmund smiled at the drowsy satiation making her voice husky and enhancing her accent as he dropped kisses across her shoulder blade. So much for not waking her up.

'Go back to sleep,' he whispered. 'I'll be back in an hour. How do you like your coffee?'

Her hand slipped up and behind, anchoring around his neck, the sheet slipping down, giving Ed full access to her breasts—an invitation he wasn't about to ignore. He might have to be up and away very soon but he could linger for a little longer. He brushed a thumb across the brown tip, pulling a moan from her throat as she arched into his hand, the action thrusting her ass cheeks against his erection.

It took all his willpower not to *grind* as he played some more, urging her nipple into a hard peak. 'Edmund…' she said, barely audible as she rubbed the cleft of her ass against the aching hardness of his shaft.

Shutting his eyes to quell the sudden hot rush of desire, Ed kissed her neck and removed his hand. 'Later,' he whispered. 'Hold that thought.'

She protested sleepily as Ed reluctantly dragged himself from the bed, looking over his shoulder at the soft golden hue of her skin exposed from her shoulder to the cleft of her buttocks, the long stretch of her spine a tantalizing trail between. He wanted nothing more right now than to kiss his way up—or down—that golden road and it took all his willpower to turn away and leave the bed.

A quick *cold* shower helped dampen his ardour and ten minutes later he was dressed casually in ochre chinos and an untucked polo shirt with the Institute logo stitched over his left pectoral. It wasn't his usual work attire of business shirt, trousers and tie but he *was* still officially on vacation.

Finding both his bed and the room empty, he called, 'Xio?' as he made his way out.

Pulling up short in the doorway, he spied her on the far side of the open-plan living room, bending over to retrieve her handbag from the floor, where he did not recall it being dropped. From this vantage point he was able to see the rounded outline of her ass pressing against the fabric of the skirt as it fell forward and he looked his fill as he idly wondered if she was still commando underneath all those layers.

So much for that cold shower.

'Looks like I arrived at the right time,' he said.

Righting herself, she shot him a rueful smile as she turned to face him, her curls settling around her head as she slid her handbag over her shoulder. 'Why, Dr Butler—' she tutted as she gave him one of those *regal* looks she'd so perfected '—were you checking out my bottom?'

Ed grinned at how *proper* she made ass sound, even knowing it was deliberate. 'One hundred percent.'

'That's exceptionally uncouth of you.'

'I know, right?'

She laughed and it was light and tinkly and it made Ed grin even more as he shoved his hands in his pockets and just looked at her, his morning-after princess, her metaphoric tiara a little tainted after last night.

When her laughter settled, she asked, 'Can I catch a lift into the hospital with you?'

Oh. *Damn.* Ed had been hoping she'd be here when he got back but he supposed, given she'd been by Phoebe's side through everything, that she'd want to be there for the ultrasound too.

'You don't have to call your bodyguards?'

She smiled. 'Technically. But—' she shrugged '—I don't always do what I'm told.'

Edmund chuckled as he leaned into the doorframe. *Amen to that.* She certainly wasn't the put-together compliant princess he'd witnessed on Castilona or the attentive royal courtier from the hospital yesterday. She looked like a woman who did as she pleased. She looked loose and messy and sated. She looked like she'd been well and truly ravaged.

And his heart kicked in his chest, knowing he'd been the one responsible.

'Umm, don't you think it'll be suspicious us arriving together?'

'No.' She frowned. 'I knew you were going to do the ultrasound at six and Phoebe wants me there for it. They'll just think we've run into each other on the way to the room.'

Ed laughed out loud. 'Xio. You're in the same clothes. I've known you for five days and never seen you in the same set of clothes. They'll know.'

She shrugged. 'They're pretty distracted right now.'

'Sure,' he conceded. 'But I still think one look at that thoroughly kissed mouth of yours will have Phoebe's female intuition pinging wildly.'

Smiling, she advanced towards him, slinking right into his space, her body pressed intimately against his, and Ed's breath hitched. He slid a hand onto her ass, holding her to him as a fresh surge of desire washed through his system. Her gaze fixed on his mouth as she raised a hand to it and trailed her index finger along first his bottom, then his top lip.

'The same could be said for yours.'

His lips tingled in response and Ed couldn't help himself,

he opened his mouth and sucked her finger inside. The flare of her nostrils, the glow of those golden flecks in her eyes sent an electric charge through every last cell he owned.

She slid her finger from his mouth, trailing it down his throat as they stared at each other for long moments, the air pulsing with that charge now a tangible force between them.

'Right,' Ed said, clearing his throat as he brought himself back from the edge. 'My point exactly. They'll probably put two and two together. Distracted or not, they seem pretty smart.'

Her hand dropped away. 'Do you...' her brow crinkled '...not want them to know?'

Ed blinked as a subtle kind of tension permeated her frame. What? *No.* That was *not* what he'd meant. 'No.' He shook his head, his eyes locking on hers. 'Not at all,' he assured her. 'I just...didn't think *you'd* want them to. I assumed you kept things like this clandestine?'

Her body oozed against him as her tension eased. 'It's a bit hard having a clandestine anything when my security detail knows where I am and that I planned to stay the night.'

Okay, that *was* a good point.

'I suppose so.' He frowned. 'Don't you find that weird? That two people other than us know exactly what we were doing last night?'

He couldn't imagine a life where some third party was privy to what was essentially private information. To know his every movement. To know what he was doing behind closed doors.

'Oh, it's very weird.' She smiled but there was a resignation to it that put an itch up Ed's spine. 'But... I'm used to it. And their discretion is absolute.'

'So, they don't have to report your movements to the King?'

Her face scrunched into a horrified mask. 'Absolutely not.' She shuddered. 'I may be born into a royal family but I am an adult woman. Their job is to protect me, not to inform on me. The only time they would share details about my movements would be if something happened to me.'

Ed quirked a brow at that titbit. 'What do you mean? *Happened* to you?'

'Like an attack or an abduction.'

She said it so casually. Attack. Abduction. As if the threat of violence was just another part of her life. It made him want to wrap her up and never let her out of his sight. It made him grateful for her protection, as weird and unnatural and intrusive as it felt.

'Has that ever happened?'

'No.' She shook her head, her curls jostling at the movement. 'Mostly they protect me from photographers. The Castilona royal family is hardly well known, but there's a group of the paparazzi who make their living from snaps of young European royals. Although when I was younger, when my father was Regent, plans were uncovered for a kidnapping but—'

'*What?*' Ed gaped at her casual announcement.

She shrugged. 'They were early plans and the people were amateurs apparently.'

Ed shook his head, not quite able to absorb the enormity of a kidnap plot. It was the stuff of fiction and yet this was Xiomara's life. 'How do you live like that?'

She smiled and raised herself on her tippy-toes. 'One day at a time,' she murmured against his mouth then kissed him lightly. 'Now—' she dropped back onto the soles of her feet, her hands sliding to sit flat against his pecs '—don't we have to get to the hospital?'

Clearly, she was done talking about the strictures of her

life but Ed couldn't help being a little freaked out. 'Are you sure we shouldn't call your bodyguards? You were followed by the paparazzi yesterday, remember?'

She'd told him about their James Bond drive to his apartment in bed last night and they'd laughed at the anecdote. But in the cold light of day, with the knowledge of much more sinister happenings, it wasn't so funny.

'Positive.' She nodded with absolute certainty. 'We gave them the slip. Nobody knows I'm here.'

'How can you be sure?'

'Because they'd have probably already found a ladder or hired a crane or something to get a picture through your windows.'

Ed shuddered. 'That's terrible.'

'Yes. It is.'

Her acceptance of the bizarreness of it all was probably the most grounding thing of all and ordinarily he'd just dismiss it with a *rather you than me* quip. But Xiomara wasn't some tabloid princess from a faraway land any more. She was flesh and blood. She'd been in his bed. He'd kissed *every* inch of her body. He'd been *inside* her.

She was real. And he *liked* her. A lot.

'It's okay,' she whispered conspiratorially, a smile playing on her mouth where she'd dashed some of that demure, princess-pink gloss. 'It doesn't happen that often. Now—' she took a step away and held out her hand '—we should go or we're going to be late.'

He smiled and took her hand but all Ed really wanted to do was throw her over his shoulder and take her back to his bed and give her some kind of reprieve from *that* kind of life. Offer her shelter in *his* life.

And hell if that wasn't new.

No woman had ever made him contemplate making room

for anything other than his work—he had one ex-fiancée
to prove it. Ed supposed that should be a cause for alarm.

Strangely, it wasn't.

At this hour of morning the two-mile drive was barely affected by traffic and Ed turned into the doctors' car park
twelve minutes after pulling out of the basement parking
garage at his Kensington apartment. There were only a few
other cars there as he drove into his dedicated parking space,
shaded by the vibrant summer foliage of one of the many
plane trees that bordered the parking area.

There was no sign of any paparazzi on the street across
the road from the hospital entrance as there had been when
he'd left yesterday. Hospital security had moved the clutch
of photographers off the grounds but hadn't been able to
do anything about them setting up camp on the opposite
side of the street.

Clearly, though, they'd got what they came for. That, or
it was just too early for them.

Ed offered Xiomara his hand as she had offered hers in
the apartment and the fact she took it as easily as he had
put a zing up his arm and a glow in his chest. He couldn't
remember if a woman had ever had such a visceral, electrifying effect on his body.

Sure, he'd desired women before that he'd felt in physical
ways. But not like this. Like a magnet vibrating with potential as the right pull entered its electrical field.

The sky was a soft gauzy mauve, promising to deepen
and flourish into a decent summer's day, as they headed for
the entrance. Her steps slowed, however, as they neared and
she drew to a halt as she shot him a nervous smile. 'Please
tell me this is all going to be fine. I feel bad that I've given
this zero thought all night.'

Ed liked that he'd been the one responsible for keeping Xiomara preoccupied enough to forget about the twins for a while. She'd been intensely focused on them and finding a solution to their condition since it had been identified only days ago, which was incredibly selfless. But the correct procedure had been performed in an expert and timely manner so she'd deserved a break from the mental load of it all.

He smiled reassuringly. 'I have every confidence.' He locked his eyes on hers so she could *see* his confidence—lean into it. 'But if you're asking me for a one hundred percent assurance that the procedure was a success, I can't give you that.'

It was the truth. He couldn't. And it was important to acknowledge that sometimes things didn't go according to plan. Something he'd already discussed in great depth with Octavio and Phoebe.

'But I've done this hundreds of times, and complications have been *exceptionally* rare.'

The thing was, *he* knew *she* knew what they were because Xiomara's research had been thorough. And now they were faced with finding out, it was only natural those things would be on her mind. They were in the back of his mind as well, despite being extremely happy with how the procedure had gone.

'Okay.' She gave him a wobbly smile. 'Thank you.'

Ed returned the smile as he slid his hand to her face, cupping her cheek, his finger furrowing into her hair. 'Please tell *me* your cousin and his wife know how lucky they are to have such an amazing advocate.'

'It has been mentioned,' she murmured, a smile curving her mouth as his lips lowered towards her.

He kissed her then, in the middle of the deserted car park, because it seemed like an age since he'd kissed her in the

apartment and he was swept up in her heart and her empathy and well…he couldn't *not*. He couldn't, it seemed, get
enough of her mouth.

'Okay now?' he asked as he pulled away.

She nodded. 'Okay now.'

Sliding his arm around her shoulders, he said, 'Let's go
look at some royal babies.'

First, though, they had to run the gauntlet of royal security.

There was a different guy in black stationed outside the
door with Xavier this morning. 'Your Royal Highness,' different guy greeted, his accent thick. 'You were supposed to
call us to come pick you up.'

Xiomara smiled prettily. 'I know.'

Ed blinked as Xiomara morphed into the princess before
his eyes. All demure and charming, like butter wouldn't
melt in her mouth. Like she hadn't ridden him like a cow-
girl last night. He wondered how often she used that façade
to get out of trouble.

Or get her way.

'I'm so sorry, Felipe,' she continued. 'But Edmund was
coming here anyway. It seemed pointless and such an imposition, not to mention entirely environmentally unfriendly
to have two cars out on the road.'

Felipe's expression remained impassive. 'It is never an
imposition, Princess.'

'Never,' Xavier reiterated as his gaze settled on Ed.

There was no outward sign that he was hacked off, but
Ed could feel the disapproval coming off him in waves.
Not that he could blame the guy. It was his job to protect
Xiomara and, given what he knew now, Ed was grateful
that there were trained people who had her back. 'We take
Her Royal Highness's protection very seriously, *sir*. We'd

appreciate your cooperation so we can do our jobs and ensure her safety at all times.'

In his peripheral vision, Ed could see Xiomara's lips pressed together, clearly amused at the achingly polite dressing-down by her bodyguard. He ignored her but absolutely planned on making her pay a little bit when he got her alone later.

Ed inclined his head in acknowledgement of Xavier's more than reasonable security request. 'Absolutely. You have it.'

'Apologies again, Xavier,' Xiomara said, shooting him another one of her pretty smiles before turning to Ed. 'Shall we?'

She didn't wait for his answer, just sailed past all three men as she headed for the door of the hospital suite as if she was walking a rope line somewhere and not all sexily dishevelled from rolling around in his bed. And hell if that wasn't a very inconvenient turn-on.

Ed was right about Phoebe counting down the minutes until he arrived. He entered the room about a minute after Xiomara, pushing the hefty piece of ultrasound equipment he'd arranged to be left outside the room. Phoebe greeted him with a huge smile that did little to hide both the flood of relief and the anxiety underpinning it all.

'Good morning,' he said as he smiled at her and Octavio.

They returned his greeting but neither of them looked particularly well rested.

'Good morning, Dr Butler,' Xiomara murmured in her cool princess voice with her best *resting royal face* firmly in place as he manoeuvred the machine to her side of the bed.

The closer he got, though, the clearer he could see the daring imp dancing in her gaze. She was obviously enjoying the clandestine flirting and the undercurrent flowing like a river of lava between them.

'Morning,' he said with a nod, all cool professional despite the *I'm-going-to-get-you-for-that-you-little-minx* look he shot her as she moved out of his way, rounding to the other side of the bed, taking up position next to her cousin.

Getting his head back in the game, Ed made all the usual enquiries of Phoebe as he fired up the machine. How did she sleep? Had the epidural completely worn off? Had she eaten and been to the toilet? Did she have any pain? Any contractions? Any discomfort? Any leakage of fluid? Any decrease in the foetal movements?

All the things the royal couple had been advised to watch for and call him should any occur.

As soon as the machine was ready, Ed got straight to it, knowing from their stilted replies that neither King nor Queen had the heart for small talk.

'There they are,' he said as he slid the transducer through the gel he'd squirted on Phoebe's bare belly.

A grainy flurry of arms and legs bobbling around in their watery world filled the screen and three sets of eyes homed in on the picture on his screen. There was no large wall-mounted TV in this suite so Ed angled the machine, giving everyone access to his screen.

Octavio kissed his wife's forehead as she said, 'How does it look?' her voice slightly tremulous.

'One moment, let me just—' Ed moved the transducer around a little until he got the view he was after—the donor twin's bladder. He smiled triumphantly. 'I see urine.'

'You do?' Phoebe said with a sniffle.

'That's it there?' Octavio asked, pointing at a black bubble that had not been on yesterday's ultrasound.

'Yes, that's it,' Ed confirmed with a grin, as relieved to

see it as everyone else in the room if the collective release of breath was any indication.

He'd been confident in the way that being an expert in his field afforded him, but he also knew that very occasionally the procedure wasn't successful or a rare complication might arise so it was always good to have this confirmation.

'And I can see there's already been an increase in the donor amniotic fluid,' Ed added as he returned his attention to the screen, pushing some buttons to accurately calculate the volume for comparison.

'Oh, thank God,' Phoebe muttered, pressing one hand to her chest as her husband kissed the other and held it close. 'I've been trying to stay positive but it's hard not to worry.'

'Of course,' Ed assured her. 'That's only natural.'

His gaze slid to Xiomara, who was smiling at him not with relief or gratitude, but with *pride* shining from her eyes. 'See,' she said as she looked at him lingeringly before switching her attention to Phoebe. 'Didn't I tell you two he was the best?'

Phoebe laughed. 'You did. He's a miracle worker.'

Octavio turned relieved eyes on him. 'You just might be. I don't think I will ever be able to thank you enough for what you've achieved here.'

Ed shrugged off the compliment. Yes, what he did was highly specialised and he *was* the best in his field but, at its core, it was a simple enough procedure. It wasn't complex like open-heart surgery or complicated like putting a smashed bone back together or convoluted like organ transplantation.

He wasn't superhuman. Or a superhero. Or a miracle worker.

And because Xiomara wasn't looking at him like he was any of those things but looking at him like he was first and foremost a *man* and with *pride* instead of relief and gratitude it meant more than the King's praise.

'Okay.' Ed moved the transducer to get a look at the recipient twin. 'Let's just do some more checks while we're here.'

Fifteen minutes later, he was wiping goop off the royal belly, chatting with two very different people, loose and laughing and relaxed now.

'You can leave as soon as you're ready today to go back to the consulate,' he said. 'But please take it easy for these next few days. You are at a higher risk of pre-term labour and membrane complications due to the procedure.'

Ed had already been through the risks associated with the surgery—both during and after—but he repeated them again because he understood that parents weren't often in a state to absorb information about post-op management when they hadn't yet been through the procedure. Their focus was understandably on the more immediate issue.

'I will make sure of that,' Octavio confirmed in a gruff voice, giving his wife an uncompromising look. Not that she seemed inclined to argue. This pregnancy complication had obviously shaken her.

'If you'd like to come in tomorrow for another ultrasound? Maybe—' he slid a quick glance at Xiomara '—not quite so early?'

Phoebe laughed then apologised. 'Absolutely. So sorry about getting you out at the crack of dawn. What time would suit you? You name it—' she smiled at Octavio '—we'll be here.'

'How about…' Another quick look Xiomara's way was executed without being noticed and Ed was thankful that the royal couple seemed too caught up in their relief and jubilation to notice the undercurrent between him and Xiomara.

She mouthed, '*Nine.*'

Nine sounded perfectly respectable.

'How about nine? I dare say you could use the sleep-in,' he said, knowing full well the King and Queen of Castilona weren't the only ones in the room who could use the extra sleep.

A certain princess could, too. He wouldn't say no either. Or they could wake early and have amazing morning sex, all sleepy and tender, and not have to tumble straight from bed to the hospital.

'Perfect,' Phoebe agreed.

'What time shall I order the car for?' Xiomara asked Octavio as she pulled her phone out of her bag. Not waiting for his reply, she turned to Phoebe. 'And would you like some of those ah-mazing little pastries from Harrods you love so much?' Her thumbs flew over the keys. 'I don't think it'll be too late to get them delivered for morning tea.'

'Xiomara—' Phoebe laughed, stilling the rapid-fire tapping of her fingers '—it's fine. You don't have to do any of that. You've gone above and beyond for us but Octavio is perfectly capable of taking care of me. Why don't you ring some of your friends? Go out on the town? It's London. You *love* London. Go have some fun.'

Ed tensed at the thought of her *having fun* out there in his city that didn't involve him. Yeah, that wasn't going to happen. If she wanted to go out, *he'd* take her. But he needn't have worried. One look at Xiomara's dumbstruck expression told him not only that she hadn't been expecting the directive but the idea didn't appeal.

'Oh.' She blinked then waved her hand dismissively. 'I'm having fun.'

Her gaze slid his way and a frisson passed between them that lifted the hairs on his nape. It was so palpable, Ed felt sure the other two occupants of the room must also be able to feel it, but it appeared not. Phoebe did, however, intercept *the look,* her eyes suddenly narrowing as they moved back and forth from Ed to Xiomara and back to Ed.

Just as he had suspected, once the cause of Phoebe's preoccupation was resolved she'd likely not miss much, so he tried really hard to *not* look like he'd spent all night debauching the Princess of Castilona. But the more he tried to empty his mind, the more unhelpful images it delivered.

Phoebe frowned at Xiomara. 'Isn't that the same outfit you were wearing yesterday?'

'Oh.' Xiomara glanced down at her clothes. 'These? Yeah... I'd slung them over the chair next to the bed last night and then I overslept my alarm this morning so I just grabbed them and threw them on.' She shrugged as if it was no big deal. 'I'll change when we get back to Belgravia.'

Phoebe's gaze met Octavio's, and he raised an eyebrow as if he didn't quite know where this was going but that something was definitely hinky with his usually put-together cousin. Returning her attention to Ed, Phoebe continued her friendly interrogation. 'And your plans for the day?' But before he could answer she said, 'More... Netflix?'

Ed wasn't sure how to play this. He was thirty-four-years-old, not some spotty teenager who needed to account for his every move to his girlfriend's suspicious friends.

But then he'd never slept with a princess before.

Phoebe got in again before he answered. 'Or maybe a little—' another look at Xiomara, and a very definite twitch of her lips as if she was having a little fun now '—chill?'

Octavio narrowed his eyes as Phoebe looked pointedly at Xiomara. Ed recognized the minute the penny dropped for the King, a slow smile lighting his face.

'Maybe,' he lied, still hedging even though he knew for damn sure there was going to be a lot of *chill* going on today.

'Hmm.' Phoebe crossed her arms and stared at a fixed point in the air for a few beats as if contemplating something, before returning her attention to him. 'You know who loves TV?'

Octavio, getting in on the matchmaking action, chimed in. 'Xiomara does.'

Ed couldn't help but smile as he finally glanced at Xiomara. 'I mean...' he shrugged '...if the Princess wanted to join me...'

Xiomara grinned. 'The Princess would.'

It was somehow old-fashioned to be having this deliberately roundabout conversation and yet that was part of its appeal. Ed felt as if he'd been given some kind of royal stamp of approval. Not that he needed one—he and Xiomara were both adults and this was just *chill* after all—but it was surprisingly nice to have.

And he was far too old to be sneaking around. Xiomara's security considerations were more than enough cloak-and-dagger for him.

*More than enough.*

# CHAPTER SEVEN

XIOMARA LINGERED THE following morning after Tavi and Phoebe had left Edmund's rooms, where the second ultrasound had taken place. They'd both been practically walking on air as the results confirmed that the TTTS was slowly improving. Edmund had been quick to reiterate that it usually took two weeks for the condition to completely resolve but he was clearly pleased that things were heading in the right direction.

As were Tavi and Phoebe.

Xavier was waiting outside to accompany her to the car. She was following the royal couple back to the consulate for a few hours to play hostess for Tavi as he welcomed a dignitary from the European parliament who'd requested an urgent meeting regarding agricultural subsidies whilst he was in London.

Unfortunately, wherever in the world Tavi travelled, his job always travelled with him. And no matter what was going on in his personal life, the people of Castilona expected their King to attend to matters of state. That was just the way it was and it wasn't something, as members of the royal family, they ever really questioned. Dedication to subjects and country was not only a birthright but a privilege.

On top of that, Xiomara knew that Tavi felt he had to be

especially accessible and steadfast in these early days after the mercurial whims of her father's reign.

Since their marriage, Phoebe had done the hostess duties but Tavi had insisted she rest and that he could handle it himself. And, of course, he could. He was a superb leader and diplomat for their kingdom. But Xiomara knew the role upside down and inside out. It was what she'd been *born* to do and, as such, could converse on a wide range of topics from the frivolous right through to more serious matters of state with the intuition to know which was required when.

So, she didn't mind stepping in for Phoebe. As with Tavi, her duty to Castilona was paramount.

But she'd also be counting down the minutes until she could be back in Edmund's bed. The last two nights had been magical in a way she'd never had before. Her lips curved thinking about them. And it wasn't about the sex. Or not *just* the sex anyway because that had been spectacular. It had been how anonymous she'd felt.

How she could just be herself.

Like any other woman in the first flush of a giddy sexual fling, when the only thing on her mind was the next encounter. Not whether the person she was with was going to sell the details to a gossip blog. Or whether he was genuinely interested in her for her or for her royal pedigree and royal bank account. Or whether he expected her to be a princess between the sheets.

Which meant she stuck to a particular circle of people. *Who all knew each other.* No anonymity there. She'd always been Princess Xiomara with any other guy. But not in Edmund's apartment. Not in his bed. Not in his arms. She wasn't a princess when she was with him.

She was a *woman*. And that was exhilarating.

She just wished they could have that outside his apart-

ment, too. Being in bed twenty-four-seven was no hardship
but, as Phoebe had said, Xiomara loved London and she'd
love nothing more than to step out into it with Edmund at
her side. This was his hometown after all—how amazing
would it be to see it through his eyes?

How amazing would it be to just be able to walk outside
the apartment with him, go for a stroll, get some fresh air?
Laze in Hyde Park with all the other people watching the
row boats on the Serpentine. Jump in a glass bubble for a
spin around the Eye. Wander through Borough Market. If
they'd been in Castilona together, she'd have taken him all
over.

But London was a whole other ball game security-wise.

Except maybe if they got out of the capital. Away from
the gaggle of paparazzi on the hospital *and* consulate door-
steps. The next ultrasound wasn't for five days…and as long
as they didn't go too far in case of complications, why not?
Her lips curved into a smile at the thought of being anonymous *outside* his apartment. Wandering around like lovers
in the English countryside without a single person knowing who she was.

'I know what you're thinking.'

Two big arms slid around her waist from behind as Edmund nuzzled her temple and Xiomara's smile grew. Turning in his arms, her breath caught in her throat. She kept
forgetting how classically good-looking he was and how
his whiskery scruff enhanced his sexiness. But it was the
*way* he looked at her that truly robbed her of her ability to
breathe.

Not because he knew who she was, but because he liked
what he saw.

Xiomara locked her green gaze with his amber one. 'You
want to get out of here?'

He laughed. 'Sure. But don't you have that thing you have to do?'

'I mean after. Let's get out of the city. Somewhere away from the capital. A quaint little village, or a pebbly beach. Within an easy drive of London, of course, but away from it all. There's five days until the next ultrasound and your holiday *did* get interrupted.'

'Like…camping?'

He was teasing but she didn't care. She'd rough-it for him. She'd lie down under any roof with this man—even a canvas one. 'Anywhere.'

He didn't immediately jump in and proclaim it a fabulous idea and a sense that she'd got things wildly wrong filled the silence. She'd been so swept up in the abandon of the last two nights she'd thought that meant he'd want to spend the rest of her time in London together.

She winced internally. Rookie move, *Princess*. This was sex. They weren't dating.

'Oh God, I'm sorry,' she apologised, feeling like an idiot. 'That was very presumptuous of me. Forget I said anything.' Xiomara pushed against his chest to be released, mortified.

But Edmund's arms only tightened, 'Hey. No.' He slid a hand onto her cheek as he captured her gaze. 'Xio.' He smiled softly before dropping a string of soft kisses on her mouth that soothed and stirred in equal measure. 'Not presumptuous. Not even a little. I think it's a wonderful idea.'

Another kiss this time and Xiomara leaned into it as it deepened, relief and the low rumble of his groan igniting the embers of passion. Her heart was racing when he eventually dragged his mouth from hers.

'My only concern,' he said, his forehead pressed to hers, his breath fanning her face, 'is your security detail. It's hardly a romantic mini-break when there's two guys in black shadowing us everywhere.'

The R word did little to calm Xiomara's pulse. She hadn't thought of it as a *romantic mini-break* but she loved the sound of it. It seemed so terribly English. Something regular, normal, ordinary English *couples* did.

And she wanted that with him so very much.

Xiomara pulled away a little so she could look into his eyes. 'Trust me, they can be a lot more discreet than that.'

But he had a point.

Xiomara trusted Xavier with her life—literally. He was efficient and strategic but also flexible, aware that things often changed at a moment's notice, so he had contingencies for everything. Pretty much the way his mother had once run the royal kitchens! But, more than that, she'd got to know him personally after several years of travelling together and she liked him. Hell, theirs was probably the longest relationship she'd ever had with a man.

But she didn't want him along for *this* ride.

'I can ask Tavi to have it withdrawn. He won't be a fan, neither will Xavier, but Phoebe is definitely team *Ed.*' She smiled at him. 'So, I think he could be convinced.'

Edmund chuckled and it was deep and warm and rich and Xiomara wanted to curl up and purr. 'Yes, but...' his brow crinkled '...*should* you?'

Xiomara had been aware when she'd shared the information about her near kidnapping as a child that it had disturbed Edmund, but she hadn't realised quite how much. She tended to forget that security guards with guns weren't *normal.*

'There's no current credible threat to me as far as I'm aware so it's really only paparazzi we have to worry about. I doubt Tavi would consider my request if we were staying in London. Not with the paps knowing the de la Rosas are in town and especially not after the statement concerning the health of the royal babies goes out this afternoon. There'll be a bit of a flurry to get first pics.'

She rolled her eyes. Sometimes even she couldn't believe her own life.

'But if we can give them the slip, which is generally easy enough, and stay away from major centres, it should be fine. Xavier will put a bunch of contingencies in place in case things go pear-shaped but I've done it before when I've been away with friends. I'm not that well known here, not like one of your royal family.'

'What does *not that well known* mean? Exactly how recognizable are you?'

She quirked an eyebrow. '*You* didn't recognize me.'

He chuckled. 'Yes, but I'm hardly in that demographic, am I?'

'I doubt I'm recognizable at all here unless you're a pap or someone who's really into the royal-watching scene. If I wear my hair back and some sunglasses when I'm out and about, my own cousin would probably walk straight past me.'

'So…don't pack your tiara?'

Xiomara laughed. She loved how casual…how flippant he was about her pedigree. As if being a royal princess was the least interesting thing about her. Most non-aristocratic men she'd dated would have already peppered her with questions about who she did and didn't know in those circles. But not Edmund. He'd never once asked her if she knew Meghan or Harry.

'Exactly.'

'All right. Let's do it.' He smiled then and it was slow and lazy and promised all kinds of wicked things that made her insides loop-the-loop. 'A good friend of mine has a small holiday cottage in Cornwall. It's on a headland overlooking the sea and St Ives, and the weather for the remainder of this week is supposed to be sunny. I could find out if it's available?'

Xiomara's heart sang at the suggestion. 'It sounds great.' In fact, it sounded perfect.

*Just like him.*

Six hours later, Xiomara was watching the sparkle of sun on the ocean as Edmund navigated the clifftop road. It might be almost five in the afternoon but the sun of high summer was still several hours off setting. She couldn't believe she was here and had to stop from pinching herself.

It hadn't taken long to get Tavi on board but, as expected, Xavier had been more hesitant. Still, ever the professional, once the King had approved it, he had set about ensuring that Xiomara could get away undetected and have some plans in place should she need to be extracted quickly.

And here they were, almost at the cottage Edmund had arranged.

Xiomara had felt guilty about leaving Phoebe, who was essentially confined to the consulate. They had become close friends over the past six months, and she was in London, in part, to be a companion, a lady-in-waiting figure for Phoebe when Tavi couldn't be around.

Phoebe, though, had been insistent that Xiomara leave. 'I'm a grown woman,' she'd said with a roll of her eyes. 'I don't need a *companion*.'

As the new Queen, Phoebe had settled well into royal life but Xiomara knew she found the strictures and traditions both surreal and jarring.

'You like him?' she'd asked.

'Yes.'

'*Like* him, like him? Or just, *I'm-in-town-for-a-week* like him?'

Xiomara had smiled. Phoebe was clearly thrilled to see Xiomara enjoying herself but it was just as clear she was worried about Xiomara potentially getting hurt when they headed back to Castilona and Edmund went to Africa. But Xiomara knew it could be nothing more than a pleasant interlude and had assured Phoebe of such.

The car slowed. 'Almost there,' Edmund said.

He turned off the main road onto a bumpy narrow lane, changing Xiomara's view to the nearby clutter and colour of St Ives at the bottom of the headland. The sun reflected off the strip of white sand and the windows of the houses and shopfronts that lined the area between the two piers. Fishing boats bobbed at anchor in the shallow harbour, the water a clear, tranquil aquamarine, the seaweed-encrusted mooring ropes on the sandy bottom clearly visible even at a distance.

'Tide's in,' Edmund said. 'When it goes out the entire harbour empties.'

Xiomara had never been to Cornwall before. In many ways it was similar to Castilona—old buildings, harbour, beaches. But that was where the similarities ended. The Mediterranean light was different—warm and golden, drenching the land beneath it in a heat that spoke of summer grape harvests and long, lazy siestas. Still, she was excited to explore this very English seaside setting, although she'd have been excited to explore anywhere with Edmund.

They passed several cottages strung along the lane before he pulled up outside a small white-washed building with blue detailing around the door as well as several large windows that dominated the front aspect and on top of the low white-washed wall that formed the front fence. There was nothing but fields behind them and a view of cliffs, ocean and town in front.

'Oh,' she said on a sigh. 'This is beautiful.'

He leaned across, slid a hand to her nape and kissed her and Xiomara melted into it, into him, her heart light as air in her chest. 'You're beautiful,' he muttered against her mouth, his voice deliciously husky as he pulled away, her red lipstick now almost completely kissed off. 'Come on, let's have a look around and then go into St Ives for some dinner. The seafood here is amazing.'

Xiomara exited the car, the sun warm on shoulders covered only by the shoestring straps of her floaty yellow sundress, a light breeze ruffling her curls. She slipped her hand into his as he rounded the vehicle and they walked through the little gate that led to a stone path that took them straight to the front door, which wasn't locked.

Edmund's friend had arranged for the cottage to be readied for them, including a supply of groceries to be delivered that were sitting in shopping bags on the island bench when they walked inside.

'This is perfect,' Xiomara said as she took in the very modern open-plan living, dining and kitchen area that had obviously been renovated to a very high spec.

Thick walls, half whitewashed, half exposed to reveal a glorious honey stone hinted at its age as well as adding character. Large weathered honey-brown flagstones formed the floor. The sea side was dominated by two large picture windows, one in the kitchen, where the sink was located to take full advantage of the view, the other in the living area, the natural wall thickness creating a cosy window seat and providing an unspoiled panorama of cliffs and ocean.

The other side of the living area was dominated by an

inglenook fireplace that would no doubt keep the little cottage toasty when the winter evenings drew in and the sea turned squally.

'The bedroom is through here,' Edmund said.

It wasn't huge but with a large bed sporting plush bedding sitting against the wall opposite and another picture window looking out to sea, it was all they needed. On the wall behind the bed a doorway led to a roomy en suite bathroom with a walk-in shower *and* a clawfoot tub situated in front of yet another huge window that looked out over the fields beyond.

It was a stunning view. And the bath was big enough for two!

'It's not a palace,' Ed said as Xiomara stepped back in the bedroom. 'But I reckon it'll do for a few days.'

She quirked an eyebrow. 'Do you think I need a palace?' Sure, she *lived* in a palace and she was used to luxury, but that didn't mean she couldn't appreciate the charm and beauty and all the love and care that had obviously gone into renovating this cosy space.

But mostly, she hated that he might think her so pampered that only luxury would do.

He shrugged. 'I…don't know? Do you?'

It was a fair question, she supposed, but it still stung. Sure, she'd landed in a helicopter and plucked him off a beach in the middle of the Indian Ocean, but she'd thought she'd proven to him at least the last two nights that she didn't need buglers and gold toilet seats wherever she went, and she didn't expect airs and graces.

'No.' Although what came to the tip of her tongue was *I just need you.*

Crossing to the hip-high window that extended almost to the ceiling, she stood and admired the vista, placing the flats of her palms on the deep ledge. She leaned close to the glass, her eyes tracking down the lane they'd taken, across the grassy expanse of the clifftop dotted with yellow and white wildflowers to where the town dipped towards the ocean. Edmund snuggled his body in behind hers and she sighed contentedly.

A remote control gadget sat in the corner and she reached for it. 'What's this for?'

Taking it from her hand, Edmund flicked the button, causing the entire window to frost over, cocooning them in a bubble of privacy.

'*Nice,*' Xiomara murmured in appreciation.

'Yep. Triple-glazed to reduce the noise from the howling winds and squalls that can batter this place. And electrochromic for complete privacy. All the windows are the same. Thacks and Vi thought of everything.'

He flicked it again, the glass becoming transparent once more, the ocean and cliffs appearing as if by magic. Placing the remote down, his palms slid onto the ledge, caging her against the sill as his mouth brushed her temple.

'I never get tired of this view.'

His voice was rich with innuendo, leaving her in little doubt it wasn't the outside he was talking about as the heat of his gaze fixed on the rise of her breasts, outlined perfectly in the firm yet stretchy shirring of the bodice of the dress. But her smile faded as Xiomara wondered suddenly, did he actually mean something different?

'Have you been here before?'

He seemed to know a lot about it after all, and this was a cottage for *lovers*.

Had he brought some other woman here? Had he laid her on the bed behind them, rolled around with her, gone down on her? Had he stood at this very window and ground against her?

'Yes,' he murmured as he dropped kisses down the side of her neck.

'With a...woman?'

Xiomara hadn't meant for her voice to be quite so high on that last word but it obviously cut through Edmund's ardour as he stilled.

'Xio,' he murmured, his warm lips brushing her cheekbone. 'Are you jealous?'

He sounded amused but his enquiry caused a mini riot inside her head. No. Yes. Oh, dear...*was she*? Or had his palace quip just made her hypersensitive?

*Gah!* This wasn't her. She *wasn't* hypersensitive and it was none of her business.

But she wasn't sure she could stay here if he had. Which was stupid, she knew. And possibly exceptionally spoiled of her. Just because she'd never been on a romantic mini-break before didn't mean he hadn't. Possibly right here. And, like a ghoulish spectator at a car crash, she couldn't look away.

She needed to know.

'Curious,' she said evasively. 'Have you?'

His arms circled her waist as he propped his chin on her head. 'I've been here twice,' he confirmed, his voice matter-of-fact. 'Once for a weekend, when a bunch of us helped with the internal painting when Thacks and Vi were renovating, though we all slept at an Airbnb in St Ives. The second time when they held a housewarming to celebrate it being done and it was the middle of a heatwave and we all camped under the stars in the field out the back.'

Xiomara shut her eyes on a wave of relief.

'Okay?' he murmured.

He didn't sound angry or impatient that she'd asked. He

wasn't getting all moody and he hadn't walked away. She'd asked, he'd answered. Done.

She nodded. 'Okay.'

'Good. Now—' His hands slid to her breasts. 'Where were we?'

He squeezed them and a low moan rolled from her throat, a wave of heat cascading south from the tip of her nipples and intensifying as it crested straight between her thighs.

'You want to try out the bed?' he whispered as his mouth buzzed her ear.

'No.' Beyond the cliffs and the town the ocean was big and vast and wild and it drove something equally wild and reckless inside. 'Here.' She slid her hands over the top of his as he kneaded.

'Mmm,' he muttered. 'Get the window.'

'No,' she repeated, then yanked the shirring of her top down, her unfettered breasts spilling out, exposing them to full view of anyone who might be passing by.

Okay, the road was hardly a major thoroughfare, but the thought that somebody *could* be out walking on the cliffs was a wicked little thrill cranking her arousal. This was not something Princess Xiomara could ever contemplate doing, taking something so private and flaunting it in a very public way. There could be telephoto lenses trained on them.

Prying eyes.

But here on the rugged Cornish coast she was just Xio and he was just *Ed* and a feral kind of abandon coursed through her system.

'*Xio,*' he groaned, his hands cupping the lush spill of her, his fingers rolling her rapidly hardening nipples.

She cried out at the exquisite torment of it, pressing back into him as she lifted her arms and circled them around his neck, thrusting her breasts into his palms.

'You want this here?' he muttered into her hair, his voice thick with arousal as he rubbed his thumbs over nipples that were now tingling with an urgent need that could well drive her out of her mind. 'In full view of the window?'

'Yes,' she panted. *One hundred times, yes.*

'There's a car coming.'

There was no hitch in his voice, no alarm or concern that they were going to be caught in flagrante delicto. It was more a low, lazy hum as he pinched the peaked tips of her breasts, shooting an entire quiverful of flaming arrows straight to her clit, lighting up the pleasure centre of her brain. She cried out at the pure delicious twist of it, arching her back, thrusting her chest, rolling her hips in pure hedonistic pleasure.

Xiomara vaguely saw the flash of sunlight on paintwork as the car made its way ever closer along the pockmarked road but she was so tuned in to the magic of Ed's touch and her baser desires she didn't care. Didn't care that she was half-naked in the window, being groped from behind by a fully clothed man like some debauched scene in a Renaissance painting.

She was here for a few blissful days with this man and no one knew or cared who she was. Or even where she was, for that matter. Apart from her security detail, of course.

'Still time to switch the window,' he whispered, his breath hot in her ear as the car drew closer, her nipples now clamped between dual pincer grips, one meaty quad pressing between her legs, parting her thighs.

'No,' she repeated as she ground back into his thigh.

Reaching behind, Xiomara pulled her dress out from where his knee was pinning it to her body, gathering it up to give him access to the back. He muttered something low and dirty as the skirt cleared her ass to reveal the lacy T of her thong and two bare cheeks. He unhanded her temporarily to squeeze those cheeks, her breasts falling softly, the air abrading her excruciatingly sensitive nipples causing her to whimper.

'You have the most perfect ass,' he muttered, palming the flesh as he used his foot to widen her stance, nudging her legs apart, hitching her higher against the thick thrust of his leg. His hands grabbed her hips and pulled them back a little, hinging her slightly forward, driving the rim of his kneecap into the heat between her legs.

Xiomara gasped at the exquisite torment, her arms slipping from his neck to splay on the sill, her hair tumbling forward, her breasts swinging with the movement as the car passed by.

Did they see her, exposed and aroused, her red mouth gaping open?

She didn't know. She didn't care. All she could feel was him surrounding her, touching her, her pulse a drum in her chest and a hammer through her ears.

'Edmund,' she gasped as she flexed her hips, riding the thick nudge of his leg, her eyes shutting at the delicious sensations swamping her body, the free swing of her breasts an erotic kind of torment. 'Please.'

His knee jammed high and hard against her, pinning her to the sill as his hands left her hips. Xiomara moaned in protest but just as quickly they were back in place, his fingers branding the soft, round flesh as his wallet landed on the sill beside her hand.

'Condom.'

It wasn't a request—it was an imperative. A sexy, gravelly one that had Xiomara moving automatically to comply, her lungs heavy as wet sand, her hands shaking. Somehow, she found the dexterity to both open his wallet and locate a foil packet although she didn't know how as his knee kept up a maddeningly relentless grind as she tore the packet open with her teeth and shoved it behind her in his general direction.

He took it, easing his leg from between hers, her heart slamming in her chest, her desire building with every rapid-fire rat-a-tat of her pulse as she waited.

And waited.

Didn't he *burn* like she was? Didn't he know she needed him inside her *now*?

Finally, she heard the metallic give of his zip and it was too much, she needed to touch him. Reaching behind, she knocked his hand away, seeking him out, her eager fingers breaching his underwear and hitting pay dirt, a triumphant sound tumbling from her parted mouth as she grasped his erection and brought it out to play.

'*Xio.*' His forehead thunked against the back of her head as she stroked up and down the satiny length of him, revelling in the thick, steely core. 'I can't think when you do that.'

Xiomara moaned at both the feel of him and the thick note of arousal she heard in his voice. She hoped he didn't think *she* was capable of coherent thought because she wasn't. She was just following the backbeat of lust thrumming through her system.

'Edmund.' She rolled back into him, rubbing herself along his shaft, her desire for him evident in her slickness. 'I need you now.'

Another unintelligible mumble fell from his throat as he knocked her hand aside, his knuckles grazing her ass. Xiomara moaned, splaying her hands on the sill again as her knees threatened to give out. But then he was done, lining himself up behind her as he yanked aside the lacy strip of nothing masquerading as underwear with one hand and jerked her hips back with the other, lifting her high on her toes.

He thrust then, in one quick move, entering her with a decisive stroke that tore the breath from her lungs and rocked her forward, her breasts swinging, her elbow giving out. Reaching for the windowpane for purchase, she flattened her palm against it, crying out at the pure unadulterated ecstasy of his complete possession.

No other man had ever *owned* her the way he did.

Before she could catch her breath, his hand slid onto her jaw, turning her head to his mouth, kissing her, hot and hard and wet, his tongue licking the seam of her lips, seeking entry as he withdrew from her body, being granted it as he plunged back inside, swallowing her gasp as his hand moved to the back of her thigh, urging it *up, up, up* until her knee rested on the windowsill, opening her completely to him as he slid in and out for a third time, her new position allowing him *deeper*.

Tearing her mouth from his, Xiomara gasped at the depth, at the way his girth stretched her and his length tested her uppermost limits. 'Edmund…' she moaned, barely able to drag her eyelids open from the pulse of pleasure kicking off deep and low. 'I…you… I…'

He chuckled at her incoherent mumbling, his breath hot on her neck. 'You want some more, Xio?' He didn't withdraw, he just *flexed* his hips in a grinding motion as his spare hand slid over the top of the palm she had flattened against the windowpane, his fingers interlinking with hers. 'Can you take me deeper?'

Xiomara moaned at the intimate pressure, her eyelids shuttering, lights popping behind. She was pretty sure Edmund had gone as far as he could, but if she had any more it was his. 'Deeper,' she muttered, her voice not much more than a ragged pant. 'More.'

The hand that held her thigh moved then, pressing between her shoulder blades, urging her down until her torso hovered off the sill, her stiff nipples lightly grazing the not-quite-smooth plasterwork, her hips angled even further until she was practically en pointe.

He withdrew then and thrust again, filling her once more, her body jerking with the action, her curls spiralling in disarray. Xiomara cried out at the erotic rub of her nipples against the sill. '*Yes*,' she said on a moan. 'Yes. Like that.'

And he gave it to her *like that*. There in the window of the cottage on the hill, looking over the clifftops and the sea and the town—not that she was conscious of any of it—thrusting **and** rocking and pounding, stoking and stoking until one **tiny** pinpoint of pleasure suddenly erupted into a wide crevasse of liquid bliss and she was pulled into it, clenching tight around him, dragging him into the fissure and drowning with him together.

At some point the pleasure receded and Edmund collapsed against her, the thump of his heart perfectly aligned with the thump of hers, his uneven breath hot in her hair as they lay there against the windowsill, joined in the most intimate way possible, exhausted but sated.

Xiomara stirred first as Edmund's body grew heavier and heavier in the drowsy post-coital haze, levering herself up onto her forearms.

'Sorry,' he murmured, his gravelly voice making her smile because *she'd* been the one to make him sound so thoroughly sated. 'I'm squashing you.' He kissed her bare shoulder blade as he also levered himself up, not separating from her but rising onto his palms, taking his own weight.

It made it easier to breathe but, perversely, she missed the intimacy of his dead weight.

Xiomara shut her eyes as his lips nuzzled her hair then drifted down her nape. 'I didn't know you were an exhibitionist,' he murmured, his warm breath ruffling the fine hairs there.

She laughed. 'I'm not.' Only with him, apparently.

'Did you want to go into St Ives?'

Xiomara did not. As soon as her legs returned to some semblance of normal control, she wanted to go to bed, directly to bed, and spend the rest of the day doing exactly *this* with this guy she couldn't seem to get enough of.

'Maybe tomorrow?'

She could feel his mouth curving against her skin as he dropped a kiss near her ear and murmured, 'Good answer.'

# CHAPTER EIGHT

AFTER A LONG night twisting up the sheets, Xiomara woke late to the aroma of coffee as a steaming mug was placed on her bedside table.

'Morning, sleepyhead.' Edmund's low voice rumbled near her ear as he dropped a kiss on her bare shoulder. 'Sit up, I prepared some breakfast.'

Xiomara smiled to herself as she did his bidding, internal muscles protesting a little at the movement, causing her smile to widen. She caught a glimpse of his naked back and legs and taut buttocks clad only in boxer briefs as he disappeared from view and sighed happily.

This mini-break had been a *very* good idea.

He was back seconds later, tray in hands, affording her a front view, which was just as magnificent. 'Eggs, toast and fruit,' he exclaimed, striding towards her looking deliciously rumpled.

'Good in bed and the kitchen,' she teased.

Laughing, he deposited the tray on her lap. 'I'm a man of many talents.'

Yes, he was. Surgeon extraordinaire. Accomplished lover. Chef. And—she glanced at what appeared to be a crystal shot glass on the tray that had been transformed into a vase boasting four yellow and white wildflowers—florist.

*Oh.* Her heart gave a funny little twist in her chest. 'You picked me flowers,' she murmured, stroking the petals as she glanced up at him.

Xiomara had been the recipient of many flowers over the years. They had been delivered to her from all kinds of people for all kinds of reasons—usually flattery or favour—not to mention the fact she was surrounded by them in the palace every day. Vases of them everywhere sourced from the renowned royal gardens.

But these four simple wildflowers touched her deeper than any arty floral display.

He shrugged. 'They reminded me of you at the window yesterday. Beautiful. And free.'

Xiomara's breath hitched at the statement as simple as the flowers and yet somehow managing to wrap around her like a warm hug.

'Thank you,' she whispered.

Smiling, he touched her cheek gently for a brief moment before his hand fell away. 'Eat up, the sun is shining and the day is ours.'

The hug intensified. Xiomara liked the sound of that very much.

It was a fifteen-minute stroll into St Ives, where they delighted in playing tourist.

Xiomara wore a white cotton kaftan-style dress that flowed loosely around her body with cute, boho, crotchet trim around the flutter sleeves and the deep V of the neckline. With it she'd teemed a pair of tortoiseshell Cartier sunglasses and a colourful red scarf to secure her hair back in a ponytail at her nape. Edmund wore a white shirt and the floral print board shorts from the Seychelles.

Xiomara couldn't help but feel they looked like a couple who'd been together for ever instead of having only known each other for just over a week, which was fanciful, she knew, but made her feel all warm and glowy inside, anyway.

They walked to the end of Smeaton's Pier, dodging people, cars and stacks of lobster pots to take a selfie in front of the white-washed lighthouse on the end. They ducked in and out of the artisan shops along Wharf Road and Fore Street, selling everything from clothes to handicrafts to candy.

Xiomara bought a silver necklace sporting a large piece of amber sea glass. It reminded her of Edmund's eyes and the woman who sold it to her had not only crafted it herself but had also picked up the piece of glass on nearby Porthmeor Beach. Edmund helped her put it on, the glass pendant sitting snug just above her cleavage, and Xiomara knew she would treasure it always.

She might have access to the Castilonian crown jewels and always took care to wear jewellery by local Castilonian artisans when on official duties, but this piece would forever remind her of St Ives and the guy who'd somehow managed to steal a little piece of her heart in such a short amount of time.

Once they'd explored all the galleries and shops and with the tide on its way out, they strolled hand in hand along the harbour beach, the calm water occasionally lapping at their feet. They licked ice cream cones as they dodged the throngs of holidaymakers, mostly young families enjoying the sunny weather that was, according to Edmund, ridiculously unusual. Apparently, summer weather in the UK wasn't as predictable as it was in the Mediterranean.

'This has been a great day,' she said as she popped the tip of the cone in her mouth and crunched.

'It has, hasn't it?' Edmund agreed, sliding his arm around her shoulder, kissing her upturned nose without breaking stride.

Xiomara's heart filled so big in her chest she was afraid it might bust right out. Her life had been packed full of amazing life experiences—people, places, things—and she was grateful for the privilege, but they had only enhanced her appreciation for the simple joys.

She knew they were often the sweetest and this day was no exception.

A toddler ambled drunkenly into their path. She was wearing a pink and purple swim shirt that covered all the way to her wrists, swim pants with three rows of ruffles on the butt and a white bucket hat perched at a precarious angle on her head as if she'd attempted to take it off then abandoned the action in favour of a stroll. Or rather, a totter.

Xiomara smiled as she and Edmund, their hands still clasped, separated to avoid a collision, allowing the little girl to pass between them, but somehow, she managed to stumble and overbalance anyway, plopping to the sand on her frilled bottom.

'Upsy-daisy,' Xiomara said as she dropped Edmund's hand to crouch down to check the little girl was okay. The hem of her kaftan was getting wet and sandy but she didn't care.

The cherub-cheeked little one stared at her with great affront, her bottom lip quivering as if her ignominious fall had been a huge insult to her ego.

'Oh, hey there, little one,' Xiomara crooned. 'No need to cry. The sun is shining and you are ah-dorable.' She smiled as she gently straightened the skew-whiff hat on the toddler's head. 'Here—' she held out her hand '—I'll help you up if you like.'

The wobbly bottom lip stopped as the toddler looked at Xiomara's hand curiously then at Xiomara for long solemn moments before breaking into a gappy grin and putting her arms out in the universal sign for *pick me up*.

Xiomara laughed. How could she resist that?

Pushing to her feet, Xiomara took both the toddler's hands and gently pulled her off the sand and back onto her wobbly legs. 'Where's your mama and papa?' she asked, looking around at the crowds of people, trying to see if anyone was looking for a runaway toddler.

'I think that's them,' Edmund said, pointing to two frantic people pushing through the clumps of beachgoers, rushing towards them.

The woman was upon them in seconds, scooping the toddler up and hugging the child to her fiercely, pressing kisses to her temple muttering, 'Thank God, thank God, thank God...'

The little girl, clearly unconcerned by the frantic reunion, squirmed in her hold.

'Hey,' said the guy who pulled up seconds later, looking just as harried as the woman. He put his hand out to Edmund and they shook. 'Sorry...we just turned our back and my wife thought I was looking out for her and I thought she was looking out for her and she...was just gone.'

The little girl held out her arms to the man and said, 'Dada.'

He smiled at his daughter and took her, slipping an arm around his wife's shoulder and planting a kiss on the top of her head as they huddled together for a moment.

'Thank you so much,' the woman said after a moment, her voice tremulous. 'Don't ever have kids, you two, they'll give you grey hairs.'

Xiomara glanced awkwardly at Edmund, cringing internally at the woman's assumption, about to rush in and explain that they weren't together like that in case Edmund felt put on the spot or embarrassed, but he just laughed and said, 'We'll take that on board.'

Which caused a funny little hitch in Xiomara's pulse.

The couple moved off, the toddler waving a pudgy little hand at them, and she and Edmund laughed as they resumed their stroll, his hand sliding into hers once again. 'You were good with her,' he said.

Xiomara glanced at him, surprised. She'd expected the conversation might be a little stilted after the mother's incorrect conclusion as to their relationship status. Or that he'd avoid any mention of the incident.

'I think it's the accent,' she said dismissively.

'You want to have children?'

Okay…he *was* going to go there.

'Yes,' she said simply. She wanted children. With the right man. There'd been too many *suitable* men pushed in her direction to not want *the one* for her baby daddy.

'And…you?' she asked tentatively.

She thought he might demur. He did not.

'It's complicated for me,' he admitted as he popped the last of his cone in his mouth, crunching and swallowing before he continued. 'I grew up in areas where poverty was everywhere. Babies, little children, their mothers, trying to eke out an existence in famines and wars.' He shrugged. 'That tends to skew a person's view. I think the world population is hugely problematic for sustaining the planet and it's an issue that's only going to get worse, and that worries me.'

Xiomara knew from her background research that Edmund had grown up in a world of famines and wars so it made sense that he would have a very different perspective. It sounded as if there was a *but* though. Otherwise, it wouldn't be complicated. It'd just be *no children* and he wouldn't have a problem with it because she'd learned that about him the past week.

He was decisive.

'But?'

'But… I see parents every day in what I do who are fighting tooth and nail for their baby. Or babies. I see new life come into the world all the time and it always hits me in the chest. The incredible wondrousness of it all. And I understand that as humans we have a basic drive to procreate.' He shrugged. 'I just…don't seem to feel that for myself. Or I haven't anyway. When I think about my life, I think about all the things I can do as a doctor, the people I can help. The technologies and possibilities of the future. It sounds conceited, I guess, but that's what excites me, drives me, and I worry that there isn't room for anything else.'

Xiomara heard the passion in his voice for his work and knew enough about his career to understand that the world needed people like Edmund Butler. But she still heard that note of uncertainty as if maybe he was trying to convince himself. Or wasn't as sure as he liked to be.

And that was possibly something new?

He gave a self-deprecating laugh as they avoided several seagulls fighting over a chip that had been tossed in their direction. 'I told you it was complicated.'

He wasn't on his lonesome there.

'It's complicated for me, too.'

She slowed and then stopped as he turned to face her, their fingers still intertwined, a question in his eyes. 'How so?'

Xiomara stared at the ocean over his shoulder for a moment before focusing on him, her heart giving a funny little flip at his earnest attention. She wasn't used to being heard. For so long she had felt voiceless. 'Children just aren't children for me. They are *literally* the lifeblood of monarchy and I have been raised to be a…royal breeder.'

'That sounds like a lot of pressure.'

'Indeed.' She smiled at his understatement. 'Having babies because you *want* them and believe that they are the ultimate expression of love between two people doesn't exactly fit with the royal succession plan.'

Being a hopeless romantic had been difficult when she'd been born into a system that privileged pedigree over personality, lineage over love.

'I imagine the twins have eased that burden a little.'

She nodded. *Enormously.* 'Especially given they're boys.'

'Castilona has a male succession line?'

'Yes.' She gave him a wry smile. 'We have not yet caught up with your British royals, who changed that rule.'

'Seems to me that kind of change might be something a new young monarch might be able to effect.'

'Indeed.' Xiomara smiled again.

It certainly would never have happened under her father's rule. Tavi had ascended the throne with many things to do to set the house of de la Rosa in order and had accomplished much in his short reign. Laws of succession had been way down on the list but it was something she planned to raise with him once hc'd settled into his role.

After his sons were born.

Not because she ever wanted to be Queen herself but because, had there been a scenario where she was thrust into the position, she could have just as ably ruled as any man.

Xiomara started to walk again, their hands still clasped. 'Is that why you split with your fiancée?' she asked as the question came to mind. 'Did she want children?'

Given his eyebrow raise, it was perhaps a question she shouldn't have let out without proper examination. *Well done, Xiomara.* Still, she had been curious about the woman since she'd read the factoid in the report. For a moment she thought she might have erred but then he chuckled.

'I keep forgetting you have this secret dossier on me.'

She laughed. It was hardly secret. But the question was out there now and she was dying to know the answer.

'That was some of the reason, yes,' he admitted.

'And the rest?' It was none of her business, but Xiomara couldn't stop now.

'I was twenty-four. Kelly wanted a much smaller life. And I don't mean that in a condescending way. She's a good person who knew what she wanted. A house in the suburbs, two kids and a dog. But I was driven even then, eager to see where my career might take me and none of it involved her vision. Not at twenty-four, anyway. At that point I was still thinking maybe I'd follow in my parents' footsteps and she definitely wasn't keen on that.'

'So why get engaged?'

'It was a mistake. We'd been together for a few years and known each other for much longer and all our friends were getting engaged and her expectation was that we'd be next and it *did* seem like the next logical step so I took it. But then I worked a shift in the emergency department where a woman with a twin pregnancy presented at twenty-four weeks with TTTS and one of the babies had already died, which was—'

He shook his head, his features suddenly bleak as if he was right back there again instead of on a Cornish beach on a sunny summer's day, and Xiomara's stomach dropped, thinking about Tavi and Phoebe's twins.

'Just so, *so* tragic,' he continued. 'And a couple of months later an opportunity came up for me to intensively study placental vasculature in the US for three months and I could feel in my bones that I was *meant* to do it, that I *had* to. Like a calling. Like my parents had felt called to humanitarian work. Kelly didn't want to leave and she didn't want me to go either and I suddenly felt...*caged*. So, I broke it off, which was about as awful as you can imagine and hurt her incredibly.'

A heavy layer of regret laced Edmund's voice and Xiomara could sense it had been a turbulent time for him. Clearly not something he'd done lightly and still felt remorse over. But the incident with the twin pregnancy had clearly affected him and knowing what she knew about him, witnessing how his skills and knowledge had saved her cousin's two unborn babies *because* of the path he'd chosen, she was grateful he'd felt compelled to follow his *calling*.

She squeezed his hand but didn't say anything and they walked in silence for a beat or two before he spoke again. 'What about you?' He glanced at her. 'Anyone serious in your past? I imagine it's not just any guy who can date a princess.'

'Well, *theoretically*, anyone can. It's just...harder in practice.'

He laughed. 'I can only imagine.'

'And it...can be hard to know who's genuine, even amongst my peers. So... I'm usually fairly cautious with men.'

She hadn't been with him though. She'd thrown herself into this—fling? liaison? flirtation?—headlong. Maybe because she'd realised straight from the get-go that Edmund Butler wasn't like any other man she'd ever met. He was a *unicorn*. And a woman from her world could only ever have one chance with a guy like him.

'That sounds both wise and a little sad.'

'And my father, of course, had his own ideas about suitable matches for me.'

His brow crinkled. 'What do you mean, suitable?'

'A match that would advance Castilona's interests. Joining two royal houses together through marriage and then, of course, linking them permanently, through children.'

'Okay...' Edmund gave a half laugh that reeked of disbelief, as if he might just have stepped into an alternate reality.

Except it was *her* life.

'That sounds very *Game of Thrones*.'

Xiomara laughed at the analogy. 'Kind of, yes. Thankfully, my mother vetoed them all. Which is why—' she let go of his hand and spun around slowly a couple of times as she walked, turning her face to the sun '—I get to be with you, here.'

She really didn't want to talk about the convoluted nature of her life any more. Not today. Not on this beach in this beautiful place. Not with him. Her father's constant interference was in the past and she didn't want to besmirch the memory of this place with thoughts of him.

Taking the hint, Edmund tucked her into his side. 'What say we head up there—' he tipped his chin to the area where several cafés and bars beckoned from beneath colourful awnings and tall glasses of orange drinks glowed in the sunshine '—get us one of those fancy drinks and watch the world go by?'

'I think that sounds perfect.'

Edmund was about as relaxed as he'd been that day in the Seychelles before Xiomara had swooped in and completely disrupted his peace—in more ways than one. Sure, this was a busy street café in a bustling Cornish seaside town in high summer, not a secluded Seychelles beach. But the knowledge he got to spend these next few days just enjoying this woman's company was surprisingly more restful than any seclusion.

She was fun and funny, engaging, articulate and bright. And so, so sexy. She was incredibly tactile and playful and eager, with a confidence in her body and the way she moved that was both sensual and bodacious. And refreshing. In his experience, too many women today were dissatisfied with their bodies to some degree or other and he'd have expected a woman who had grown up in front of the paparazzi to be even more so.

Especially one who was soft and curvy with hips and thighs and boobs in a world where *skinny* was fashionable and anyone with a keyboard could be a critic.

But Xiomara de la Rosa seemed inordinately comfortable in her skin.

Maybe that came from her innate privilege. Being able to afford anything you desired to look and feel good about yourself and the luxury of people kissing your ass all day. Whatever it was, Ed was here for it because just being around her was relaxing.

He didn't feel as if he was just marking time when he was in her company. The constant drive to push himself quietened in her presence. That might have terrified him a week ago, but today he revelled in it.

Revelled in this *thing* between them. That had been there since the Seychelles. That he didn't think he'd ever felt with another woman and made him exceptionally grateful her father had never succeeded in his attempts to marry her off.

A *suitable* guy?

Xiomara deserved someone of intellect and passion, not lineage and position.

He was almost at the bottom of his Aperol when Xiomara's phone rang and her eyes widened in alarm as she glanced at the screen, which yanked him out of his relaxation by the roots of his hair.

'It's Tavi.'

The apprehension in her voice was echoed in the sudden double beat of his heart. Octavio, wanting his cousin to completely get away from it all, had promised phone silence—so had her security—but they had insisted Xiomara have her mobile on at all times for tracking purposes, which she'd complied with more than happily.

So, something had to be wrong. Was it Phoebe? And, if so, why hadn't the King called Ed? He had insisted Octavio call him if there were any concerns regarding the Queen's health. Had he been trying to call and not been able to get through? Ed checked his phone as Xiomara answered hers.

'Tavi?' Xiomara's high voice betrayed her anxiety. 'What's wrong? Is it Phoebe?'

Ed was only privy to one side of the conversation but it was quickly evident, by the way Xiomara's shoulders dropped and the look of relief sweeping across her face, that Phoebe was fine.

'*No* way.' Xiomara glanced at him, irritation flashing in the flecks of her eyes.

'What's wrong?' he mouthed.

She shook her head at him as she said, 'But how?' And then she dropped her face into her hand and rubbed her forehead. 'Okay…yes…okay. Send them through. Okay… Ask Xavier to give me half an hour before he calls?' She nodded a couple of times. 'Uh-huh… Yes, thanks. Talk soon.'

A harsh exhaled breath ruffled a couple of curls that had escaped the red scarf tied at her nape to bounce around her forehead. She shot him an apologetic look. 'I'm so sorry, Edmund,' she murmured. 'The game is up.'

Ed frowned. 'What does that mean? What's he sending through?'

Her phone chimed then and she held up a finger as she scrolled on her screen. Despite her annoyance and irritation, Ed couldn't help but smile. She was used to having that finger obeyed and the temptation to lean in and suck it into his mouth was a living breathing beast inside him, but her softly muttered, 'Oh, no…' cut it off at the knees.

Sliding his hand across the table to cover hers, he said, 'What? Now you're worrying me.'

Reluctantly, she passed the phone across the table and Ed picked it up with his spare hand. There on the screen was the front page of a well-known tabloid. And he was on it.

*What the hell?*

It was a little grainy, clearly taken with a telephoto lens, but definitely him. It wasn't the first time Ed had ever been in a newspaper—not by a long shot. Over the course of his career there had been many articles written about him. So much so the Institute had a press kit on their website for media to easily access carefully curated images of himself both formally and in a work setting.

This was not that. This was the first time he'd been in a newspaper kissing a woman. Under a headline that screamed: *The Princess and the Posh Doc!*

'What the hell?' he said, aloud this time, as he looked up from the phone.

'Yep.'

'Is that the—' Ed scrutinized the picture a little closer. 'That's the hospital car park, the morning after we…' It was hard to believe it was only three days ago.

'Yep.'

'But there were no paparazzi around when we arrived.'

'It seemed that way. But I should have known. There's always one. I'm sorry I was a little too...'

Ed glanced up as her voice trailed off. Her cheeks were glowing and she was biting her bottom lip. He quirked an eyebrow as he interlinked his fingers with hers. 'A little too...?'

He knew exactly what *a little too* she was. A little too *sexed up*. Just as he had been. A little too full of all the intimate new things they'd discovered about each other swirling between them on residual heat and hormones.

'Distracted,' she said, with a twitch of her lips.

'Yeah.' Ed grinned. 'Me too.'

He supposed it was wrong to be grinning at each other in this situation, but he was right back at that kiss and he was pretty sure he'd have still kissed her in that moment whether he'd known they were being watched or not.

Staring at him for a beat or two longer, she murmured, 'There's more. Swipe left.'

Two more images confronted him on the next two screens. One was him leaving the hospital the day he'd done the laser surgery on the twins. The other was of Xiomara on the same day, being sneaked out of the back entrance by her security. The photographers had managed to get a decent shot of her—decent enough to support the gist of the article.

Ed scanned the article. It had apparently not gone unnoticed that the *royal clothes horse of Castilona* was in the same outfit both days. From that and the car park kiss the next morning, they had come to the very accurate conclusion that Xiomara must have stayed the night with the doctor that had performed *heroic lifesaving treatment on the royal heirs.*

The statement that had been released yesterday from the

King and Queen hadn't named Ed as the doctor or even the TTTS specifics but, given the picture of him and Xiomara kissing in the car park the morning after, they had definitely joined all the dots.

One part of Ed admired the way they'd put the *story* together. They'd obviously had to do some digging to identify him then piece together the car park kiss, the hospital and the royal statement to figure out the full picture. The tone was ridiculously sensationalist and exceptionally unkind—*royal clothes horse* indeed—but they had essentially got it right.

'Okay.' He handed the phone back. 'So, what do we do?'

She blinked. 'You're not freaked out?'

'That I'm on the front page of a paper kissing a beautiful woman who knocked on my door the day before with ravage-ment on her mind?'

Her cheeks warmed some more as she fought the urge to smile, and hell if that didn't give his heart a little kickstart. 'I'm being serious.'

'Sorry.' He smiled at her, not remotely sorry. Hell if he didn't want to kiss her right now. 'It is what it is, I guess. I'm more concerned about what it means for you.'

'Well…the hunt will be on now, that's for sure. Every pap in the country will be trying to figure out where we are. There'll be a bounty on our heads.'

'Okay, but…' He shrugged. 'None of them know we're here, right?'

'No. But Xavier will be calling soon and I'm pretty sure he'll try to talk me into coming back. Or him coming here anyway. He takes his job very seriously.'

'Of course he does. I'm *glad* he does. But I repeat: none of them know we're here. And I doubt any of them are going to think "let's go to Cornwall just in case". We're probably safer way down here in the West Country than in London.'

'You'll be surprised how they can ferret things out, the tricks they use. And with the pictures in every gossip mag and news site, it won't just be the paps to worry about. The public might notice us now too.'

Ed looked around at the café, where not one single person was paying them any attention. The only thing they appeared fixated on was the food, the sunshine and that view.

'So...' He shrugged. If she thought he was going to let this spoil their time together, she was wrong. He'd already had one break cut short; he wasn't going to let it happen again. 'We'll be careful.'

'Edmund.' She sighed and it was one of deep forbearance. This was obviously not her first rodeo. 'You don't know these people.'

Maybe he didn't know them personally, but the British people knew intimately how persistent they could be and how their antics to get that one perfect picture could endanger people's lives. And this was the reality for Xiomara and it made him want to break things at the thought of how it *narrowed* her life.

Sure, on the outside she appeared to have enormous privilege and freedom, but in reality, she was attached to a gilded retractable leash that was only so long before it yanked her back.

'Do you feel unsafe here with me?' This seemed to be a paparazzi issue only, not some legitimate threat to her life from someone who would do her harm. That was an entirely different matter and Ed would happily go back or move Xavier onto the couch at the cottage.

Whatever she wanted.

'No.' Her fingers tightened around his. 'Absolutely not.'

'Do you *want* to go back?' If she wanted that, then of course they'd leave immediately.

Slowly, she shook her head. 'No.'

Ed smiled. 'Why don't I duck back to that shop from earlier and buy you that enormous floppy hat you tried on?'

She regarded him for a few moments as if she was seriously considering his proposal, a smile slowly curving the plush red outline of her mouth. 'We should probably lie low for a day or so.'

'Oh, no.' Ed clutched his heart as he feigned disappointment. 'Whatever will we do?'

# CHAPTER NINE

Ed was aware that Xavier wasn't very happy with their plan to lie low and stick it out in Cornwall, although he had conceded it was probably less visible than being in the capital. Surprisingly, Ed wasn't as irritated by Xiomara's pedantic security guy as he would have thought. He was comforted knowing that long after their time together was a faint memory, Xiomara would be safe, that someone had her back.

And in the meantime, he had Xiomara all to himself.

*Un*surprisingly, they had no problem filling the next day inside the cottage. The weather had turned overnight, becoming cool and blustery—so much for summer! But the change made it conducive to staying in bed and they burned up the sheets as the wind howled around the cottage and the rain lashed the windowpanes.

Although the sheets weren't the only things being burned…

He and Xiomara took advantage of the couch *and the* rug perfectly positioned in front of the roaring fire in the inglenook. The shower got a workout too, as did the bath, the floor a puddle of water by the time they were spent.

Finally, at almost ten p.m., they emerged for a proper meal, suddenly ravenous from a day of…not a lot of eating. With a supply of gourmet food that would probably outlast a small apocalypse there was plenty of choice, but they decided to keep it simple as they worked side by side preparing the meal.

'I'm impressed you know how to cook,' Ed murmured as he sliced an onion in nothing but his underwear. The cottage was cosy so there was no need to rug up.

She laughed as she cut fat slices of bread. 'I wouldn't get too excited. It's just a toasted cheese sandwich.'

'*Gourmet* cheese, artisan *sourdough* bread *and* onion,' he corrected. 'And anyway, I love a cheese toastie.'

'Me too.'

Hallelujah to that. The last woman he'd dated had avoided meat, dairy, gluten, sugar and carbs. Not because she was allergic but because she thought it was *healthy*. As a doctor, Ed knew that wasn't true and it made eating out a nightmare but she'd been cool and interesting and arty and not looking for anything long-term and he'd enjoyed her company otherwise.

Then she'd started commenting on his food choices when they dined out, which generally goaded him into choosing the most unhealthy things he could find and he realised life was too short for such passive-aggressive crap and that no amount of cool, interesting, arty and commitment-phobia could compensate for silent judgement over his medium rare steak.

Picking up her glass of wine, Xiomara took a sip, the orange flame of the fire in the background causing it to glow a deep ruby red. 'I used to love visiting the palace kitchens as a kid,' she said. 'The head cook—Carlota—she's Xavier's mother, she was an absolute wizard.'

Ed raised an eyebrow. 'You knew Xavier before he was on your detail?'

'Not really, no. I caught sight of him a few times as a kid but he's older than me so we never really met properly. Although Carlota used to talk about him all the time. Anyway…' Xiomara continued '…*she* could make the most amazing delicacies and put on a meal at short notice for impromptu guests without breaking a sweat. But she always said mastering the art of a *toastie*—' he smiled at how her accent imbued the humble dish with a Mediterranean *je ne sais quoi* '—was a skill all people should have up their sleeves. And she taught me her secret.'

'Oh, yeah?' Ed put down the knife as he slid in behind her, placing his hands either side of the bench, caging her between the hardness of the stone top and the hardness of his erection. She hummed appreciatively as her hair tickled his face. 'What's that?'

'Thick bread. Fresh herbs. Don't skimp on the butter.'

'Or the cheese, by the looks of it,' he murmured as he took in the thick, fragrant slabs of the Keltic Gold sitting next to the fresh thyme on the cutting board.

'Well, if you're going to have a cheese toastie, there's no point skimping on the cheese.'

Ed couldn't agree more. 'Hear, hear,' he muttered as he nuzzled the side of her neck, rubbing against her, the shiver that raised goosebumps down her neck passing straight through him as well.

He was all for no skimping when it came to food. Or other pleasures of the flesh.

From his vantage point he could see straight down her shirt. Or *his* shirt as the case might be. It was from his old alma mater and had been with him since his first year at Cambridge. It covered enough of her to be considered decent—sitting just under the curve of her ass cheeks—but there was nothing decent about Xiomara in his shirt, the sea glass pendant sitting temptingly at the V of her cleavage. And he knew for a fact she was wearing no panties.

She looked sinfully, decadently indecent.

'That T-shirt looks far better on you than it does on me,' he mused, noting the way her hardening nipples beaded against the fabric as she layered up the sourdough.

'In that case, you won't mind if I keep it?'

Ordinarily, Ed *would* mind very much. The shirt was a favourite, worn soft and thin over the years. But the thought that Xiomara would be somewhere in the world, wearing his T-shirt? Yeah, that was worth the sacrifice.

'It's all yours.'

Right now, though, as the insatiable need to touch her rode him again, his only interest in his shirt was getting her out of it as quickly as possible. Removing one hand from the bench, he slid it down between her thighs, where he found her bare and wet and ready.

'Edmund…' she gasped, gripping the bench '…the toasties.'

'What about them?' He stroked her as he bit gently into the slope where her neck met her shoulder.

She moaned as his other hand slid under her shirt and moved north, cupping a breast, teasing the nipple. 'I thought you were hungry?'

'I am.' Unhanding her long enough to spin her around, he ravaged her mouth as he pushed the cutting board aside and urged her up onto the kitchen bench. 'Very hungry,' he muttered as he broke the kiss, sliding the shirt up her thighs, exposing her to his view as he dropped into a crouch and feasted until she was drumming her heels on his back and crying out his name.

They stayed inside another day, the inclement weather conducive to the decision, but when the sun was shining the next morning they decided to venture out for a drive. Ed had been more than fine to stay inside again but Xiomara had taken one look at the blue sky and declared they *had* to get out for some fresh air. And Ed was happy they had as they left the seaside behind, driving at a leisurely pace from St Ives to the Lizard peninsula, stopping to stroll through quaint, less busy villages on the way.

They stopped at a thatched roof pub for lunch, where there were only a handful of people dining in the sunny beer garden, paying zero attention to the woman in the floppy white hat. Ed, on the other hand, couldn't take his eyes off her. There was something about Xiomara incognito and the way that she kept peeping at him from under the brim that was super sexy but also just…made his lungs feel too big for his chest.

It made him feel like he was the luckiest man in the world.

By mid-afternoon they were back at the beach but one of the less popular ones, not far from St Ives. There were only about a quarter of the people compared to three days ago, and fewer family groups given the surf was still up from the recent squalls despite the sunnier weather.

And nobody recognized them, so they just lazed in the sun on the towels they'd thrown in the boot this morning. With Xiomara's head on his chest, her curls brushing his chin, Ed shut his eyes and drifted off to sleep. There hadn't been a whole lot of sleep going on at the cottage—actually, since he and Xiomara had been sharing a bed—and the sound of the surf and seagulls and the warmth of the sun lulled him into a doze.

He wasn't sure how long he'd been asleep when he first heard the commotion but people yelling soon yanked him out of his slumber. For a disorientating moment, he thought someone had recognized Xiomara and he gathered her protectively in his arms as she also stirred. But then he realised there were people running towards the water. Towards a man who was running out of the ocean, calling for help as he carried a very floppy-looking child out of the waves.

It took no time at all for Ed's medical instincts to kick in and he shot to his feet, quickly covering the distance to where the rescuer had placed the child on the sand.

'Stand aside,' he ordered as he pushed through the small knot of people that had gathered around the child, the control he always felt in these situations taking hold. Adrenaline buzzed through his system but Ed knew how to hone it and use it to his advantage. 'I'm a doctor, stand aside.'

He was vaguely aware that Xiomara had followed him as the crowd parted and he knelt in the sand quickly, casting his eye over the child, who lay wet and shivering on the sand. He looked to be about eight or nine and had been placed on his side although not in any kind of useful way. He was breathing, but only just, his skinny shoulders shrugging as he coughed ineffectually and gasped like a fish, his lips dusky, his eyes wide with fright.

Ed felt for the carotid pulse, which was slow but present. 'Somebody call an ambulance,' he demanded.

'I will,' someone from the crowd said as the guy who had pulled the child from the surf grasped Ed's arm.

'Help him,' he begged. 'Please help him.'

'What happened?' Ed asked as he positioned the child correctly, lifting his chin for proper jaw support, which brought the airway into anatomical alignment and almost instantly improved the boy's breathing and the colour of his lips.

'He was there beside me one minute, we were only shallow, just jumping the waves. We were having fun. We do it all the time. He loves it. Then a big one hit and his hand was ripped from mine and I couldn't find him. Oh, God—' His voice cracked. 'Is he…did he drown?'

'No.' But he nearly had. And would have, had he not been found in time. The undertow could be deceptively strong after storms. 'I'd say he probably hit his head as the wave churned him around and knocked him out briefly. He probably inhaled some water. Are you his father?'

'Yes.'

'What's his name?'

'Alfie.'

'Okay, Alfie.' Ed lowered his head to murmur in the boy's ear as he gently stroked his wet hair with his spare hand. 'You've taken some water on board and you're a bit dazed but you're going to be okay now.'

'Ambulance is ten minutes away,' said a voice from behind somewhere.

Ed nodded. Barring unforeseen circumstances, Alfie would be okay, but he'd give anything for some oxygen and his stethoscope right now.

The child gave a weak cough, his shoulders shrugging with the effort as his father knelt over him. 'Hear that, Alfie? You're going to be fine. The ambulance is almost here.'

Ed felt for Alfie's pulse again, which was less bradycardic now. His skin was cold to touch however and goosebumps stippled the boy's flesh. He raised his head to ask for something to keep Alfie warm but it was already there.

'Here.'

He looked up to find Xiomara passing him her sun-warmed towel. 'Thank you,' he said, smiling at her as he handed it to Alfie's father to do the honours.

Ed noticed a few phones out taking snaps and for a moment he thought it was to do with Xiomara, before he realised they were taking pictures of a prostrate Alfie. He frowned as he angled his body to block their shots. What on earth were they going to do with pictures like that? Put them on their social media?

'Okay, folks.' He looked around the concerned faces. 'Everything is under control now. Let's give the lad some privacy.'

The innate authority in his voice dispersed the crowd to a point. Most still watched the spectacle from close by, standing in small groups, clearly discussing what they'd just witnessed. Xiomara knelt beside him then as Alfie's father reached across and clasped Ed's shoulder. 'Thank you, thank you,' he said. 'I'm Raymond.'

'Ed. And this is Xiom… Xio.'

Not that Raymond noticed the stumble over her name as he stroked his son's head but Ed silently berated himself. Xiomara wasn't exactly a common name in the UK.

As if she knew he was beating himself up, she gave his arm a squeeze and smiled at him, mouthing, 'It's okay.'

'I'm so sorry to interrupt your day like this,' Raymond apologised to Xiomara as he glanced up from his boy. 'But I don't know what I would have done—' his voice cracked '—without your man, here.'

*Your man.* It had been less than two weeks and not exactly what was happening, but hell if Ed didn't like the sound of that.

'Please don't concern yourself about that,' Xiomara said in what Ed was coming to think of as her *princess* voice. Soothing, gracious, diplomatic. 'We're just grateful to have been in the right place at the right time.'

'Yes,' Ed agreed.

'Will he need to stay in hospital?' Raymond asked.

'I imagine they'll want to monitor him overnight,' Ed confirmed as a siren wailed in the distance.

Within five minutes, Ed was handing over to two paramedics as he assisted them with Alfie. They had an oxygen mask in place and Alfie on a monitor pronto. His heart rate was now within normal limits but his saturations had been in the low nineties prior to commencing the oxygen therapy. One of the paramedics loaned Ed a stethoscope and he listened to the boy's chest which was, as he suspected, full of crackles.

They'd definitely want to monitor him overnight with his lungs being so irritated from the seawater and the possibility of pulmonary oedema.

A few minutes later Ed and Xiomara, along with everyone else—and their phones—on the beach, watched as the paramedics stretchered Alfie, swaddled in a space blanket that reminded him of the dress Xiomara had been wearing during their first meeting, to the waiting ambulance. Raymond followed, holding his son's hand.

'My hero,' Xiomara murmured in his ear. 'You're kinda hot when you go all doctor.'

Ed grinned as he turned to look at her, dragging her close, his hands moving to her ass. 'You ought to talk, coming in there with the towel before I even asked for it, like a scrub nurse who knows exactly the right instrument to pass up at exactly the right time. That was very hot.'

He swooped in and kissed her, high on a combination of residual adrenaline, a good outcome and the scent and the taste of this woman who already seemed to be able to read his mind. Heat sparked between them that was really more appropriate for behind closed doors.

'Excuse me, mister?'

Reluctantly, Ed dragged his mouth off hers, although he didn't let go of Xiomara, his body still buzzing from their insane chemistry. Three teenage girls were looking at him curiously and had he had his wits about him, he might have been more wary than irritated. 'Yes?'

Clearly the leader of the trio, the teenager who'd addressed him stepped forward. 'Aren't you that couple that's been all over the news?'

Ed's heart skipped a beat as his awareness broadened out to the wider beach area, noticing people pointing and murmuring, their phones no longer trained on the ambulance in the parking area but on them.

'You're that Castilonian princess,' she continued, looking at Xiomara. 'And you're the doctor that saved the royal babies' lives?'

'No, no,' Xiomara denied in her unruffled princess voice even as she tensed in his arms.

Ignoring their denials, one of the other girls stepped forward. 'Could we get a picture?'

'Time to leave,' Xiomara murmured.

'Uh-huh,' Ed agreed as more phones came out.

'Sorry,' Xiomara said, easing out of his arms. 'We're on holiday. I'm sure you understand.'

She tugged on his hand then and Ed followed as they trudged to where they'd left their things, pausing only for him to quickly scoop them up and for Xiomara to cram the floppy hat on her head before they hurried off the beach.

Something disturbed Xiomara early the next morning as the first light of dawn broke through the window, although she wasn't sure what. Her body was loose and supple from another late night of naked times, the sheets twisted around her body. Edmund, lying on his belly and barely covered at all, had one arm flung across her stomach. It was heavy in his slumber but she smiled to herself, loving how good it felt, how possessive it felt pinning her to the mattress.

She stretched languorously, her muscles liquid, her body feeling as if she'd been marinated in heated honey, a warm glow in her chest.

The noise came again and she frowned, a sudden itch up her spine. It sounded distant. Maybe the patter of rain against the triple-glazed windowpane? The meteorological app had predicted more sunshine and, after their day had been cut short yesterday, she'd been hoping for continued fine weather for their trip to Bodmin, which they'd discussed last night.

After she had reported yesterday's incident to Xavier, he had suggested they lie low again in case the pictures taken on the beach managed to alert the paparazzi to their location. *And they would.* It was hardly going to be busy where they were going and they'd planned on taking a picnic lunch.

With them having to head back to London tomorrow for Phoebe's ultrasound, they only had one more full day together and she wanted to make the most of it.

They hadn't talked about what came next. They hadn't needed to. Because she'd go back to Castilona, where the planning for the Fiesta del Vino de Verano would be in full swing—as patron, Xiomara was heavily involved in its organisation. And Edmund would go to Africa and then back to his normal life doing important work. *Very* important work.

She was his holiday fling and everybody knew they didn't survive past the plane trip home.

More pattering noises had Xiomara lifting her head off the bed. Unfortunately, what she found was *not* the wet splat of rain running down the glass but about a dozen photographers standing on the other side of the stone wall, merrily snapping pictures through their zoom lenses of her and Edmund through the window.

What. The. Hell.

'*Mierda*,' she cursed under her breath as a heavy knot of dread pulled taut in her stomach. '*Edmund*,' she whispered, although why she didn't know—it wasn't as if they could hear her outside. But she didn't want him to make any sudden movements and possibly give the paparazzi a full-frontal view of his naked form. For sure it was impressive but she was certain he didn't want the world to know what the renowned foetal surgeon was packing. She just needed him to reach out, grab the window remote that was on his bedside table and block those bloodsuckers out.

He stirred a little, his hand shifting from her stomach, moving south as he nuzzled her neck. The fine nerve-endings beneath her skin twitched as a familiar heat flared between her legs and she shut her eyes tight, fighting the urge to undulate into the treacherous slide of his hand.

Instead, she clamped down hard on it and, keeping her voice low, said, 'Edmund, I don't know how, but there's a bunch of guys out there with cameras taking pictures of us. Can you reach the window remote?'

Edmund's hand froze. She hadn't heard him say the four-letter word he muttered against her neck before but she couldn't agree more. The mattress shifted a little as he reached across the bed, groping for the remote. Xiomara could tell when it was done by the sounds of protest audible, if a little distant, through the triple glazing.

She blew out a breath. There went all their lovely peace and quiet.

Edmund levered himself up onto his elbows as he looked into her face, his eyes roving over her hair and her mouth before coming to lock with hers. 'I guess they found us, huh?'

'Yeah.' Xiomara grimaced. 'Sorry.'

His brow crinkled. 'How on earth did they find us at the cottage?'

Xiomara shook her head. 'I've given up working out how.' Being filmed and photographed at the beach was one thing, tracking them down here was entirely another. 'They've probably asked about us in town. Flashed our pictures around. Maybe someone from the other cottages along this lane recognized us?' They'd been out walking a couple of times and waved at people in passing cars who had waved at them.

Stroking his fingers down her neck, Edmund ran his thumb over the warm bulk of her sea glass pendant sitting pretty in the middle of her chest. 'Are they allowed to take pictures through the window like that?'

'Technically, no. But they're on the other side of the wall so they're not trespassing and we left the window uncovered so...'

'Yeah.'

He seemed as resigned as she was and Xiomara wanted to open the door and pelt eggs at the gutter press. *Damn it.* These past few days had been so incredibly fantastic and she wasn't ready for them to end. But she knew it was over. There'd never be able to shake them now. And the thought of them cooped up inside here with a bunch of photographers camped outside, idly speculating about what they were doing *and* how many times, made her skin crawl.

It had been nice while it lasted but it was over now.

'What do you want to do? How do we handle this?'

Xiomara sighed. 'I'll call Xavier. They'll come get me.'

'I can drive you back.'

'No.' Xiomara shook her head. 'The paps will follow us and it takes a special skill set to drive safely for yourself and everyone else whilst they're driving recklessly around you trying to get a good shot.'

Edmund didn't argue. He just nodded then dropped his forehead to her chest, his breath warm on her cleavage.

'You should be able to get away okay. A few of them may hang around for a while after I leave, but I doubt they'll stick around for long.'

'Yeah,' he said, his voice a warm burr against her skin. 'I'll wait till the coast is clear.'

'I'm sorry,' she said again as she combed her fingers through his hair, staring at the ceiling, a heavy kind of wretchedness descending.

'Me too,' he murmured. 'Me too.'

# CHAPTER TEN

THE TEXT CAME through to Xiomara's phone at five that afternoon, during a discussion she was having with Tavi and Phoebe about baby names.

Hey Xio. Finally home.

Xio… She blinked hard as the message went blurry and she fought a thickening in her throat. She was going to miss hearing him say that.

Xiomara shot back a quick reply.

Was traffic bad?

She'd thought he'd have been back in London hours ago.

Three little dots danced on her screen as he replied, his message landing within fifteen seconds.

The paps didn't leave until almost two. Don't know how you put up with them. You want to come over to the apartment? I also make a mean cheese toastie.

Xiomara's stomach dipped. *Don't know how you put up with them.* And therein lay the rub. She didn't have a choice.

In her world it was the cost of being born into a particular type of privilege.

To be fair, the interest was never usually this intense. She was, after all, just minor European royalty. But it always intensified if it looked like romance was on the cards.

The mere hint of some action for the Princess or, God forbid, an actual *boyfriend,* the paparazzi went into overdrive. And the last thing she wanted was for Edmund to have to endure that. Unfortunately, there was only one way to stop it and that was stop feeding the beast.

She replied with a heavy heart.

Can't. We're hosting a dinner here tonight for some innovation entrepreneurs wanting to invest in Castilonian viniculture.

It was a lie but she couldn't bear the thought of dragging it out. Their goodbye in Cornwall had been awkward enough. With the paparazzi at the front wall and Xavier and Felipe out in the living room, it had been about as intimate as a student house party.

Their little Cornish bubble had been resoundingly burst and maybe that was for the best.

She added to her text.

I'll see you tomorrow morning. At the ultrasound?

And hit send.

It took ten minutes before his reply finally landed. In the meantime, those three tantalising little dots undulated before her eyes and despite Xiomara lecturing herself about being sensible and smart about the reality of their relationship, her hopes were buoyed.

Was he scripting an impassioned plea to keep seeing her? Hatching a plan to make it work between the two of them? Because God knew, she'd like that very much.

She'd expected some kind of tome for the amount of time it had taken but...no. It turned out he was not.

See you then.

Xiomara stared at those three little words until her eyeballs stung from not blinking. It was perverse to be feeling so devastated—she'd known him less than two weeks—to wish that he'd at least tried to rebuff her decision. But she couldn't help the way she felt. Which was why she should never have let herself get involved with someone *normal*. Someone not used to the life. Who didn't understand its strictures.

Because it was too easy for them to walk and too hard for her to leave.

Tapping the thumbs-up emoji—about as impersonal as an emoji got—she put down her phone and rejoined the baby name conversation as if a little piece of her heart hadn't just sheared right off.

It was a cold, grey morning the next day, which was a perfect match for Xiomara's gloomy mood as she walked into Edmund's rooms to be with Tavi and Phoebe for the ultrasound. She'd taken the coward's way out, arriving a few minutes after the royal couple had entered and with Xavier by her side. There'd been no need for him to accompany her into the room and he had looked momentarily puzzled when she'd asked but he had, of course, obliged.

She didn't feel great about using Xavier as a barrier between herself and Edmund but nothing demonstrated the disparity in their lives like arriving with personal security in tow. And thank God she had, because just the sight of Edmund was like a brick to her heart, a rush of feelings almost felling her at the knees.

How could she feel so…*much* after such a short acquaintance?

He was still dressed casually, in a navy pair of chinos and a grey polo shirt, but he'd shaved, she noted absently, the scruff he'd been sporting since she'd met him nowhere to be seen. She liked the scruff. She liked the scruff *a lot*.

She liked that he knew exactly how to use it to its most lethal effect.

But she liked the cleanshaven version of him too. He looked more formal, more businesslike, more *renowned foetal medicine specialist*. This was the guy she'd first seen on the internet. Not the guy from the Seychelles. Or the apartment in Kensington. Or the cottage in Cornwall.

This guy was one hundred percent Harley Street, and God knew she needed that right now.

'Good morning, Xio,' he murmured from his position at the ultrasound machine.

In her peripheral vison she saw Phoebe and Tavi exchange *a look*. The kind of look married couples exchanged in that weird ESP thing that seemed to go hand in hand with a gold band.

Xio. Why…why? If he'd called her Xiomara she'd have been on the front foot. But *Xio* put her right back in the cottage, in front of that window, her breasts bared to the world, her head tossed back, as he came inside her.

And she suspected he knew that.

'Good morning.' Xiomara put every ounce of demure princess she had into her reply as she left Xavier's side. She'd pulled her hair back into a severe ponytail and she was conscious of it brushing between her shoulder blades as she crossed to Phoebe, who was already on the bed, her shirt rucked up, a sheet covering to just under her bump.

She slid in beside Tavi, which put her directly opposite Edmund.

'How was your dinner last night?' Edmund asked Phoebe conversationally as he squirted warm goop on her belly with one hand whilst twisting a couple of knobs on the console with the other.

'Well, I had a hankering for a Super Club from Pret so we got a delivery.'

Xiomara briefly shut her eyes at being caught in a lie. When she opened them again it was to find Edmund watching her, one eyebrow slightly raised.

'Octavio got a Chicken Caesar and bacon,' Phoebe continued, oblivious, 'which I quite fancied when it arrived so I ate half of that.' She shot her husband an apologetic look. 'And Xiomara got her usual posh Cheddar and pickle, but she only ate half of hers and handed it over to Octavio to finish, but I intercepted it and ate that as well because I'm suddenly ravenous all the time.'

His gaze lingered on her for a beat longer before Edmund turned his attention to Phoebe and he said congenially, 'My favourite is their egg and mayo.'

Xiomara could have kissed him for that. Not for not calling her out but for running with Phoebe's detailed conversation about what they'd all eaten last night, which he surely didn't care about but he didn't try to interrupt either. It was as if he knew, as Xiomara did, that Phoebe was apprehensive about the ultrasound and was letting her chatter calm her nerves.

'Ooh, yes, that one's good too. Also, their Hoisin duck wrap is chef's kiss.' She gave an apologetic little half laugh.

'Sorry, I'm rambling. But we don't have Pret in Castilona *or* New Zealand and they make really good sandwiches.'

'They do,' he agreed with a warm, reassuring smile. 'Now, shall we do this?'

'Oh, yes—' she breathed a relieved sigh '—please.'

Flicking the nearby wall switch, he killed the overhead lights and, with one swipe of the transducer, the twins were, once again, on the screen. Phoebe made a throaty noise and grabbed Xiomara's hand as Tavi pressed a kiss to her forehead.

'There they are,' Edmund announced. 'Oh, yes, that looks much better.'

'Really?' Phoebe asked, her voice suspiciously husky.

Edmund grinned. 'Really.' He angled the transducer as he fiddled with the console. 'The amniotic sac of the donor twin is significantly bigger and he has a full bladder.'

The ultrasound continued, with Xiomara sure that Edmund was spending much longer for the sake of allaying parental anxiety than he might normally and, again, she could have kissed him. He answered all their questions and took his time examining everything, reiterating several times how happy he was with the results.

By the time he'd wiped off Phoebe's belly, she and Tavi were a very happy King and Queen.

'Now, let me stress,' he said as Phoebe pulled her shirt down, 'TTTS usually takes a couple of weeks to fully resolve, so I want you to have another ultrasound next week in Castilona. I will be in touch with Dr García and will make sure she gets all my notes and copies of the scans.'

'Thank you,' Octavio said, holding out his hand. 'I don't know what we would have done without you.'

Tavi's statement took Xiomara right back to the beach the day their identity had been blown. Was it only two days ago?

That was what Raymond had said about Edmund, too. Except he'd said *your man*. Those two words had caused a tiny little flutter at the time but now they made her heart ache.

Edmund waved the compliment aside as he continued. 'I'm going to be in Africa for four weeks from Monday. I'll be fairly remote and mostly uncontactable.'

Xiomara had known he was going to Africa and the fact he would be out of range should be welcome news because that meant it would be a clean break. Not that they'd been *together* to break up, but it would be cold turkey. No one a.m. *miss-you* phone calls or long texting sessions.

Despite the knowledge, her heart ached a little more.

'Too remote for Xiomara to land in a helicopter?' Octavio asked, a smile on his face.

She tensed as Edmund flicked a gaze his way. 'Even for her, yes,' he said with a slight smile before returning his attention to Octavio. 'But I'll make sure that Dr García has contact details for a colleague of mine—Kimberly Kwan. In case anything crops up—' he put up his hand as Phoebe opened her mouth and smiled gently '—not that I think it will.' Phoebe shut her mouth and smiled ruefully. 'Just for some peace of mind, that's all,' he assured her. 'Or even if you want to discuss anything or have *any* kind of worries or concerns, Kimberly is excellent.'

'Thank you,' Octavio said. 'That's most appreciated and I know Lola will also value the backup.'

'When are you flying back to Castilona?' he asked as he absently wiped the transducer with an anti-bacterial wipe.

'The plane is leaving in a few hours,' Phoebe confirmed.

It was probably only Xiomara who noticed the way Edmund's hand faltered a little as he wiped. But it would be stupid to read too much into it.

'I was just wondering how much activity Phoebe should

do between now and the end of the pregnancy?' Octavio enquired. 'Our calendar is always full but with the revelries for the annual festival starting next week, it's more so than usual. A lot of different events, early starts, late nights.'

'I would advise trying to take it as easy as possible,' Edmund said as he slotted the transducer back in its holder. 'Twin births always carry a higher risk of early labour and the TTTS adds an extra layer to that risk. Are you able to take a step back, just as a precaution?'

Phoebe nodded as she rubbed a hand absently over her belly. 'I can work with my team to see what can be moved around and modified.'

'Nonsense.' Octavio shook his head. 'Of course you must step back.' He tipped his chin at his cousin. 'Xiomara can take over your commitments.'

'Tavi.' Phoebe gave a half laugh as she shook her head at her husband. 'Xiomara is already busy enough as patron of the festival and maybe—' she bugged her eyes at her husband '—she has other things she'd rather be doing.'

Xiomara's cheeks grew warm at the implication and she daren't look at Edmund. 'Of course I can do that,' she jumped in to assure Tavi. There was no hesitation on her part. It was a no-brainer. It was what Xiomara did as part of her service to the family and her country—made things as easy as possible. It was what she'd *always* done. Even now, she was shifting dates around in her head.

The fact that Edmund's eyes were hot on her profile only made her more determined. The extra workload would keep her so busy she wouldn't have time to miss him, that was something.

'Xiomara—' Phoebe shook her head as she briefly side-eyed Edmund '—no.'

'It's fine,' Xiomara assured her breezily as she squeezed

Phoebe's hand and tried to convey with her eyes that everything was okay. That *she* was okay. That she and Edmund had been a dalliance but it was over now and she was *fine*.

That her first priority was always Castilona.

'Good.' Octavio nodded. 'That's settled.'

Phoebe sighed as she looked between the cousins then rolled her eyes as she glanced at Edmund, which caused his lips to quirk. 'Take the offer,' he said. 'Trust me, twin pregnancy can be extra tiring. By the time your little ones are born, you'll be pleased you did.'

Once again, Xiomara found herself wanting to kiss him. She knew Phoebe still struggled with the demands royalty made on their lives and found it slightly bewildering. Also, weird. She didn't understand how hereditary service was ingrained in the fabric of their lives. How could she? No one could, unless it was imprinted into their DNA.

'Seeing as how everyone has ganged up on me, I guess I'll have to,' she said. But she was more bemused than annoyed.

Octavio kissed her forehead. 'Don't worry, there'll be plenty more years for Castilona to see their Queen.'

A kick somewhere in the vicinity of Xiomara's heart had her looking away from the frank display of love and devotion, which was a mistake as her eyes landed squarely on Edmund, who had also averted his gaze—to Xiomara. Suddenly, they were looking at each other and she felt as if every moment they'd shared these past few days was replaying on an invisible strip of celluloid between them.

Every touch, every kiss, every intimate moment.

But also, the walks along the beach and the even longer conversations as they lazed in bed, all loose and warm in a tangle of limbs. The picnic and cooking together. Trinket shopping in St Ives.

His gaze dropped to where the sea glass pendant hovered at the rise of her cleavage and the air in her lungs turned to molten heat, each breath viscous as honey.

'C'mon, *querida*,' Octavio said, 'let's get back to the consulate and get ready to fly out.'

Edmund dragged his attention back to the royal couple. 'It will be nice to get back home.'

Octavio smiled. 'You have no idea. Your city is grand and exciting but I miss the slower pace of life and the predictable mellow sunshine of our summer.'

'Yes—' Edmund grimaced '—our summers can be a bit of a mixed bag.'

He helped Phoebe down from the bed and Xiomara was grateful for the distraction as a flurry of thank-yous and goodbyes ensued. She accompanied them to the door, Xavier close on her heels.

'Can you give me a moment?' she said to Tavi as he passed her by. 'I'll be down shortly.'

He glanced over his shoulder into the office. 'Everything okay?' he asked her in Spanish.

No. Everything was not okay. But it would be. She nodded and replied, 'Of course, won't be long,' also in Spanish.

Xavier raised an eyebrow. 'Do you want me to stay?' He also spoke in Spanish, his voice a low murmur.

'No.' She shook her head. 'Thank you.'

He lingered for a moment and she gave a little nod for extra reassurance, teaming it with a small grateful smile for the man who she'd probably spent more time with than any other in recent years. With one last glance at Edmund, Xavier slipped out of the door and it clicked shut.

Long drawn-out moments of silence followed the click as Xiomara's eyes drifted to Edmund, who was now sitting on the edge of his desk, his leg swinging a little. Staying near the door, her gaze ate him up, roving over the casual fall of his hair to the rangy brawn of his frame to the perfect delineation of his leg muscles in those chinos.

Despite their short acquaintance, she'd come to know every inch of him so intimately and the thought of never seeing him again sat like a lump of cold porridge in her stomach.

'So—' he cocked an eyebrow '—this is the final goodbye, huh?'

Part of Xiomara had expected him to challenge her over her little white lie from last night. Many other men would have but she should have known he wasn't one of them. He wasn't some petulant, feckless rich-boy who was too used to, and overly fond of, attention. He wasn't about to pout and make a scene. He was a grown man with his own life to lead.

He'd clearly understood why she'd avoided going to his place, or at least that she had her reasons that were none of his business. Because they weren't in any kind of relationship, which meant she wasn't accountable to him. And he wasn't accountable to her.

'Yes.' Xiomara swallowed against the lump in her throat.

*Final.* It sounded so, well…final.

But this being anything other than a two-week fling would be absurd. Even thinking it *could* be more was absurd. She wasn't some giddy, flighty *girl* who thought every man who kissed her was *the one.* She'd known what this was going in and nothing had changed. It had been spontaneous and thrilling and opportunistic but it had been a *liaison* and nothing more.

Yes, it had been like nothing else she had ever experienced and just looking at him flushed her body with a kind of yearning that was more than physical, but wishing and hoping and dreaming was for other women. Not for princesses with obligations and commitments and subjects who expected her focus to be on them and their beloved Castilona.

Still, she was pleased she'd dressed for the occasion in a silky bronze pants suit that clung and moulded to her hips and breasts, the cleavage daring, the solid weight of the sea glass pendant drawing the eye. She'd made an impression the day she'd walked into his life; it was only fitting that she left him with an equally flashy impression the day she walked out of it.

'That is a very great shame,' he murmured.

It was, it really was. She just hadn't expected him to feel the same way, let alone say it out loud. Her stomach lurched at his admission and she tensed her legs and straightened her spine lest she somehow betrayed her inner uproar.

She forced herself to shrug casually instead. 'This was never anything more than an affair of convenience.'

But even as she said the words, Xiomara knew they were wrong. So wrong they clawed at her throat. It was never *meant* to be anything but, right from the start, their chemistry had been more than sexual.

There'd been synergy as well.

'We both knew that,' she added for good measure because he couldn't know that she was feeling more things than she should after such short acquaintance.

She might be royal and trained to display poise and dignity at all times but she suddenly felt terribly gauche in front of this very accomplished man and couldn't bear the thought that he might think her asinine or silly for allowing herself to *catch feelings*.

He regarded her for long moments, his leg gently swinging, but didn't say anything. Xiomara wished she could tell what he was thinking like she'd been able to in Cornwall, when there'd been an openness between them she'd relished. But there was a reserve there now and she just didn't know.

'It seems like you're going to be busy.'

Xiomara nodded. And so was he. It was the perfect way for them both to move forward and not look back. 'August is always busy. Planning for the festival will be in full swing upon our return and as the patron that takes up much of my time.'

'And now you have Phoebe's engagements too.'

'Yes.' Xiomara nodded. 'There'll be plenty to do.'

He folded his arms. 'And is that what you want?'

She frowned. 'To be busy?' Hell, yes, it was exactly what she wanted.

'To be at the King's beck and call?'

Xiomara blinked. He'd challenged her similarly on the first day they'd met and here he was almost two weeks later, challenging her again. *Only he knew her better now.* He knew how intrinsically she was entwined with Castilona. How it wasn't just the place of her birth and where she lived but how she'd been raised to *serve* it as a member of the house of de la Rosa.

She was Castilona. Castilona was her.

And it wasn't fair of him to reduce her life to one of brainless royal subservience. It might look like that to him, but *the King* was her cousin and newly ascended to the throne. If she could ease his burden while his focus was split between the demands of his people and the anxiety over his wife and unborn babies, then that was what she'd do.

Because that was what *family* did.

A spike of irritation needled at her brain and she could feel herself morphing into the haughty princess from that beach on the Seychelles, gathering her carefully chosen clothes and famous royal composure like armour around her. 'Castilona is my country. Everything I do is for my *country*.'

He nodded. 'It just…seems to me that the diplomacy required in what you do has given you this extraordinary skill set as well as incredible connections that could be useful in many fields of employment.'

Xiomara raised an eyebrow to cover her confusion. 'I have a job.' Sure, it wasn't exactly defined and she often felt like a jack-of-all-trades-master-of-none, but variety wasn't a bad thing. And she *was* going to speak to Tavi about clarifying her position—after the babies arrived.

'Princess?'

She stiffened. There was no contempt in his voice. It was very matter-of-fact. But Xiomara couldn't help but feel judged by him, just as she had that first day. 'Yes?'

'What if I was to offer you a job? With the Institute.'

Xiomara blinked. Okay…*that* she hadn't expected. But her pulse did a crazy little tap dance anyway as her brain grappled with what the offer meant. Had he put it out there because he wanted to see her again? It was a tantalizing thought—too tantalizing—and she quashed it before it could take root. Sure, plenty of minor European royals held down jobs, but they didn't have a full schedule of royal commitments as well.

So, how would that even work?

'I don't understand…' Xiomara shook her head as she leaned against the shut door, its solid presence at her back exactly what she needed after the startling suggestion. 'What kind of job?'

'Well…' his lips curved into a warm smile '—the Institute has just come into possession of one million pounds. You could help us spend it.'

Xiomara returned the smile despite the riotous state of

her feelings. There was something about the laidback way Edmund didn't take himself too seriously that had her body lighting up from the inside and she was glad once again for the solid support of the door. She'd seen him at his serious professional best and yet he had a knack for knowing when to let that all go.

Yes, he was driven and committed but it wasn't his *whole* being.

Unlike herself, who found it impossible to separate out the princess from the woman. They were one and the same. Except maybe when she'd been wrapped up naked in Edmund's arms.

Everything in her life, it seemed, was serious, every element weighed down by such enormous responsibility and... *gravity.* Maybe that was why Edmund's suggestion felt so damn seductive.

Or maybe it was just the thought of being around him.

'The charity side of the Institute is always looking for ways to raise funds. There's a large committee that coordinates all these activities and there are any number of events that you could be involved with from an organizational standpoint or in an ambassadorial role. Certainly, your presence at functions would add a level of gravitas that tends to loosen the grip on wallets.'

*Oh*...

Time stood still for a moment as a hot spike of disappointment lanced straight through Xiomara's middle. So, he wanted her *gravitas.* Not her. Not what they'd shared.

He wanted her *royalness.*

Foolishly, she had thought Edmund was the only person who'd ever seen the woman first, not the princess. Who hadn't given a hoot for her pedigree.

Apparently not...

# CHAPTER ELEVEN

XIOMARA GOT IT, of course. It made sense.

A real-life princess associated with your charity was quite the coup and would indeed lead to increased donations. But that didn't stop the tsunami of dismay body-slamming her from every direction, her heart thudding loud and slow like a warning gong.

'So, you think I should…' Xiomara was careful to keep her voice light and not betray how much his suggestion had hurt '…be at *your* beck and call instead?'

Her raised eyebrow and calm smile would have won her an Oscar had she been an actress in a movie. It certainly felt like she was playing a part now, existing somewhere outside her body as she mentally shored up her disintegrating poise.

'No… Xio.' He stood, pushing away from the desk. 'I'm sorry, I didn't mean…'

He prowled towards her and if Xiomara could have backed up more she would have. As if sensing the tension in her body, Edmund slowed and stopped when he got within touching distance. 'That came out all wrong.'

He shoved a hand through his hair, which bulged his pecs and biceps, and Xiomara wanted nothing more than to rewind a day so she could just slide her arms around his waist and lay her cheek on his chest. But perhaps this was for the best. This awkwardness.

'Apologies. What I should have said is that you're young and accomplished and articulate. You're more experienced in many ways than most people your age and you're not intimidated by anything or anyone. Which is a rare thing. And you don't take no for an answer.' His lips lifted in the ghost of a smile. 'You'd be an amazing asset to *any* organisation or workplace.'

His gaze captured hers, blazing with sincerity, his words mollifying her a little. But they didn't change the facts of her life. Smiling graciously to acknowledge his clarification, she said, 'Thank you, but I'm happy with what I do.'

She *was* happy, damn it. And after the twins arrived she'd look at carving out a role for herself that didn't just involve smiling, waving and making small talk, that was more than ornamental.

'Okay.' He nodded. 'Just…food for thought.'

Xiomara had no doubt she'd probably think of little else. That this conversation would become like a burr in her shoe, niggling and prickling. Still, that was far preferable to thinking about him hot and hard and naked, the span of his chest and the swell of his shoulders rising over her as he drove her to climax night after night.

'Well…' Xiomara shook the images from her head as she straightened, the support of the door gone now, the action edging her a little closer to Edmund, charging the air with a very familiar frisson '… I really shouldn't keep Xavier waiting any longer.'

Another nod from Edmund as his gaze sought and locked on hers, the charge intensifying as they stared at each other, all that had been between them pulsing bright and reckless in a moment heady with anticipation. He leaned in then and Xiomara's breathing stuttered for a beat.

Oh, no…he was going to kiss her.

*Step back.* She needed to step back. But Xiomara didn't know how to resist this pull he exerted. He inched closer and she was in his thrall, her breath strangling in her throat. But then he stopped, imperceptibly at first, then obviously as he reached for her hand.

For one crazy moment, Xiomara thought he was going to shake it. *Pleased to meet you. Have a nice day.* Which would have crushed her. But he didn't. Instead, he turned her hand over, lifted it to his mouth and, with his eyes fixed on hers, pressed his lips to it.

He kissed her hand like countless men—dignitaries, heads of state and Castilonian subjects—had done before. But nothing like that at the same time. There was nothing formal about the action. He kissed her hand like a man who had kissed her in many other, much more intimate places and they both knew it.

Smiling as he straightened, he murmured, 'I'll never forget you, Xiomara de la Rosa.'

Swallowing the rapid thickening in her throat, Xiomara smiled like she'd been taught to since she was old enough to understand it was required of her. 'Nor I you.'

Her tone was wistful as she pulled her hand from his. It was the last thing she *wanted* to do but it was the *sensible* thing. Ignoring her heavy heart, she opened the door and stepped outside, shutting it behind her with a final resounding click.

Shutting him out, literally and figuratively.

'Are you okay?' Xavier asked gently as he inspected her face.

She smiled and nodded even though the effort not to cry *burned* her eyes. How could she be okay when her stupid, feckless heart was breaking? It had been less than two weeks.

*How was that even possible?*

* * *

Xiomara sat at the table, staring absently out of the plane window as Tavi and Phoebe sat opposite and continued their baby name discussion. She was barely listening as the crystal-clear waters fringing Castilona came into view. The sight of her home from the air had always called to her. The tranquil lap of sea on sand filled her with peace and joy and contentment. The island had been her anchor, grounding her in history and tradition and family.

But today it felt more like a chain.

Especially with that hand kiss playing over and over in her mind. It was as chaste as any first kiss and yet she was obsessing over it just as much. In their brief acquaintance, Edmund had kissed her so much more intimately and yet there was something so…reverential about that kiss that clogged her throat with emotion and pricked at the backs of her eyes.

Had he felt the same level of emotion that she had over their parting? Confusion, reluctance, yearning. The look in his eyes as his mouth had brushed her skin had seemed to be saying *Don't go,* but she didn't trust her ability to interpret anything when it came to the enigmatic doctor she'd known for such a short time.

She was far too enamoured to trust her instincts where he was concerned.

And what if she'd been free to stay in London? Would he have wanted that? If she was a normal everyday woman, would he have just *asked* her to stay?

Or asked to see her again, at the very least?

The captain came over the intercom announcing their descent, bringing Xiomara out of the quagmire of her thoughts to once again focus on Tavi and Phoebe's conversation. She'd lost track of the number of boys' names that had been bandied around, from the traditional to those that would pay homage to Phoebe's New Zealand roots. There was also debate about the difference between the first-born twin's name and the second because the first would be King one day and the name should be given extra special consideration.

Which Xiomara understood on one hand, but made her want to shred her skin on the other.

Her father had been Tavi's father's twin. The second-born. A cosmic roll of the dice that had embittered her father and driven a wedge between the brothers. And it *had* been her father that was responsible for the ill will. Her Uncle Miguel—*King Miguel*—had been gracious and understanding and had tried to breach the gap on so many occasions. She remembered how often he had reached out the hand of peace during her childhood, only to have it rebuffed.

It had been *her* father who hadn't been able to handle the trick of fate that had been no more Miguel's fault than it had been his. But he'd taken it very personally and not only let it define him but let it fester. Even let it shape his decade-old reign as Regent while waiting for Tavi to come of age.

Castilona had become more isolated under her father's regency. More inward-looking. Less prosperous. It had taken a back seat on the global stage as it had become more protectionist. And that had had ramifications. International relations had suffered. Business and trade had suffered. Their wine exports had taken a massive hit.

But that had all, thankfully, changed with Octavio's ascension. Within the first month he had reestablished old trading links and ushered in a new age for Castilona. And the world had embraced them with open arms. So, the last thing Xiomara wanted to see was history repeating itself with these two precious baby boys.

Brothers should be close. They should be loving and supportive. They should build each other up. Not have one working behind the scenes to tear the other down. Not that Xiomara thought Phoebe and Tavi would allow such a rift to develop or that the degree of regalness of a name alone could cause a rift. But the twins would not grow up in a vacuum.

Tavi was now running through all the King's names for the past several hundred years and giving Phoebe a potted history of their reigns, looking for inspiration from the past. Phoebe had studied the history of Castilonian monarchy after her and Tavi's hasty nuptials but there was only so much a person could learn from books.

'Who cares about historical precedent?'

The impatient words were out before Xiomara could call them back, spilling into the space between them, abruptly ending the conversation. Phoebe's kind eyes blinked owlishly as Tavi's eyebrows raised.

'I think the people of Castilona might.'

It was on the tip of Xiomara's tongue to say, *So what?* Too much of Tavi's life—*her* life—was dictated by Castilonian expectations. The monarchy—even under the more austere regency of her father—was beloved amongst the people and Tavi and Phoebe's wedding and the impending birth of their babies had added a much-needed sprinkle of fairy dust to the institution of the monarchy.

The Castilonian people adored their new King and Queen, so surely none would begrudge the young royal couple the experience of naming their own children without regard to centuries of tradition.

'Call them what you want, what any other parents would call their kids. Call them Beavis and Butt-Head if you like.'

Phoebe laughed, clearly tickled by the idea of a King Butt-Head. Tavi, on the other hand, was more serious. 'But we're not just any other parents.'

And that was it, right there. Like herself, Tavi could never disassociate himself from his role. He could never truly just be Octavio. Every hair on his head, every cell in his body, belonged to Castilona. And every action he took was predicated on how it would affect his people.

'Just…' Xiomara let out a heavy sigh '…choose something you like. Don't let this decision be dictated by royal protocols and what their futures might be.'

Xiomara knew that was a big ask as silence settled over the table. Husband and wife exchanged a puzzled look.

'Xiomara?' Tavi's voice was gentle when he eventually spoke. 'What's going on?'

She wished she knew. She wished there wasn't this surge of discontent and resentment over the strictures of royal life, simmering like a witches' brew in her gut and almost overwhelming her with the desire to scream.

'I just would hate for them to feel any kind of *heir and the spare* divide.'

Phoebe's swiftly indrawn breath had Xiomara wondering if she'd gone too far. Luckily, gone were the days when speaking truth to power could put a person's head on the chopping block.

'We would never make them feel like that,' she said quietly.

'Of course, you won't.' Xiomara gentled her voice as she reached across and squeezed the other woman's hand. Phoebe was new to all this, it was easy for her to be idealistic, whereas Xio and Tavi had lived the reality. 'But society *will*.'

She glanced at her cousin. 'Had my father been born two minutes earlier, he would have been King—not just a temporary Regent—and the fact that he was born second had a huge ripple effect on everyone around him, including the country.'

Tavi nodded and Xiomara could see he was thinking about

those years too. How the poison of that perceived slight had leached into every decision Mauricio had made as Regent, regardless of the ramifications. How he had spent so much of these last months untangling all her father's bitter knots.

'I'm aware. It's just…a lot easier in theory than in practice. Balancing the personal with the traditional.'

'Tradition.' Xiomara shook her head in disgust.

Her entire life had been dictated by tradition. When she'd been younger she'd taken comfort from it, knowing it provided some kind of road map to follow. It was only as she'd grown older that she could see it for the double-edged sword it was, and suddenly Xiomara was impatient for change.

She knew that Tavi's goal to modernise the monarchy had been derailed by much bigger matters of state, not to mention the royal wedding and the complications with the babies. But, if anything, the royal babies had only amplified the issue.

'What if the twins were a boy and a girl?'

Tavi's brow furrowed as if he wasn't sure where this was going. 'Okay?'

'And the girl was born first, making her the elder. But according to our succession laws she cannot rule because she's a girl and that privilege would go to her brother.'

As a female de la Rosa in a male primogeniture system, Xiomara was especially sensitive to the topic. Not because she wanted to be Queen, but because it rankled that she— or any female—was considered less *able* merely because of her gender. It rankled even more so today with Edmund's job offer replaying over and over in her brain.

'Do you not think she would be just as capable of ruling as her brother? Do you not think *I* would be just as capable of ruling as *you*?'

'Of course you would be.' He cocked an eyebrow. 'You… want it?'

Xiomara huffed out a breath. '*No*, Tavi, I don't want it.' It was the last thing she wanted. 'But I don't think I or any other female de la Rosa should be excluded from it either, just because of our gender. I don't think girls in our family should be made to feel inferior and that their only worth is in the male babies they can produce for the line.'

'Hear, hear,' Phoebe murmured.

Tavi glanced between the two women fixing him with their gazes and held up his hands. 'You get no argument from me.'

'Good.' Xiomara nodded. 'You want to modernise the monarchy? Then start there. Do something about our archaic male succession laws. The British Royal Family altered theirs over a decade ago. It's about time we brought ours in line for future generations of de la Rosas.'

'You're right. I'll get onto it first thing tomorrow.'

Xiomara smiled at her cousin but the victory felt hollow and did nothing to take the edge off her irritability. Two weeks out of her normal life and suddenly everything about her existence felt meaningless and it *gnawed* at her.

'Anything else I can do for you?' he queried, amusement lighting his handsome features. 'Would you like a national holiday named after you? The keys to the city?'

He was joking but Xiomara was in no mood for jokes. 'Yes. I want a job. A proper job.'

Xiomara hadn't planned on putting any of this on Tavi's plate right now. Changes to the succession and a job for her could have waited. The last couple of weeks had been stressful and she hadn't wanted to add to that. She'd been fine with waiting until after the babies arrived and all was well. But he'd opened the door and she was too vexed by the lack of direction in her life and her own inertia to stay quiet any longer.

'I don't want to cut ribbons any more or take a visiting dignitary's wife on a wine tour or read out some innocuous speech that someone in the royal protocol office has written. Not *all* the time anyway. I want something I can get my teeth into. A role I can call my own. And I want to write my own damn speeches.'

The plane touched down then, startling Xiomara a little. She'd been so caught up in the conversation and the squall of emotions inside her, she hadn't been paying attention to the plane's descent. It was impossible to speak then as the muffled roar of the reverse thrusters reverberated through the cabin and the plane rocked and vibrated as it rapidly slowed. But she was aware of both Phoebe and Tavi watching her carefully—one curious, one concerned.

Phoebe was the first to speak as the plane slowed to a taxi and they could hear each other again. 'You seem unhappy.'

*What?* No. She wasn't unhappy. How could she be? That would be ridiculous, given her life of enormous privilege. But she wasn't…satisfied either. She *had* been, but the last two weeks had changed everything.

'I'm not,' she assured them with a quick smile. 'It's just… I'm twenty-seven years old. I want to do more with my life. Something meaningful.'

Tavi met her gaze. Xiomara knew that he, more than anyone, understood what she meant. Everyone assumed that being born into royalty meant you had no other life ambition, but that simply wasn't true. And she wasn't going to let it dictate her life any more.

'Good idea.' Tavi smiled. 'Something else to talk about tomorrow?'

Xiomara nodded. She could wait a day.

# CHAPTER TWELVE

THE PLAZA CENTRAL was awash with sunshine and alive with merriment on the last Sunday in August. Throngs of people wearing wreaths of vine leaves in their hair were out enjoying the culmination of the Fiesta del Vino de Verano. Bunting of mini Castilonian flags crisscrossed overhead and fluttered in the light breeze. Building edifices, shop-fronts and cafés that faced the square were decorated in vine leaves dripping with grapes, as were lampposts, flag-poles and bollards. Statues and figurines in fountains were given the same treatment.

Laughter was everywhere as children ran in between groups of festivalgoers and both local and tourists alike took their turn at stomping grapes with their bare feet in the plethora of wooden half barrels that littered the cobble-stoned square. Guitar music drifted from somewhere, add-ing to the general hubbub along with a mix of languages, Spanish and English predominantly, but also a smattering of other European languages, giving the event a truly in-ternational feel.

Ed hadn't planned on being here. In fact, only yester-day he had a flight booked from Dar es Salaam to London. And then he'd arrived at the airport and just…changed his mind. On a whim.

Sure, he'd told himself, he needed a break before he went

back to work in a few days. His time in Africa had been its usual mixed bag of rewarding and gruelling and a few days chilling on a Mediterranean island was just what the doctor ordered. Especially considering his last island holiday had been cut short.

He also needed to deliver an apology to Xiomara. To *Xio*. For his gaffe the day they'd parted in London. What on earth had possessed him to offer her a *job,* he had no idea. All that had done was trivialise her time-consuming role in the royal court.

But, in truth, neither of those were the real reasons he'd not boarded that plane to London.

He'd come to Castilona because he couldn't *not*. Because he *had* to see her. Because he'd missed her and hadn't been able to stop thinking about her. He'd known her for less than two weeks and been apart from her for four and they had been *interminable.*

It was ridiculous. He'd been *engaged* to Kelly and had never felt this constant restless, *reckless* need to be with her. To see her. To just be in the same room as her. It had invaded every moment of his days in Africa, from teaching in sophisticated university auditoriums, to performing life-saving foetal surgery in rudimentary hospitals, to pitching in at maternal health clinics held under mahogany trees on the outskirts of villages or in white tents in refugee camps.

*Xio* had formed a relentless drumbeat in his head.

*Xio. Xio. Xio.*

Her smile, the way her hair bounced around her head when she laughed, her graciousness. The way she talked and dressed and moved. The way she was with people. Sure, she'd been cool and haughty with him originally, but he knew her well enough now to know that was her façade for when she felt out of her depth. The more she was unsure of herself, the more she disappeared behind her princess veneer.

She'd not been like that with the parents of the little girl who had fallen at her feet on the beach. Or the father of the boy who had nearly drowned. Or with Xavier. Who was essentially *staff* and yet she treated him with deference and respect.

And Ed couldn't wait to see her again. He just hoped she felt the same way.

He hadn't let Xiomara know he was on Castilona because he knew that, as festival patron, she'd be busy and he didn't want to interfere with her day. He'd call her this evening and let her know he was here. In the meantime, he was content to wander for a while, soaking up the sights and sounds. And, as he scooped another spoonful of delicious paella into his mouth, the tastes.

He'd purchased it from one of the many market stalls that was stationed along one of the access roads to the plaza. It was rich and spicy and he sighed contentedly at the burst of flavours on his palate.

But then he heard the laugh—*her laugh*—cutting through the murmur of the crowds and the food suddenly turned to ash in his mouth.

*Xiomara.*

It *was* her laugh. He knew the sound intimately. He knew every inflection of it. The snort laugh when she was watching something funny on the television, the tinkly laugh when something delighted her, the hysterical laugh when she was being tickled, the low, self-deprecating laugh when she was poking fun at herself.

This laughter was pure joy and he turned, homing in on it, spotting her standing in a barrel in the middle of the square, encircled by a crowd. She was in a stripy boho dress, her arms bare, the skirt tucked up at the sides to lift the hem to just below her knees. The amber sea glass pendant she'd bought in St Ives played peekaboo with her cleavage.

There was another woman with her, also laughing, as they held each other's shoulders for purchase and watched their feet as they crushed grapes, their knees rising up and down, their calves splashed with dark red juice.

On her head, sitting atop her curls, was a simple leaf wreath. It was far from the tiara she'd been wearing in the photograph he'd found online the day they'd first met and, standing in a barrel with the hem of her dress splattered in grape juice, she was far from the formality of *that* princess.

But the people milling around clearly didn't care. They were smiling—beaming, actually—and clapping as they called out, *'Viva!'* and took pictures on their phones, clearly enamoured with their Princess getting her feet dirty. There were some paparazzi too, snapping away, but not many, and none were yelling her name or bothering her, as he had witnessed in the UK. Certainly, Xiomara wasn't paying them any heed—nobody was.

Well, almost nobody. Xavier, who Ed had spotted off to one side, was keeping an eagle eye, but there was no tension in his body like Ed had witnessed in London.

Ditching his finished food in a nearby bin, Ed let his feet take him in her direction, aware of the sudden extra beat of his heart. He made his way slowly, hanging back a little to just watch her and the utter joy on her face. Xavier clocked him but, if he was surprised, didn't show it, just tipped his chin in acknowledgement before returning his gaze to his protectee.

The woman in the barrel took a selfie with Xiomara, who grinned at the camera before she was helped out and two little girls with wreaths in their hair, one slightly older than the other, were lifted in—by their parents, he presumed—to join the Princess. She smiled and chatted to them in Spanish and held out her hands for them to take, which they did, smiling up at her, as dazzled as the rest of the crowd by her exuberance.

Xiomara led the girls around in a circle, reciting some song he didn't know, the girls giggling in response as they stomped with extra enthusiasm. More pictures were taken, then the girls were lifted out and an elderly man, his trousers rolled up to his knees, was helped in. Xiomara leaned close to hear what he said, then she laughed, a big hearty sound as if the old man had told a risqué joke, and Ed swore he could see the old guy's eyes twinkling from here.

They stomped then, Xiomara's curls bouncing as she got into the action, and his breath caught. She was *radiant* in the sunshine and he was in love with her.

There it was. As plain and simple as that.

Part of him wanted to dispute it because how could he possibly know *that* after such a short acquaintance? But it was indisputable. Overwhelmingly *irrefutable*. It was there in every in/out chug of his breathing, every lub-dub of his heartbeat. Somewhere in those two weeks he'd fallen hook, line and sinker for the Princess.

No. Not somewhere. *Day one*. That moment she'd stepped from that helicopter and strode across the white sand of a Seychelles beach, looked at him imperiously and demanded he go with her. She'd *wowed* him that day for sure, but he recognized now it had been much deeper than that. In that one bold move she had totally snatched his heart.

He'd been a goner from *that* moment, he just hadn't realised it until *this* moment.

And for a few seconds of pure utter joy, love flooded his system like a thousand laser lights all humming on together, the possibilities of a life together stretching endlessly in front of him. Then he looked around at the adoring crowds and the indulgent smiles and the sheer buzz surrounding her and he realised he wasn't the only one who loved her.

*They* loved her, these people. And *she* loved them. Princess Xiomara de la Rosa could never ever truly be only his.

The laser lights switched off abruptly, deflating his chest, the joy in his heart turning to an ache. The crowd noise around him seemed to amplify, making it impossible to think. The high of moments ago crashed to a brutal low, his gut churning, his temples throbbing.

It wasn't that Ed didn't want to share her. Seeing her like this with her people filled him with pleasure—he could watch this all day. But he knew already he loved her too much to ask her to leave. Or to split her life, her loyalties, in two.

If, indeed, she even felt the same way.

And even if she did, how could he ask that of her when she was *incandescent* with happiness right now? When every part of him could see that she *belonged* here in Castilona?

His heart heavy, Ed slowly backed away, tamping down on his instinct to rush in and blurt out his feelings, sweep her up and carry her off. Xiomara's royal status added a level of complication that, now reality had set in, he knew deserved deeper thought and consideration. He was a logical guy—his job demanded it of him—there was no reason why this issue couldn't have a logical solution, too. He just had to go away and come up with a plan before he came back for her.

Because he would be back. Once he'd figured it out.

Turning away, he shuffled through the crowd, head down, not really looking where he was going as he started to turn the problem over in his mind. Someone stepped in his path and he sidestepped to avoid a collision, only to find two big black boots blocking his path again.

Frowning, Ed glanced up to discover Xavier standing in his way. 'Oh…hey.'

'Hey.' Xiomara's bodyguard nodded. 'Where are you going?'

'I'm heading back to London.'

He cocked an eyebrow. 'Without saying hello to the Princess?'

Both the eyebrow and the tone of voice left Ed in no doubt that Xavier was judging him. But he could live with that.

'I shouldn't have come today. She's busy with the festival. I'll call her next week.'

Xavier regarded him for long moments, not saying anything but not moving either. 'So, you're just going to let all this—' he glanced around the plaza '—intimidate you?'

Ed supposed he should be annoyed that Xavier was overstepping but the bodyguard obviously felt it was his role to look out for Xiomara in more than just a physical safety sense.

'Not at all,' he denied. He *wasn't* intimidated, but it made rushing in more complicated. Ed's gaze returned to the centre of the square, where he could just see Xiomara through a throng of people, her curls bobbing as she stomped on grapes with yet another person. 'They love her very much,' he said, his eyes fixed on her.

'They do.'

'And she loves them.'

'She does. But that's not the kind of love that keeps a person warm at night.'

Ed dragged his eyes from Xiomara to her bodyguard. 'No.'

'She hasn't been the same since returning from London.'

The news lifted Ed's heart. Was Xavier trying to tell him that Xiomara reciprocated his feelings? The mere thought made him a little dizzy. But that still didn't remove the hurdles he could see at every turn. He hesitated. 'It's…complicated.'

'It is.'

Xavier's simple acknowledgement of the situation was appreciated. 'I need some time to think how we might navigate a life together.'

'I understand.' He nodded. 'But maybe—' he glanced at Xiomara again '—two brains are better than one?'

Ed followed his gaze at the same time the crowd parted a little and a ray of sunshine flooded her in warmth, holding her in its glory. It was like a sign from on high and his heart just about exploded out of his chest. Xavier was right. Ed had come all this way; he couldn't leave here without talking to her. Without telling her he loved her and begging her to love him back.

He didn't want to.

He'd spent four weeks in Africa wanting this—to see her—and now he was here he wasn't going to let hurdles and complications get in his way of holding her again.

Ed glanced at Xavier and stuck out his hand. 'You're right,' he said as they shook. 'Two brains are better than one.'

Xiomara was fine, *perfectly* fine. She'd been busy this past month, too busy to think about Edmund. Which had been a good thing. She'd proved to herself that she didn't need him, that it had been a one-off. An infatuation caused by his utter competence and proximity. And today was the culmination of Castilona's month of celebration and she was happy, damn it.

She would *not* think of him.

There was sun on her face and grape juice between her toes and she was home on Castilona, surrounded by people who loved her. She didn't need anything else in life. But then she looked up from her feet and Edmund was striding towards her in quad-hugging shorts and a pec-emphasising T-shirt, looking even better than she remembered…and she knew. She *one hundred percent* knew.

This wasn't infatuation.

This was *love*.

'Edmund?' she said breathily as he halted in front of her, the curious looks of the crowd around her fading away as he stared at her so intently she thought she might faint from how hard and fast her heart was beating.

'*Xio*,' he muttered, his amber eyes darkening to tawny.

And then he was reaching for her and she was reaching for him and his mouth was on hers, kissing her deep and hard, filling up her senses with his taste and smell, uncaring of their audience. Heat and lust and love coalesced into a raging torrent, flowing through her veins, deluging her every sense as she held on and leaned in and moaned and opened to the quest of his tongue.

She'd missed him so damn much.

Hooting and hollering finally penetrated and Xiomara remembered where they were. Breaking off, she looked around at the crowd, who were teasing her good-naturedly, and she didn't even care that there were several paparazzi here who were going to cash in on her today.

Xiomara didn't care if the kiss was splashed over the pages of every newspaper and magazine and social media site in the world.

She loved Dr Edmund Butler and she *wanted* the world to know.

Smiling goofily at him, her heart did a little giddy-up to see him returning her smile with one equally as goofy. But what she craved was a very different kind of look that was not for public consumption. Glancing to her right, she found Xavier. 'Do you think you could find us somewhere close by?' she asked him in English.

The palace was too far away and she hadn't come in a car today. She didn't need to say *somewhere private*. Xavier knew what was required.

He nodded briskly. 'Follow me.'

Xiomara apologised to the crowd as Edmund helped her out of the barrel. She promised to return shortly as she dried off her feet and shoved them into her strappy flats. No one seemed to mind her hasty departure from the scene as they beamed at her knowingly.

How could they *not* know after that very, *very* public display of affection?

She and Edmund followed Xavier, who was walking at a reasonable clip. People greeted her as they passed by. They smiled affectionately and regarded Edmund curiously but they must have looked like they were on a mission because no one tried to detain them.

Still, it probably took a minute before Xavier turned into a deserted side alley. *The longest damn minute of Xiomara's life.* Then, almost immediately he stopped and opened a blue door to the right, flanked either side by pots of red geraniums.

'No one's home here,' Xavier said as he stood aside for them to enter. 'I'll wait outside.'

Xiomara didn't question the location and only barely remembered to say thank you before dragging Edmund inside the cool, dark interior, pushing him against the closed door and kissing the hell out of him, revelling in his groan and the wild thrill of his hands locking on her ass and holding her firm against the hardness of his body.

They didn't talk—hell, they barely came up for air. After four weeks without him, Xiomara was *starving*, almost beside herself with the need to touch and taste and feel him. And if the way he dominated the kiss and the rough heave of his breathing was any indication, he was just as desperate.

How had she lived apart from this man for four weeks? How had she survived? She couldn't get enough. She couldn't stop.

She *never* wanted to stop.

Unfortunately, he had other ideas, eventually breaking away from the kiss, to her mewled protest. Xiomara went back in for seconds but he cupped her face and held her firm, their harsh, erratic breaths mingling as he stared into her face.

'More,' she muttered, her gaze roving over his lips, wet from her kisses.

He chuckled at her impatience but quickly sobered. 'Soon,' he whispered. 'I just want to look at you for a moment.' And he did, he looked at her like she was his *everything,* and Xiomara knew she never wanted to be apart from him again. 'I love you,' he murmured.

Xiomara's breath caught on a sob. He *loved* her. This wildly accomplished man who had saved the lives of two precious babies and performed the same such miracles every day *loved her.*

And she loved him back.

'I'm in love with you,' he repeated, a slow smile lifting the corners of his mouth. 'And I know it's only been such a short time and I don't know how we're going to make it work, with my job and you being *a princess* and all, but if you're in love with me too then I know we'll figure it out, because I don't want any version of my life that doesn't include you by my side.'

If hearts could truly sing, Xiomara's was playing a symphony. One of those achingly romantic ones that rose to a crescendo and brought tears to her eyes.

'I am.' She gazed at him through two shimmering puddles. 'Wildly, deeply, desperately in love with you.'

She grinned then and suddenly they were back to goofy smiling.

'Same,' he murmured. 'Wildly. Deeply. Desperately.'

'Are you sure?' she asked, taking a moment to put aside the thrill and goofiness of it all to be serious. 'I don't want you to feel caged again.'

'The thing about cages,' he said as his eyes romanced over her face, 'is that when you find someone you want to be with for ever it doesn't feel like a cage any more. It just feels like home.'

*Oh*. This man. He undid her.

But… Her brow crinkled. The realities of her life were very different to most. 'My life is not exactly normal, so you need to be really sure.'

'I'm sure.' His gaze was earnest as he brushed his thumb across her cheekbone. 'Hell, Xio, I'm *that* sure I want *babies* with you.'

Xiomara was momentarily nonplussed. Now *that* she hadn't expected. 'You do?' He'd been so genuinely conflicted in Cornwall.

'Yeah.' He nodded. 'I get it now. I get why people change their minds about having children when they find that one special person. I want to create something amazing from this love and I want to watch our babies grow inside you and I want to love them and raise them in our home together. Wherever that might be.'

He smiled at her then, slow and sincere, and she believed him.

'There's so much to figure out,' she whispered, her head light and spinning but her heart solid and true.

'There is,' he agreed. 'But we'll do it together, okay?'

Xiomara nodded. 'Okay.'

And that was all she needed in this moment as their lips met because together started now.

# EPILOGUE

*Three months later...*

THE LUSTY CRIES of Rafael Miguel de la Rosa—the baby
that would one day be King of Castilona—filled the operating theatre as Ed, scrubbed and gowned and assisted by
Lola García in similar garb, eased the second royal baby
boy out of his watery home.

'And here's number two,' Ed announced.

The baby blinked at the bright light, snuffling a little as
Lola clamped and cut the cord, and Ed indicated for the
drape to be lowered a little so his parents could see their
son as he held him up. Phoebe, an oxygen mask on her face,
smiled through tears as Octavio, whose eyes were suspiciously glassy, kissed her forehead.

'You did it, *querida*,' he murmured. 'They're here.'

'What name do we have for this little one?' Ed asked.

'Rodrigo,' Octavio said. 'Rodrigo Tomas de la Rosa.'

Ed smiled although he knew it couldn't be seen behind
the mask. Xiomara had told him all about their beloved
Uncle Rodrigo who had finally been able to return earlier
this year to his island home after almost two decades of
exile thanks to her father. Sadly, he'd returned only to die,
but his name would now forever live on in Octavio's son.

'Congratulations, mum and dad,' Ed said as he passed

the babe, who was also now bawling as loud as his brother, into the warmed sterile towel being held by a waiting nurse. 'You have two beautiful baby boys.'

Of course, they were red and wrinkled and covered in blood and vernix but their lungs were obviously healthy and the fact they'd made it to thirty-eight weeks and were both almost seven pounds after their TTTS complication had given them the very best start in life.

He'd been honoured a week ago when Phoebe had asked him if he had some time in his schedule to perform a C-section at the clinic. It was well below his paygrade but Ed never got tired of that moment he pulled a small wet body into the world and his connection to these two small wet bodies made this moment even more special.

He and Xiomara had flown out of London yesterday afternoon, slipping into Castilona without fanfare to spend the night at the palace. This morning he'd been scrubbing up beside Lola at the clinic by eight a.m. and now, not even twenty minutes later, he'd delivered two new lives into the world.

'Okay,' he said. 'Let's finish up here so you can go spend some time with your babies.'

'Yes, please,' Phoebe said.

Indicating that the drape should be raised, Ed and Lola quickly delivered the placenta then closed. At nine a.m. Phoebe and Tavi and the babies were being rolled out of the door. Fifteen minutes after that, Ed emerged from the swing doors of the theatre to find Xiomara in the anteroom where she'd been waiting for news. She was talking to Xavier who, since Xiomara had moved to London, had become head of security at the Clínica San Carlos.

After much discussion between the royal protection detail and Octavio, Ed and Xiomara had taken up residence in the private royal apartment at the Castilonian consulate in

Belgravia. It fulfilled her security needs and also gave her the perfect base for her new job, which entailed representing Castilona at various cultural forums throughout Europe.

The first few weeks after the news of their relationship broke had been a little ridiculous with the paparazzi but then some private royal drug-riddled rave in Slovenia had been busted by the police and the paps had quickly moved on.

She stood and smiled at him as he entered and Ed's heart did its usual thunk at the sight of her, still not quite able to believe how lucky he was that she'd chosen him to share her life. Between the two of them they travelled a fair bit for their jobs and Xiomara usually returned home to Castilona every few weeks to fulfil what she called her 'part-time princess role' but that only made their reunions more intense.

Every time he saw her, his feelings got bigger and bigger. He'd never thought that could be possible but he was living, breathing proof that love multiplied. And multiplied.

'Is everything okay?' she asked anxiously as she crossed to him.

'Everything is perfect.' He grinned. 'Mother, babies *and* daddy are all doing well.'

She threw her arms around his neck and kissed him. Kissed him in a thoroughly indecent manner that made him forget entirely they weren't alone. Although by the time they came up for air, the room was empty.

'*Dios,* you look sexy in a pair of scrubs,' she murmured.

Ed chuckled as his feelings grew bigger again. 'I love you, Princess Xiomara Maria Fernanda de la Rosa.'

'I love you too, Dr Edmund Butler.'

Then he kissed *her.* And his love multiplied and multiplied and multiplied.

\* \* \* \* \*

# ONE NIGHT
# TO ROYAL BABY

JC HARROWAY

MILLS & BOON

To AA and CC, if only the gorgeous Mediterranean
kingdom we created existed off the page…
Perfect location for a field trip!

# CHAPTER ONE

DR LOLA GARCIA read her typed letter of resignation, her mouse hovering over the send button. As clinical director of *Clinico San Carlos*, an exclusive private hospital renowned for world class care, she answered only to the board of directors, astute businesspeople who would likely thank her for her years of service while swiftly and efficiently appointing her successor. But even as restlessness tugged increasingly at her consciousness, she glanced around her well-appointed office, thinking of her achievements in building the clinic's current reputation.

Just because she secretly hankered for a new challenge, maybe to make a difference in the less privileged parts of society, didn't mean her position there wouldn't be highly coveted. The island kingdom of Castilona was the Mediterranean's jewel in the crown. Her job would be snapped up in a heartbeat.

A knock sounded at her office door. Lola quickly locked her computer screen, the message unsent, and sat a little straighter.

'Come in,' she called, glancing up expectantly.

The door swung open and Xavier Torres, head of hospital security, filled the doorway. His dark brooding stare, broad shoulders and imposing height were enough to make even the toughest of villains hesitate. He wore slim-fit black trousers and a matching polo shirt bearing the hospital's logo, which hugged his athletic build in a way that made Lola aware of how long it had been since she'd last gone on a date. But regardless of her attraction to the man their interactions during the six months they'd worked together had remained polite, professional and never too friendly.

'Xavier, come in.' Discretely clearing her throat, which always seemed to clamp up when speaking to this strong silent hulk of a man, Lola stood and offered him a seat.

'Thank you, Dr Garcia.' He eyed the chair but declined with a tilt of his strong, clean-shaven jaw.

'I've told you before…' she smiled patiently, her body tingling with the awareness of him, '…you're welcome to call me Lola away from our clients.' The 'clients' being the hospital's private and wealthy patients.

She'd yet to persuade him to drop the formality. When they first met Xavier had worked as part of the royal family's personal protection detail, accompanying Princess Xiomara and Dr Edmund Butler, the world-renowned expert on intrauterine endoscopic laser surgery, to the clinic.

Lola's instantaneous attraction to Xavier had been easily dismissed. Her high professional standards were legendary and were directed nowhere more vigorously than towards herself. Her career was everything. She'd once even chosen it over marriage to a man she'd believed she'd loved.

'Yes, Dr Garcia,' he said, staring at the window behind her head while standing with his hands behind his back in that habitual way of his that reminded her that he'd once been in the Castilonian army before he was discharged on medical grounds.

Perhaps he hoped the stance would help him blend into the background. A skill handy while working for the royal family. But Xavier Torres' presence was far too electrifying for him to be invisible. He filled up any room he was in with his magnetic aura.

'I wondered if we might discus the weather, ma'am,' he went on.

'The weather?' Lola concealed a sigh. The only thing that grated more than his refusal to use her first name was when he called her *ma'am*. It made her feel...ancient. And asexual! And with him around, she felt every inch a woman in her sexual prime. Maybe that was the reason for her restlessness—her self-imposed lack of a personal life.

She glanced at the window where a constant deluge of rain had turned the normally crystal-blue sea and sky to grey.

'Yes. Cyclone Gabriel,' he said.

Rather than sit back down behind her desk, Lola perched on the front edge facing him. 'I thought the forecast predicted it would blow east.'

Tropical-like cyclones or *medicanes*—a portmanteau of Mediterranean and hurricane—usually occurred at this time of year, although rarely.

'The latest indications are that wind directions have changed and it's heading straight for us,' he said, finally meeting her stare, his unreadable as usual. 'I suggest we prepare for worst case scenarios, ma'am. In my experience it's better to be safe than sorry.'

Lola shuddered at the moment's exhilaration that occurred when their eyes met. But there were always more important matters to address than her love life, or sad lack of one, an impending cyclone an excellent case in point.

'Yes, I agree,' Lola said, her mind racing through lists of possible contingencies. 'Let's make sure we're prepared.' She stood, setting aside her irrelevant attraction to the clinic's head of security. 'Please speak to maintenance and ensure the hospital's backup generators are ready to go in case of a power cut.'

'Yes, ma'am.' He jerked his chin in a nod.

She rounded her desk and reached for her mouse to wake up her computer. 'I'll speak to each head of department and suggest that all superfluous staff be sent home to be with their families before the storm strikes. We can manage for one night with a skeleton staff.'

'Yes, ma'am.' Rather than leave her office, he hesitated, his lips pressed together, a minute clenching of the muscles of his jaw. Then he met her stare once more, and she saw the concern he usually did well to hide whenever some metaphorical fire or other required extinguishing. Like her, he took his work very seriously.

'Was there something else?' she asked, grateful he was so good at his job. Excellent in fact. She suspected this role at the clinic wouldn't satisfy him for long or challenge him sufficiently. There was a restless, prowling quality to him that made her curious to know about his private life, his past and his dreams. Not that there'd ever been the time or opportunity for that. It was just as well. She'd devoted herself to her career these past fourteen years since breaking off her engagement to Nicolás.

'No, ma'am.'

'Don't worry, Xavier,' she said. 'We are built to last. This building was once a medieval monastery. It's been here for centuries, I'm sure it can weather the storm. And at least we haven't the acute and emergency admissions of the public hospital to worry about.'

Xavier nodded once more and turned for the door.

'Wait,' she said, stalling him. 'Can you please make a call to your counterpart at St Sebastian's?' she asked, referring to the larger fully public hospital. 'And I'll do the same. Offer them any support or extra equipment they might need and liaise with our porters to transport items there before the weather deteriorates further and the storm arrives in earnest.'

'Yes, Dr Garcia.'

'And Xavier, if you need to be elsewhere, you can head home too. We should be fine with only one security guard tonight.'

'I'd prefer to stay,' he said. 'To ensure everyone remains safe.'

'Very well.' Lola nodded, wondering again at his relationship status. Did he—like her with the exception of her cat Albie— live alone?

'Should *you* leave in case the coastal roads become inundated?' he said, a flattering hint of concern in his eyes.

'I prefer to stay too,' she said, her stomach fluttering. She was fiercely independent, once rejecting a married life of wealth and status to pursue her career because her fiancé had, rather chauvinistically, insisted she couldn't do both. She'd never regretted that choice. But for some reason seeing that this man cared for her welfare brought a return of the discontent that had prompted her letter of resignation.

'I'm the clinical director,' she said finally. 'The buck stops with me.'

Something like admiration flitted over his expression. 'Then let's prepare for whatever the night might hurl at us,' he said confidently, as if he could handle anything.

As the door snicked gently closed behind him, Lola

released another sigh, her thoughts returning to the well-being and safety of everyone under her care—staff and patients alike. Yes, hopefully, no matter what Cyclone Gabriel threw at them, *Clinico San Carlos* would remain as steady and immovable as their mysterious head of security.

# CHAPTER TWO

THREE HOURS LATER, as night fell, Xavier's gut feeling about the storm had proved accurate. While for now, all seemed calm and business as usual inside the hospital's sturdy stone walls, outside Cyclone Gabriel rattled the entire island as if Castilona, from its coastal fishing towns to its mountainous and forested interior, were trapped inside a vigorously shaken snow globe.

From the security office adjacent to the hospital's reception, where his colleague Antonio was stationed, Xavier listened to the live news feed and weather reports, unease building as he anticipated a night of damage limitation. The rain, present for most of the day, had turned torrential. Reports of flash flooding and land slips all over the island made news. Tidal surges had taken out the main coastal road between the clinic and the island's main port, *Puerto Reyes*. Several fishing boats had been torn from their moorings and smashed onto the rocks. Wind gusts of up to a hundred miles per hour were ripping terracotta tiles from rooftops, felling trees as if they were matchsticks and causing all sorts of infrastructure issues.

Having heard enough bad news, Xavier left the office to perform his rounds. He was about to head to the lower ground floor to check on the kitchen staff who'd stayed behind to cater for the patients and staff working the night shift, when the emergency pager he wore on his belt at all times, whether he was on duty or not because he liked to be kept aware of everything that happened at the clinic, screeched out an alarm. A cardiac arrest call on the post-op ward.

Xavier took off running, his military training kicking in. He arrived at the emergency breathless from taking the stairs at full pelt, but mentally calm and able to quickly assess the situation.

Directed by one of the nurses, he entered the private room occupied by a retired statesman from a neighbouring European country who'd recently undergone a plastic surgery procedure at the clinic. Lola was already there. Dressed in the same elegant trouser suit she'd worn all day, she was kneeling on the edge of the bed performing chest compressions on the unconscious patient.

Sensing him enter she glanced over her shoulder, her stare revealing she was relieved to see him.

'Is there anything I can do to help?' he asked, noting that wisps of her normally immaculate chestnut brown hair had escaped her tight bun and her cheeks were flushed from exertion.

'Can you take over here?' she asked without a second's hesitation, her voice calm and in charge.

Xavier nodded, glad that he could be of some use. But of course, she knew his history. Knew he had medical training from his time in the army. And everyone employed at *Clinico San Carlos* had undergone mandatory CPR training prior to commencing work.

Xavier relieved her of her efforts with the chest compressions, quickly scanning the room to find that while there were two ward nurses present, Lola was the only doctor.

Lola stepped aside and Xavier timed his chest compressions to coincide with the nurse inflating the man's lungs with a bag resuscitator.

'He's in asystole,' Lola said, meeting Xavier's stare, letting him know that the heart showed no sign of electrical activity and was in an unshockable rhythm that didn't require defibrillation.

'Does he have a cardiac history?' Lola asked the nurse as she prepared a syringe of adrenaline.

'No. His only medical history is diabetes,' the nurse confirmed.

Lola checked her watch. 'Check for a pulse please,' she instructed, supervising the arrest protocol now that she was free from administering the chest compressions.

Xavier felt the man's neck for a carotid pulse and Lola did the same on the other side, their eyes meeting after a second. Xavier shook his head, his respect for this woman multiplying. Over the past six months, he'd come to see that she ran the *Clinico San Carlos* with the utmost professionalism and integrity. No detail was too minor to escape her notice. Every staff member, from the cleaners to the consultants, was treated equally. Under Lola Garcia's clinical directorship, patient care featured at the forefront of her every decision.

To say he found her fascinating, and a little intimidating, would be an understatement.

'Resume CPR,' she said, administering adrenaline into the man's IV cannula, her expression carefully devoid of emotion.

But inside, she must be concerned for this elderly man. Not that she wasn't fully capable of dealing with any medical emergency. But maybe because Xavier was a soldier, maybe because he'd seen the worst and the best of humanity through his work, he recognised the hint of fear and concern in Lola's amber eyes. Like most, Lola Garcia had probably gone into medicine to help people. Losing a patient, tonight of all nights when they were operating under special circumstances, would take its toll. No matter how calm and efficient she appeared under pressure.

After another three minutes of resuscitation where the man's heart remained stubbornly unresponsive, they repeated the cycle. Pausing to check for a spontaneous pulse and respiration. Administering more adrenaline to try and restart the heart. And resuming CPR. With every cycle, Lola looked to him, her expression growing more desolate. Xavier tried to convey his non-verbal support, but after another ten minutes of futile efforts, the atmosphere in the room turned heavy and sombre, all eyes looking to Lola for guidance.

Xavier watched in growing empathy as Lola's shoulders slumped despondently. He shared her helplessness, but the situation was a sad fact of life. This patient had age and a pre-existing medical condition against him in addition to a recent general anaesthetic, which wasn't without risk. Of course, as the only doctor in the room, Lola would take full responsibility.

'Check for a pulse please,' Lola said, her voice thick with contained emotion. He and the nurse did as she asked, one by one shaking their heads to indicate that their efforts to revive the man had been in vain.

'I'm going to call it,' Lola said, bravely tilting up her chin. 'Any objections?' She glanced around the gathered staff who shook their heads.

No one ever wanted to give up CPR. But sometimes, despite everyone's best efforts, nothing more could be done to revive the patient. He'd essentially died the minute his heart and breathing had stopped.

Lola glanced at her watch. 'Please record time of death as twenty-one-forty-three.'

She swallowed and Xavier itched to put his hand out and touch her. To tell her she'd done a great job. But she wouldn't need his comfort. She was an intelligent and experienced physician. They weren't even friends. He'd deliberately kept his distance from day one on the job, knowing that his attraction to her was far too fierce and therefore dangerous. He only ever dated casually and Lola Garcia was a woman who epitomised every man's gold standard.

'I will personally inform Mr Ortega's next of kin,' she added, addressing the nurse who'd provided the patient's medical history.

As the team disbanded, returning to their other chores, Xavier hesitated. He watched a distracted Lola walk away from the ward, her posture ever so slightly less confident than usual.

Before he'd realised he'd moved, he sprinted after her. 'Dr Garcia...'

She turned, her dulled eyes lighting up expectantly. He hesitated, uncertain because as a result of his upbringing, he habitually kept people out emotionally. Having never known his father Xavier had grown up feeling as if he didn't fit. Anywhere. But his time in the army and his security work had taught him to put other people's safety and wellbeing above his own and he liked and respected Lola.

'You did everything you could,' he said, fighting the urge to touch her, as he'd been fighting it every day for months. Some attraction was just too powerful to be casual.

'I know.' She nodded, her stare dropping to the ground before meeting his. 'I'm not used to running the arrest protocol alone. But thanks for your help. I really appreciated it.'

Xavier said nothing. He might be calm in a crisis, but working so closely with a woman he felt thoroughly drawn to was bound to push him out of his comfort zone. Normally he avoided Lola Garcia like the plague. Not because she was an aloof or tyrannical boss. Quite the opposite in fact. The woman seemed to have a warm, open smile for everyone, while also managing to run the clinic with proficiency and professionalism. But there was something about her, beyond the fact that he found her incredibly attractive. He admired her. She was smart and intuitive and could relate to anyone with ease. Whereas Xavier considered himself an emotional island. As self-contained as Castilona itself. The island upon which he stood. The island he called home and had once patriotically considered it an honour to serve.

'I'd better call his family,' she said, her big brown eyes haunted as she turned away.

He watched her leave, torn. There was no place for dangerous personal interactions where Lola was concerned. She wasn't his usual type of woman. Even now, when his overriding instinct was to ensure she was okay after losing a patient, he knew he should leave well alone and walk away.

He had years of discipline training to fall back on, so ignoring her while the storm held them captive there should be a piece of cake. But he had a bad feeling about tonight and his gut was never wrong.

Back in her office, Lola hung up the phone, sighed and dropped her face into her hands, suddenly exhausted.

She'd never grown used to breaking devastating news to a family member. In this instance, the patient's death was unexpected and therefore even more shocking.

Thinking back to the arrest, she recalled the same look of devastation on the faces of her team. Even stoical, unshakeable Xavier had been affected. That he'd reassured her afterwards had affected her just as deeply. Being trapped there overnight, the storm forcing them into a closer working relationship, she could no longer tolerate the polite but distant rapport they'd established over the past six months.

She needed to know this capable man better. Thinking about his calm, quiet strength, she removed the hair grips from her bun and brushed out her hair at the mirror in her en-suite bathroom. It had been a long time since any man had looked at her the way Xavier had as he'd checked up on her. Maybe even close to two years when she'd last dated. Did he find her attractive? Glancing at her slightly dishevelled appearance in the mirror, she wondered what he saw. At thirty-three, she kept fit and active. Her face was ordinary but symmetrical. Her dark hair thick and lustrous, considering she kept it tamed and professional Monday through Friday.

Just then, a knock at the door startled her. She automatically reached for the suit jacket she'd removed after returning to her office. Then she abandoned it once more reasoning the caller was unlikely to be a relative at this time of night, with the enforced hospital lockdown and the walls all but rattling under the force of the storm outside.

She opened the door to find Xavier once more on the threshold, her pulse accelerating excitedly. He wore a sheepish expression she'd never seen before and held out a small tray she recognised as coming from the kitchen, bearing a teapot, a cup and saucer and a milk jug.

'Is everything okay?' she asked, anticipating some other crisis because the cardiac arrest and phone call to Mr Ortega's brother had left her a little shaken.

'I… I brought you some tea,' he said with a frown that left her wondering if he regretted the thoughtful impulse.

'Thank you.' Touched, Lola self-consciously ran a hand over her hair, which she usually always wore up for work. Maybe she should have slipped her heels back on before answering the door. Without them he seemed to tower over her. She stepped aside, forcing him to enter and place the tray where she indicated, on the coffee table in her office's seating area.

'You are a lifesaver, Xavier,' she said while he hesitated, clearly uncomfortable despite his thoughtful gesture.

'You look…tired,' he said his dark stare taking in her casual appearance. 'Is there somewhere you can get some rest?'

She looked down to see that her blouse had popped an extra button at the neckline, presumably when she'd been trying to restart Mr Ortega's heart.

'I'm okay.' She self-consciously refastened the tiny pearl button aware of the spicy scent of his aftershave. 'I'm just normally tucked up in bed by now with a cat curled up on my lap. Please join me,' she said refusing to take no for an answer. She collected a second cup and saucer from the sideboard before sinking into the sofa. 'I have a bad feeling that it's going to be a long night.'

She poured strong tea into the two cups while Xavier folded his big body into the armchair and accepted the cup and saucer, which looked ridiculously delicate in his large, manly hand.

'I share your intuition,' he said, sitting on the edge of the chair as if ready to spring into action or escape.

'We've avoided getting friendly, you and I,' she said. 'I don't know anything personal about you. If we're going to spend the night here together, I'd like to know you a little better.'

Xavier froze, his expression comically horrified, as if he hated talking about himself.

'Are your loved ones safe tonight?' she asked, easing him into the conversation, eager to know him beyond what she could learn from his employment file.

He didn't wear a wedding ring and she'd never seen him so much as smile at any of the pretty young hospital staff, which only added to his mystique. Maybe he was like her, practically a workaholic.

'My mother is safe and sound at her home.' He held her stare, his expression settling to the bland neutral one he wore so often it could be a mask he slipped on with his uniform. 'She still lives on the palace estate, despite being retired, so she has someone she can call if she's concerned.'

'That's good.' Lola curled her feet up next to her. 'My parents and twin sister are in Spain, which is where I'm from, so I don't need to worry about them. And I live alone here. I'm hoping Albie, my cat, will have the good sense to wait out the storm curled up asleep.'

She paused, eyeing him over the rim of her cup as she took another sip of tea. Her breathing a little faster as she waited for another exhilarating personal detail. She had of course memorised his employment record. He was Castilonian born and bred and had served ten years in the army before being medically discharged following a head injury that left him partially blinded. Upon which time he joined the royal family's personal protection detail protecting the King's cousin, Princess Xiomara.

'I also live alone,' he confirmed, his tea untouched. 'Not even a cat for company.'

'I hope you're not a workaholic like me?' Lola smiled, glad they had more in common than a professional desire to help others. 'Have you ever been married?'

She could no longer deny her curiosity for this wary and watchful man who clearly had many hidden talents beyond security.

'No. Have you?'

She shook her head. Her heart hammered that her curiosity was reciprocated. 'I was engaged once,' she admitted, 'but I called it off.' She placed her cup and saucer down on the coffee table. 'I was far too young, only nineteen. Nicolás came from a wealthy family and expected a traditional wife.' She made dismissive finger quotes around the last two words. 'Even back then I had ambitions beyond being a trophy or a puppet, hosting luncheons for the right people and running the domestic side of his ancient historic estate.'

His eyes narrowed, glittering with something like admiration. 'I'd say you made the right call.'

His comment, the implied compliment that she was good at her job, caught her off guard. 'Thank you. I really appreciated your calm competence earlier. Dr Lomas left to help out at St Sebastian's,' she said of their lead physician who would normally have answered the arrest call. 'I understand they've been inundated over there with storm-related admissions placing strain on the system.'

'I'm happy to help.' He took a swallow of tea and

placed the cup on the coffee table. 'Although you didn't need me. You had the situation well in hand.'

Lola glanced at her lap to stop her from admitting how grateful she'd been when he'd shown up. There was something very lonely and desolate about emergencies that occurred in the middle of the night. An extra layer of responsibility. An awareness that there was no one else to call.

'Losing a patient never gets any easier,' she said, unexpectedly responding to his quiet strength, despite her usual self-sufficiency. 'The man most likely had a massive coronary event, or maybe a post-operative pulmonary embolism, but it's harder to accept when a death is…unexpected.'

'It was just timing.' His stare met hers, his dark eyes penetrating, as if he saw her all too well. 'I doubt the outcome would have been different with a full complement of staff on board.'

She shrugged, saddened that in this instance, her best efforts to revive the patient hadn't been good enough.

'You disagree?' he challenged.

'No. I simply hate failure,' she admitted with a sigh. 'I'm a dreadful high-achiever, I'm afraid.' The standards she imposed, not only on her work at the clinic but also on herself, were perhaps a response to need to prove that her choice in giving up the life Nicolás had offered to pursue her career had been the right one.

'So, you were an army medic for a time?' she asked, changing the subject.

His company was easy and undemanding. There was something comforting and fascinating about him, as if he was exactly the right person to have around in a crisis.

The storm, being trapped at work overnight, was making her unexpectedly uneasy.

'I was,' he replied, succinctly.

'Do you miss the…adrenaline?' she asked, secretly frustrated by his brief answer.

He tilted his head in challenge. 'My work here stimulates me sufficiently for now, otherwise I'd do something else.'

'Like what?' she asked, curious that she might have touched a nerve but finding his fortitude wildly attractive. Xavier Torres was not a man to be underestimated. He was clearly a man of action. A man comfortable in his own skin. 'You like to help people. To keep them safe.'

'Don't you?' he asked, his stare narrowing as if he found her equally fascinating.

She shifted, his observation making her flush. Were they finally going to acknowledge that their chemistry was mutual?

'I do,' she said. 'It's why I became a doctor. Although I never imagined I'd stay so long in *this* particular job.'

Surprise registered in his expression. 'Because it's lost its challenge?'

Lola's face heated that he'd been so perceptive. 'Don't get me wrong,' she said, 'I'm proud of what I've achieved here.'

'As you should be. You've made *Clinico San Carlos* a world class facility and attracted influential benefactors with bottomless pockets. Anyone who works in the health sector would agree that's no mean feat.'

'Thank you.' She accepted his compliment graciously.

'What else would you do?' he asked, his stare intense as if he couldn't bring himself to look away.

Wasn't that the million-dollar question? She shrugged,

embarrassed that she had no definitive reply. 'Sometimes I have a hankering to help the other parts of society. Those…less affluent,' she said carefully. 'I'm proud of the public wards we have here. The free care we offer alongside the private. But I don't know… Lately I see myself doing something bold. Maybe working overseas for a medical relief charity.'

A few beats of silence followed her statement. His curious gaze sent more blood to her cheeks. She'd surprised him, that much she could tell. But otherwise, he was his usual hard to read self. His thoughts locked behind that dark, brooding stare of his.

Then he said, 'There are many ways to help others. You could do anything you chose, I'm sure.'

'So could you,' she countered, a delicious moment of understanding connecting them like a thread.

Suddenly, her skin became sensitive to every air current in the room, goosebumps raising on her arms as if they'd just admitted they wanted each other sexually.

Before either of them could say more or look away, a commotion sounded in the main foyer. Startled from what might have been an unsettling staring match, Lola rushed from her office with Xavier at her side.

The main entrance to the hospital was located across the marble-floored foyer. Still in her bare feet, Lola hurried towards the noise of someone pounding on the glass.

'Let me deal with this,' Xavier said, his hand on her arm drawing her to a halt before the hospital's security doors, where a soaking wet and bedraggled man was hammering at the glass with his balled fist.

'Someone must need help,' she said, hurrying after Xavier as he strode to the panel beside the door and inserted his master key to disarm the lock. 'He looks desperate.'

The minute the doors slid open to admit a blast of frigid air and driving rain, the man held out his arms, pleading. 'Please help me. It's my wife. She's injured.'

The frantic man indicated the car behind him, which was parked haphazardly, slanted across the circular cobbled driveway outside the clinic.

'We have a farm,' he explained. 'She was securing the animals. I came home from work to find her on the ground next to one of the sheds, which had been damaged by a fallen tree.'

In the passenger seat, sheltering from the torrential rain, sat a woman clutching a blood-stained towel to her forehead indicating an obvious head injury. And more alarming still, she was heavily pregnant.

Lola's heart leapt but she didn't hesitate. 'She's bleeding,' she told Xavier, urging him to assist the man. 'Help him bring her inside. They shouldn't try to make it to St Sebastian's in this weather. Not in her condition.'

Xavier rushed to the passenger side of car, while Lola retrieved a wheelchair from the porter's office behind reception. When all three of them had the woman transferred to the wheelchair and inside the warmth and shelter of the hospital, Xavier re-locked the doors and radioed for someone from maintenance to come and mop up the puddle of rain from the tiles.

'What's your name?' Lola asked the woman, quickly assessing her cognition and level of consciousness, her concerns that she'd sustained a significant head injury.

'Maria,' she said, clutching a towel stained with blood to her forehead. 'My husband's name is Diego.'

'Do you know where you are, Maria?' Lola asked, quickly taking her pulse.

'*Clinico San Carlos*,' the woman said, telling Lola she was aware of her surroundings.

Lola nodded and, after asking for permission, laid a hand over her abdomen to assess the tone of the uterus. It had been a while since she'd delivered a baby, but she could do it if she had to. 'Any pain or contractions? How many weeks are you?'

'No. I'm thirty-seven weeks,' Maria said.

'Did you black out?'

'I don't think so,' Maria said. 'I just saw stars and it took me a while to get up, then I slipped back down in the mud and kind of gave up.'

'Okay, I need to take a closer look at your head. We'll take her to a treatment room,' she told Xavier. 'Would you mind collecting my theatre shoes from the closet in my office?' She was still barefooted.

While Maria's husband pushed the wheelchair, Lola directed them to a nearby fully equipped consultation room. Xavier quickly returned with her shoes and she slipped them on, feeling instantly more capable.

'Right, let's get you up on the bed,' she told Maria, pulling on some gloves.

Removing the sodden towel from Maria's hand, Lola revealed a six-centimetre gash at the woman's hair line. Without the pressure, the wound began to bleed heavily.

'This is going to require stitches I'm afraid,' Lola told Maria, glancing at Xavier. 'Can you unlock the drugs cupboard? I'll need local anaesthetic and antibiotics.'

Maybe it had been a mistake to let most of the staff go home. But during a state of emergency most people's thoughts turned to their family. If Lola had a husband

and children she'd want to be home with them on a night like tonight making sure they were all safe.

'He's going,' Maria exclaimed, pointing to Diego. 'He's not good with blood.'

The husband wobbled unsteadily on his feet, bracing one arm on the wall. But before he could hit the floor in a faint, Xavier hauled him under the arms as if he weighed nothing.

'Let's sit you outside,' Xavier said. 'There's a couch. You can lie down until you feel better.'

Lola shot him a grateful glance. The last thing she needed were two head injuries to deal with.

When Xavier returned a few minutes later saying Diego was feeling better and sipping a glass of water, Lola put him to work. 'I'll need you to assist I'm afraid.'

'No problem.' He unlocked the drugs cupboard for her and washed his hands, pulling on his own pair of gloves.

'Can you keep the pressure on the wound?' she asked, passing him some sterile gauze.

Xavier did as she asked while Lola drew up the local anaesthetic in a syringe and poured iodine into a kidney dish.

'This might sting a little,' she said to Maria.

While Lola cleaned the wound, Xavier offered Maria his other hand. The woman took it gratefully and talked about her husband who'd been having Eye Movement Desensitization and Reprocessing or EMDR in order to overcome his fear of blood so he could attend the birth of their first child.

'He's going to be fine,' Xavier reassured her with a smile, taking her mind off the injection of local anaesthetic Lola placed around the wound. 'His most important role will be to hold your hand like I'm doing.'

He was such a natural leader. So good with people. Lola wanted to marvel at the rare sight of his smile but maintained her focus.

'Can you keep the pressure on either side of the wound while I suture?' Lola asked him, impressed when he did her bidding while still holding the patient's hand. Multitasking like a seasoned pro.

Together, they closed the wound and kept the patient's mind occupied with a steady flow of chatter. Then, while Lola completed a thorough examination of Maria's neurological system to exclude a significant head injury and took her blood pressure and temperature, Xavier went to the kitchen to make more tea. Lola watched him leave with a sigh. The man was a jack of all trades. Lola was so grateful for his calm reassuring presence. She had no idea what she'd have done without him tonight.

'I'm going to admit you to our obstetrics ward here for observation,' Lola told Maria as soon as Diego rejoined them, looking better if a little embarrassed. 'It's just a precaution but you took a nasty knock to the head.'

Maria looked as if she might protest, but one glance at Xavier and her husband silenced her.

'Thank you, Dr Garcia,' Diego said.

'Sir, if I could have your keys,' Xavier asked the man, 'I'll move your vehicle to the car park.' He held out his hand and Diego handed the keys over.

Lola stepped out of the room with Xavier. 'Thank you again,' she said, squeezing his arm. 'I don't know what I would have done without you tonight and it's not over yet.'

His forearm tensed under her hand, his physical strength and warmth comforting.

'You're welcome, Dr Garcia.' He stepped back, putting some distance between them, as if her touch bothered him.

Momentarily taken aback by her body's violent reaction to his proximity and the warm earthy scent of his cologne, she dropped her arm to her side. But maybe because tonight was unlike any other night she'd known in the nine years she'd worked at the clinic, maybe because she'd seen another unexpected side to this man she responded to more than any man she'd met in years, she couldn't let it go.

'What's it going to take for you to call me Lola?' she pushed, suddenly desperate to hear her name on his lips now that she'd witnessed that killer smile of his.

He paused, turned and shrugged. 'Like you said, the night isn't over,' he said cryptically. 'And neither is the storm.'

She watched him walk away, a sigh of something like longing trapped in her throat. Xavier Torres was the kind of man who made a woman like her all too aware that there was more to life than work. Maybe there was more than one thing missing from her life, beyond professional challenge. But fixing that would need to wait. Xavier was right. There was more work to be done.

# CHAPTER THREE

By HALF PAST midnight, an ominous calm had descended, at least indoors. Outside the hospital the storm raged on. The news reports cataloguing the extensive damage all across the island, to roads, trees, power lines and property.

Lola had just completed a round of the wards, checking in with each one, when she returned to her office and found Xavier waiting outside.

'I thought you probably hadn't eaten,' he said, holding out a plate of sandwiches and fruit covered with plastic wrap.

Lola took the offering with a groan of gratitude. 'Thank you. I'm starving. Have you eaten?' she asked, unlocking her office door, preceding him inside.

'The army taught us the importance of keeping energy levels up and staying hydrated,' he said in a non-answer.

She smiled at his seriousness. 'Well, they trained you well. Come in. I need an update.'

She washed her hands and sat on the sofa, inviting him to sit too. It seemed her office had become their unofficial storm command post. 'What's going on out there?' she asked. 'Anything I should know about?'

Peeling the plastic wrap from the plate, she invited him to share before helping herself to a bunch of grapes.

He declined with a shake of his head. 'I've eaten something, thanks.' Then he began his report. 'The government has declared a national state of emergency, effective from midnight. Civil defence have deployed the armed forces to assist in search and rescue, crisis management and temporary shelter for those who've had to abandon their homes due to flooding and other damage.'

Lola nodded for him to continue as she wiped her mouth with a napkin.

'Currently, there is no damage to the hospital's property, although I suspect the grounds will be a mess when all of this is over.'

Lola shrugged in agreement, selecting a sandwich while he went on.

'There have been no breaches of security to report,' he said. 'All of our communication systems are operative and maintenance say there's enough fuel to run the backup generators for a week, which hopefully won't be necessary.'

'Thanks, Xavier.' She sighed, leaning back against the cushions. 'I'm so glad you stayed to help. I really appreciate you.'

He jerked his chin in a small nod, then glanced at the TV screen on the wall. Lola had muted the sound earlier, but now she adjusted the volume so they could listen to the latest news update.

'Isolated reports of damage have been trickling in over the past few hours,' the newscaster said. 'Three people were injured when a tree fell on the vehicle they were travelling in. Flash flooding in the *Cazorla Valley* has inundated homes and farms, prompting emergency evacuations. And two fishermen and their boat are missing off the *Costa de las Estrellas*, search and rescue operations being severely hampered by four-metre swells.'

Muting the sound again, Lola retrieved two bottles of mineral water from the fridge and handed Xavier one. 'Have there been any more requests from St Sebastian's? I wonder how they're coping.'

'No, ma'am. One of my team, Antonio, the security guard on duty tonight, is married to a nurse who works in the emergency department there. I understand it's predictably busy.'

She sighed. 'It's at times like this when I wish I could do more to help.'

'You are helping. You're a doctor and you're needed here.'

'Yes,' she stated simply. 'I guess the storm has made me even more restless.' Something was missing from her life and, short of moving overseas to work for that medical relief charity, she had no idea how to figure out exactly what it was or how to fix it.

'Storms will do that,' he said. 'Do you…miss your family?'

At the mention of her loved ones, Lola smiled, astonished that she'd finally got him talking. 'I do. We're very close. Especially me and my twin sister, Isla. Do you have siblings?

'I'm an only child,' he said.

'I'm very lucky,' she said, 'especially as I see them often. My parents love Castilona. Mum is retired, apart from her charity work. Dad is a landscape artist so he takes inspiration from everywhere he travels and he always brings his sketchbook and paints when he visits.'

Xavier nodded. 'No shortage of stunning scenery

around here. Let's hope the storm hasn't caused lasting damage to any of it.'

'Your country is beautiful. I guess that's why I'm still here. It will be hard to move away if I decide to change direction.'

'How long have you lived here?'

'Nine years. I worked at St Sebastian's after leaving medical school in Spain then took a job here. I became clinical director three years ago.'

'Is your mother a doctor, too?'

'No. I don't know where my career aspirations originated. I think it was from reading that series of famous books, *Medical Magic*, as a child.' She laughed softly, heartened when he smiled. 'What about you? Did you always want to be a soldier?'

A veil fell over his expression, tension returning to his mouth as if he disliked her question or didn't care to answer. 'Not really. But I grew up seeing quite a bit of palace life and state traditions, so it was a logical step for someone like me.'

'Someone like you? What does that mean?'

'Someone patriotic and free of family ties.' His eyes hardened a fraction, his posture stiffening. 'I was raised by a single mother. I never knew my father. Instead of going off the rails as a teen, I signed up to join the army.'

'And they taught you discipline and medical skills?'

'And most importantly self-respect.'

'I see,' she said, her voice a croak. The clinic's head of security had demons she could never fully understand. Maybe that was why he kept his feelings to himself and kept people at a distance. 'I understand from your employment records you were medically discharged.'

He sat a little taller. His voice, when he spoke again,

devoid of emotion. 'I was injured in an explosion. I sustained a head injury and was knocked unconscious. When I woke up, I was diagnosed with a detached retina in one eye. I had surgery but it didn't help. The injury had gone too far.'

Lola nodded, instinctively knowing that would have had a massive psychological impact on him. 'That must have been difficult for you. I'm sorry it happened,' she said. 'How does it affect you?'

He hesitated for a second, as if he didn't want to talk about it, but then he said, 'I have blurred vision and some peripheral visual field loss on that side. I compensate by turning my head to the affected side, but I've learned to adapt over the years. Fortunately, I'm still able to drive.'

'I see,' she said, instinct telling her the limitation would bother a man like him, especially given his work and personality. 'You don't like talking about yourself much, do you?'

'I don't know you,' he said.

'Which is why I'm asking questions. Tonight has been…unusual.'

'What else would you like to know?' he asked, his stare bold and unwavering, as if he knew the contents of her head.

'What makes you tick,' she said, raising her chin.

'I'm a simple man. What you see is what you get.'

'I very much doubt that.' She paused, instinct telling her that was only half his story. 'I think we all have hidden depths. Things we keep from people because we find them uncomfortable.'

'And what's yours?' he asked without missing a beat. Xavier didn't shy away from confrontation but, in deflecting, he'd cleverly avoided sharing *his* secret.

Lola took a deep breath, liking that he wasn't afraid to challenge her. She was being nosy and he'd turned the tables. 'I'm scared,' she said boldly. 'Scared that if I don't keep going, keep striving, I'll somehow lose myself.' As she'd almost done when she'd agreed to marry Nicolás.

He held her stare, a moment of honest connection between them. 'I think you know who you are and what you want.'

Lola stilled, her pulse bounding. His observation made her feel naked. Her attraction to him doubling. She *did* know what she wanted. She craved independence and professional success. But she was also a woman attracted to a man. *This* man.

'If that's all,' he said, standing. 'I'll continue my rounds.'

'Of course.' Lola stood too, disappointed that she'd confessed more than she'd learned. 'Perhaps when you've finished your rounds you should try to get some sleep.' As much as she enjoyed his company, it had been a long day so far.

'I'll be fine,' he said, securely in control of himself.

Just then, her phone rang and she jumped, the ring tone far too loud for this time of night. Snatching it up from the desk she answered.

'Dr Garcia,' someone said, 'Maria Fernandez, the patient you admitted for observation following a head injury, is in labour. Her waters broke five minutes ago and she's already eight centimetres dilated.'

Lola's gaze flew to Xavier's. He'd stayed in the room, waiting and listening to her side of the conversation, presumably to offer help if required.

'I'm on my way,' Lola said, hanging up the phone.

'Ever delivered a baby?' she asked him in answer to his questioning look.

'I have actually, once,' he said shrugging, unconcerned by the prospect of helping.

'Good. The last babies I helped to bring into the world were the royal princes. But that was in an assisting capacity with a world leading obstetrics expert leading the procedure and in a fully equipped theatre. I'd appreciate your calming influence,' she told him, reaching for her stethoscope.

'Then I'm all yours,' he said, filling her with confidence, and together they headed for the obstetrics ward.

'And here's your baby,' Lola said from behind her mask as she raised the newborn girl into her mother's waiting arms.

Xavier swallowed, a lump in his throat the size of a football. That the delivery had gone without a hitch, tonight of all nights when there was only a skeleton staff on the obstetrics ward given there hadn't been any planned deliveries, was testament to Lola's amazing skills as a physician. She was incredibly talented. He felt...euphoric that the delivery had gone so smoothly, so he could only imagine how the parents felt.

For a moment, Lola glanced up and met his stare, her eyes crinkled in the corners so he knew she was smiling in gratitude. But all he'd done was hold Maria's hand opposite her husband and observe the foetal heart rate monitor for signs of distress as Lola had instructed.

He smiled back, wishing he could tell her 'well done', not that she needed his praise. But the more time he spent with her, the keener he was to get away. She was slowly wheedling her way under his ever-present guard. Push-

ing to get to know him. Sharing parts of herself as easily as she shared her smile and her compliments. It was
messing with his head, making him imagine things he
shouldn't. Making him want things he didn't need, like
connection.

With his hand holding duties complete, Xavier stepped
away from the bedside, allowing Maria and Diego time
to bond with their tiny daughter. He moved towards the
door, shutting down the pointless emotions the delivery
of a baby had stirred up. He'd often dreamed of fatherhood, but every time the thought popped into his head,
he shut it quickly down. Firstly, he'd never had a relationship serious enough to warrant the dream and secondly,
he never wanted to be like his own father—an absent,
self-serving, narcissist. The only thing his mother had
ever told him about the man was that he hadn't wanted
to be involved.

Xavier paused at the door. Lola and the midwife were
busy, and while the unexpected arrival of baby Fernandez made this a night Xavier would always remember,
he didn't really belong there. Truth was, he wasn't sure
where he belonged. Never had been. But he'd made his
peace with that long ago. No point wishing for something
he'd never had. Better to do everything in his power to
make his life secure. And now that he was thirty-five,
he certainly had no need for a father. Especially not one
who would callously abandon and reject his own son.

He was just about to leave the room and get back to
work when the lights flickered out. Everyone froze for
a second.

'Don't worry,' he said. 'There must be a power cut.
The generator will take over soon.'

Sure enough, in the next second, the lights flickered

back on and Lola shot him another of those grateful looks over her shoulder. A man like him could get used to the way she looked at him. As if he was something special. But tonight was just one of those nights. The storm creating an artificial environment where it was easy to believe that normal rules failed to apply.

But his rules kept him safe and in control of his own existence. His support network, the people he allowed close, was small. Except Lola's gentle questions, and the chemistry that had become glaringly obvious was mutual, kept nudging him just out of his comfort zone.

'I'll check in with maintenance,' he told Lola, removing his mask and apron, determined to keep his head around this woman, who was after all, his boss. Just because tonight had thrown them together, didn't mean he should act on the attraction he'd been struggling to ignore since the first day they'd met.

'Can you do a circuit of the wards, too?' she asked him. 'Make sure all vital equipment is functioning properly. See if they need anything while I finish up here.'

'Of course,' he said, glad to have a reason to distance himself from her as he set off on his rounds. It had been a pretty intense night so far and it wasn't over. Lola Garcia had a kind of freaky intuition. As if she knew human nature and could see right through him, see that deep inside him there would always be a fear that his father had left because Xavier was lacking somehow. He didn't want her to see those dark places in him. He'd spent most of his adult life keeping people out emotionally. There was no reason to change that now, no matter how amazing and sexy the hospital's clinical director was.

# CHAPTER FOUR

THIRTY MINUTES LATER, after a shower and a change of clothes into a clean uniform he kept in his locker, his head was clearer.

Storms often made people behave out of character. Unless Lola specifically called for his help he would steer clear of her for the rest of the night. No more food deliveries simply because he recognised how hard she worked and how she put everyone around her first. No more personal chats where he allowed himself to be lured by her openness into sharing more than he normally would. No more enjoying her lingering looks of appreciation and gratitude. It was time to claw back some distance.

He'd just secured his locker in the staff quarters—a central communal lounge and a fully equipped kitchen, surrounded by a series of en-suite bedrooms for staff to sleep if working overnight—when there was a knock at the main door.

Wondering if Antonio had lost his key pass, he pulled open the door to find Lola on the threshold. She'd changed too. She wore a set of the clinic's navy blue scrubs and her hair was pulled back into a neat ponytail, the ends damp as if she too had showered after the delivery of baby Fernandez.

'Dr Garcia,' he said, shocked, his manners deserting

him as he kept her on the threshold and tried not to gaze at her body, which was killer—even in the scrubs. He'd never once seen her in the staff quarters. 'Is everything okay?'

He checked the walkie talkie he kept on his belt, worried he'd missed a call. But the charge light was green showing the device was in full working order.

'I just wanted to check on you,' she said looking up at him with a smile, her straight white teeth scraping at her plump lower lip. 'That all happened rather quickly and then with the power going out... You left in a hurry. Are you okay? Not too traumatised by the birth?'

'I'm fine,' Xavier said automatically, trying to recall the last time someone other than his mother had worried about his welfare or state of mind and coming up blank.

His personal relationships were always casual. The last woman he'd slept with was some aide to a visiting ambassador who had made it perfectly clear that all she'd wanted from him was an orgasm or two. And that had suited him just fine. He'd been too focussed on building a career and a comfortable life for himself to chase love and commitment. Which, unlike security and knowing who he could trust, were things he could do without.

'Thanks for asking,' he said, clearing his throat. 'How's the...um, little one doing?'

What was wrong with him? Was he starstruck by Lola because she was good at her job? Her position as his boss had forced him to ignore their chemistry these past six months. But if they'd met under different circumstances, if he'd acted on his attraction, it might be out of his system by now.

'She's good.' Lola smiled again and leaned against the door jamb, obviously in no hurry to leave. 'A little small, but that's normal for her gestation. So tell me about the baby you delivered.'

'I was deployed overseas with the army,' Xavier said. 'My unit came across what we assumed was a deserted building until we heard moans. I went in to search and found a local woman labouring alone.'

'So you helped her? Just you?' Her stare shone with admiration.

'She did all the work,' he said. 'I simply stayed and provided an extra pair of hands when it came to catching the baby and dealing with the umbilical cord. Then we transported them both to the hospital.'

'Wow. That's…impressive.'

'Apologies,' he said, stepping back and swinging the door wide, finally recalling his manners. 'Would you like to come in? There's no one else here, but there's a kitchen. Tea and coffee. Snacks in the cupboard.'

The last thing he needed was any more of her company. Lola Garcia, while insanely hot, already saw him far too clearly for comfort. But still, he found himself hoping she'd accept the invitation.

'Thanks.' She nodded and stepped into the room, glancing around. The staff quarters, like the rest of the clinic, were comfortable bordering on luxurious compared to some accommodations he'd seen.

'Do you have any Marcona almonds?' she asked referring to the gourmet Spanish snack, her eyes bright with excitement as she bypassed the lounge and headed for the kitchen. 'I have a soft spot for those as they remind me of home.'

'Let's find out,' he said, pulling open cupboards and drawers to reveal an array of options. Maybe if they found the snack, she'd leave and he could set about forgetting the way she looked at him as if she *did* indeed know what she wanted and knew only he could give it to her.

Peering over his shoulder, she stepped so close he was bathed in the scent of her shampoo and something else— the warm natural fragrance of her skin.

For a terrifying second, he feared he might forget himself and dip his face to the side of her neck, inhale that honey scent that had been plaguing him all night long as they'd worked together, then kiss her skin. It had clearly been too long since he'd been with a woman.

'There they are,' he said, having spied the almonds near the back of the drawer. He reached for them and almost wept for joy.

At the exact same moment, Lola squealed with delight and did the same. Their hands collided. He froze, tensing every muscle in his body while desire hot and insistent ransacked him. When you worked security, stillness was your friend. The human gaze was naturally drawn to movement. And if ever there was a moment he needed to be invisible, it was now. Otherwise, she might look at him with another impassioned look. He might drag her into his arms and taste those soft, pouty lips. Test whether she'd taste as good as he imagined. Drag out a moan from her cultured mouth.

Beside him, Lola gasped and withdrew her hand as if she'd been burned by his touch. Her stare flew to his. Her pupils dilated. Her breathing shallow and fast.

Swallowing discreetly, he held out the bag of almonds to her. It wasn't too late to gloss over that accidental touch that had awoken every nerve ending in his body. He could pretend it hadn't happened, pretend they were both oblivious to the hair-raising crackle of sexual awareness and the warm scented cloud of pheromones engulfing them.

But she hadn't stepped away. If anything, she appeared to have leaned closer.

She blinked up at him. 'Thanks,' she said. Her fingers closed around the snack held between them. Neither one pulling away as the seconds stretched and Xavier's mind blanked to all the reasons kissing her would be a bad idea.

He stared, willing her to take the almonds and leave. No good would come from the way she was looking at him. As if she too wanted a couple of orgasms and nothing more. But maybe because of the intense and unexpected events of the night, they seemed bound by a new kind of understanding. As if here and now, for this single moment in time, they were just a man and woman. Insanely attracted to each other. No boundaries. No differences. No expectations.

Xavier waited. A primal instinct building inside him. Urging him to act on the impulses he'd experienced every day since first meeting her. He wanted to know if she'd moan when he kissed her. If her skin would feel as good as it smelled. If, when he pushed inside her, she'd gasp his name.

'You should go,' he said, dragging the words from some disciplined corner of his mind that was still in control. He didn't need her acceptance. What he wanted from her was far more animalistic. Would the sophisticated doctor be shocked if she could read his mind?

Expecting her to nod, to agree or move away, he braced himself for the loss of her body warmth, the soft rasp of her breath, the way her pupils swallowed almost all of her amber streaked irises. But as much as he would regret her absence, he wanted her gone before he did something stupid. She was his boss. A woman who frequented the world of wealth and privilege. A world he'd been around his entire life but to which he could never belong and that was fine by him. Finally, in his thirties, he knew who he was—even if he only understood half of his heritage.

'I hate being told what to do,' she said softly, her tongue swiping her bottom lip as her gaze dropped to his mouth and he knew instantly that they *would* kiss. It seemed inevitable. An unspoken agreement.

'Then do what you want,' he said, certain that this independent and driven woman had always made her own destiny. Something he could relate to and something he found so attractive.

She stared for a handful of seconds, her breasts rising and falling with every breath. Then she tugged the almonds from his grasp and tossed them carelessly onto the counter.

Before she could step closer—he'd read her intent in the lowering of her eyelids, the half-step she began in his direction, the start of a soft moan at the back of her throat—he gripped her face between his palms and covered her mouth with his. Tasting those lush lips, parting them. Touching the tip of his tongue to hers when she offered it and it sliding deeper into her mouth as her hands, rested on his chest, curled into his shirt.

She moaned. A low, needy sound that lured him deeper into madness. He'd been right. She tasted fantastic and she wanted this too. Wanted him. As reckless as it was, he couldn't stop himself from indulging, just for a second, in the passion of their heated kiss. Growing more determined, she surged up on to the balls of her feet and pressed her gorgeous body to his. Her breasts against his chest. Her stomach aligned with his groin where his erection stirred. Her hands gripping his shoulders and tugging him closer.

'Xavier,' she said, dropping her head back, her eyes closed. Her hands raked his back, her fingers curling into the belt loops on his trousers to hold their bodies flush as if she couldn't quite get close enough. But Xavier had discipline in spades.

'Tell me what you want from this,' he said, unable to stop himself from sliding his lips over the soft skin below her ear where her natural scent was strongest and then down the side of her neck so she moaned again, those full lips parted. He wasn't anyone's for ever and he needed her to understand that.

'I want you,' she said on a sigh, her eyes still closed as he tunnelled his hands into her hair and angled her head to give himself better access to her neck. Her body pressed to his was driving him wild. 'Just one time,' she added. 'No strings.'

A groan rumbled inside his head. She was perfect and so sexy. He was struggling to think of anything beyond that condom he always kept in his wallet.

'You sure?' he asked, one arm around her waist holding her close. His other hand cupped her breast so he could thumb the nipple that peeked through her clothes as if begging for his touch. 'Because I only do casual. I'm not the romance type.'

Love was all about belonging and he'd made himself content to emotionally drift.

'Yes,' she said, emphatic. Her body writhed restlessly against his. Her hand slipped between them to rub at his erection. 'I only do casual too. I value my work and my independence too much for anything else.'

He kissed her again and her eyes drifted closed, a dreamy look on her face as he stroked her nipple, as if she'd been fantasising about this every bit as much as him. But if they were doing this, he needed her to be certain. He worked his hand underneath her scrub top to where the lace of her bra cupped her flesh and pulled back from her lips.

'Lola, open your eyes,' he said.

At this command, the sound of her name on his lips, she did just that, looking up at him with such heated desire he almost groaned aloud at how royally screwed he was. Now that he'd kissed her, tasted those soft lips, heard those breathy moans he'd fantasised about and learned the shape of her curves, his resistance was crumbling fast.

Still he clung to the last shred. 'Normally, I'd point out that this is a terrible idea. We work together. You're my boss.' His arm flexed around her waist, bringing her closer so the heat and softness of her body melded to him.

'It's hardly a normal night,' she challenged. 'And I know what I want.'

Because her stroking was driving him to distraction, he dived for her lips once more. Her tongue surged against his. Her hands sliding inside his shirt. Her nails lightly scraping his back, urging him on.

Certain that they wouldn't be interrupted, he gripped her waist and sat her on the kitchen counter. 'I need to see you,' he said, standing between her spread thighs while he raised the scrub top over her head, casting it aside impatiently.

Her breasts were perfect pale, creamy mounds encased in a sexy black lace bra. He filled his hands with them, his thumbs rubbing over the nipples so she gasped and scraped her teeth over that bottom lip again as she watched, thrusting her chest forward into his touch.

He kissed her again, popping the clasp on her bra so he could remove it. Her breasts filled his hands perfectly, her nipples hard and responsive as she moaned louder and tugged at the hem of his shirt.

She threw his shirt to the floor and ran her hands and eyes over his chest and shoulders, pressing her warm skin to his so he feared he might combust.

'Hold tight,' he said as she wrapped her arms around his neck and he scooped her from the counter, carrying her with her legs around his waist as he made for his room.

The staff bedrooms were designed for sleep—sparsely furnished with a king single bed, nightstand and small closet. But Lola didn't seem to care about the room's minimalist functionality. The minute he laid her down against the clean bed linen, she tugged eagerly at his neck and brought him down on top of her.

'Hurry, I want you,' she said, shoving the waistband of her scrub trousers over her hips.

Xavier extricated himself from her wild kisses. He took one nipple in his mouth, smiling when she sighed and speared her fingers through his hair, holding him in place, moaning his name, demanding more.

He took his wallet from his pocket and removed the condom. They each removed their trousers and underwear so they were completely naked, tossing everything in a pile on the floor. Xavier knelt between her bent legs on the bed. His gaze scouring every inch of her glorious body. His hands gliding along her thighs and hips up her ribs to cup her breasts.

She sat up, her arms around his back, and pressed kisses and swipes of the tip of her tongue to his chest and abs. Dipping lower and lower. He closed his eyes for a second, burned alive by the passion of her touch. Then her hand encircled his erection and she took him in her mouth. His eyes suddenly opened. His jaw clenched hard against the intensity of the pleasure.

'Lola…' Her name came easily now, no deference required. Here, like this with naked need the only thing between them, they were equals in every way.

She looked up at him and smiled. He pulled back, grabbed the condom and slid it on, too impatient to enjoy her mouth on him any longer.

She pushed him back into a sitting position against the wall and straddled his lap, gripping his shoulders as she slowly lowered herself onto him. Her lip snagged beneath her teeth and her eyes locked to his so he saw the desire and determination there. Was there any sight sexier than a woman who knew what she wanted and wasn't afraid to chase it?

Xavier gripped her hips, controlling her descent and the depth of his penetration. She gasped and moaned his name as he filled her.

'You feel so good,' she whispered against his ear.

He crushed her to his chest, his arms banded around her back, his face buried between her breasts as he forgot to breathe in the face of such powerful pleasure. Lola tunnelled her fingers through his hair, cradled his head and began to move. Rocking her hips, driving him wild, sending licks of flame streaking from his groin to his gut and down his legs.

Her moans intensified as he caressed her buttocks and directed the speed of her rocking hips to a rhythm that sent stars sparking behind his eyes. She might have been made for him, so tight was her grip on him. So attuned were their movements. Their desire for each other so in sync.

Needing more friction, needing her untamed, he gripped her thighs and flipped her onto her back in one deft move, still buried deep inside her. She gasped, her mouth open, her stare on his as he took over. His shallow thrusts growing deeper and faster, riding them both hard as she gripped his arms like he was the only thing grounding her to Earth.

'Xavier,' she cried, her breath catching. Her breasts bouncing enticingly.

He kissed her deep. His tongue duelling with hers as his entire body stretched taut, braced for the explosion and the euphoria that lay just out of reach. She engulfed him. Her tight heat agonising torture. Her scent clinging to his skin so he'd smell her long after this was over. Her taste as addictive as the sounds of her unrestrained desire.

Tearing his mouth from hers he dived for her nipple, sucking it into his mouth. Flicking the tip of his tongue over the bud as he raised her thigh over his hip and thrust faster, deeper, harder until she cried out in ecstasy. Her elegantly manicured fingernails dug into his shoulders as her orgasm struck and he let go, joining her in the moment of ecstasy.

With a harsh groan he couldn't hold inside, he surrendered. His body rigid as he came. His head full of the sound of her fading cries and panting breaths as they clung to each other until every last drop of pleasure was spent.

# CHAPTER FIVE

A WEEK LATER, Lola bade farewell to Castilona's royal family after their visit to the clinic. The baby twins, Princes Rafael and Rodrigo, had passed their six-month health check with flying colours.

'Xavier will accompany you to the car park, Your Majesty,' she told King Octavio, a handsome and imposing man clearly besotted with his queen, Phoebe, and his adorable sons.

'Thank you, Dr Garcia,' he replied, warmly shaking her hand. 'For everything.'

Queen Phoebe added her thanks and the family, accompanied by their own team of security and not one but two royal nannies, stepped into the private elevator that would take them directly to the secure underground car park so they could leave the hospital unobserved.

Before the elevator doors closed, Lola glanced at Xavier, their eyes meeting. Her breath halted. A delicious shudder quivered in her stomach as it had done every time their eyes met since *that* intense but incredible night.

Thanks to the storm, Lola's normal workload had increased. What with minor repairs, and the clean-up of the hospital's grounds, there'd been no time for a private conversation with Xavier. In fact, as agreed, they'd kept their distance from one another, acting as if the intimacies of that night hadn't happened.

The lift doors closed and Lola released the breath she'd been holding, her mind ensnared by the exquisite memories. She'd never known passion like it. After the first time, they'd showered together and he'd gone down on her in the cubicle, one thigh over his shoulder, his hands gripping her backside and the water pounding them both. If he hadn't held her upright as he groaned out his encouragement, she'd have collapsed to the tiles so astounding was her second orgasm.

After she'd returned the favour to him, glorying in how thoroughly she'd reduced such a tall and powerful man to a shattered wreck, they'd dressed in silence and then agreed to put that night behind them and resume their cordial working relationship.

Now, Lola returned to her office on shaky legs. Standing at her desk, she'd just opened her emails when she spied Xavier across the main foyer having returned from the car park. He strode across the marbled tiles, headed her way. Every step he took shunting her pulse higher, as if her body recognised and anticipated the source of such incredible pleasure. Heat flooded her system, centred most insistently between her legs.

She straightened her spine and tried to shut down the memories of him holding her so close she thought she might not be able to breathe. Of him moving inside her, desire darkening his stare to almost black. Of the expression of sheer determination on his face as he'd looked up at her in the shower, his tongue and clever fingers thrusting her once more into oblivion.

'Come in,' she said, when he reached the open door.

'Did their departure go to plan? Without incident?' Her voice cracked and she prayed he hadn't heard it.

'Yes, ma'am. The wolves have left the den,' he said using the code name supplied by the palace security team. He stood erect, feet spread, arms clasped behind his back, reminding Lola that despite that incredible night, they'd agreed to resume business as usual.

Except every time he addressed her as ma'am, or Dr Garcia, all she heard was him groaning *Lola*.

Closing the door, she sat on the edge of her desk facing him, her eyes meeting his. 'Good. I wanted to touch base now that things have returned to normal after Gabriel,' she said, although the cyclone had ravaged the island, leaving considerable damage in its wake. 'We haven't worked together much this week.'

'I've been on night shifts,' he confirmed, clearly back to his restrained self. All evidence of that torrid passion concealed.

She nodded, wishing he'd look at her the way he had that night. As if he hadn't been able to stop himself from wanting her, no matter how hard he'd tried. But she needed to follow his example. To put all that from her mind and act professionally. After all, she was his boss at least for the next few weeks. She'd finally got around to sending that resignation email that morning, setting the wheels of her departure from *Clinico San Carlos*, and from Castilona, in motion.

'So we're good?' she asked, hesitantly. 'You and I, I mean?' Her breathing sped up, an itch of frustration spreading over her skin because he was still staring at the window over her shoulder.

He glanced her way then. His expression bland. His dark stare unreadable. 'We're good, Dr Garcia.'

Lola concealed her sigh. She was being unreasonable and selfish wanting more than his usual polite competence. She wanted to see his fire. His abandon. That glorious moment when his restraint had snapped and he'd dragged her into his arms, kissing her with such ferocious need that she'd instantly known he'd been smothering his attraction for her since the day they'd met.

'Good,' she said instead as she stood and took her seat behind the desk. 'One more thing, I wanted to let you know that I've handed in my resignation.'

A frown slashed his brows. 'Why? I hope it's nothing to do with...that night.'

Ignoring the regret she'd probably imagined in his eyes, she rushed to reassure him. 'No, no. I've been thinking of it for a while. The board will, I'm sure, accept my resignation. If they have any sense, they'll appoint Dr Lomas to the position of clinical director. But whomever they appoint, I'm sure that you and all the other staff will find the transition a smooth one.'

A few beats of awkward silence passed during which she wished she could tell what he was thinking. But Xavier was clearly practised at keeping people out. He might have momentarily lowered his guard and slept with her, but it seemed they weren't going to be friends.

'Where do you plan to go?' he asked, showing no indication that he cared one way or another.

And that was fine. They'd shared an amazing night and neither of them wanted more. Except for a brief moment afterwards, as she'd tried to put herself back together, that restlessness she'd been experiencing had lessened.

'I've ended my tenancy on my home here,' she said. 'I'll go back to Spain in the first instance. Then...well, we'll see. Maybe overseas for a while.'

She didn't have all the details figured out yet, but she'd been looking at medical aid charities, or maybe considering pursuing a master's degree.

Xavier nodded. 'Then I wish you well, Dr Garcia.'

'Thank you.' She looked up to find his stare was trained on the window once more. The matter, what they'd meant to one another that night, resolved. 'I'll let you get back to work.'

He nodded and left. And just like that, their connection, be it real or imagined, seemed severed.

*Three weeks later*

Xavier knocked at the back door of his mother's cottage and entered her warm and fragrant kitchen. After weeks of trying to forget that night with Lola, of shoving aside unsettling thoughts of her impending departure for Spain, he finally had another thing on which to focus—the contents of the disturbing letter clutched in his tight fist.

'Not working today?' Carlota asked on spying him. She dusted her floury hands on her apron and greeted him with a warm embrace before she resumed kneading dough for her *telera*, the Andalusian white bread she'd baked for him every day of his childhood and beyond.

'I've taken the week off,' he said, dragging in a patient breath laced with the sweet smell of baking, for which he had zero appetite. 'I need you to explain this to me, Mamá.'

Keeping a grip on his temper, he placed the letter on the counter, his mind still spinning at its unbelievable contents.

Carlota Torres read the letter, her hand steady at first, but then trembling as her eyes scanned the page. Xavier's stomach knotted tighter. Her shocked reaction, the flush of shame on her cheeks, all the confirmation he needed that the letter's claims were genuine.

She met his stare, her hand covering her mouth. 'I'm so sorry. I wanted to tell you. I almost did, a million times.'

'So it's true?' he asked, his mind rebelling because he'd spent his entire life wondering where he'd come from, who he was related to, and all this time the answer had been there in front of his face.

Carlota sank into a kitchen chair and looked up pleadingly. 'I was young. He was handsome and charming back then,' she said about Mauricio de la Rosa, the King's uncle, a man Xavier had feared growing up because he'd never witnessed anything other than a disappointed scowl from him.

Tears slid down Carlota's cheeks. He crouched before her, gently taking her hands in a silent plea. He hated to see her cry. He wanted answers, not to upset her. But with a secret of this magnitude, he guessed upset was inevitable.

'He seduced me,' she said. 'And I was flattered. I didn't know until it was too late that he was already engaged to someone—Xiomara's mother.' She cupped his face lovingly, the way she'd always done, as if Xavier was her pride and joy. 'When I found out you were coming, I went to him and told him. I'd never seen him angry until that moment when he finally showed me his ruthless side.'

Xavier swore under his breath, positive that if the hateful man hadn't already died from a stroke three weeks ago, as he had according to the letter, he would have personally hunted him down and throttled him for his treatment of Carlota.

'He wanted to…fix the problem—' she said, tremulously, '—but I refused. I wanted you. I told him I'd raise you alone. That was when he persuaded me that it was in your best interests to never know who your father was.' She gripped Xavier's hands tighter, as if begging him to understand. 'He said if the world knew the scandal, you'd be a target. You'd never be able to live a normal life. You'd be hounded by the media. You might even be at risk of harm, given his status.'

Confused and reeling, Xavier shook his head. 'You should have told me anyway, when I was old enough to understand.' He hated what she'd endured, but he'd spent all those years wondering. What difference might it have made to his life if he'd known the truth?

Carlota nodded, swiping aside her tears. 'I should. But by then I was ashamed that I'd ever fallen for the charms of someone so poisonous. He'd matured into the selfish, power hungry and cruel regent.' She held his stare, her eyes hard. 'You are *nothing* like him. Nothing. I didn't want you to think for one second that you were.'

Xavier stood and collapsed into the seat facing hers. How many nights had he slept in this house, wondering about the man who should have been there to guide and raise him when all along that man had known of his existence, had practically watched him grow and had still chosen to disown him?

Reaching for his hand, his mother, leaned close. 'I should have told you. You're right. But I wanted to keep you safe. From his world and from him. You saw what he was. How he treated people. Even his own daughter.'

Xavier sucked in a breath. Princess Xiomara. Technically, this news made her his half-sister... No, having worked for her for years he couldn't think of her that way.

'So why didn't you move us away?' he asked, confused and nauseous, the full implications dawning on him. Would the princess accept this news, or reject him too? He liked and respected her, but theirs had always been a transactional relationship. One where it had been his job to protect her.

'With you on the way, I needed the money,' Carlota said, raising her chin in determination. 'This job was secure, well-paid and it came with this house for life. Besides, Mauricio didn't live at the palace until years later. After his brother died. By then you were in the army. A grown man. He'd never shown the slightest interest in you, so I figured he would leave you alone. Which thankfully he did.'

'Until now,' Xavier said bitterly, pointing at the letter she'd discarded, which had arrived from a Spanish law firm and contained the details of his heritage, including the results of a paternity test and the inheritance left to him by a man who'd ignored him his whole life. Casa Colina was a hundred acre vineyard estate that came with an aristocratic title of *Marqués de Moro*.

'What will you do?' his mother asked hesitantly.

'With his estate? The title? The money?' He shrugged, furious, certain that de la Rosa's gift was intended to cause pain and havoc. 'Reject it…' The way his so-called father had rejected both his mother and him, not that he wanted to emulate such a hateful man. Carlota was right there.

She glanced at the letter. 'Who's been running things since Mauricio fled to Spain?' she asked quietly as if she was thinking about the jobs and welfare of the estate's employees, who numbered over sixty.

'I understand there's an estate manager in charge,' he said, already feeling the weight of the responsibility that had been thrust upon him. 'I'll find out the situation, then make some decisions.'

Carlota nodded, touching his arm. 'I know you will do what's right. You always have, which is how I know you are one hundred percent mine, as you have always been.' Her eyes blazed as she looked at him and just like every other day of his life, he felt her unconditional love and strength.

For an unguarded moment, Xavier closed his eyes on a wave of grief. But it was for a man that had never existed, apart from in his childhood imaginings. The reality of his father was nowhere close to those imaginings. The man had been totally unworthy of this kind, loyal, hard-working woman who'd raised Xavier alone while he'd lived a life of privilege.

'I'll leave you to your bread,' he said, hugging his mother goodbye. He needed time to think, to assimilate what he'd learned and figure out who he was in the face of this new information.

Before she released him, she gripped his face in her floury hands. 'I love you, my son.'

He nodded. 'Love you too, Mamá.'

That would never change. Even if, with the arrival of that letter, everything else in his life had.

# CHAPTER SIX

ON HER FIRST Saturday off since the storm, and blind to the half-packed boxes cluttering up her entire apartment, Lola forced herself to catch up on some much needed life admin. The most pressing of which was her late period.

She wasn't religiously regular and she and Xavier had used a condom, so she fully expected the test she'd purchased that morning to be negative. But she preferred to have it confirmed over wasting time wondering and worrying.

She stared at the blue plastic stick on her bathroom vanity unit, trying to stay calm while she awaited the result. Logically the chances of her being pregnant were slim. She wasn't on birth control—she hadn't dated for two years—and she and Xavier had certainly put that one condom through its paces. But they'd been safe.

Thinking over the past few weeks, Lola paced to the bedroom, a ball of restless energy making her limbs jittery and her head full of pressure. She and Xavier had barely seen each other since she'd told him she was leaving. She'd been busy with the extra workload pertaining to the storm damage and her resignation, and he'd taken some annual leave, so she was unlikely to see him for a while longer. But the lack of interaction was a good thing.

Helping Lola to move on from that night, even if she was still struggling to forget.

Pacing back to the bathroom, Lola glanced at the stick. Her hand flew to cover her mouth as she read the word in the window, which was clear and undeniable—*pregnant*.

Her other hand automatically dropped to her stomach, resting there protectively as a deluge of emotions washed through her—shock and disbelief uppermost. She was pregnant. With Xavier's baby.

Collapsing onto the edge of her bed she sniffed away the choked feeling in her throat as she thought about the tiny life growing inside her. She'd always wanted a child one day. She'd imagined it would be with a man she'd fallen in love with. A man who wanted her for the person she was. Not for how she might slot into his life, like Nicolás.

But this, she and Xavier, was an entirely different situation. They weren't in love. They weren't even a couple. He'd even dodged her attempts to get to know him on a deeper level. The only real thing she knew about him, besides his employment history and a bit about his past, was his prowess as a lover.

But this was happening and her first instinct was to call Isla, her twin sister.

'*Cómo estás?*' Isla answered, in her usual cheerful voice.

'I'm not sure...' Lola replied, swallowing. 'I... I've just discovered that I'm pregnant.' They were as close as it was possible to be so she didn't bother building up to the news.

'What?' Shocked silence followed Isla's question.

Lola wished she was there with her sister, in Spain, where she could seek the comfort of a hug.

'I know.' Lola scrunched her eyes closed, her face warm with embarrassment. She was a mature professional woman. A doctor. How could she have let this happen?

'I didn't know you were seeing anyone,' Isla said, warily.

'I'm not. It was a one night thing. Remember that cyclone we had…?'

'Ah…blame it on the storm.' There was no judgement in Isla's voice and Lola laughed mirthlessly.

'So what are you going to do?' Isla asked carefully.

Lola rubbed at her temple. 'I don't know. Have a baby I guess.' She was still in shock but already felt better having confided in her sister.

'Well, I'll be here to help you, not that you'll need it,' Isla said offering the kind of unconditional support that brought tears to Lola's eyes.

'Thanks, *manita*.' Suddenly ferociously homesick, Lola pressed the phone closer to her ear, wishing Isla was there.

'Have you told the father?' Isla asked.

Lola's stomach dropped. Xavier… How would he react? Would he want to be involved in their baby's life, or would she be doing this alone? It didn't matter. As a financially independent woman, she didn't need his input. But she owed it to him to tell him all the same. Could she stand to wait until he returned to work?

'No. But I will.' Maybe she should do it today. Get it over with so that in the few weeks she had left in Castilona, before she visited her family in Spain, they could come to some sort of arrangement.

Realising that the job with a charity organisation that serviced refugee camps, providing humanitarian aid, emergency health care and immunisation clinics, she'd applied for might no longer be suitable for a pregnant woman, she paced nervously.

'I need to go,' she told Isla.

Ever the pragmatist, she preferred action over contemplation. Better to tell Xavier right away, then she could figure everything else out.

She finished her phone call, then with a trembling hand, she dialled the number she had for Xavier, but it went to voicemail. Maybe he'd gone overseas on holiday. Logging into her work computer, she brought up his file and checked that the number was current. Then, because she preferred to have her answers today over tomorrow, Lola typed his address into the GPS app on her phone, grabbed her car keys from the bowl on the marble topped table in her hallway and headed for her car.

She might be in shock, but she was going to have this baby regardless of the timing. The sooner she informed Xavier, the sooner she'd know if he wanted to be involved or not and the sooner she could formulate a new plan.

Following the directions to the address from his file, she drove along the coastal road that clung to the side of the steep cliffs like a swag of ribbon on a Christmas tree. Slowly ascending the hill where the honey-coloured stone and terracotta rooftops of Castilona's hillside homes became more expansive. The million-euro views more and more breathtaking.

Near the top of the road, just before it flattened out to begin its descent down the other side, Lola pulled the car onto the indicated driveway. On the pavement opposite, a small group of photographers loitered, their cameras pop, pop, popping as they pointlessly recorded her arrival. There was nothing newsworthy about her, but her trepidation increased. Perhaps Xavier was living there with some sort of celebrity.

Confused by the grand ornate wrought iron gates blocking the drive, she lowered her window and pressed a button on the intercom box on the wall.

'*Hola,*' a female voice said. 'Welcome to Casa Colina.'

'My name is Lola Garcia. I'm looking for Xavier Torres,' Lola said hesitantly, wondering if she'd made a mistake. 'Do I have the correct address?' Maybe she'd typed it in incorrectly.

'*Sí,*' the woman replied. Seconds later, the gates swung open.

With her heart pounding, Lola followed the winding, tree-lined drive until a stunning sprawling villa came into view. Sitting atop the hill, the building had an almost three hundred and sixty degree view of the ocean, which from up here looked dyed turquoise as if someone had washed out paint from a giant paintbrush there.

Lola parked and exited her car, taking a moment to appreciate the beauty of the expansive, creamy stone villa, which was surrounded by terraces—some tiled for outdoor seating, some boasting manicured Mediterranean gardens and one composed entirely of an exquisite infinity pool that ran the length of the house.

A crunch of gravel sounded. Lola spun on her heel to find Xavier a few feet away. He was casually dressed in worn ripped jeans and a grey marl t-shirt. His strong square jaw covered in sexy scruff, his dark hair ruffled and his eyes wary.

'Lola,' he said, a small frown pinching his brows together and tugging down his lovely mouth. A mouth she could still taste if she didn't take care to concentrate on stifling those memories.

'You...haven't been at work,' she said, her voice accusing despite the real reason she was there.

'No. Would you like to come in?' he asked, looking far from comfortable as he slipped his hands into the back pockets of his jeans so his biceps flexed. She remembered exactly how it felt to be held in those strong arms. To feel his weight on top of her and the tenderness with which he'd cupped her face for the last time that night and brushed a goodbye kiss over her lips.

She hesitated, wishing she'd simply continued to call. After all, a woman had answered the intercom. Perhaps he was involved with someone now. Perhaps they lived in this stunning house together. Perhaps Lola was about to ruin his day and that of his new woman in his life with her news.

'I don't want to intrude...' she said, more uncertain of him in this environment because whenever she thought of his private life, she'd never pictured him living in a home like this.

'You're not,' he said. 'Come inside.'

Without waiting for her to ask any more questions he turned and led the way to a side entrance that after a few turns down cool, dim, stone flagged corridors, led into a sun bathed kitchen.

'Would you like something to drink?' he asked, leaning against the counter, his hands curled over the edge besides his hip as if he felt both at home and uncomfortable.

'No, thank you,' she said, embarrassed that his unease might be due to her just turning up out of the blue when they'd agreed to move on. 'I won't intrude for long. Is... is this *your* house?' she asked, his reticence irking her and making her paranoid. 'It's breathtaking.'

But he needn't worry. She hadn't come to beg for more

sex or suggest they date. Of course, she was also stalling. But maybe because she'd once rejected a life of wealth and privilege as Nicolás's wife, she just couldn't picture Xavier living here. It was throwing her off, shoving the very important reason she'd come aside.

'Yes,' he stated simply.

'I don't understand,' she said, glancing around the state of the art designer kitchen that definitely possessed a woman's touch—a giant vase of Hydrangeas on the island counter, a soft throw draped over the sofa in the adjoining conservatory where tropical house-plants and culinary herbs spilled healthily from numerous terracotta pots.

'Neither do I,' he said glancing at his feet then back at her, his eyes stormy.

'I thought you lived in an Old Town apartment,' she pushed, certain he'd mentioned that when he'd first applied for the position at the hospital. Why was he acting so weird?

He nodded. 'I used to, until recently.'

'Okay,' she said, still unsatisfied. Not that he owed her any explanation. Not that she was likely to get one either. 'You seem upset. Is the reason you haven't been at work because—' She glanced at the hallway and lowered her voice to harsh whisper, '—we slept together?'

His stare held hers. 'No. Who are you looking for? I live here alone.'

Lola placed a hand on her forehead, her own news shoved aside in the face of his cryptic responses. 'I just... I assumed...' She met his stare. 'I'm surprised, that's all. I didn't picture you living somewhere like this.'

'I inherited this house recently,' he said in explanation. 'From my father.' He spat the word with contempt and the pieces began to fall into place. 'I haven't yet decided if I'll be keeping it,' he went on, 'or torching the place instead.'

'Your father?' She stared, incredulous, her heart racing anew. 'You told me you never knew him.'

'I didn't.' His jaw clenched so she could practically hear his teeth grinding together. 'And fortunately, I never will. He died a month ago. This—' he spread his arms wide, '—is my legacy. The house, the estate, the title, the private beach down there...' He pointed to where the gardens sloped towards a picture perfect crescent-shaped bay. 'Not to mention the yacht, the cars and the very lucrative winemaking business that comes with it.' He pressed his lips together and scowled in disgust.

'Wow... That's quite the inheritance.' But why wouldn't he keep it? And why did he seem so...angry? 'Why would you torch such a stunning home?' She was procrastinating now. Finding any excuse to avoid telling him why she'd come. But she'd never seen him angry before. He was intimidating enough in his usual, neutral state. Would he be receptive to her life-changing news in his current frame of mind?

He stepped closer, passionately making his point. 'Because no manner of wealth, land or expensive toys can make up for thirty-five years of pretending that I didn't exist,' he said, a quiet kind of fury rolling off him like waves. 'He had all of this and more and yet never gave my mother a single euro to help raise me. Even though he knew of my existence.'

'I see,' she said quietly, her curiosity turning to dread and her stomach churning. 'I'm sorry.'

Her timing couldn't be any more appalling. He was clearly going through something momentous emotionally. How could she tell him about the baby now?

'Do you see?' he demanded, bracing his hands on the counter of the island. 'Because I can't get my head around it.'

She shrugged. 'Well…not really. I mean I understand how you must be feeling hurt, rejected, perhaps even grieving for someone you never had the opportunity to know, but—'

'I'll never grieve for that man,' he said, coldly. 'If I hadn't seen the paternity test results he had done on me when I was a child, with my own eyes, I'd deny that we could ever be related.'

'Why?' she asked frowning, nervous that his anger might extend to the paternity of *her* baby once she told him her news. 'Was he so bad? Wouldn't most people consider a legacy like this akin to a lottery win?'

He leaned closer, his stare burning into hers, like a jungle cat about to pounce. 'Do you know who once owned this house, the estate, the title? All of it?'

Lola shook her head, her stomach in knots. 'No, why should I? I'm a doctor. I don't move in these circles.' Not since she'd ended her engagement to Nicolás.

'Mauricio de la Rosa,' he said. 'King Octavio's uncle.'

She gasped, her hand covering her mouth. 'Are you serious? *He's* your father?'

He laughed bitterly. 'I'm afraid so. I'm the illegitimate son he always knew about but disowned and ignored.'

She reached out and touched his arm, her heart pounding with shock. His muscles tensed under her fingers as he gripped the edge of the counter once more. A wave of empathy washed over her and she wished she could hold him in her arms. But theirs wasn't that kind of a relationship.

'Xavier, I'm so sorry,' she said instead. Her heart ached

for him. Both for the boy and the man who, she imagined, had always felt lost because he'd only known half his story.

Xavier tensed under her touch. His feelings too volatile to untangle in the face of the fierce intensity of his ongoing attraction to her, which should have faded but only seemed stronger. He had no idea why she'd come to his home when they'd agreed that their one night would be the extent of their relationship. When she was leaving Castilona soon. But desperate to be free of the turmoil of the past week—during which he'd discovered his true parentage, been slapped with this insult of an inheritance and had his entire world turned upside down—his body had responded to her the minute he'd seen her in his driveway. As if he were a drowning man in the ocean and she was the only life raft for miles.

'That must have been a terrible shock,' she said quietly. The scent of her fanned the craving he'd experienced daily since the night of the storm, when he'd discovered just how flammable their chemistry was. But unlike back then, when she'd looked at him with desire and wonder, as if he was something special, now he saw only pity in her eyes.

'What are you doing here, Lola?' he asked, changing the subject, the idea that she might treat him differently because he was the illegitimate son of the late regent who'd ruled for a time until his brother's son had come of age, adding to his frustration. Was this to be his life now? A title, land and an estate he didn't want? His actions compared to those of de la Rosa? His so-called father's reputation for ruthlessness would probably long outlive the man. But Xavier would fight, tooth and nail, every day for the rest of his life to be nothing like him.

'I…' She dropped her hand from his arm and blinked up at him, uncharacteristically hesitant where he'd never known her to be anything other than calm and confident.

'Lost for words?' he asked, tauntingly, shutting down his confusion and hurt, wishing he could once more lose himself inside her the way he had that night. But discipline was his ally. Just like he'd needed it every day for the past month in order to stay away from Lola Garcia and stick to their deal, he would employ it now that she was standing in his kitchen.

'Not at all.' She stood taller. 'I'm wondering what you plan to do?' she asked, swallowing as if her mouth was dry.

He glanced down at her soft red lips, desperate to hear them cry his name. Desperate for her to look at him with desire and infatuation. The way she had as he'd made her body sing, shoving her headlong into two orgasms that had utterly undone her polished, poised exterior.

'Will you resign as head of security at the clinic now that you have all this?' she asked, glancing around the luxurious space.

'Why would that be your concern?' he asked, sneering because he took pride in being judged by his actions, not his net worth. 'You're going back to Spain.'

Whereas Xavier was more confused about where he belonged than ever. Nothing about this inheritance felt right. He'd only moved into Casa Colina because the staff had questions about their jobs and needed reassurance that he wasn't certain he could give in the long term.

But having Lola this close, his entire body ached to crush her in his arms and to kiss her until she moaned and looked at him as if he was just a man she desperately wanted.

'Maybe I'll sell all this,' he said. 'Go back to my ordinary life.' He shrugged, his gaze clinging to her features. To the slope of her neck and the swell of her breasts. 'I don't need it. I'm just a simple guy after all.'

All he really wanted was to forget—his past, his renewed sense of rejection and betrayal and this stifling legacy he had no idea what to do with. Even Lola, who was after all moving on.

'Perhaps I'll donate the money to charity,' he went on. 'Change my name and move overseas so I can be anonymous again, because as soon as word spreads, there will be a lot more people looking at me with stunned contempt, as you're doing right now.'

Lola frowned and shook her head. 'I'm not looking at you that way. I'm shocked, yes, but all I feel for you is empathy. To not know your father all these years then to be left this...'

Xavier hadn't had a restful night's sleep since they'd slept together. Waking most nights from sweaty dreams, hard and aching for more of her passion. He reached out, cupped her jaw and tugged her bottom lip from under her teeth with the pad of his thumb. Tilting her eyes up to his so he saw a flicker of that passion she'd unleashed from her professional, put together demeanour that night.

'You still haven't told me why you're here,' he said, finding himself a step closer. 'Did you decide that one night wasn't enough? Or have you come to say goodbye?'

At the reminder he might never see her again, desire roared through him, demanding he touch her until her moans of pleasure and the way she'd cried his name drowned out the fury and impotence in his head. He too was tempted to go back on their deal, if only to distract himself from the sharp turn his life had taken. Everything was crumbling. He'd always imagined that knowing who his father was would free him and slot his missing piece back into place. But if anything, he felt more unsettled. Adrift like those missing fishing boats taken by the storm. Who was he supposed to be with a title, land and a princess as a half-sister? With an estate to run and a historic aristocratic title to measure up to? It felt more like a cage than a lottery win.

'No,' she said, her stare clear and bold and full of her signature determination he found so compelling. She tilted her chin up. 'I came to tell you that I'm pregnant.'

Xavier's hand fell to his side. The breath whooshed out of him as if he'd been winded by a blow to the chest. 'What?'

'You heard me correctly,' she said, sounding instantly defensive. 'I'm pregnant and the baby is yours.'

Xavier reeled, his legs unsteady, his heart wrestling its way out of his chest as he gripped the edge of the counter. 'We used a condom,' he said, stunned, blurting out the first rational thing that came to his spinning mind.

'It happens,' she said with a shrug he was certain she didn't feel. 'I know. It's a shock.' Finally her voice turned sympathetic. 'I only took a test this morning, so I'm still reeling, too. But I wanted to tell you as soon as possible. Obviously, I knew nothing about what you've been going through here, otherwise I might have left it for another time.'

Confused, Xavier latched onto her words in an attempt to claw back some control of his life.

'What does that mean?' he asked, adding dread to the other emotions spinning inside him like a whirlwind.

'You're supposed to be leaving Castilona for Spain soon. When else would you have told me?'

Would she have left the country with his baby? Maybe even raised it alone and kept it from him? His stomach churned. It was as if history was repeating. As if she might leave and force Xavier into the absentee parent role his sperm donor had chosen. Force Xavier to be like the man he felt no connection to whatsoever. Well he might be stunned by her news, but one thing was for certain— *his* child would know exactly who its father was.

'I don't know,' she snapped. 'I'm here telling you now, aren't I? But don't worry. As far as I'm concerned, nothing's changed. I don't want anything from you.' She raised her chin. 'I don't need anything either. I work hard so I can support myself and the baby. And you're right, I'll be going home to Spain soon, so I'll have my family to help out.'

Xavier stiffened, not sure he was hearing her correctly. 'Hold on a second…' He held up his hand, the room all but tilting. 'You're *still* leaving Castilona?'

This week just kept getting better and better… She'd not only dropped this bombshell when he was trying to come to terms with the fact his entire life had been a shameful secret, but she'd also decided she didn't need his help and was taking his baby away.

She flushed. 'Of course. As soon as I finish working my notice. I've applied to work for a medical relief organisation, although they probably won't want me now… so I'll have to think of something else. I might go back to university.'

He stepped closer, narrowing his eyes, taking no satisfaction from the way her pupils dilated as she looked up at him. 'So this was just a courtesy call before you leave the country with our baby? What if I want to be a part of my child's life? Where do I fit into the equation, Lola?'

She frowned, blinking. 'I assumed—'

'You assumed that because I never knew *my* own father, I would want nothing to do with my son or daughter?' Fury left him deadly still. 'How very presumptuous of you.'

'No…of course not.' Her frown deepened and her cheeks coloured. 'I didn't mean that. It's just that we're not a couple, so I assumed this would be complicated… That we'd need to come to some sort of custody arrangement.'

'We will.' Xavier nodded. His resolve strengthened because in a split second the world he'd felt was crumbling had settled, its pieces sliding back into place. He was going to be a father. Something he'd never really considered because he'd always shied away from serious relationships. But now that it was happening, there was no way he'd inflict the same fate he'd experienced on his own child.

'How are we to come to any sort of arrangement if you're in Spain?' he asked. 'Or worse, performing medical procedures in a tent in some war-torn country, which is dangerous and frankly ridiculous?'

Her stare narrowed, determination flattening her mouth. 'It's possible. Women can do more than one thing in this day and age you know,' she said sarcastically. Then she swallowed, looking contrite. 'But you're right. I haven't figured everything out yet.'

'I guess I should be grateful for the fact you didn't simply keep this to yourself, leave Castilona and never tell me about my child. Never tell our child who its father is.'

When he'd confided in her that night of the storm, he'd never imagined it would be used against him this way.

She gasped, horrified. 'I would never do that. That's abhorrent. I can't believe you're even suggesting it.'

'You'll forgive me,' he said bitterly. 'My experience with fathers is limited, as you know.'

She winced then and moved closer. 'Look… Why don't we talk again in a few days when we've both had a chance to come to terms with this news. We both have a lot going on at the moment. I don't know…maybe you can visit me in Spain and we can…come up with a plan.'

'A plan?' he asked, incredulous, the idea of him having no contact or say in the life of the baby they'd made together making him panic. 'You can't take my child out of the country, just like that,' he said, still stung by the fact that his own mother had kept his paternity from him although her motivation had been to keep him safe. The de la Rosas were a powerful family and Mauricio had been the most ruthless of them all. As a cook in the palace kitchens, Carlota Torres had been at a distinct disadvantage, both emotionally and financially.

'Well I can't leave it with you either, can I?' she snapped, placing one hand on her hip. 'And don't forget, I'm my own person too.'

They faced each other angrily. All the pent-up frustration he felt at his change of circumstances boiled over, directed at Lola. 'You can delay your departure, until we sort things out,' he said, his mind racing.

She shook her head adamant. 'I dislike being told what I can and cannot do. And besides, I've ended my tenancy on my rented house. I have to leave. I have nowhere else to live.'

'I'm not telling,' he said, moderating his tone of voice. 'I'm suggesting.'

But now that the initial shock had worn off, the full implications of this came at him, thick and fast. If she left with his baby, he might never see either of them again. Not to mention that now he'd inherited all this, he'd begun to attract media attention. There were paparazzi camped on his street as they spoke. He knew how intrusive they could be from his years of keeping Princess Xiomara safe. There was no way a child of his would be exposed to that. If nothing else, he would keep his baby safe.

'Do you realise…' he started to ask, his voice calm while panic slithered through his veins, '…that if the Castilonian laws of secession change, as is currently being debated by parliament, this baby, *our* baby, will effectively be fourth in line to the throne after the twin princes and Princess Xiomara?'

She paled, her eyes wide. 'No…' she whispered.

Xavier nodded. 'It's time for a reality check, Lola. Even if our child is never recognised as legitimate because Mauricio de la Rosa was a scoundrel who knocked up the palace cook and then persuaded her it was in my best interests to never know my parentage, our child will still have royal blood. Still have all of this one day.' He stretched out his arms, now certain exactly what he would do with the unwanted legacy he'd inherited. 'Whether we like it or not, that will make our child a target and safety is my job.'

'Don't say that,' she said, shaking her head in disbelief. 'That's not true.'

'I assume you saw the paps outside?' Xavier pinned her with his stare. 'They've been there all week since news of Mauricio's death. Our baby will move in ruthless circles that are all about power and wealth. He or she will need protection from stalkers, kidnappers, the press. I, for one, will do anything to ensure their safety.'

'But I'm just an ordinary woman,' she cried. 'A doctor. You can't hold me captive simply because *you've* inherited a legacy that two minutes ago you didn't even want.'

There was less fight in her voice and more fear. He wished he hadn't needed to put the latter there, but she needed to understand the consequences of their one night together, which transcended both of them.

'I'm not imprisoning you Lola,' he said quietly, stepping back to appear less threatening. 'But you should know this—I will be a father to our child. Every day for the rest of my life.'

'Of course,' she said. 'I'd never stop you from seeing the baby.'

He nodded, nowhere near appeased. 'I'm glad to hear that. Because my second job, after being a father, will be to keep our child safe,' he went on as if she hadn't interrupted. 'Even if I have to fight you to do it. I'd prefer that we worked together, but it's your choice.'

'But… I…' She clenched her fists in frustration and searched his stare.

Xavier held his ground, still processing the news he'd never have imagined when he awoke that morning.

'Oh… I can't talk to you right now,' she said petulantly. 'Not when you're being so…unreasonable. I'll be in touch in a few days.'

And with that, she stormed out.

# CHAPTER SEVEN

As the outgoing clinical director of the *Clinico San Carlos*, Lola had been invited to the annual Royal Garden Party at the palace a week later—an event coveted by every member of the Castilonian elite. Not that she was in the mood for a party, but it wouldn't do to decline highly influential benefactors like King Octavio and Queen Phoebe.

Seeking solace from the crowds, Lola traipsed through the stunning rose gardens at the palace, her bare shoulders warmed by the spring sunshine, which was putting on its best display for the event. Taking a sip of her perfectly chilled and refreshing virgin mimosa, Lola marvelled at the sheer number of heavily scented varieties in bloom. But her mind wasn't distracted for long. She was still confused by her last conversation with Xavier and was still childishly ignoring his calls.

She tried to see things from his point of view, but how dare he tell her what to do. She understood how his inheritance must have come as a massive shock, but she was a modern woman with a career. Not an aristocratic brood mare, happy to pump out children to keep some ancient family line going.

At that mean-spirited thought, hot shame washed over her. Xavier wasn't Nicolás. He didn't want a wife. And he must be feeling so conflicted about his inheritance given his father's former years of rejection. Of course he would want to be a better father that that, which wouldn't be hard… She guessed she should be happy that he wanted to be involved with their baby, but it was so…complicated.

'Ignoring my calls won't change the facts,' a voice said. *His* voice.

She spun, startled, her reply dying on her tongue as she took him in. Apart from that one time at his home, when he'd been wearing worn jeans and t-shirt, she'd never seen him out of his security uniform of black trousers and polo shirt. Now, dressed in taupe chinos, a blue dress shirt open at the collar and an olive green linen sports jacket, he looked utterly delicious. Every inch a member of the European aristocracy.

'I needed some space,' she said, trying to shut down her body's instantaneous reaction—her blood overheating, her breathing tight, her pulse surging. 'We gave each other quite a lot to think about that day. And as it stands right now, I'm not sure I have anything new to say to you,' she said, noticing how he'd had his hair cut a little shorter at the collar, making it seem a little longer on top. His facial hair was neatly trimmed. The perfect amount of sexy scruff to make her want to kiss him, just to feel the scrape of it against her skin, because as much as she disliked his heavy handedness, their chemistry was as inarguable as ever. And never more irrelevant.

'In that case, I hope you managed to clear your head,' he said, watching her from behind his dark sunglasses.

How dare he look so handsome and composed when she was so instantly flustered.

'What are you doing here?' she asked changing the

subject. 'Not at the garden party, but here in the rose garden. Shouldn't you be over there making small talk?' She assumed his recent status change had prompted his invitation to the party unless he was there as a former member of staff.

Xavier slung his hands casually into his trouser pockets and glanced to where most people were gathered on the immaculate lawns, enjoying chilled champagne and gourmet canapés delivered by formally attired wait staff.

'I…um…seem to have reached my capacity for small talk,' he said. 'As a newcomer to both elite society and wine growing, what I can offer to the conversation is limited anyway. I have no idea which socialite is marrying which billionaire this summer or how fruitful the grape harvest is likely to be this year.'

Taking pity on him, because he was clearly out of his comfort zone despite appearing as if he belonged, Lola stepped closer, smiling slightly. 'It's easy,' she said, lowering her voice. 'In my experience, people with power, wealth and influence like to talk about themselves. All you have to do is ask them what they do for a living and they'll fill in any conversational blanks. Then it's simply a case of nodding occasionally.'

Neither of them truly belonged here, among the famous and influential and royal, although Lola had yet to see the King and Queen who were purported to be joining the party at some point.

'Thanks for the tip.' Rare amusement twitched his lips.

She wished he'd remove the sunglasses so she could see his eyes.

'But I'd much rather talk to you,' he said quietly. 'How are you feeling?' His gaze dipped to her stomach as if she was already showing, which of course she wasn't. But with the exception of Isla, the baby was their little secret.

'I'm okay,' she said with a small sigh, unable to stay angry with him now that he'd lost the bossy tone of the previous week. 'Sore boobs, going to the toilet all the time and this morning I felt decidedly nauseous. Apart from that, I'm awesome,' she finished sarcastically.

She left out the hormonal mood swings that left her wanting to throttle him one minute and have sex with him the next. Sadly neither was an option.

'Is there anything I can do to help?' he asked, his lips pursed in a small frown, his concern for her wellbeing obviously genuine.

'I think you've done enough, don't you?' She laughed softly.

He didn't laugh along, merely clenched his jaw and glanced at the ground. 'I… I want to be there for you both, which is probably what I should have said last week. I might have come over a little harsh the last time we spoke. So…apologies.'

'A little?' she teased because she could see that he was trying and neither of them had planned this.

'There was a lot coming at me,' he said, serious, his voice turned gruff with repressed emotion. 'But I meant what I said—I want to help raise our child. I want to… protect you both. I hope we can talk and find a way for us to figure this out together.'

Lola shuddered, his protectiveness awakening some primitive desire in her that she would have previously denied. Common sense told her he'd included her in his statement because for the next eight months, wherever she went, their baby went too. But no matter how hard she tried, because she was a strong, independent woman, she couldn't forget the way she'd felt wrapped in those strong arms of his—safe, seen, respected. The way he'd groaned her name in that gravelly voice as he'd climaxed. The way he then turned tender, holding her face in his palms and staring into her eyes as if they'd just shared something special. Which, as it had turned out, they had. They'd made their child that night.

'Of course, Xavier,' she said, her voice breaking. 'I want that too.'

They stared at each other in silence. A kind of truce forming. But then just as they seemed to be entering new conciliatory territory, there was a crunch of gravel behind them.

'Dr Garcia,' a breathless uniformed staff member interrupted. 'There's a medical emergency with one of the guests. Are you able to come to the drawing room right away?'

'Of course,' Lola said, thrusting her glass of juice at the young woman.

'I'll come too,' Xavier said and they hurried after a second staff member who showed them the way.

They ran through a series of exquisite rooms and marble tiled hallways, finally entering a vast elegant drawing room with a large marble fireplace, art bedecked walls and French doors framed by billowing white drapes that opened onto a terrace.

The patient, a man in his sixties, was seated on the edge of a cream upholstered sofa. A similarly aged woman fretted at his side.

'I'm Dr Garcia,' Lola said, reaching for the man's wrist and taking his pulse, which was fast but regular. 'Can you tell me what happened?'

'Pain…' the man said, clearly breathless and sweating, his complexion alarmingly grey.

'He has a pain in his chest,' the woman supplied. 'His name is Lorenzo and I'm Carmen, his wife.'

'Does your husband have any medical history?' Lola asked, aware that Xavier stood just behind. She noted that Lorenzo was overweight. His rotund belly stretching at his shirt buttons.

'Just arthritis,' she replied, concerned.

Lola turned to the steward in the room. 'Has an ambulance been called?' The party continued outside, but the last thing they needed was for a full-blown medical incident at the palace.

'Yes, Dr Garcia,' the man said.

'Do you have any aspirin at the palace?' she asked as Xavier helped Lorenzo loosen his tie and the top button of his shirt.

'We've sent for the palace's first aid box, ma'am,' the steward replied. 'Ah, here it is now.' He took the large box from another man and placed it on the table beside them.

Lola opened the box, finding a fully equipped medical kit, including a blood pressure machine, a stethoscope and even an automated external defibrillator, or AED.

'Aspirin,' Xavier said, holding up the bottle. His stare on hers was calm and reassuring, as it had been the night of the storm, filling her with confidence that no matter what was thrown their way, they could handle it together.

'Can we have a glass of water?' Xavier asked the steward, who nodded and retrieved one from a sideboard at the end of the room.

Lola fitted the stethoscope in her ears and, with Xavier's help, raised the man's shirt so she could listen to his chest at the back.

While the patient swallowed the aspirin, and with her examination complete, she drew Xavier aside. 'I think he's having a myocardial infarction,' she whispered, glancing nervously at the door. 'I'd feel happier if the ambulance and paramedics were here.'

Xavier wrapped his hand around her elbow, his touch warm and comforting. 'You stay with Lorenzo. I'll speak to the steward and ensure that we can admit the ambulance to the palace grounds with the minimum of delay. The guests and press outside are a logistical problem, but there's a rear way out. We can transport him to the ambulance that way, avoiding a scene.'

Lola nodded, her hand covering his before she was even aware that she'd moved. 'Thank you.' She held his stare for a few seconds, yet again grateful that he was there to help. Even if she'd been free to speak in that moment, she doubted she'd find the words.

While Xavier discreetly discussed logistics with the palace staff, Lola returned to the patient. 'I'm concerned that you might be having a heart attack, Lorenzo,' she explained to the man and his wife. 'The aspirin should help before the ambulance arrives, but what we really need is for you to be assessed at hospital where they can run blood tests and look more closely at your heart.'

'Should I drive him there?' Carmen asked, clutching the pearls at her throat.

Lola shook her head, but before she could add that waiting for the ambulance was safest, Lorenzo slumped to the side and rolled onto the floor, unconscious.

'Xavier,' Lola called.

Xavier bounded over and knelt opposite her while they each felt for a pulse.

'Help me roll him over,' she said, struggling with the

patient who had turned into a dead weight and was too heavy for her alone.

With the patient lying on his back, she felt again for a carotid pulse, her suspicions turning to dread when she failed to find one. 'No pulse,' she told Xavier, their eyes meeting for a split second.

Xavier looked up from listening for breath sounds. 'No breathing either.'

'He's in cardiac arrest,' Lola said to the steward while Xavier delivered two rescue breaths via mouth to mouth. 'Have someone re-call emergency services to let them know and unpack the defibrillator,' she instructed, while commencing chest compressions.

At the count of thirty, she paused for Xavier to administer another two rescue breaths, a horrible sense of déjà vu coming over her. Last time they'd been in this position, the night of the storm, they'd lost the patient. Lola couldn't bear the idea of that happening again, here at the palace with the man's wife watching on as she sobbed into a lace trimmed handkerchief.

Beginning another cycle of chest compressions, Lola glanced at Xavier, whose expression was calmly neutral. But because she knew him better, she saw he was thinking the same thing. By the time of her next pause, the steward had switched on the defibrillator and Xavier had stuck the electrodes onto the man's chest. Lola observed the heart's rhythm displayed on the machine's small screen.

'He's in VF,' she told Xavier who nodded, delivering two final breaths.

When the machine instructed them to stand clear, they removed their hands from the patient to allow the two-hundred-volt shock to be given.

To Lola's relief, the heart returned to sinus rhythm. 'There's a pulse,' she said as Lorenzo groaned, still groggy and semi-conscious, as he tried to bat them away.

'The paramedics have arrived,' the steward said in a panicked voice, moving to a door on the other side of the room and swinging it open to admit the ambulance crew.

As the paramedics placed an oxygen mask over Lorenzo's face and transferred him to a stretcher, Lola gave them a brief history of events. Within minutes, they'd whisked both the patient and his tearful wife from the room, leaving Lola, Xavier and the steward alone.

'Thank you, Dr Garcia,' the steward said, clearing away the equipment they'd used so the elegant, sun-bathed drawing room was once more immaculate, showing no sign of what had transpired there. 'Do take your time. You won't be disturbed here.'

He discreetly left and closed the door.

Drained of adrenaline and unusually emotional, Lola shivered, goosebumps erupting over her bare arms. From behind, Xavier silently draped his soft linen sports coat over her shoulders, the fabric giving off the warmth from his body and the scent of his after shave.

'Come on,' he said, his arm around her shoulders. 'I'll drive you home. One of my old security guard buddies can deliver your car later.'

'Thanks,' she said, meekly following him from the room to the parking area at the rear of the palace, away from where the garden party continued unsuspecting.

'I don't know what's wrong with me...' she said as she clicked her seatbelt into place.

'It's just shock,' he said, reaching for her hand and squeezing. 'You came here expecting to socialise in the sun, not to resuscitate someone in the palace drawing room.'

She nodded, grateful once more for his calm, reassuring presence.

'We're making a habit of tackling medical emergencies together,' he said as they headed down the palace's rear driveway, hoping to make her smile because she'd fallen pale and quiet.

Grateful for his inherited car's tinted windows, Xavier paused at the electronic gates before he drove past the handful of paps loitering outside the palace hoping to photograph a member of the royal family or someone rich and famous leaving the party, and headed for the city.

She glanced over at him, a ghost of a smile on her lovely lips. 'I agree. We really have to stop meeting like that.' She sighed tiredly and frustration coiled tight inside him.

He fought the instinct to touch her again. Things were complicated enough between them without indulging the pretty constant need to kiss her to see if it was as good as he remembered. Not that he needed the test to be certain of the outcome.

'Apart from the unforeseen cardiac arrest…' she said, glancing his way with a little more colour in her cheeks, '…how was your first official social event as *Marqués de Moro*? I saw the story announcing the death of Mauricio on the news.'

Xavier paused at traffic lights, shooting her a mocking look. 'If I admit that I hated every second until I found you in the rose garden, would you be shocked?' he asked, his pulse accelerating because she looked lovely, her slim figure draped in a floaty summer dress.

He'd done his best to hide from the breaking news, from the paps eager to get a shot of the shocking illegitimate heir no one knew about, but they'd still somehow found him, snapping pictures outside the hospital as he'd arrived for his shift.

'It's surely not that bad.' Lola watched him for a few seconds, until he looked away and pulled off once more.

'I don't belong,' he said with a shrug. 'And what's more, I don't care. But everyone else knows I'm a fish out of water and they *do* seem to care. For the moment at least, until I become old news.'

'I understand how you feel you know,' she said quietly. 'Maybe better than you think.'

When he shot her a quizzical look, she went on. 'I told you I was engaged,' she said pensively. 'If I'd gone through with it, I'd have married into that kind of family—obscenely wealthy, influential, titled. Nicolás and I were young when we met, but then after we got engaged, his expectations changed. I began to see that as far as he and his family were concerned, my dreams, my ambitions, were irrelevant. He talked about us running the estate together. About raising our family to take over one day. And when I insisted that I still wanted to go to medical school and become a doctor, he laughed.'

'Why would he laugh?' Xavier scowled, annoyed on Lola's behalf.

'He said that as his wife, I wouldn't need to work. He completely missed the point that I wanted to do something I could be proud of. Something for myself. When I kept pushing for his agreement that I could follow my own dreams, he gave me an ultimatum.'

Xavier held his breath, knowing strong, spirited Lola would have hated that.

'He said if I loved him, I'd work with him. When I pointed out that it worked both ways, that if he loved me and the person I am he'd want me to do whatever made me happy, he refused to see it.'

'So you called things off?'

She nodded. 'I went to medical school, became a doctor and embarked on a fulfilling career. I'm proud of what I've achieved.'

'Do you have any regrets about…the relationship?' he asked, keeping his eyes on the road. She didn't belong to him, but because she was having his baby, because he couldn't wipe that night from his mind, he couldn't ignore the panic that came whenever he thought of her leaving Castilona. The idea of her past feelings for this other man burned his chest with hot stabs of jealousy.

'No,' she said. 'I always imagined having a loving relationship like the one my parents have. My mother's family wanted her to marry someone professional, but she fell in love with my dad, an artist, and married him anyway. Nicolás obviously didn't love *me*. And I thought I loved him but realised I hadn't known the real him at all. I wanted more than to fill my days with charity work and running his ancient estate in which I had no interest. Of course the irony of the fact that, before I knew I was pregnant, I'd resigned from my job to work for an overseas charity isn't lost on me.' She huffed softly, her eyes falling to her lap. 'So you see, I understand how you feel about your inheritance. How on the surface it can seem like a gift, but if it's not who you truly are it becomes more like a cage.'

Xavier nodded, her heartfelt admissions leaving him unsettled. But she was right. She could understand that what appeared from the outside as a very generous and life-changing gift could, from the inside, feel claustrophobic.

'If it wasn't for the baby,' he said quietly, 'I seriously would have donated the entire estate to charity.'

'You still could…' she said, her hand resting over her belly.

He nodded grimly, because in some ways, he had no choice but to accept the legacy. 'I don't plan on disowning my child. Do you think once the media, those paps back at the palace, learn of our child's existence that we'll be able to walk away from its birthright? That title has been handed down from father to son since the sixteenth century. I have a theory that that's why de la Rosa passed it on to me. He had no legitimate son and, as power hungry as he was, his ego finally outweighed his need to reject me as his.'

She touched his arm. 'It may not be that simple…'

'Even if I refuse the inheritance,' he went on, ignoring the misplaced credit she attributed to de la Rosa, 'the estate and title will be kept in trust for our child. And besides, since I've moved in to Casa Colina and seen how the estate is run for myself, I've had to think twice about throwing it all away. There are many families whose livelihoods are tied to the estate. They are reliant on the income to feed their children and pay their mortgages. It's no longer just about me and my wants.'

'I see,' Lola said. 'But then life is never straightforward, is it?'

They drove in silence for a few minutes, through the busy streets of the capital. Xavier pulled up outside her apartment and turned off the engine.

'I'll walk you in,' he said, jumping from the car and opening her door.

'Thanks.' She took her key from her purse. They entered the building and climbed the stairs to the first floor.

Inside her apartment, the entire place was stacked with packing boxes, a sickening reminder that she was moving on. Lola removed Xavier's jacket and, shivering again, reached for a hoodie from a pile of folded clothes on the sofa before slipping it on.

'I hope you've employed a moving company,' he said gruffly, those protective urges returning. She was so independent and he had all these…urges. He wanted to make her tea, run her a bath and carry all her possessions for her. What the hell was happening to him?

'I will,' she said, collecting his jacket and holding it out to him.

He took it, their fingers brushing for a second, before they each pulled away. But that second of contact was enough to all but choke him with a surge of desire. How could he still want her so badly when they'd agreed to move on? When everything was complicated now, because she was having his baby? When nothing was settled and she might soon be leaving the country?

'I guess I'll need to find somewhere else to rent,' she said, 'until…you know, we sort everything out. Not that I'm sure what I'll be doing next…'

'Aside from becoming a mother.' Xavier stepped closer, as if his feet weren't under his control.

'Yes.' She smiled. 'Aside from that.'

'You could stay with me,' he said, stunning himself. 'That house has twenty-two bedrooms and a separate, self-contained guest house. It's so big we wouldn't even run into each other.'

If she moved in, he could help her out and be involved. Of course, there'd be pros and cons to having her under the same roof. He could protect her and gain the peace of mind that would come with knowing she and the baby were safe. But, conversely, the physical proximity might become a form of torture. His restraint would only stretch so far.

'I don't think that's a good idea,' she said, as if she could read his mind.

He nodded. 'I agree… It was just a suggestion.'

She shot him a look of surprise.

'But we could avoid each other if we had to.' His stare dipped to her lips, which were parted, her breathing fast and shallow. 'I've been trying to avoid you since I came to work at the hospital so I'm well practised.' His admission made his pulse buzz in his fingertips, but the time for pretence had been and gone. They'd proved how badly they'd wanted each other. They'd even made a baby.

'Why?' she whispered, a small frown tugging at her mouth.

Xavier paused, not sure she'd like his answer. 'What happened between us the night of the storm,' he said, 'I'd wanted you since we first met.'

Her breathing sped up, her lips parted. 'And that's a bad thing?' she asked, looking confused and so beautiful, he couldn't breathe.

He shrugged, wishing she would step away, because he seemed to lack the strength. 'I told you. I only do casual. I assumed you were a for ever kind of woman, not to mention you were my boss.'

Xavier imagined he saw a flicker of something like disappointment pass over her face. 'I guess I am a for ever kind of woman, with the right man.'

Xavier nodded, that jealous twist of his gut returning.

'I knew it,' he said, trying for humour. But he didn't feel like laughing.

Of course *he* could never be the right man. He'd never been in love. Not even close. Love was all about belonging. Something he knew nothing about. He'd just about come to terms with who he was and then bam, the letter from de la Rosa's solicitor had arrived. And now he was going to be a father, another thing of which he had no experience. What if he turned out to be like his father? No, he would never allow that to happen.

'I'm sorry I ignored your calls,' she said quietly.

'It's okay.'

'I guess I've always known where I was headed and now... I'm all over the place,' she said.

He nodded, compassion squeezing his lungs. 'We're both going through some changes.'

'Yes.' She looked uncertain. He'd never seen her that way.

If he didn't leave soon he might touch her, hold her and struggle to stop there.

'Have something to eat,' he said instead, stepping back at last. He draped the jacket over his arm and shoved his hands into his pockets. 'Drink tea maybe. You still look...pale.'

She inhaled, as if she was about to say something more, then appeared to change her mind. 'I...will.'

At the door, he paused, turning to face her once more. 'When you're next free, I'd appreciate a chance to talk about the baby. There are plans we need to make.' He would start as he meant to go on with fatherhood, be fully involved from the beginning, letting his child know exactly how much he or she was loved and wanted.

'Okay.' She followed him to the threshold. 'Thanks for your help earlier and for the lift.'

'Get some rest,' he said, fighting the urge to press a kiss to her cheek, because they weren't friends and he couldn't trust that he'd be able to resist.

Instead, he walked away, tossed his jacket on the passenger seat and drove home, the scent of her perfume she'd left behind taunting him every mile of the journey.

# CHAPTER EIGHT

THE FOLLOWING MONDAY, after a weekend spent pointlessly reliving every second of her final frustrating conversation with Xavier, Lola was at her desk when she
received a summons to the hospital's security office.

Embarrassed by the eager clack of her heels against the
marble tiles as she hurried there assuming the call had
come from Xavier, she paused outside the room to pull
herself together and steady her excited breaths.

'Dr Garcia,' Antonio, one of the regular security
guards, said standing as she entered the small room,
which was equipped with a wall of screens capturing
images from the multiple cameras around the hospital.

'You wanted to see me,' Lola said with smile, hiding
her disappointment that Xavier was absent.

'Yes, ma'am. We have a situation.'

With a couple of mouse clicks, Antonio brought up an
enlarged image, the live feed of the camera that faced the
hospital's main entrance. Across the street stood a clus-
ter of paps, smoking, chatting and raising their cameras
to their faces every time a car slowed as if it might pull
into the clinic's private driveway.

'They've been there since five a.m.,' Antonio said.

'Who do they want?' she asked, peering closer, her
stomach flopping with dread. It could only be Xavier.

There was no one else particularly newsworthy currently on the premises.

'I don't know, ma'am. Shall I call the police?' Antonio asked.

Lola straightened, frustration whipping through her. 'No. They're on a public footpath. They're not breaking any laws. Let's just hope they soon get bored or hungry or dash off to bother someone else.'

Just as she was leaving the security office, she came face to face with Xavier. Unlike at the garden party the weekend before, he was now clean shaven, but just as devastatingly handsome.

'Dr Garcia,' he said, his stare shifting over her face and briefly lower to the V-neck of her blouse, reminding her of the way he'd looked at her when he'd dropped her home the other night—as if he was struggling to walk away. But maybe he simply wanted to discuss the baby again.

'I hope you had a restful weekend,' he said, as if oblivious to the havoc he'd caused with his casual comment about wanting her since they'd first met. It shouldn't have made any difference, but she hadn't been able to stop thinking about him all weekend.

'Thank you. I did,' she said, her stomach swooping at his proximity. 'Would you walk with me, please?'

She headed back towards her office with Xavier at her side. 'Have you seen our friends across the street?'

He nodded, his mouth pressed into a line. 'I have, I'm afraid. I think this time, they're after me. They've also been camped opposite my gates since I moved into Casa Colina.' He paused at the threshold to her office and faced her. 'Which is why you'll find my letter of resignation in your email inbox.'

Shocked, Lola stepped inside her office, gesturing

him to follow. 'You're leaving us?' she asked ridiculously given that she too was leaving *Clinico San Carlos*. 'Are you sure?'

The paps would soon lose interest. Hopefully...

He stood just inside the door. 'Yes, ma'am.'

'Do you have another job lined up?' It wasn't what she wanted to ask. She wished he'd closed the door so they could have a personal conversation, but she was desperately trying to stay professional. Trying to keep her distance as effortlessly as he was able, even though sometimes, she wanted to hurl herself into his arms and kiss him.

'No,' he said, his stare holding hers. 'I'm going to be concentrating on some personal matters for the time being.'

They stared at each other, some kind of weird telepathic communication connecting them. Was he saying he'd decided to embrace his inheritance? Or was he talking about fatherhood? Either option left her itchy, as if his choices had consequences for her independence, which she guessed they did in a way. He would likely have the same reservations about her leaving Castilona, which, if she imagined the tables were turned, wasn't that unreasonable. She wouldn't tolerate him taking their child overseas without her, either.

Lola swallowed her throat dry as doubts filled her head. 'Then I wish you well, Xavier,' she said, her voice thankfully steady. 'I'll happily provide a reference, should you ever need it in future.'

'Thank you.'

He was doing that military stance thing again. His hands clasped behind his back as they stared at each other. She wanted to rattle him as he effortlessly flustered her with his reasonable requests, honest admissions and potent virility.

Before she could inappropriately raise their personal issues, he stepped closer, his stiff posture softening. 'Have dinner with me tonight,' he said quietly. 'So we can talk.'

Lola's heart galloped with excitement, even as the urge to point out that he was telling her what to do again built on her tongue. But he was too close, smelled too good, the look in his eyes both vulnerable and expectant. She couldn't disappoint him.

'What time?' she asked, enslaved suddenly by the crackle of sexual tension that had always existed between them and had in no way diminished since they'd slept together.

'Why don't we leave here together tonight, sneak past the paps. My car has tinted windows.'

'Okay,' she said, a thrill of anticipation fluttering in her stomach. But it was just a meal and a conversation. If only her hormone-ridden body understood that.

'If that's all then…?' he asked, effortlessly resuming his professional role where Lola was left achy and breathless, her body pityingly desperate for their physical connection. She needed to be careful. Surrendering to lust was one thing but losing her head over a man who was always in control of his emotions…that would be a very stupid mistake.

Later that evening, Xavier carefully poured Lola a glass of iced lemonade made by his housekeeper, Tia. The cavernous kitchen somehow felt warmer and more inviting now that Lola was there to share it. Their journey from the clinic to Casa Colina had of course attracted interest from the photographers camped across the street. His car was recognisable and several paps had followed them on mopeds. But thanks to the clinic's underground car park, as well as Casa Colina's electric gates and long drive, they'd been able to get a head start and hopefully avoided providing any profitable photos. That hadn't eased Xavier's concern though. He knew firsthand how...persistent some of them could be.

'I wondered who you might have told,' he said, sliding the lemonade across the counter. 'About the baby?'

He returned to the hob, lowered the burner under the vegetable paella and gave it one final stir.

'I've told my twin sister, Isla. That's all,' she said, watching him cook with a slightly impressed expression he enjoyed.

'If it's okay with you...' he said, '... I'd like to tell my mother. I think she's pretty much given up hope that I would meet someone I'd be serious about, so she's going to be thrilled to be an *abuela* at last. She will, of course, be discreet. Working at the palace she's had plenty of practice. And I'll make sure to explain that we're not together.'

'Of course,' Lola said, glancing over her shoulder. 'Is she here? Will she be moving in?'

'No. She's still coming to terms with all of this,' he said, trying and failing to keep the bitterness from his voice. 'De la Rosa seduced her when she was young and vulnerable then got angry when she told him she was pregnant. He convinced her to keep his secret, said it was for my own protection, but no one benefited from that more than him.'

'Her hesitation is understandable,' she said. 'Have you considered how he might have done you a favour, even if it was for his own ends?'

'By leaving me a tainted legacy you mean?'

'No. More like his selfishness gave you a chance to grow up in private and follow your own dreams. I imagine having those paps follow you everywhere is pretty tedious. Just imagine if you'd had to cast aside your dreams of the army to come and work here, making wine because that was expected of you and not a choice.'

'I hadn't thought of it that way,' he said. 'And you're right about the paps. Nothing sells like a scandal. I think they'll lose interest in me soon though. Would you like a tour of the house?' he asked, removing the paella from the heat. 'Given that all of this will belong to our baby one day.'

With every day that passed, Xavier grew more and more comfortable in the role of caretaker. That he could someday turn an unwanted legacy from a man he'd never known into a safe and secure future for their child, helped him to rationalise it all.

'Sure,' she said, sliding from the stool.

Before they'd left the hospital, she'd changed into a long sun dress that might have been designed specifically to torture him given the way it caressed her figure, outlining her perfect breasts and trim waist, the flare of her hips and sexy backside. And she smelled like a meadow of flowers baked by the sun.

Trying to keep his distance, Xavier led her from the kitchen through the terracotta tiled hall to a whitewashed living room with French doors that overlooked the terraces of the garden.

'I hired some decorators to freshen up the place. It was a little dated,' he told her as they walked along.

'There's a library through there,' he said pointing down

another corridor off the living room. 'A home office, gym and indoor pool too.'

'It's stunning,' she said, glancing around impressed, taking in the luxurious furnishings and original art on the walls.

Taking the stairs, he moved the tour to the first floor. 'There are four bedrooms at this end of the house. Eighteen more throughout the guest wing. Although who would ever need that many guests is beyond me,' he muttered, embarrassed by the extravagance he couldn't quite believe was his. Xavier was a simple man with simple needs.

'Might be useful for parties,' she suggested, laughing at him when he glanced her way in horror.

Then she poked her head into the first two bedrooms, her eyes wide. 'Very nice.'

'This staircase brings you to the back of the house,' he said leading the way. 'There are quarters for the housekeeper,' he said, breezing past Tia's rooms. 'And here,' he swung open the door to a tiled courtyard and the separate, self-contained chalet beyond, 'is the guest house. Just in case you have even more guests, I guess.'

She shot him a sympathetic smile. 'It's impressive,' she said quietly as if mindful of his turbulent feelings.

'It's unnecessary,' he replied, sighing. 'Would you like to eat out here? The courtyard is sheltered from the breeze.'

'That would be lovely,' she said.

'Take a seat and I'll be back in a second.'

Xavier loaded up a tray with two plates of paella, the lemonade and glasses, cutlery and napkins. When he returned, Lola was staring out at the ocean, watching the sunset.

'So what do you plan to do now that you'll no longer be working security at the hospital?' she asked when he'd taken the seat next to hers.

'The estate supports sixty staff.' Xavier loaded up his fork with paella. 'As much as I'd love to board the place up and sleep in a hammock in the garden, I don't want to create any unemployment. There are staff here who've worked for the estate manager for close to twenty years.'

Lola nodded. 'That makes sense. So you're going to become a winemaker?'

Xavier scoffed softly. 'I might need to get some qualifications to do that. I'm told it's a cross between an art form and a science, neither of which I know the first thing about.' He topped up her lemonade. 'In the short term, I'll spend some time here, learn how things work and figure out where I can be most useful. It might be by staying out of the way.'

'I'm glad,' she said, watching him carefully. 'Glad that you'll make something positive out of your past, out of a situation you had no control over that wasn't your fault.'

Xavier hesitated, stunned at how intuitively she'd touched a nerve.

'It doesn't mean I forgive him,' he said, bluntly. He doubted he'd ever be able to do that. 'But our baby has given me a reason to think about the importance of heritage. Just because I wish I wasn't related to de la Rosa, doesn't mean my child will feel the same way. He or she deserves the chance to make their own decisions about all of this. About who he or she is and where they belong. Don't you think?'

Lola watched him, blinking, her eyes shining with emotion. 'I guess… Although it's a pretty intimidating legacy for one so small.' She rested her hand over her belly as if their child needed protecting from the enormity of all this, which he guessed it did.

Xavier swallowed and glanced away pretending to find his paella fascinating when, in reality, his appetite had vanished to be replaced by doubts. What the hell did he know about being a father? But just like he would take viticulture classes to learn about wine, he could also learn about parenthood.

'So… How are we going to tackle this situation?' he asked quietly.

Lola sighed and his stomach knotted with dread. She wasn't ready to talk about the details, he'd sensed that. But he needed to plan, to think about logistics like babyproofing the house and beefing up estate security.

'We're both mature, responsible people,' she said, evenly. 'I think we can figure things out, don't you?'

'I hope so.' He glanced down at his barely touched food. 'I… It goes without saying, but I want to be fully involved.' He met her stare, his heart pounding, his body rigid with contained feelings. 'I want to be a better father than he was.'

Lola smiled softly, tilted her head and reached out her hand, covering his. 'That wouldn't be hard. For what it's worth, I think you're going to be an amazing father. Our baby will be lucky to have you.'

That she hadn't dismissed his fears made his respect for her soar through the roof. That she saw him capable of loving their child, choked him to the point of breathlessness. How could she be so certain? He wasn't. He knew he would protect the child with his life, that he'd try to ensure that it was happy and healthy and had every opportunity in life, but what if the love didn't come? What if he'd spent so long shutting people out, uncertain of who he could trust with his feelings, guarding them against rejection and betrayal, that he was incapable of love? What if deep down, he was more like de la Rosa than he knew?

'I don't know what I'm doing,' he said, his doubts so huge, they made a verbal bid for freedom. 'But I want to be there, which is why I wanted you to stay here in Castilona.'

She nodded, falling silent.

'That being said,' he went on, 'if you do permanently move back to Spain, then I'll move there too. I can leave all of this to manage itself, as de la Rosa did, and help you to raise the baby…if that's okay?'

Lola nodded, her stare shining. 'That's fine by me, Xavier. But we have plenty of time. We don't have to decide right now where we'll end up living, do we?'

Xavier shook his head and she relaxed, began eating, while he felt light-headed with relief and doubt, because everything was still up in the air. But he wouldn't push her any more tonight. He would feed her then take her home and try his best not to kiss her goodnight. Because the only constant in his life at the moment, the only thing he could rely upon, was that around her, he was consumed by burning need.

# CHAPTER NINE

USING AN ESTATE vehicle rather than his personal one to avoid being followed by the paps, Xavier had driven Lola home. After such an emotional evening, she hoped that a warm shower before bed would lull her into a restful sleep, one where she slept through any erotic dreams about Xavier. She'd just pulled on her favourite silk pyjamas when the buzzer to her apartment sounded, jarringly.

Lola hurried to the intercom near the door, fear clutching at her throat. Who would be on her doorstep at this time of night? The couple of female friends she'd made in Castilona would only call this late if it was something urgent. Perhaps Xavier had forgotten something after dropping her home.

Seeing a dark male figure she didn't recognise on the security screen, she warily pressed the intercom. 'Yes?'

'Dr Garcia, I wondered if you would give an interview to *Estilo Magazine*? I can pay you for your time, but we'd love to do a feature on your relationship with the new *Marqués de Moro*.'

Lola gasped, rearing away from the intercom in shock. She stepped backwards as if physical distance would erase this from reality. How had they found her? Had someone at the hospital leaked her home address? And what did they want? She had no intention of talking to anyone.

Ignoring the man, Lola moved to the window and peeked through the blinds, gasping once more as she saw the group of paps on the street, looking perfectly at ease. Chatting, sipping takeaway coffee and chain smoking as if they planned to spend the night camped outside her apartment block.

The man who'd rung the bell leaned on the button so the buzzer sounded continuously, making her jump as it echoed around the otherwise silent room. She had no personal experience of this. She was an ordinary woman. Yes she'd managed the press as part of her role at the clinic, but this was different. Intrusive. Threatening. And if they could find out where she lived, when her and Xavier weren't even a couple, what would stop them finding out about the baby?

She dropped a protective hand to her abdomen. Then with trembling fingers, she called Xavier.

He answered after a single ring. 'Are you okay?'

She winced at the panic in his voice, feeling silly for calling so late. 'I'm fine. But there are journalists and paparazzi on my doorstep. I don't know what to do.' The one who'd knocked continued to press the buzzer so she put her finger in her ear so she could hear Xavier over the horrible sound.

'Don't answer the door,' he said, his voice firm but calm, making her feel instantly better. 'I'll be there in ten minutes.'

'No… I'm fine.' She back-pedalled. It wasn't as if she was in any danger, although she'd never be able to sleep through that noise. And would they still be there in the morning when she left for work? 'I was just on my way to bed but I doubt I'll be able to sleep now, especially as one of them hasn't stopped pressing my doorbell. Can you hear it?'

'You can come back here,' he said, his voice breathless as if he was running while he spoke.

'There's no need for that,' Lola said. 'What do they even want from me? How did they even find me?'

'They must have followed us when I dropped you home. I'm sorry. I thought we'd lost them.'

'Should I call the police?' she asked, her paranoia building.

'I'll be with you in eight minutes,' he said, obviously driving now.

'Okay,' she said in a voice that sounded far too small for her liking.

'Pack an overnight bag,' he said. 'You won't be disturbed at Casa Colina and I can keep them away from you there.'

When she hesitated and said nothing he went on. 'You've seen the layout. You can take any of the bedrooms you like. Even in the guest house you'll be safe.'

Lola glanced around her small apartment, stacked with moving boxes. She'd once loved this place, but now it felt tainted somehow. As if she'd been burgled, her possessions rifled.

'Don't speed,' she said, heading to the bedroom and taking out her overnight bag from the closet. 'There's an underground garage. The code is six-three-eight-seven. They won't be able to follow you there.' She threw some work clothes, underwear, toiletries and her toothbrush into the bag.

'Don't count on it,' he said bitterly. 'You won't believe

the lengths some of them went to just to get a shot of Princess Xiomara.'

While Xavier stayed on the line, Lola quickly changed out of her pyjamas into jeans and a sweatshirt, slipping on her comfiest ballet flats.

'I'm pulling into the garage now,' he said. 'Stay in your apartment. I'll come up and meet you.'

She topped up Albie's food and water, although she knew the cat sitter would do that too, and when she finally opened the door to Xavier, having verified his presence through the peep hole, she almost sagged into his arms with relief. She prided herself on being a strong, independent, capable woman, but being pregnant made her feel more vulnerable somehow. As if she was keeping two lives safe, which she was.

Taking her bag, Xavier rested his hand on her shoulder. 'Have you got everything you need?'

Suddenly his intimidating height, his physique and training and calm assurance filled her with confidence. She nodded.

'Lock up,' he instructed, 'and let's go.'

With her hand gripping his, she followed him to the garage. They made it to the car without incident, but as the electronic grill-style exit gate raised and they pulled out onto the street, the car was swarmed by paps all pointing their cameras at the windows and yelling their names.

Lola sank down into the passenger seat, her heart pounding with adrenaline, her first instinct to cover her face.

'It's okay,' Xavier soothed, steering single handedly so he could reach for her hand and squeeze it. 'I won't let them get anywhere near you.'

Not hesitating for a second, Xavier drove away, leaving

the paps to scramble, jumping onto mopeds and giving chase. Xavier drove as if they weren't there, confident in the features of his modified luxury car—driver attention monitor, tinted bulletproof glass and a three hundred and sixty degree camera system.

It was only when they'd finally pulled through the double automatic gate system back at Casa Colina that Lola was able to breathe easy.

Xavier's entire body remained tense as he ushered Lola inside, fury boiling through him that they'd gone after her to get to him.

In the hallway, he gripped her shoulders and scanned her from head to toe. 'Are you okay?'

Choked by fear, he wanted to ask about the baby but couldn't. He wanted to drag her into his arms and hold her until the panicked pounding of his heart had eased. He wanted to dedicate the rest of his life to making sure she and their child were safe. But he was acting crazy and getting ahead of himself. Lola hated being fussed over.

'I'm fine,' she said, looking pale and tired. 'I was just shocked. Sorry if I worried you.'

He dropped his hands from her shoulders, not trusting himself to drag her into his arms and never let her leave. 'I'd rather you were here, where there's a wall and security gates to keep people out.'

'Thank you. For rescuing me,' she said attempting a smile. Then she stepped forward and embraced him, her arms around his waist and her head on his chest.

Xavier froze, one hand between her shoulder blades, the other at his side holding onto her overnight bag. His body reacting to her closeness and how right she felt in his arms with her heart beating against his. For a dangerously indulgent second, he dipped his head and inhaled the scent of her shampoo, closing his eyes as the desire he'd been denying all these long weeks since the storm rushed through him, like fizz from an uncorked bottle.

Using all his strength, every scrap of his discipline, he stepped back. If he didn't put some walls between them soon, he might do something stupid. He wasn't trying to seduce her. He needed to protect her and their baby. He wanted them to work on a respectful and mature relationship as parents. That had to be his priority.

'Would you prefer the guest house,' he asked, 'or one of the rooms upstairs?'

Lola frowned as if upset he'd ended their embrace. But she surely didn't want to reopen that closed door, did she? Not when things were so much more complicated between them now compared to the night of the storm.

She crossed her arms as if she was cold. 'Where do you sleep? I… I'd feel safer in a guest room in the main house if that's okay.'

Maybe she just wanted comfort. She must be spooked by what had happened tonight.

'Of course it is,' he said, wondering how in the hell he'd manage to sleep with her so close by. 'I'm on the first floor, one of the smaller rooms you looked into earlier. Why don't you take the master bedroom? It's at the end of the hall, so I won't disturb you, and you won't be alone in the guest wing, which by the way is perfectly safe and fitted with the same alarm system as the rest of the house but feels…lonely I guess.'

Lola nodded gratefully, relaxing slightly. 'Okay. Thank you.'

With his mind full of plans to increase security at Casa Colina, Xavier showed her the way to the master bedroom, a room he'd rejected for himself. One because he was a simple guy with simple needs and two because he'd guessed that de la Rosa had used it once. Even though he'd had it redecorated when he'd first moved in, purchasing brand new furniture, he still preferred the smaller room.

On the threshold, he passed over her bag. 'I'm right down the hall if you need anything. There's also an intercom beside the bed, which connects to Tia, the housekeeper, if you want a drink or something to eat.'

Lola shook her head, her eyes dark and haunted in the dim light of the room's lamps. 'I won't need anything, but thanks.' She stared, as if she might say more but didn't.

Swallowing down the turmoil inside him—the lingering fear for her safety, the arousal from holding her, the innate need to do the honourable thing—he forced himself to step back. 'Sleep well. See you in the morning. I'll take you to work.'

His stare swept over her one final time, then he headed downstairs to his office where he placed a series of calls to some recently discharged army buddies he would trust with his life, offering them a salary they couldn't refuse to join the estate's security.

Safety was his job, and the one thing he could do for Lola and his child, and he intended to do it to the best of his ability.

# CHAPTER TEN

BY THE END of the week, after Lola had been sleeping at Casa Colina for a few days, Xavier was certain that he was losing his mind. Having her there, driving her to work every day, sharing breakfast or dinner with her, reassured him that she and the baby were safe. But his peace of mind came at a high price. He was just about ready to crawl out of his skin with sexual frustration. He wanted her. Ached for her. Awoke from dreams where he was either searching the house for her in vain or rolling around naked with her, their passion for each other obliterating everything he stood for in life. There seemed to be no reprieve from the way being around her made him feel…unstable. And he had no idea what to do about it.

Glancing up from his laptop in the cool of the air-conditioned library, he spied her out by the pool and muttered a curse under his breath. Dressed in one of those long, flowing sun dresses she liked to wear when she was off duty, her shapely figure and slim legs visible through the sheer fabric, which was virtually see-through in the sunlight, made his mouth water.

The only thing worse than that torture, was when she donned a worn pair of cut-off denim shorts, pairing them with a simple white tank top that left him in no doubt that she was braless beneath, her breasts fuller than he remembered and nipples poking through the fabric, as if begging for his attention.

He looked away with a snort of self-disgust, trying to return his focus to the spreadsheet before him. But the numbers, a balance sheet of expenditure and profit predictions for the coming wine growing season, swam before his eyes, which once more sought out Lola.

'*Dios...*' he muttered, seeing that she'd now removed the filmy dress to reveal a sexy black bikini, the tiny triangles of fabric barely covering her gorgeous breasts and the haven between her legs. The small swell of her abdomen called to that primal part of him that needed to protect her and his child. If he hadn't memorised her body's shape from the night of the storm, obsessing over the images he'd stored like a fanatic, he doubted he'd be able to tell that she was pregnant.

Before drool could leave the corner of his mouth, Lola dived into the pool, sinking from his view, gifting him a few moments of respite from the hell in which he was trapped. Instead of returning to estate business, he checked the property's security camera feeds, all eighteen of them, which covered the walled and fenced perimeter of the property, every entrance and exit and the first and ground floor hallways.

Unsatisfied with what he saw, which was nothing more than another stunning Castilonian spring day, he picked up the walkie talkie and radioed the security team he'd employed the day after Lola had moved in.

'Status update,' he said, knowing his ex-army colleagues would think nothing of his abruptness. They, like him, understood the world in a way that most people were insulated from.

'All clear at the front,' one guard, Carlos, responded.

'Rear secure too, over,' the other, Marco, replied.

Xavier tried to console himself with their reassurance, but ever since the night he'd rescued Lola from the paparazzi on her street, he just couldn't seem to relax. Ever.

'Mrs Torres will be arriving shortly,' he told Carlos who was manning the front gate. 'Please let me know when she gets here.'

He'd invited his mother for dinner so he could introduce Lola and tell Carlota about the baby. After another ten minutes of fruitless work, Xavier abandoned his laptop and headed for the kitchen, where Tia was busy preparing a dinner of *albondigas*—Spanish meatballs in a garlic and tomato sauce, *patatas bravas* and a Mediterranean salad.

'Mr Torres,' she chided as he opened the cabinet, retrieved a water glass and filled it with ice from the fridge. 'If you tell me what you need, I will bring it to you, sir.'

'Please call me Xavier, Tia. And while I appreciate everything you do here, I have legs. I can fetch my own glass of water.' He doubted he'd ever become accustomed to having someone do things for him.

The older woman, a widow with two university-aged children, tilted her head in a way that told him he'd won this skirmish, but the war would be protracted and fiercely fought.

'My mother is on her way,' he told her. 'I'll warn you now that she has never once visited me empty handed, so please don't be offended if she brings enough food to feed the entire estate.'

'Her cooking is legendary.' Tia smiled. 'I hope to part her from some of her famous, well-guarded palace recipes.' Tia's smile widened, her stare landing on someone over Xavier's shoulder.

Xavier turned, already certain it was Lola from the

light floral scent of her perfume and the uncontrollable quickening of his pulse.

'Nice swim?' he asked, noting that she'd changed into another floaty dress that showed off her gorgeous figure. Her hair looked freshly blow dried and she'd scooped it into a casual top knot he wanted to undo while he buried his face against her neck.

'Blissful,' she said, helping herself to an olive from the bowl Tia had set next to a sweating jug of home-made lemonade. 'Dinner smells delicious, Tia. I'm ravenous.'

Giving his hands something to do that wasn't touch Lola and satisfy her other appetites, Xavier collected the tray of lemonade and suggested they sit in the conservatory to wait for Carlota.

'I wanted to ask you,' he said carefully, 'if I can tell my mother about the baby tonight? I can't risk her finding out from the media. I hope that's okay.'

Lola nodded, looking a little guilty. 'Of course. That's fine by me. I just… I hope she understands.' She licked her lips nervously.

Xavier glanced at her hand, fighting the urge to hold it. 'That we're not a couple?' he asked instead, the unease that had rumbled inside him since he'd discovered that Lola was having his baby increasing because while they'd agreed in principle to raise this baby together, they had none of the finer details planned. Whatever Lola's plans turned out to be, the estate was entering its busy season with the vines full of spring growth and the cellar door open for tastings and sales of previous years' vintages. It would take some planning for him to follow her if she decided to head back to Spain, permanently.

'Yes,' she said. 'I hope she understands that we didn't plan this. That I didn't set out to trap you or something…'

'Please don't worry,' Xavier said. 'She was a single parent herself. I guarantee she'll be delighted by the news. Although I might be scolded in private for being…careless.'

Discussing the moment they'd conceived, inevitably brought erotic memories flooding in. Had he ever connected so fully with a woman? The desire for her was becoming increasingly persistent. It might actually kill him.

'You weren't careless,' Lola said, looking at him in that way of hers—with intelligence and intuition, as if she saw through him to the places even he was scared to probe. 'I used to be on birth control, but I haven't dated for two years and I hadn't planned on sleeping with you. And I get the occasional migraine so didn't want to take unnecessary medication.'

Hearing her talk about her dating life only increased his restlessness. 'Did you want a child eventually?' he asked cautiously. Since she'd moved in, they'd avoided discussing the practicalities, but they each knew that conversation loomed.

'Yes. My family are very close,' she said. 'My parents are still wildly in love even after forty years of marriage. What about you?'

Xavier swallowed, unused to discussing his feelings. 'I've never had a relationship serious enough to give it any thought.'

'Not ever?' she asked, her intelligent stare appraising him.

'No. Like you I've been focussed on my career. Focussed on building a secure life for myself, living with my vision limitations.' Letting someone get close came with risk and he'd had enough rejection to last a lifetime, thanks to de la Rosa.

Just then, the radio he'd taken to wearing on his waist-band crackled to life. 'Señora Torres has arrived, sir.'

'Thank you,' Xavier replied then stood. 'Ready?' he asked Lola, who ran a nervous hand over the escaped wisps of her hair and nodded. 'Don't be nervous.' He swept his gaze over her. 'You look beautiful. She's going to love you.'

Xavier headed outside to meet the car, Lola at his side. Knowing that Carlota rarely followed celebrity gossip, all he'd told her was that a friend from work had come to stay at Casa Colina. As soon as he'd mentioned Lola's name, and Carlota discovered the friend was a woman, her voice had turned high pitched with hope. He'd never lived with a woman before, nor introduced Carlota to anyone he dated.

When Carlota climbed from her car, he made introductions. As he'd known she would, Carlota warmly embraced Lola as if they were old friends. While Xavier carried in the two foil-covered plates from the back seat, Carlota looped her arm through Lola's as they walked back inside, already chatting about the weather, dinner and the amazing views from the house.

With everyone once more seated in the sun room, and after a brief period of small talk where Carlota asked Lola about her work and her family, Xavier cleared his throat.

'Mamá, I have some news,' he said, glancing Lola's way, catching her small nod of encouragement. 'Lola and I are having a child.'

Carlota gasped, her hand reaching for Lola's arm as her eyes filled with the shine of tears. 'Really? Is it true?'

Lola nodded, blinking with emotion. 'Yes. We have the first scan next week, but I think I'm almost eight weeks along.'

Carlota threw her arms around Lola's neck and hugged her. Then, standing, she embraced Xavier tighter than he ever remembered being hugged.

'Don't get too excited,' he warned, sliding another glance Lola's way. 'We're not actually dating or together. It just…happened. The night of Cyclone Gabriel.'

Carlota waved her hand dismissively. 'I don't care how or when. I'm just delighted. But how are you feeling, *amado*?' she asked Lola, retaking her seat.

Lola glanced at Xavier and smiled. 'I'm fine. A little more tired than usual, but otherwise good.'

'And you're getting plenty of rest?' Carlota pushed, casting him a look he easily interpreted—*take care of her.*

'It's wonderfully relaxing here,' Lola said. 'I'm very comfortable and have been enjoying swimming in the pool after work.'

Carlota nodded with enthusiasm. 'So have you told your family? Are they planning to visit?'

Xavier winced. This was the tricky part. The details that he and Lola had yet to discuss and agree on.

'I've told my twin sister, Isla,' Lola said. 'But my parents will also be delighted to be grandparents.'

'Good.' Carlota clapped her hands together. 'I'm so happy for you both and for myself of course. An *abuela* at last.'

The women beamed at one another. Xavier stiffened, his doubts returning. Surely he and Lola could successfully navigate parenthood in a mature and respectful way. He'd have to make it work. He couldn't afford to mess this up because he'd have the most to lose.

Just then, there was a cry from the kitchen. Lola's startled stare shot to Xavier's. They both stood, hurrying into the other room to find Tia standing over the kitchen sink, her hand wrapped in a towel.

'Oh, Mr Torres, I'm so sorry,' she said. 'The knife slipped and I've cut my hand. So careless.' She winced at all three of them, her cheeks flushed with embarrassment.

'Tia, please don't worry,' Xavier said. 'How bad is it? Let us see.'

Tia gingerly unwrapped the towel, her cupped palm instantly filling with a pool of blood.

'Sit down,' he told her, quickly reapplying the towel and exerting pressure while he steered Tia over to a chair.

'I think it's going to need stitches,' Lola said once she'd examined the wound, looking up at Xavier over the top of Tia's head.

'I'll drive you to the hospital,' Xavier said, collecting more towels from the drawer.

'No,' Tia wailed. 'Your dinner…your mother.' She glanced at Carlota who was near the door, keeping out of the way. 'Please do not trouble yourself over me.' Tia stood but Xavier pushed her gently back down. The last thing they needed was her passing out and hitting her head.

'I have a suture kit in my medical bag,' Lola said. 'If you want, I can do it here. But you must attend the accident department at St Sebastian's tomorrow for a tetanus shot and some antibiotics,' she told Tia, who nodded meekly.

Lola met Xavier's stare. 'My bag is in the closet of my room.'

'I'll get it.' Xavier rushed to fetch it and when he returned, the three women had moved to the sink in the downstairs cloakroom.

'Let me take over with compression,' Xavier said, once he'd washed his hands and pulled on some gloves. He applied pressure to the wound while Lola also washed up and pulled on gloves.

Just like the night of the storm when she'd sutured up the wound to Maria Fernandez's head, she and Xavier worked together now while Carlota left the room, returning to the kitchen to remove dinner from the oven.

Lola injected local anaesthetic around the cut while Xavier did his best to staunch the bleeding.

'Don't worry,' Xavier playfully told Tia, 'I've seen Dr Garcia do this before. She's very neat with the stitches.'

Lola smiled at them both, her eyes lingering on Xavier. Something like respect shone in her stare as if she was grateful for his presence, just as she'd been the night of the storm.

'I'm so embarrassed that I ruined dinner,' Tia said.

'Are you kidding?' Xavier said softly, trying to take her mind off the procedure going on. 'My mother's probably out there right now adding the finishing touches. She's only happy when she's in a kitchen and she'd have inserted herself into the preparations one way or another.'

Tia smiled at him and touched his arm. 'You're a good man Mr Torres. Thank you for coming to Casa Colina. Your energy has changed the place and let in more sunlight. All the staff are happy.'

Feeling Lola's eyes on him, Xavier stiffened, unused to compliments.

Lola, busy placing a neat row of sutures to close the wound, didn't seem to notice that his chest felt too small for his lungs. In the few short weeks he'd lived there, he'd come to know every one of the staff the estate employed. How de la Rosa had inspired such loyalty, he had no idea, but he considered himself honoured to know these kind-hearted, hard-working people.

While he tried to pull himself together, Lola covered the wound with a sterile dressing. 'There. All done.'

She met his stare and he looked away, feeling raw. 'No more work for you tonight,' Xavier told Tia, who looked like she might argue.

'Take some painkillers,' Lola said. 'And get some rest. If you shower, pop your hand into a plastic bag to keep the dressing dry.'

When Tia hesitated, looking as if she wanted to clean up the bathroom before she retired to her rooms, they shooed her off together.

'I'll ask Mamá to bring you a plate of whatever smells so good in the kitchen,' Xavier said.

'Thank you, Mr Torres. Dr Garcia,' Tia said as she left the room.

When they were alone, he and Lola set to cleaning up.

'She's right you know,' she said quietly about Tia, placing the equipment she'd used into a sealed biohazard bag and a small portable sharps bin. 'I know you didn't ask for all this, but you're a natural at leading people. You're fair, compassionate and down to earth. Having met your lovely mother tonight, I can understand why. She adores you.'

Xavier stiffened, his pulse leaping, the urge to pull her into his arms and hold her until everything made sense, stronger than ever before. What she and Tia had said was compliment enough. But the words they hadn't said were even more devastating because what he'd heard was *you're nothing like him*.

'You're pretty good with people yourself,' he said gruffly, placing the soiled towels in a rubbish bag. If he didn't leave her company soon, he was going to do something they might both regret and with so much at stake—

the baby, their relationship as parents, the future—he needed a clear head.

Lola smiled as she sprayed down the vanity with disinfectant spray. 'We do make a good team.'

It was true. But more than that, their chemistry, his near constant need for her, just wouldn't be silenced. They left the tied-up rubbish bag and Lola's medical bag in the laundry, and washed their hands at the sink.

'I'll help your mother finish dinner,' she said, her smile taking him back to the night of the storm.

'Good luck with that.' Xavier replied, doubtful that the ravenous hunger in him could be satiated by food alone.

# CHAPTER ELEVEN

LOLA STARTLED AWAKE. Someone was gently shaking her shoulder. Gasping, she opened her eyes to find Xavier leaning over her in the gloom of the darkened living room.

'It's okay,' he said. 'Just me.'

His hand fell away from her shoulder and she almost cried out, her body eagerly craving his touch, as it had since that night of the storm.

'I fell asleep,' she said instead, sitting up, taking a moment to recover from her disorientation.

Xavier had left thirty minutes ago to drive Carlota home. Lola had checked on Tia then sat down with a book to wait for his return. After Tia's accident, he'd been quiet throughout dinner, barely eating a thing. She wanted to make sure he was okay. After all, he was used to having his own space. He'd insisted she stay there, but maybe he was struggling, because things seemed to be moving so fast—the house, the baby, them living together.

But no matter how often she told herself it would be a mistake to submit to her need for him, it beat at her in relentless waves. Each look, each touch, each considerate thing he did for her weakening her resolve. Xavier, on the other hand, seemed oblivious as if he'd well and truly moved on.

'Sorry to wake you,' he said, stepping back, his posture rigid. 'I didn't want to leave you here all night.' His eyes were almost black in the dim light from the lamp, his body tense as if coiled with energy.

'Was Carlota okay?' she asked, sitting on the edge of the sofa. She felt wary of him because ever since she'd moved in, her hand forced by the persistent paps, there'd been a weird forcefield between them, binding them somehow but also creating an emotional distance she didn't like. It made sense. For her their chemistry was still exhaustingly intense, but Xavier was an expert at keeping her out and personally they had a lot to discuss.

'She chatted about the baby all the way home,' he said, his voice indulgent. 'It's not even born yet and she's already going through her family, suggesting names for us to consider.'

'She's lovely,' Lola said, feeling closer to him now that she'd met Carlota, who clearly adored her son and had raised him to be the strong, capable, selfless man he was. 'I couldn't have wished for a better *abuela* for our baby. She's clearly very proud of you.'

Xavier shrugged. 'I'm an only child. There's no one else for her to focus on.'

He was deflecting, clearly uncomfortable with compliments.

'She'd be proud of you if she had a hundred children.' Lola stood stretching out her back and shoulders, which were stiff from falling asleep on the sofa.

When Xavier's gaze dropped to her breasts, which she'd accidentally thrust out, she froze, keen anticipation and excitement flooding her body.

'Why didn't you go to bed?' he asked, not moving away, his intense stare hooded.

'I wanted to make sure you were okay,' she admitted. 'You were quiet tonight. More so than usual.' She offered him a small smile, but her heart wasn't in it. She felt too volatile, strung out on the way he made her feel both safe and reckless in the same heartbeat. But wanting him was more dangerous than before. They were living together. They had the baby to consider. They had a future to plan.

'You waited up for me?' he asked, gruffly, adding no further explanation of his strange mood.

'I tried…' She said with a shrug and another half-hearted smile. Her expression slipped because, danger or not, something had shifted between them, making her heart flutter erratically and her stomach hollow with fear and longing, as if what happened next was vital— a crossroads.

'You should go up to bed,' he said, making no move to leave, his intense stare shifting over her face as his breathing sped up, as if he too was waiting for something to happen and was unable to walk away.

Lola sighed, certain that he felt it too, this building pressure they'd danced around and dodged for the past few weeks, since the storm.

'Are *you* going up?' she asked, her body swaying towards his.

Even as she craved him, desperation making heat pool in her belly and between her legs, she couldn't stop herself from challenging him, testing him, pushing him for more.

'Not tired yet,' he said, his fingers twitching at his sides as if he wanted to touch her, to kiss her. As if he could read her mind. Then his tongue darted out to swipe at his lip.

Lola moaned silently, recalling the brush of that clever

tongue over her skin, her nipples, her clit. Excitement energised her. She wanted him. Surely they were mature enough to navigate both sex and sharing a home while keeping feelings off the table. Xavier excelled at the latter and she could handle herself.

'You know I always do what I want, not what I'm told,' she said, boldly stepping closer, because he was too far away and she was full of hormones and only he could appease her neediness.

'Lola…' he warned, his voice a low rumble, his facial muscles bunching as he clenched his jaw. But he held his ground, his breath gusting through flared nostrils as he stared her down.

She was playing with fire. But if she had to stay in his home while also carrying their child, had to see him every day both at home and work, there ought to be some payback. It was only fair.

'I'm turned on,' she said, her breaths coming short and fast. 'You made me pregnant and now I'm a slave to my hormones. You invite me to live with you, dangling yourself in front of me like a forbidden snack. What are you going to do about it, Xavier?'

She'd never done well with self-denial. If she wanted something, she made it happen. And she wanted him. Now. Tonight. A reprieve from this tension that had pulled taut to snapping point.

'Ignore it,' he said in a low voice. 'That's the sensible thing to do.' But he leaned closer, as if he couldn't stop himself. As if he wanted her too just as much.

'I've tried since the night of the storm,' she said, 'and it's no longer working.' She took another step closer until she felt the warm gusts of his breath brush over her parted lips. Felt the heat of his body bathe her in his scent. Felt the delicious anticipation in the way he held back. 'If we have to be under the same roof, it makes sense that we shouldn't have to suffer. I'm tired of fighting. It's just sex. We moved on from it before. We can do it again.'

She raised her gaze from his mouth to his dark, unreadable eyes. But this time, she saw what he was trying so hard to conceal—fire, desperation, barely contained restraint.

'We agreed on one night,' he said, showing his superior mental strength, as if he was desperate to do the right thing.

'Minds are for changing,' she whispered, certain that she couldn't go another day in denial.

'Lola…' he groaned, panting hard now, clearly struggling, wavering, torn. He curled his hands into fists at his side.

'Xavier,' she moaned, reaching for his wrists, bringing his hands up to her tingling breasts. 'Touch me,' she begged. 'I'm achy and it's all your fault.'

When he did as she asked, she bit down on her lip and sighed. Only he could put her out of her misery. Only this, them taking what had begun the night of the storm and harnessing it, made sense.

With another groan of defeat, he dragged her into his arms. His hands spread over her ribcage as he lowered his mouth to hers in a fierce kiss that filled her with electrifying triumph. She parted her lips and met the surges of his tongue with her own. Clinging to his neck to keep her body pressed to his, desperate to find as much contact and as much friction and heat as possible. She wanted to burn, safe in his arms, knowing he'd not only take her there, but also catch her as she fell apart.

'Yes,' she cried, dropping her head back to give his

mouth access to her neck as his hand slid the strap of her sun dress from her shoulder.

He cupped her bare breast, his thumb brushing over her sensitive nipple, spreading tingles throughout her body, adding to her desperation. Her fingernails dug into his upper arms as she clung to him, willing him to continue, needing his touch as much as she needed air. Wanting to break him because his mere presence had broken every one of her good intentions.

'You're sure this is what you want?' he asked, his arm banded around her waist so she felt his erection against her stomach while that thumb rubbed and teased. Desire darkened his eyes to black.

'Yes,' she cried, eyes wide open, her body restless against his. 'Positive.'

He cupped her chin, raised her face, lowered his stare to her half-naked chest. 'You wore that bikini on purpose today, didn't you?' he said, impatiently raising her breast to his mouth, his tongue lashing the peak over and over in punishment until her legs almost buckled.

She gripped his biceps to hold herself up, riding his hard thigh to try and appease the viscous throb between her legs. 'I knew you were watching,' she said on a moan. 'I felt your eyes on me.'

'Did you want my eyes on you?' he asked, sliding one hand under her dress and along her thigh.

'Yes,' she said, shoving at the hem of his black t-shirt until he removed it, desperate to see him naked once more. 'I want it all.'

Denied his sublime body since the storm, Lola pressed kisses to his chest, her hands caressing his flexed abs, her nails lightly scoring his muscular back, her skin picking up the gorgeous scent of him. She covered his nipple with her mouth, laving and sucking as he'd done to her until he groaned, walked her back towards the sofa and pulled her down astride his lap as he sat.

'I've wanted this every day, since the storm.' He peeled down the other strap of her dress, exposing her from the waist up, his stare devouring her nakedness. 'Are you sensitive?' he asked, cupping her breasts, toying with the nipples, leaning down to capture one with his lips and stroke it with his hot tongue.

'A little,' she moaned, thrusting her chest forward. 'It's wonderful. Don't stop.'

He rubbed one nipple harder, his tongue laving the other. Gasping in delight, Lola rocked on his lap. Seeking the friction of his hard length between her legs and frustrated by the barrier of his jeans and her underwear.

'Xavier, I need you,' she begged, uncaring that he'd hear the desperation in her voice. This chemistry had been between them from the start. Now, when she was living in his house and carrying his baby, was no time to deny it. But just because they were acting on it, didn't mean either of them wanted more than sex.

He leaned back, peering up at her with desire, his hands sliding up her thighs under her dress. She rocked her hips, unable to keep still with him looking at her as if he wanted to devour her. His fingers brushed her clit through her underwear and she moaned. She closed her eyes as he slipped them inside the lacy barrier to where she was unashamedly soaking wet for him.

'Don't stop,' she said, biting her lower lip as he stroked her and pleasure streaked like lightning down her legs and up to her nipples.

'Look at me, Lola,' he said, pushing his fingers inside

her while his thumb kept on brushing her clit, over and over so her muscles clenched around him.

Lola did as he'd asked, her hands braced on his shoulders. Their stares locked as he took her higher and higher, his other hand on her hips to hold her firm. But she was going nowhere. This had been building between them since that first night, as if they had unfinished business and needed some sort of physical closure.

Collapsing forward, she kissed him, wildly riding his hand as he held her in his strong arm. His thighs steel beneath her bottom. His groans encouraging her to take what she needed.

Her orgasm came swiftly, her muscles gripping his fingers and her cries ringing out through the silent house as the unbearable tension finally eased.

When she was spent, he removed his hand from between her legs, encouraged her to stand on her shaky legs and stripped her naked. His dark stare touching every part of her body, the way it had that first time, as if he couldn't look away.

'Do you want me to use a condom?' he asked, his voice thick with lust. 'I'm tested regularly.'

'No,' she said, a ghost of a smile tugging at her lips. 'That horse has kind of already bolted.' Then because he had too many clothes on and she was naked, she dropped to her knees between his spread thighs and unzipped his jeans where he sat. He raised his hips and together they removed his jeans and boxers. He groaned low in the back of his throat and cupped her face when she took him into her mouth, ruthlessly pleasuring him, sucking him the way he'd done to her that time in the shower. She hummed, enjoying the way his fingers curled into her hair as he watched, the soft grunts of pleasure he made, the way every muscle in his body had turned as hard as marble, as if he was clinging to his control by his fingernails and she'd put him there.

Then, as if he'd reached his limit, he pushed her away, scooped his arm around her waist and dragged her under his big powerful body on the sofa.

For a few seconds, their eyes locked, their hearts banged together, their breaths mingling as they panted. Lola burned everywhere their skin touched, that fire centring once more between her legs as he slowly pushed inside her, filling her up. She gasped, smiling at his long-awaited possession. He groaned, his face twisting in agonising rapture as he held himself still, as deeply as possible. Because she wanted more, Lola crossed her ankles in the small of his back and he sank lower, deeper, right where she needed him, where she ached anew.

'Xavier,' she whispered, cupping his face, spearing her fingers through his damp hair to drag his mouth down to hers.

His kisses began slow, his tongue thrusting inside her mouth as his hips moved shallowly at first.

'Don't hold back,' she said against his ear when they'd come up for air. Just because she was pregnant didn't make her fragile, nor did it lessen her overwhelming desire for him. In fact, it made it stronger.

He reared up on his forearms, his lips capturing her nipple once more. Pleasure boiled in her pelvis, spreading, burning, making her gasp and moan as he thrust faster and deeper, finally giving her what she'd craved all this time.

'Xavier,' she cried, letting him know that she was close again as she clung to his shoulders and spread her legs wider.

With a harsh groan from him and a cry from her, they came together, crushing each other, their hearts thundering in harmony so it seemed as if they were one being, not two, each needing the other to survive.

But as good as they were together, Lola also clung to their limitations. They weren't a couple. He'd never needed a serious relationship or love. She needed her independence and had almost made a catastrophic mistake once before. She needed to keep sight of what this was, because neither of them wanted to ruin what they could have as parents or end up hurt.

After a few seconds, Xavier withdrew and stood, his chest still heaving, his eyes still dark with impressive desire. Then he scooped her up from the sofa and carried her upstairs to the master bedroom, the night obviously nowhere near over, much to Lola's relief.

# CHAPTER TWELVE

A WEEK LATER, Xavier awoke hard, his naked body curved around Lola's as early morning light filtered through the gauzy drapes. His heart accelerated, the confusing mix of arousal and fear ensnaring him. Every day since they'd finally reached their limit of endurance and denial and found each other again, began this way. Him waking, reaching for her as if automatically, then recalling all the reasons why he couldn't get used to such an astounding start to the day.

It was just sex. Incredible, addictive sex. The infatuation would fade and when it did what remained would be the most important relationship of his life. That of coparent with the mother of his child. *That* was where he needed to focus. *That* had to be his number one priority. The thing he guarded with his life.

Beside him, Lola stirred, her hand reaching back, fingers sliding through his hair at the nape of his neck as she pulled his mouth down to hers.

Xavier cupped her full breast, toying the nipple awake until she moaned and kissed him harder. But while his mind fought to stay in control, his body was weak for her. Taking what he needed. Connecting in a way that was beyond words.

'Xavier,' she moaned his name as his hand slid over

her belly and delved between her legs to where she was already slick for him.

She tilted her hips back, pressing her gorgeous backside into his groin, so his erection nestled between her cheeks. 'Have we got time?' she asked, reaching for him, encircling him in her hand, guiding him to her entrance. 'I need you.'

Glancing at the clock, Xavier stroked her faster as he pushed inside her from behind, skin to skin. His eyes closed on a wave of euphoria as her tight heat gripped him and he lost himself. He kissed the side of her neck, his tongue tasting her skin as she raised her arm over her head and clung to his neck. The position thrust her breasts forward. He groaned, desperate to take her pert nipples into his mouth because she loved that, crying out and twisting his hair.

'Come for me,' he said, stroking her faster. His free hand cupping her breast, toying with the nipple, pushing her closer and closer.

'Yes,' she cried, tilting her hips back so he sank deeper with every thrust, the frenzy building as they each chased the pleasure they found in each other's arms.

'Need to kiss you,' he said, shifting positions and laying on top of her, thrusting his tongue against hers as he pushed back inside her and their hearts banged together, chest to chest. Her nails dug into his shoulder. Her moans growing erratic as they chased oblivion together. Every part of them entwined—their legs, their fingers, their tongues. Then she was coming and he let go too, groaning as he joined her. Spilling himself inside her and holding her so tight he wondered if he'd ever again be able to let her go, even though he knew he would.

Later, he rested his head on her chest and she toyed

with his hair. A sense of contentment, the likes of which he'd never known, washed over him in a wave.

He placed his hand on her stomach, where their baby grew, certain that this sense of belonging, impending fatherhood, was behind the way he felt. It couldn't be anything else. It couldn't be feelings for Lola. He didn't know how to do that.

He must have sighed because Lola's hand stilled in his hair. 'Are you worried about your meeting this morning?' she asked as if they had all the time in the world. Whereas in reality, they needed to get up, shower and head out for the day—her to the hospital and him to the palace.

'No,' Xavier said about his private audience with King Octavio. 'He's just a man like me. I don't want anything from him. He's astute and intelligent, so I'm certain he will see that I'm no threat.'

Of course he had reservations, but only because the nature of his relationship with their monarch, a man Xavier had known his entire life, would be…redefined. Xavier was no longer an employee, but nor did he feel like the king's cousin. And with his cruel mistreatment from Mauricio as a boy, the king might not welcome de la Rosa's illegitimate son, although the king had been the one to issue the invitation.

'Are you worried about the scan?' she pushed, as if he were made of glass and she knew his every fear. They had Lola's first antenatal appointment that afternoon.

He shrugged. He *was* worried. Terrified. But he didn't want Lola to worry.

'I'm sure everything will be fine,' he said, the secret fears he had for the baby all but choking him.

As the day approached, Xavier had felt increasingly tossed back and forth between excitement to finally see their baby and fear that something might go wrong. What if there was something amiss with the pregnancy? What if fatherhood, the life he'd begun to feel might be his destiny, was ripped away? Would he survive another upheaval of that magnitude, just at the point he was starting to feel like he finally belonged for the first time in his life? Not there at Casa Colina, which was just stone and mortar, but as a father to his child.

'I'm sure it will be too,' Lola said reassuringly. 'I'm fit and healthy and not that old.'

Xavier nodded, eager to keep his concerns hidden. 'I'll be leaving for London straight after the scan,' he reminded her. 'Princess Xiomara can see me this evening. I thought we should discuss the recent revelations of my paternity face to face.' Another relationship about to change. He'd always admired and respected the princess, but he'd also been comfortable in his role as her employee. How would she feel that her father had produced a son? That he'd left Xavier an estate and title?

'I remember,' Lola said, stroking his hair. 'It's a big couple of days for you. Meeting our baby. Old relationships changing. Finding your place in a new family.'

Xavier raised his head and looked down at her, certain that he would always struggle to think of the de la Rosa family as *his* family when he'd spent his entire life on the outside, looking in. 'I'll be back tomorrow.'

Panic crowded his chest at the thought of leaving her and the baby there all alone. 'Carlos and Marco will both be on duty tonight for anything you need.' Although he'd arranged for double the normal security, a hundred security guards couldn't make up for his personal touch. But then he needed to get used to that. He couldn't be with Lola all the time. One day she'd want to move on and move out. She'd want another serious relationship, maybe even marry. Then his child would have a stepfather. He shuddered and she must have felt it.

'I'll be fine,' she said, gripping his face between her palms. 'Don't worry about me.'

Xavier bit his tongue, worry seemed to be the only constant in his life at the moment. That and desire for her. What was happening to him? His fear for Lola and the baby's safety was understandable under the circumstances. The paps still hounded his every move. But the few moments of peace he felt when he and Lola were intimate, didn't seem to last long enough, driving his need for her to mindless levels. Maybe his doubts about fatherhood were making him irrational. After all, he had no role model to emulate. What if he was no good at it? What if he messed up and got it wrong? Would his child forgive him or end up needing a lifetime of therapy?

Later that afternoon, after his surreal meeting at the palace, Xavier hurried to St Sebastian's to meet Lola. She'd chosen there for her antenatal care over *Clinico San Carlos*, eager to keep her pregnancy private from her work colleagues.

Xavier arrived before her and took a seat in the waiting room, his heart kicking at his ribs when she walked in moments later. He stood as she approached, thrown off balance by his strange morning and nerves over the scan. As if sensing his turmoil, Lola pressed a kiss to his cheek and sat at his side, pulling his hand into hers.

'How was your audience this morning?' she discreetly asked about his meeting with King Octavio.

Concern dulled her eyes. Was she nervous too, or could

she sense how scared he was of losing control of the security he'd built around himself with all this change.

'Fine,' he said vaguely, but grateful that she'd raised a subject designed to take his mind off the impending scan. 'My cousin, I guess…' He winced, the idea of calling their monarch that, laughable. But in this setting the name served as a useful code. Only Lola would know of whom he spoke. '…he graciously welcomed me into the family and asked if there was anything he could do for me.'

Xavier was still reeling, desperately trying to keep the redefined relationships in his life at a safe distance. But keeping Lola from seeing his deepest fears was his priority.

'I'm so glad,' she said, squeezing his arm. 'You must have been nervous, but now that the first meeting since the truth emerged has occurred, next time will be easier.'

Xavier shrugged. 'I didn't know what to expect,' he said. He'd always respected their ruler, but that respect had doubled after today. 'I figured my paternity would be a shock to all concerned.'

'But you realised that it doesn't matter,' she said. 'That it in no way reflects on you.'

Unable to express his feelings as eloquently as Lola seemed to be able to do, he gripped her hand tighter. 'We talked about the upcoming wedding,' he said referring to Princess Xiomara, who would soon return to Castilona to marry Dr Edmund Butler.

She nodded encouragingly.

'He…suggested I might play a small role,' Xavier said, flattered but doubtful that the princess would want that.

'Are you reluctant?' she asked, that insight of hers once more hitting the mark.

He replied shrugging. 'I want to do anything I can to make sure the bride is happy, but…'

She leaned close, dropping her voice to a whisper. 'I understand. It will take time for you to feel like they are family, no matter how long you've known them or how welcoming they are.'

Xavier swallowed. How could she do that so…effortlessly? See the things he was feeling when he himself struggled to decipher them? But of course he would likely always struggle to feel as if he belonged with the de la Rosa family. His family had always been Carlota and now included Lola and the baby.

The speed at which that thought filled his mind, caught him off guard. Had he let Lola so close he considered her a part of his team? She certainly had an intuitive knack of seeing parts of him he assumed were hidden from everyone. But if she understood him so well, if she saw how deep down, there must be something wrong with him, she could easily hurt him if she chose.

Just then, with that unsettling thought in his head, a nurse called Lola's name. She and Xavier followed the woman into a consulting room, where Lola was weighed and her height and blood pressure were recorded. Then they were directed into the sonogram room.

'You can leave your clothes on,' the young female sonographer said. 'Just undo your trousers and pull up your blouse.'

Lola handed Xavier her bag, loosened her clothing and lay on the bed, smiling over at him as if she had not a care in the world. Whereas he wouldn't be able to breathe easy until they saw that tiny heartbeat.

Xavier stood stiffly at her side until she encouraged him to sit in the chair provided and then reached for his hand.

'Okay,' the sonographer said, squirting gel onto Lola's lower abdomen. 'Let's see what we have.'

Xavier's fingers tightened around Lola's as the sonographer placed the probe into position. His stare was glued to the screen, which was currently an indecipherable mass of static—like an un-tuned television channel.

Lola sent him a reassuring look, but he held his breath, strung too taut to do anything other than breathe and focus on the ultrasound machine.

'So, here we go,' the sonographer said, positioning the screen so they could see the image more clearly. 'The black area is the amniotic sac and this is your baby.'

Xavier stared in wonder. The tiny human he and Lola had made easily recognisable now—head, spine, arms and legs.

Losing his breath as if winded, Xavier clung to Lola's hand. It was real. His baby existed. Would he be able to love it as he should? What if there was an inherited inability to love in him, passed on from de la Rosa? He'd always believed his lack of interest in romantic love came from his hang ups, the rejection he'd grown up with, the deep fear that *he* must be unlovable. But what if he simply couldn't love because, like it or not, he was related to that man?

'I'm just going to do some measurements to corroborate your dates.' The sonographer repositioned the probe and clicked some buttons, measuring the baby's size.

Xavier stared at the tiny baby on the screen. His feelings so big they were a painful mass expanding in his chest. But fear was dominant.

Then something miraculous happened. While he and Lola watched, the baby moved, its tiny hand coming into focus. An eruption of love built inside him, a wave of indescribable emotion that left him certain he would, without doubt, protect and nurture that tiny human until the day he died. So this was parental love, a sickening tumult of joy and fear, and it had already begun.

'Are you okay?' Lola whispered, a serene smile on her face and her beautiful eyes awash with emotions.

He nodded, lost for words. How could she be so calm? What if she finally saw through him? Saw that he wasn't good enough to be a father? What if she one day rejected him and took his baby away?

'Did you see it move?' she asked. 'See the tiny fluttering heartbeat?'

He nodded again, leaning forward to press a breathless kiss to the back of Lola's hand, vowing there and then that if she let him, he would always care for her and the baby to the absolute best of his ability.

'Does everything look okay?' he croaked, addressing both Lola, who would have seen scans before through her work, and the sonographer.

Lola nodded and the sonographer confirmed it. 'The baby is growing well, the size consistent with the dates of your last period.' She printed off a couple of pictures and handed them over. 'Your due date is the sixth of January. Congratulations.'

Xavier stared at the picture, his heart in his throat and time speeding up. He had approximately seven months to prepare for the biggest life-change he was ever likely to encounter. Seven months to pull himself together, to figure out how best to share their child with Lola. Because now that he'd experienced that rush of parental love, he absolutely, categorically, could not mess this up.

## CHAPTER THIRTEEN

XAVIER SILENTLY HELD onto Lola's hand for much of the rest of the appointment, which included a brief examination by the obstetrician to confirm that all was well with the pregnancy.

Her heart clenched for him. He was obviously going through some momentous feelings, not that he would share them with her of course. But as they left St Sebastian's side by side, Lola tugged his hand to bring him to a halt near her car, pushing to be let in.

'It's overwhelming, isn't it?' she said, identifying his bewildered expression, part of her feeling something similar. She cared about him the way he cared about her. She wanted them to share not just the highs of this pregnancy, but also any fears they might have. She needed him to be on the same wavelength, so they could support each other through the next seven months as well as through the birth and the newborn stage.

'I guess it is,' he said, seeming distracted and withdrawn. Maybe he was already thinking about the princess and London.

Lola sighed, a strange flood of panic washing over her. Lying in his arms that morning, she'd been filled with excitement and optimism, but now that they held photographic evidence of their baby in their hands, she was suddenly besieged by doubts.

Maybe it had been a mistake to start sleeping with him again. Because since they'd surrendered to their passion, she couldn't seem to stop. Only in the back of her mind, she knew she must and soon. She couldn't afford to develop feelings for him. Not when she was still trying to figure out where she wanted her career to take her. Not when Xavier had no interest in a real relationship. Not when each of them had set aside the search for commitment for their own reasons, hers to prove that she could excel in her career and his because he'd needed to fill a hole in his life.

He held up the scan picture. 'I can't quite believe it. I know it's true, but it feels…surreal.'

'I know.' Lola glanced again at his picture. Hers was tucked safely in her bag. 'The first scan makes it way more real. That's our baby.'

Was he having doubts, too? Was he gearing up to end their fling and focus instead on them being parents?

'If I feel it's appropriate,' he said, 'do you mind if I tell the princess, about the baby?' He still clutched his copy of the sonogram picture as if it were precious.

'Of course not,' Lola said, the reality of Xavier's earlier warnings hitting home.

That tiny baby had some big shoes to fill—a historic estate, a lucrative business, a title and royal relations. Just like Lola had once protected herself from simply slotting into Nicolás's readymade life, she would need to protect her child from the weight of such a responsibility. Every child deserved a carefree childhood. She and Xavier had both had one, and she would make certain that no matter what the future held for them as parents, their baby's happiness would come first.

'Are *you* okay,' he said, taking her hand once more, his stare searching hers so she felt close to tears suddenly.

'I'm fine,' she said. 'A bit emotional and overwhelmed. It's all finally hitting home. But sadly I need to head back to the clinic. And you have a plane to catch.'

She smiled, hiding her disappointment with the timing of his trip to London. She was secretly dreading being at Casa Colina without him, even for one night. She'd hoped they would talk about the baby this evening after they'd each had time to process the scan. She would miss him and couldn't help but draw parallels between Xavier's life and the life of duty she'd once rejected.

Xavier nodded, wrapped one arm around her neck, drawing her close and pressing a kiss to her forehead. 'I'm not telling you what to do, but please be careful. If you want, I can arrange for Carlos to pick you up from work tonight, so you don't have to face the paps alone.'

Of course he would worry about her safety. His thoughtfulness and the extra security team he'd employed were touching but practical. But it was too much to hope that he might actually miss her in return.

'Thanks, but I'll be fine.' Lola looked up at him with her brave face in place. She shouldn't want him to miss her. They weren't a couple. They'd only been living under the same roof for a matter of weeks. But they'd spent every spare moment together. They'd slept in the same bed, had sex in every one of the villa's rooms, including every single guest room. They'd eaten breakfast together, sometimes in bed, travelled to and from work together, swam and walked the estate together. Maybe she was simply emotional because of the baby.

'See you tomorrow then,' he said, looking as if he wanted to say more, but had stopped himself. Then he glanced down at her stomach. 'Both of you.'

Lola's heart leapt. Of course he was thinking about the baby. Lola knew he cared about her—he showed her that every day. But she needed to remember that his consideration was largely because she was carrying his child. It wasn't about *her*.

'Good luck with Princess Xiomara,' she said, before she could embarrass herself by welling up in hormonal tears. She rested her hand on his chest, over the reassuring thump of his heart. 'Just be yourself. Any family would be lucky to have you.'

She was certain that when the de la Rosa got to know him as a man not just and employee, they would see the loyal and compassionate man she saw. Except she doubted any of them, her included, would ever see his whole, vulnerable self.

'That's the only person I can be,' he said with confidence.

But deep down, she knew him well enough to understand that he most likely had doubts. After all, he'd once worked for the princess, keeping her safe. With his feelings for their mutual father so...resentful, he would likely struggle to feel comfortable that she was actually his half-sister.

Brushing her lips over his in a swift goodbye kiss, she said, 'Safe travels.'

She unlocked her car, desperate to get away before she blurted out something stupid, like how much she'd miss him or how she wished he'd let her in, or how, sometimes, when she was alone, she thought she might want more than sex. Praying that was simply her hormones talking, she started the engine.

Today was a wake-up call. She couldn't get used to having him around. Them living together was a temporary measure and nothing to do with feelings. Xavier didn't do serious relationships and the last time she'd trusted her instincts when it came to love, she'd almost married a man who hadn't loved her in return. Who'd only wanted her to complete some family portrait he could hang on the wall of his ancient estate alongside his ancestors.

She'd always wanted more than an empty relationship that looked good on the surface. If she wasn't careful with Xavier, who no matter what they'd shared always seemed to be holding himself back, she'd get hurt.

As she drove away, she couldn't resist one last glance at him through the rear-view mirror, a view she should perhaps, get used to.

It was gone midnight, officially the next day when Xavier finally returned home to Casa Colina. After his meeting with the princess, or Xiomara as she'd insisted he call her from now on, the idea of spending the night in a faceless London hotel, miles away from Lola, left him cold. Especially today, when together they'd finally seen their baby. So, instead of tossing and turning through a fitful night's sleep in a strange bed where he knew his doubts would plague him, he'd jumped on the last flight leaving London for Castilona.

Quietly climbing the stairs after touching base with Carlos and Marco, he already felt better just knowing they were back under the same roof. He paused outside his room and glanced down the hallway. There was a light coming from Lola's bedroom. The door was ajar.

Unable to resist checking on her, he peeked inside, his heart galloping at the sight of her asleep, an open book still clutched in her hand. He swallowed the lump in his throat, watching her breathe for a few minutes, glad that he'd gone with his instincts and returned tonight. This beautiful, intelligent woman had turned his world upside down with her news. She'd given him a wondrous gift in his child, given him the sense of belonging he'd always craved.

But now came the tricky part. He needed to treat her with care. His current physical addiction to her would soon fade and then they would have bigger issues to discuss than whether to sleep in his bed or hers.

Silently, he crept into the room and carefully removed the book from her hand, placing it on the nightstand. He was about to turn off the lamp when Lola stirred.

'Xavier...?'

'Sorry,' he whispered. 'I didn't mean to wake you. You fell asleep with the lamp on.'

She sat up, rested on her elbow and reached for his hand. 'You came home early.'

Home? He couldn't bear to tell her that this stunning villa didn't feel like home, or at least it hadn't until she'd moved in. She'd brought laughter there. Lit up the rooms with her smile. And most of all, she'd given him a reason to preserve the traditions of this place for their child. That was the one easy thing he could do as a father.

'Is everything okay?' she asked sleepily. 'How did it go with the princess?'

Xavier allowed her to pull him down to the bed and sat on the edge beside her, his hand far too comfortable in hers. But then every time they touched it gave him a buzz and left him hungry for more. What the hell was happening to him? And how could he make it stop before it got any worse? Before he let her all the way in and she saw the real him? Before she found something lacking?

Fearing it might already be too late, he focussed on his visit with the princess. 'It was fine. A bit awkward at first. She kept insisting that I drop the "princess" and simply call her Xiomara, correcting me every time I used her title.' Which was every time he'd addressed her.

'Yes, you would struggle with that,' Lola said with an indulgent smile. As if she knew him better than anyone. 'It took you seven months to call me Lola.'

'Old habits die hard, I guess,' he said, his thumb stroking the back of her hand, which was warm and soft and distracted him from the idea that he was balanced on the top of a precariously stacked pile of furniture. One wrong move and everything would come tumbling down.

'It's understandable given you protected her for so many years,' Lola went on. 'But don't forget that she's also just a person, irrespective of any title.'

Xavier fell quiet, Lola's insight hitting right at the heart of his doubts. He suspected he'd never feel comfortable around the royal family now that he no longer worked for them. Not because they were cold or superior, but because he would always feel like an imposter in their world. In his own life, the small but secure safety net he'd built around himself, he knew exactly who he was. His needs were few and simple. Those he could trust and rely upon even fewer.

'I know it's not easy for you to embrace your new family,' she said, clinging to his hand. 'But if you let them see the real you, I'm sure they'll come to value and respect you for the man you are.'

'*I* know who I am,' he said, his pulse buzzing in his ears. 'That's all that matters. I don't need acceptance from the de la Rosas. And any relationship we might have in the future will always be complicated by the past.'

'I know,' she agreed, looking hurt by his dismissal. 'But just like you deserve to know them as family, they deserve to know you, too. I know it's scary to let people in,' she said, her touch soothing the torture of her words. 'Especially after what you've been through. But you're someone worth knowing, Xavier.'

Xavier stayed silent, wishing he'd kissed her when she'd awoken so that they might be naked by now instead of dissecting his damaged psyche—his least favourite pastime.

'Does anyone know the real you?' he asked, his pulse leaping at how close she was to tearing away his final shield. His final layer of protection. 'You once said we all have uncomfortable secrets.'

She looked down at their clasped hands then met his stare once more. 'You're right. I've been scared too in the past. Not of letting someone close but of trusting myself to know when a relationship is right. Ever since I ended my engagement, I've been trying to prove to myself that I made the right choice in choosing my career over my personal life. I've been scared to make a mistake and find myself trapped in a life that isn't mine. But that means I've been denying a whole part of my life that needs attention. I don't want to be alone for ever. One day, I want it all. My career, a family, love.'

His mouth dried, jealousy for the future man whom Lola would one day love turning his stomach. 'How will you know when you've found it? This relationship that's right?' He'd always assumed seeking out commitment was too risky, but lately the idea of losing what he and Lola had seemed even more terrifying.

But he couldn't selfishly hold onto her. She deserved to be loved, to find happiness, to have it all. Of course, that would also mean some other man would be raising his child…

'I'll know, because I'll want to give it my all,' she said, making it sound so simple, highlighting their differences.

'Then I hope you find what you're looking for,' he said, knowing *he* couldn't make her any promises.

'I hope you do, too,' she said sadly, as if she pitied him. And maybe she did. Because she'd always seen him far too clearly.

Needing to show her that he would be okay without her, without the kind of love he'd never experienced and feared he was incapable of, he said, 'I think, after today, after meeting our baby, I've already found where I belong—it's fatherhood.' He met her stare, his chest tight, his emotions so close to the surface. 'A part of me was scared that I'd be like him, be a terrible father.'

Lola frowned and shook her head.

'But after today…when I saw the baby move… I don't know, something happened. I vowed that I would die trying to be the kind of father our baby deserves.' The kind that every baby deserved.

'Xavier…' Lola whispered, her eyes shining with tears. 'You're going to be amazing.'

'Don't cry,' he said, cupping her face, the ache for her he'd carried with him to London intensifying. 'I'll let you get some rest. It's late. We can talk tomorrow.' He stood, leaned over her to kiss her, but she grabbed his hand.

'Don't go. I want you to stay.' She peeled back the covers invitingly.

Xavier hesitated, that self-protective core of his battling with his desire to hold her, to sleep with her and his baby in his arms, to drift off praying that everything would work out.

The decision made, Xavier heeled off his shoes, simultaneously removing his shirt, his jeans and socks following. Wearing only his boxers, he climbed in alongside her. The bed was warm with her body heat, the linens scented with her perfume. Her silky slip-clad body fitting into his arms until their hearts rested side by side, her back to his front.

She snuggled, entwining her legs with his, her arms around his arms, which held her close. 'The house was too quiet without you,' she whispered.

'It was like that before you came to stay,' he said, pressing a kiss to her neck, breathing in the warm scent of her skin so the panicked feeling enslaving him all day, eased. 'It's just too big for one person.'

She sighed. 'I guess it won't be quiet for long, not with a baby around.'

'That's fine with me,' he said, sensing her smile, needing her promises that they would share the baby, no matter what. Because the longer they delayed the conversation they needed to have, the more space there seemed for doubts.

Telling himself that he trusted Lola, he finally allowed himself to drift off to sleep.

# CHAPTER FOURTEEN

THE NEXT MORNING, as they travelled the coastal road to the clinic for what would be one of their final days working together, Xavier asked Lola a question that had been spinning in his mind for weeks.

'I wondered if you'd come to Princess Xiomara's wedding this weekend as my plus one?' he asked. 'Not a date just… Well, apparently, it's not the done thing to fly solo and you know how I hate making small talk.'

From the passenger seat, Lola glanced his way, her expression guarded. 'Won't us being seen together create gossip, even if it's not a date?'

By laying low at Casa Colina and using Xavier's vehicles with tinted windows, they'd managed to avoid being photographed together. Xavier's hands tightened on the wheel, disappointment leaving a sour taste in his mouth. Her voice was strange. Tense. As if their talk late last night had upset her—the last thing he wanted to do. And he had no clue how to fix it. But they weren't a couple. Having spent his entire adult life avoiding close connections, he had no idea how to be that vulnerable with someone. No matter how much he might want to try.

'The reception will be held at the palace,' he said. 'Press are strictly forbidden. I only care that you'll be safe, which I'm confident you will there otherwise I'd never have suggested it. But I understand if you'd prefer not to come.'

'Okay,' she said quietly, thoughtfully. 'Can I think about it and let you know?'

'Of course,' he said, this relationship with Lola pushing him way out of his comfort zone. Lola had gently pushed and pushed since the night of the storm, exposing his feelings as if he had an endless supply to give, as if she wanted more of him than he was perhaps capable of giving. As if his best wasn't good enough or maybe that was unfair and simply his own doubts talking.

Just as they rounded a tight bend in the road, they came across a cloud of dust and a motorbike lying on the verge.

'Pull over,' Lola said, at the same moment Xavier flicked on his indicator.

'Someone's had an accident,' he said as he parked safely, leaving his hazard lights on to warn any other vehicles.

Together they hurried towards the bike, which was unattended. Xavier pulled his phone from his pocket to call the police. Lola inched towards the edge of the cliff and carefully peered over.

'There's a casualty down there,' she said, gripping Xavier's arm. 'He looks unconscious. I'm going down to him.'

'We should wait for help.' Xavier grabbed her hand, the metallic taste of fear on his tongue. 'You can't go down there. It's dangerous.'

A moment's determination flashed in her eyes. 'He needs help now. I'll be fine,' she argued, tugging her arm free and gingerly beginning to scramble down the slope, which was covered in scrub. No discernible path obvious.

'Be careful. Wait for me,' he yelled just before the call

to emergency services connected. He quickly informed the emergency dispatcher of the location of the accident. Then he hung up and followed after Lola, clutching at handfuls of grass and bracken and sliding down the slope on his backside to get to her quickly.

His fingers curled around her upper arm, relief choking him. 'You could fall too,' he said, pleading. 'Think about the baby.'

He wasn't telling her how to behave, but nor did he want to see her throw herself headlong into a dangerous situation.

'Then help me,' she cried, proceeding despite his warning, although she kept a hold of his hand so they could slowly and carefully descend together.

With one hand on Lola, Xavier clung to the vegetation as they slipped and scrabbled towards the man. He was lying lifeless on a small ledge, held in place by the trunk of a tree without which, he would have surely fallen to the rocks and ocean below.

When they finally reached the casualty, Lola felt for a pulse and listened for breath sounds.

'He's alive,' she said, opening his leather motorbike jacket to search for other injuries.

Xavier noticed the unnatural angle of his foot. 'He's got a broken leg by the looks of it,' he told her, also scanning for injuries, although the man's crash helmet prevented them from assessing his head.

When Lola's hand came out of the man's jacket covered in blood, their fears intensified.

'I think he has a penetrating chest wound,' she said, glancing up at the road as the sound of distant sirens reached them.

'There's not much we can do beyond maintain his airway,' Xavier reasoned. They had no equipment, they were perched on the edge of a steep drop and the ambulance was on its way.

'I'm not leaving him,' she said, bracing her hand on the trunk of the tree as she shifted closer. She wobbled, righting herself quickly, but Xavier's pulse exploded as he envisioned her at the bottom of the cliff.

Because of his vision issues, the bottom of the cliff was a blurry abyss. He had no concept of how far the drop actually was, but his fears for Lola and the baby intensified, a tight band of pressure around his temples.

'I'm staying too,' he said. 'Please be careful. Just stay there. Don't move. Help is on its way.'

Within tense, fear-filled minutes, the police, ambulance and fire service arrived. A fire officer and paramedic secured by ropes and safety harnesses descended the slope to join them and assess the situation up close.

'I think he's impaled on a branch,' Lola told them.

The fire officer radioed for a saw to be lowered. With the branch cut from the tree they set about securing the unconscious man to the stretcher that had also been lowered. Slowly, they hauled him up the slope inch by inch to the waiting ambulance, the paramedic following.

'Let's get you two safely up to the road,' the fire officer said. 'We don't want another accident.'

'Her first,' Xavier told him, reaching for the safety harness the team above lowered and helping Lola into it. 'She's pregnant,' he told the other man, who nodded reassuringly.

Lola shot Xavier an annoyed look he ignored. Until he had her safe on firm ground away from the cliff, he wouldn't rest.

The fire crew hoisted Lola up the slope, followed by

Xavier, the rescue complete. By the time he'd made it to the road, Lola was in the back of the ambulance, updating the paramedics.

Xavier's insides trembled with adrenaline. He wanted to drag Lola close and ensure she was unharmed. He… cared about her. How could he not? She was having his baby, living in his house, sleeping in his bed. He'd begun to wonder if, for Lola, he might break the habit of a lifetime and give a committed relationship a shot rather than lose her. But even if he could change and let her into his life, would she want him? She wanted it all. She wanted and deserved love. He wouldn't be enough for her and he might ruin what they already had—respect, a connection through their child and commitment as parents.

Panicked, he dragged in some deep calming breaths, fearing it was impossible to be objective around Lola. His feelings were brittle. His protective urges in overdrive, leaving him irrational and helpless. He'd already let her close and now she had the power to destroy him. To rip his safe world to pieces. He watched her climb down from the back of the ambulance more unsettled and confused than ever before.

Lola stepped from the back of the ambulance wiping some of the blood from her hands with wet wipes the paramedics had given her. Xavier stood stiffly waiting, his face set in an angry scowl she ignored. Together, they watched the ambulance pull away, an awful tension building between them.

After briefly giving their names and address to the police, they headed back to the car in stony silence. Late last night, when he'd shared his fears for fatherhood with her, she'd felt as if she was finally making a breakthrough with him. That he was finally letting her close. She'd fallen asleep in his arms, nursing the first flicker of hope that maybe, just maybe, they might be able to build on what they had and have a real relationship. But now, in the cold light of day and with anger and resentment simmering just beneath the surface, she simply felt stupid.

*I wondered if you'd come to Princess Xiomara's wedding this weekend as my plus one? Not a date...*

His words from earlier rang through her head, mocking how much more invested in this relationship she was compared to him. But then Xavier had always protected himself. Holding back from her, from everyone, to keep himself safe from rejection.

'I'll take you home,' he said, unlocking the vehicle and opening her door.

'I'm fine. I need to go to work.' She cast him a determined look and climbed into the passenger seat, in no mood for his mollycoddling.

'You're covered in blood, Lola,' he pointed out as if she wasn't aware.

'It wouldn't be the first time,' she said. 'And I have a change of clothes at my office.' She pulled on her seatbelt. 'I'll clean up there.'

Xavier pressed his lips together and started the engine, pulling out onto the road, disapproval seeping from him.

'You're annoyed with me,' she said after a few minutes of unbearable silence.

'I'm concerned for you,' he said in that infuriatingly calm voice. 'I know you're a doctor and you need to help people, but you won't be able to do that if you're dead at the bottom of a cliff.'

'I was safe,' she argued. 'I'm not stupid.' Apart from with her feelings, which despite her best attempts, craved more and more and more of him. Whereas he was still safely emotionally contained.

'You're pregnant,' he retaliated.

'Yes, I'm pregnant, not incapacitated.' She tried and failed to keep the mocking tone from her voice. 'It's not the Victorian era, Xavier. Pregnant women don't need to be confined to bed rest these days.'

Why were they having their first fight? Was it because with every day she woke up in his arms, every time they reached for each other making passionate love as if the end was coming, she saw things more clearly. She *was* at risk. At risk of falling for him. Whereas he seemed to only care about the baby. Not about her.

But then he'd warned her he was uninterested in anything beyond sex. If she'd imagined that his touch, his kisses, the way he held her was more than that, she only had herself to blame.

'You scared me,' he said quietly, his eyes on the road.

'I'm sorry.' Compassion welled up inside her. They were both making this up as they went along and Xavier was safety obsessed. 'That wasn't my intention. I would never have put myself in a situation I felt was dangerous.'

'So you're not planning to take our baby overseas to some war-torn country or humanitarian crisis then?'

'Of course not,' she reasoned. 'That was the plan before I discovered I was pregnant. You're just lashing out now.'

She understood he might be reeling. Coming to terms with the fact he was going to be a father when he'd never known his own father and had some pretty major hang ups about his ability to adopt the role, but if he'd only let her in, they could discuss his fears in a rational way.

'I'm not lashing out, Lola, I'm scared. I have no idea what your plans are for the rest of the pregnancy or for after the birth. For all I know you're moving back to Spain, where you'll strap the baby into a baby carrier and carry it around the hospital while you do your job. I've tried to give you space and time, but we need to discuss all of this, Lola. It's my baby too.'

'I hope you're not suggesting that I can no longer work,' she scoffed, 'just because I've had a baby.' It was as if he didn't understand her at all. As if he hadn't heard a thing she'd told him about Nicolás and the past and her need to be independent.

'Of course I'm not saying that,' he said shooting her a look of hurt and confusion. 'I would never say such a thing. You're free to do whatever you like. You're free to move out of Casa Colina. Free to take any job you want anywhere in the world. I told you I'd move with you. I'm not trying to clip your wings. I just want you to be safe. I need to know the baby is safe and I need to be a part of its life.'

'I know that.' Lola deflated, the fight draining out of her as he pulled into the underground car park at the clinic. How could she argue with his reasonable logic? Of course they weren't a couple. And he was right. She'd been putting off finalising her plans because she'd been struggling to imagine what her life would become. But she could see now how her indecision might have made Xavier feel off-balance.

'Look…' She sighed, turning to face him as he parked the car. 'I know you need answers and I wish I had them for you, but I guess a part of me, a part I hadn't even re-alised existed until we went for the scan, has been in de-nial that my life is about to change.'

He reached for her hand and Lola clung to his fingers, regret a weight on her shoulders.

'I've been restless for a while,' she said, glancing at her lap, fighting her inclination to interpret how wonderful he was as a sign that he might have feelings for *her*. 'I thought I needed a change of medical scenery. But... I don't know. Maybe I just need to step off the professional treadmill I've been on since nineteen and really examine what it is I want to do with the rest of my career. I've thought about doing a master's degree, but I'm also dealing with the fact that the baby will also bring changes.'

'We're both dealing with that,' he said softly.

She nodded, her tangle of feelings suddenly close to the surface. For days now, every time they laughed together or when they made love, the force of their passion and their connection had overwhelmed her and she realised how easily she could develop deep feelings for this man. Not just because he was the father of their baby, but because he made her feel secure. That she could always be herself because he was always himself. That he was solid and dependable and would always be there if she or their child needed him.

But of course he couldn't be the right man for her. He didn't want to be the right man. He believed himself incapable of romantic love. But he had so much more to give. Maybe somewhere along the way, while pushing and trying to get to know him, she'd lost sight of *his* needs.

'I know you're a protector,' she said. 'You need to know that those around you are safe, so I want to reassure you. I'm fully committed to us raising this baby together. I'm not going anywhere without a discussion with you first. I promise.'

Although how she would watch him be the wonderful father she knew he was capable of being and not want him still, want all of him, was enough to make her wonder if she should end their physical relationship now, before she slipped any further under his spell. Her apartment was still leased for a few more days. Maybe she should put some distance between them and move back there.

'I only want to keep those around me safe because...' He swallowed, obviously struggling to explain. 'As wonderful a mother as Carlota was,' he said, 'never knowing my father made me feel...untethered. He could have been any man I saw walking down the street. I was free to imagine every possible scenario, from the fact that he might have forced himself on my mother to the fact that he had another family somewhere and I had a sibling, which, as it happens, turned out to be true.'

She cupped his face, held his stare to hers, aware he was trying his best to be more open. 'I'm sorry. Of course you wanted your world to have boundaries, to feel secure, to make sense of something that...' she shook her head, choked, '...seems inexplicable to me.' How any parent with means could disown their own child was unfathomable. 'But he didn't deserve you, Xavier. You're a strong and honourable man. A natural leader with a huge heart. *He* was unworthy of *you*.'

His expression tortured, he pulled her into his arms, buried his face against her neck. She held him, both euphoric that he'd let her in and heartbroken that he'd spent so much of his life lost, trying to make sense of a senseless situation. Her heart clenched for him. He wanted to be a good father, to be nothing like his own. He would always love their child and that would need to be enough for Lola.

Easing away, she popped her seatbelt and forced herself to take an emotional step back. 'Of course, I can't live with you for ever. I'll find my own place again, soon. I might at some point want to go back to Spain. I might one day meet someone and want a serious relationship.' She bravely met his stare, catching sight of the same flicker of fear she'd seen last night when they'd talked about her wanting it all. But his fear was for his relationship with the baby, not for *her*. 'But I promise you we'll always figure out what's best for our baby together, okay?'

They stared at each other for a few moments. Lola emulated him, closing down that part of her that had begun to harbour hope and foolish fantasies. Where she, Xavier and the baby were a real family. But the last thing she wanted was a gloss-covered relationship like the one Nicolás had been offering. If she ever fell in love again, she wanted the grit and fire and chaos of a love that was fearless, bold and mindlessly passionate.

'I'd better go,' she said, placing her hand on the door handle, scared at how close she'd come to falling for him.

'Wait…' he said, resting his hand on her knee. 'I'm sorry, I overreacted earlier. I have no right to tell you what to do.'

Lola nodded, a part of her wishing he'd fight for her, the way she wanted to fight for him. Hungry for all of him. The parts he gave readily, like his loyalty and his protection and his passion, and the parts he held back, like his fears and his dreams and the very heart of him.

But maybe he was truly incapable of letting someone that close. Maybe he was already giving all that he could give and she was just a fool to expect more the way she'd almost made a terrible mistake before. She needed to stop pushing, to protect herself and adjust her expectations, otherwise, she *would* get hurt.

'See you tonight,' she said, leaving the car, the clack of her heels across the concrete of the car park echoing like a bad omen.

# CHAPTER FIFTEEN

THAT WEEKEND, AFTER A lavish state ceremony joining Princess Xiomara de la Rosa to Dr Edmund Butler, Xavier stood stiffly in the great hall of the palace,
where everything glittered and sparkled in celebration
of another joyous royal wedding. All around him, people wore smiles as they mingled and chatted and sipped
champagne. The newlyweds circulated, speaking to their
guests, but Xavier could barely drag his eyes away from
Lola.

She looked stunningly beautiful in a royal blue dress,
her hair artfully pinned up to reveal the elegant slope of
her neck. But she also looked nervous and a little tired.
Royal weddings were an all-day event and they were less
than half way through this one.

Foreign urges swamped him. He wanted to hold her,
to proudly introduce her to the princess, to say something—anything—to stop her slipping through his fingers. Because he felt it.

'I think they're heading this way,' Lola said, stiffening
slightly at his side as she glanced at the beaming bride
and groom.

Without thinking, he rested his hand in the small of
her back and dipped his head to whisper, 'You've met
before. Just be yourself.'

'Don't,' she said quietly, stepping out of his reach so his hand fell away. 'I don't want to fuel any gossip.'

Her stare was imploring, but Xavier winced, his heart thudding painfully, terrifyingly, as it had since the day after he'd returned from London. Something had changed. Lola seemed to be putting more and more distance between them. Her disappointment seemed to taint every gentle word she spoke to him. Her withdrawal ruined every touch and kiss. And he had no right to expect anything else. They weren't a couple. The only promise he'd made her was one of protection. He could try and hold onto her, to give her more, but what if his attempts to let her in and be what she needed still weren't enough? She deserved love. The all-consuming, unconditional, mindless kind.

'We only met briefly,' she said about the princess, her eyes on the couple. Her expression softened. 'She looks so beautiful. And happy.'

Xavier swallowed at the wistfulness in Lola's voice and the resulting spike in his panicked heart rate. Last night, they'd finally had their long overdue talk about the future. Lola had agreed to stay in Castilona until the baby was born. Xavier reiterated that, if she favoured returning to Spain for work or study after her maternity leave, he would relocate there at that point, leaving the estate under its current management.

Their civilised and reasonable talk should have reassured him, but all he'd felt since was growing dread. Fear of losing her jostled with the fear of trying and failing to be the man she deserved. Those fears hounding him no matter how often he made love to her, worshipping her body, pleasuring her into incoherence as if he could fix what he'd broken so she would once more look at him the way she had before everything began to go wrong.

'Xavier,' Princess Xiomara said, holding out her hands as she walked towards him, elegantly trailing her dress and the floor-length veil she wore. Taking his hands, she pulled him close, pressing her cheek to each of his.

When she released him, Xavier bowed at the waist, his sense of duty battling with the need to be alone with Lola. 'Princess, you look breathtaking.'

Xiomara frowned slightly at his use of her title, but she seemed far too happy to be cross with him.

'Congratulations,' he said to them both, shaking Edmund's hand. 'You remember Dr Lola Garcia from *Clinico San Carlos*.'

'Of course,' the princess said warmly, greeting Lola with the same cheek kisses. 'May I present my husband, Dr Edmund Butler, whom of course you've both met before. He wasn't my husband then, but he is now and I like saying it.' She smiled playfully at the man at her side.

'What a beautiful ceremony,' Lola said, her eyes shining with sincerity. 'I hope you'll both be very happy.'

'Thank you,' the princess said as Butler asked Xavier about the medals he wore on his uniform before engaging Lola in talk of the clinic and the new medical director.

'She looks tired,' Xiomara said in a low voice about Lola.

Xavier nodded. 'She's been a little nauseous these past few days.' Guilt added to his other emotions.

'I asked the palace housekeepers to prepare a room for your use, just in case you needed a moment to yourselves,' Xiomara said. 'Perhaps you could take Lola there before the banquet begins so she might have a lie down. These state occasions can feel dreadfully long when you're not the centre of attention.'

She smiled, but because he'd known her so long, he saw the flicker of concern in her eyes.

'Thank you. I'll suggest it to Lola.' A reprieve from the small talk and a moment to themselves might help.

'I know you're not together,' she said, carefully, 'but I must say, you make a very attractive couple. I'm sure that when he or she arrives, my baby nephew or niece will be utterly adorable.' She squeezed Xavier's arm. 'I can't wait.'

Xavier tried to smile, to let her know he appreciated her attempts to make him feel part of the family, but all he could do was nod, his gaze returning to Lola. How would things be between them by the time the baby arrived? Could they find a way to be together? Could he offer her more of a commitment and hope it was enough? The alternative, to let her go, for them to just be friends and parents felt equally terrifying.

'We'll talk later,' Xiomara told him before scooping her arm through her husband's before leading him away to greet more of their guests.

'You have the same eyes,' Lola said when they were once more alone. 'It's obvious now that you two are related.' She looked up at him, the ghost of a sad smile on her lips.

'Is it?' he said, not yet comfortable with such comparisons, which only reminded him of de la Rosa, a man to whom he never wanted to be compared, least of all by Lola. 'We're very different personalities. The princess has always been unapologetically herself, something I've always admired.'

'Yes.' Lola nodded, looking at him appraisingly. 'I'm glad that she found a way to break free of her father's influence. She seems nothing like the man I've heard rumours about.'

Xavier stilled, his heart thudding. He too, of course, was related to the man at the centre of those rumours. Were his past attempts to protect himself, the way he habitually shut people out, Lola included, turning into his worst character flaw? Was Lola now having doubts that he could be a good father to their baby?

'She's had a room prepared, if you'd like to lie down for a while,' he said, his own doubts building at the strange tension between them because he had no idea how to make things right.

Lola nodded. 'That sounds wonderful actually. I should have reconsidered the height of these heels. My feet are killing me.'

'Let's slip away,' he said keeping his hands to himself when every instinct in him wanted to touch her. But that was selfish. She didn't want his touch and didn't belong to him, no matter how badly he wanted her. He'd always respected that she was her own woman. 'Let's find a steward and locate the room,' he said, hoping that after a rest, Lola might seem more herself and he might find the right words to make her stay.

After a nap and a shower in the most lavish bathroom she'd ever experienced, Lola tied the belt of her robe and faced herself in the mirror.

The royal wedding had been everything it should be—traditional, uplifting, romantic. The palace was the most breathtaking venue for a ceremony, every meticulous detail perfection. And Lola should never have agreed to come. Looking down she breathed through the growing hollowness in her chest.

Having witnessed the joy and intimacy of other people's love today, not just the princess and Edmund, but also the King and Queen, who'd proudly each held one of their adorable twins, Lola had finally found the strength to admit to herself that she too had fallen in love. With Xavier.

Dropping her hand to her stomach, she blinked away the tears threatening to fall. She had to be strong for the baby. For herself. And she had to move out of Casa Colina. Tonight. As soon as they left the celebrations. She would move back to her apartment. Find another to rent. Maybe visit her family in Spain and return here strengthened. Ready to face him and pretend.

Opening the bathroom door, she stepped into the bedroom to find Xavier sitting at the window, the room dimly lit with lamplight. The suite prepared for them was on the ground floor, with French doors that opened to the rear gardens. A light breeze made the drapes billow and carried the scent of flowers from outside where the distant lights of coastal towns snaked out of sight around the headland.

'Feeling better?' he asked, holding out his hand for hers, then tugging her into his lap.

'Yes,' she said, the lie coming easily, because to tell the truth would be to ruin, once and for all what they had, not that any of it had been real anyway. She'd simply convinced herself that her heart was safe when the reality was she'd fallen harder than she'd ever before been in love.

Curling into his lap, she buried her face against his neck, wishing she had the strength to leave him now. But he had a formal banquet to get through, followed by dancing and an entire evening of small talk.

Forcing herself to make memories for the tough times ahead when she would miss him as if a part of her soul was lost, she breathed in the scent of his skin, closing her eyes so she could cling to the illusion that he was hers for just a while longer.

'You looked so beautiful today,' he said, his hand stroking her back as she kissed his neck, trailed her tongue up to his earlobe, slipped her hand inside his open dress shirt where his skin burned hot and his heart thudded against her palm.

'Lola…?' he said, growing hard under her lap.

She looked up and saw desire in his dark eyes, but confusion too, as if he had no idea how to interpret her strange mood. But this time, she couldn't help him. Her strength was just enough to make it through the rest of the day in his company and then leave.

'I want you,' she said, capturing his lips, kissing him, darting out her tongue to meet his when he opened his mouth. She wanted him, as always, but she also wanted more. She wanted him to love her as deeply as she loved him. She wanted the two of them to have it all—this connection she hadn't been able to fight, a family of their own and endless, passionate love.

Scared that those three little words might escape her lips, ruining the last few hours they had left together, she reached for the belt of his trousers. If this was the only part of him she could have, the only part of him she'd ever had, she would take it. Anything to delay, for a little longer, the inevitable end.

He groaned under her kisses. One arm around her waist, he slid his other hand along her leg and up her thigh under her robe. She tangled her fingers in his hair, kissing him harder as he delved between her legs where she was bare. Where she ached.

'Xavier,' she gasped as she stroked her. Then she twisted on his lap, sat astride his thighs, her back to the window and loosened the belt of her robe.

The fabric parted and his stare darkened as he took in her nakedness, his eyes devouring her the way they always had, as if he couldn't stop himself from touching. He cupped both her breasts, his thumbs rubbing her nipples into peaks. She moaned, thrust her chest forwards where he captured one nipple in his mouth and sucked.

'I need you,' she said, attacking his fly in earnest. He raised his hips and together they shoved down his trousers and underwear. Lola gripped him in her hand, tugging, stroking until his hands gripped her hips and he crushed her closer, as lost as she to this fire they generated.

She raised herself onto her knees then slowly sank onto him, tossing her head back as he filled her making her feel whole because she loved him. 'Xavier...'

His head was bent, his tongue lashing her nipple once more. She clung to his shoulders, rocking her hips, trying to ease the burning need inside. He held her hips, thrusting up into her so every stroke hit where she needed. All the reasons she must walk away from him, from this, fled her mind. Replaced by only pleasure, rightness and a longing that this could last for ever if only he'd open his heart to her.

She clung to his shoulders, crying out into the night as her orgasm struck. But still she couldn't let go, her arms banding around him as she rode wave after wave of spasms, as he stiffened, holding her just as tight and groaned his climax against her chest, their hearts thundering side by side.

'I love you,' she whispered into his hair, the words slipping out during an unguarded moment of euphoria.

He froze. His ragged breathing the only movement he made. His silence the ultimate withdrawal.

Realising her mistake, Lola untangled herself from him and stood, tying the robe closed over her nakedness.

'I'm sorry,' she said, bitterly. 'I know that's the last thing you probably want to hear...' How could she have been so stupid?

Xavier stood and zipped up his fly. His appearance dishevelled. His stare haunted. 'I...' He speared a hand through his hair and turned away from her as if he couldn't bear the way she was looking at him.

'I can't hide it any more,' she said refusing to diminish her feelings. 'I shouldn't have to hide it. I don't want to. I love you, Xavier, like I've never loved anyone else.'

He stood stiffly, silently, his back to her.

'I know it wasn't part of the plan,' she said. 'But I just realised it today, at the wedding. The bride and groom are so in love. I looked over at you during the ceremony and it hit me.'

He paced behind the chair they'd just vacated then paced back. 'What do you want me to do...to say?' he asked, looking lost like a scared child. He really had no idea.

Lola crossed her arms over her waist. 'Nothing. I guess I just hoped that you might have feelings for me in return. But I can see from your face that you don't.'

He gripped her arms, forced her to meet his stare. 'I *do* have feelings for you. I've never felt this way about anyone. Ever. I care about you. I want you to be happy. I want to protect you—'

'But you don't love me,' she said flatly. 'Not the way I love you.' She stood taller, stiffening her spine and her resolve to leave. Now. Before the pain worsened and destroyed her.

'Lola…'

'It's okay.' She shook her head, scared to hear what he had to say or wouldn't say. 'You don't have to make any excuses. But I need to leave Casa Colina. Tonight. I can't stay any longer.'

He dropped his hands, his handsome face slack with shock. 'No. It's late. Let's get through the banquet, go home and sleep on it. Talk about this in the morning.'

Lola marched to the bed where she'd left her change of clothes in her overnight bag. 'I can't. I need space.'

She pulled on clean underwear, threw on the dress she'd worn for the ceremony and reception and tossed the robe inside the bag, desperate to get away.

'You're leaving now? Leaving the wedding?'

'I'm sorry. I have to go. You'll be fine without me.' She hunted down her shoes and slid her feet inside. If she didn't get away from him soon, she was going to cry and beg him to love her.

'Lola… This is crazy. Wait.'

'It *is* crazy,' she said, all her frustration and heartache spilling free. 'I'm crazily in love with you. I want to fight for you and spend the rest of my life with you and raise a family with you and you have no idea what I'm feeling because you've kept your emotions under lock down and kept me out.'

'That's not true,' he said reaching for her again, his arms falling to his sides when she stepped back. 'I let you in. I've never let anyone else know me the way you do. I've told you things… We're having a baby. We agreed to raise it together. To make this work and now you're just walking out?'

'I'm sorry,' she said, tears finally falling. 'I want more.'

'Your independence?' he asked frowning.

She laughed hollowly, desolate that he had no idea how she felt. 'No. More of you, Xavier.'

'I…' His stare grew stormy. 'I gave you everything Lola. You pushed and kept on pushing and I gave you as much as I could. I told you about my fears of fatherhood. I shared my past with you, things I've never shared with anyone.'

'I know you tried. I know it's all you're capable of giving me and I wish it was enough. It would be so much easier, hurt so much less, if it were enough. I'm not blaming you.'

'But it's not enough?' he said, his voice dead.

'No.' She forced herself to be strong. 'I want it all. I wanted it all with you, but now I see that's not possible. That I've just made another mistake.'

'I… I don't know what more I can do.'

His words slashed her like knives. 'You can let me go. You can give me a few days to sort myself out. I need space.'

'But the baby…' he pleaded, his stare falling to her stomach.

'It's not about the baby. I promised we would raise the baby together and we will. But I can't stay loving you and knowing that you only want me around because I'm carrying your child.'

'That's not true. I…'

Unable to stay a second longer, she scooped up her bag. 'I'll be at my apartment. Please, if you care about me as you say you do, give me a few days. Then we'll talk.'

Without a backward glance, she fled.

# CHAPTER SIXTEEN

TWO DAYS LATER, the crackle of static from the walkie talkie on his desk snapped Xavier out of the trance he'd existed in since Lola had left him that night of the royal wedding. He snatched it up, his heart rate spiking with adrenaline and hope. Had she changed her mind and come back to Casa Colina? Had she decided that he was enough for her after all?

'Princess Xiomara is on her way,' Marco's voice said through the walkie talkie.

Xavier's stomach fell. Hope a wisp of smoke, gone in a second. Of course Lola wouldn't have come back to him. She'd told him that she loved him and he'd let her go, scared to open his mouth and explain everything he was feeling. Flailing because she deserved it all, everything she wanted, and he knew nothing about romantic love.

'Thank you,' Xavier replied, too bereft to wonder why the princess was there when she must be about to leave for her honeymoon.

Dragging himself to his feet, he ran a hand over his face and the two days' worth of scruff, wondering just how haggard he appeared and if Xiomara would notice. With Lola gone and Xavier once more alone at Casa Colina, time had lost its meaning. The estate work waiting for his attention went undone. Tired of throwing his untouched meals in the bin, Tia had stopped cooking for him. And sleep…forget it. He spent all night staring at the walls of his study, his mind a confusing swirl of regret, frustration and fear.

Just as he made it to the hall, Princess Xiomara arrived, a flurry of energy and floaty fabric, waving off her security guard as she breezed Xavier's way, arms outstretched.

'I came to thank you for everything you did at the wedding,' she said, embracing him with a double cheek kiss.

Xavier stiffened, too bereft to conceal his reaction to being hugged. Too confused to do more than stand and stare.

'Shouldn't you be with your new husband?' he asked at last.

'We're leaving soon, for our honeymoon…' the princess said, '…but I wanted to say *ciao*. Who knows when we might see each other next. Although I expect you to stay in touch.'

Xavier led her inside to the living room, where Tia had pointlessly flung open the French doors to let in the warm, fragrant air of a perfect sunny day.

'I always loved this house,' Xiomara said, glancing around appreciatively. She stepped around in a graceful arc, her fingers gliding over cushions, a marble topped table, the framed photo of Xavier with his army unit. 'Although I only stayed here a handful of summers. But I love what you've done with it even more. It seems so much lighter than I remember.'

'The décor was a little dark for my taste,' he said woodenly. 'Plus, back then, I planned to sell the place, so I was redecorating to appeal to potential buyers.'

And now that Lola had moved out, he knew he

wouldn't be able to stay for much longer. He saw her in every room, on every piece of furniture. Her playful smile, her challenging quips, her delighted laughter and her looks of what he now realised was love.

Xavier swallowed, sickened, choked by the realisation of what he'd had for one terrifying, euphoric second when she'd said those words and what he'd thrown away by being too scared to be as open as she needed him to be. Too scared to offer himself to her, flaws and all, and hope that he was enough.

'I know how you must have struggled with the lies and the betrayal and the hurt of the past,' Xiomara said in her forthright way.

She was much like Lola, this half-sister of his.

'But I think you might be the second best thing our father ever did,' she finished, turning to him, her eyes bright.

Xavier frowned, unable to address her compliment or the way she'd said *our father*, as if she truly considered him a sibling.

'What was the best thing?' he asked on a croak around the lump in his throat.

She pressed her hand to her chest and batted her eyes. 'Me, of course.' Then she fell serious once more. 'I can see that something bad has happened to you since we were last together.'

Xavier ducked his head, lacking the words to even begin to explain what he'd done or hadn't done, which was worse. He should have fought harder to keep Lola. He should have somehow found the right words to tell her how he felt. He should have begged her to stay.

'If you want advice from a wise little sister...' she said, '...here it is. Whatever you've done, fix it.'

His stare met hers, his body frozen with grief and indecision. Could he fix it? Was he capable? Could he say something to win Lola back?

'Don't throw it all away because that might seem like the least painful option,' the princess went on. 'It won't be.'

She might have meant the estate, the title, the wealth, but Xavier had a sneaking suspicion she meant Lola. It seemed female intuition was universal among the women of his life.

'Love is everything,' she said quietly, the truth of her words shining in her eyes. 'You'll soon learn that when your son or daughter arrives, as our cousin Tavi has learned it.'

Xavier stayed silent. Lola's accusations that he wanted her only for their child, slaying him anew. Even if there was no baby, he would feel this way, as if he'd never be the same again, because she was gone.

'What use is anything else in life, if you don't have someone to share it with?' Xiomara said, once more glancing around the beautiful home that meant nothing to him, not without Lola.

Xavier swallowed, aware that a response might be polite. 'Spoken like a true newly-wed,' he said, trying to smile while his heart cracked into pieces.

'Of course, it's not just anyone,' the princess continued, 'it's that special person who feels like home, no matter where the wind takes you.'

Xavier sucked in a breath, the princess's words striking at the heart of him. Lola was home. Without her this place was just like any other place, just stone and mortar. A shell. Or a cage. And Xavier didn't want to be trapped alone, missing her, aching for her, safe but bereft.

Because *she* was his place of belonging. *She* was the home he'd been searching for his whole adult life. She was *everything*. And he'd let her walk away because he'd been scared and desperate to protect himself.

'Lola is an impressive woman,' Xiomara said softly, as if aware of the chaos inside him, as if he were indeed made of glass. 'I hope you find a way to make your little family work.'

Xavier snapped out of his trance. Xiomara was leaving. She would take her female intuition and wisdom with her and he still needed to know how to fix it with Lola.

'How…? What…?' He swallowed and tried to get the question out. 'What does it feel like? How do you know it's enough?'

Xiomara raised her eyebrows, a small smile playing on her lips. 'Love?'

Xavier nodded.

'It feels like you look,' she said sympathetically. 'As if you're at the centre of a terrible storm, but you've never been more ecstatically alive.'

Xavier exhaled the breath he'd been holding, his body sagging with exhaustion. So this, the way he'd been feeling for weeks but denying, was love?

'I know…' Xiomara said. 'It's wonderful, isn't it?'

*Wonderful?* Xavier shook his head, feeling as if he might pass out. He'd already loved Lola but he'd let her go, too scared to say the words.

'Does she love you, too?' she whispered, perhaps sensing how close he was to utterly breaking down.

He nodded. 'She did. But…' He'd failed her, his love too little, too late. She'd finally seen through him and found him lacking as he'd feared.

'It's not too late to tell her how you feel,' Xiomara said.

He looked up sharply. 'Isn't it? How can you be sure?'

'She's having your baby, Xavier. She's been living here with you. She's put her career on hold to make this, the three of you as a family, work.'

He nodded, restless energy boiling inside him. He needed to go to Lola now. To tell her he loved her back and beg her to give him another chance, because without her, he couldn't breathe.

'I have to go,' Xiomara said. 'Remember, if you ever need anything, I expect you to reach out to your only sister, first and foremost.'

Xavier took her hands in his when she offered them.

'I'll see you soon,' she said, once more pressing her cheeks to his. 'Don't see me out. I don't do goodbyes, so *cuídate*,' she said, sweeping towards the hall as she waved over her shoulder.

And just like that, Xavier was once more alone with the knowledge that, through his own fear and inaction, he might have lost the best thing that had ever happened to him and his only chance to be happy.

# CHAPTER SEVENTEEN

FROM HER SUN-FILLED KITCHEN, Lola abandoned her untouched and now cold tea and sighed. The movers were arriving later today to put all her worldly possessions into storage. Now that she'd left Xavier and Casa Colina, left behind a relationship that was going nowhere, her life was supposed to be getting back on track. Her feelings for him dying. Except her restlessness, the certainty that she would love him for ever, grew stronger, hour by hour.

Needing to hear a friendly voice, she called Isla. The call connected and the hollowness inside her expanded as she wished more than anything, that her sister was there, in the flesh.

'Are you okay?' Isla asked, as instinctively in tune with her twin as ever, as if they shared an emotional barometer.

'I'm in love,' Lola said with a wince, her throat aching with unshed tears. 'And it's over.'

'Oh, *manita*… I'm sorry,' Isla said. 'Tell me what happened.'

Lola recounted the events of the day of the wedding, the moment she'd realised she'd fallen deeply in love with the father of her baby and he didn't love her back.

'I had to leave,' she said, recalling the look of hurt and devastation on Xavier's face when she'd told him her feelings. 'I couldn't do it any longer. Pretend. I can't love him, live with him and have no more than the thing I threw away when I was nineteen. A loveless relationship where he wants me only for the baby. Only so his massive house doesn't feel so empty. For appearances. He doesn't want *me*.'

'Did he say he doesn't love you?' Isla asked cautiously.

'No. He didn't have to.' Doubts chipped away at her memories of how he'd looked that night. 'He can't love anyone, or won't. He won't let me in.' Lola dropped her head into her hand, the look on his face when she'd told him he wasn't enough for her haunting her still. 'I can't believe I'm back here, in love with someone who doesn't love me in return. In love with someone who only wants me for the way I make his life better.' Except the situations were different. She'd hadn't loved Nicolás the way she loved Xavier.

'Is he scared?' Isla asked.

'Probably. And I get it, you know. I'm scared too. I thought I was in love with Nicolás, but that was just childish infatuation. Nothing close to the way I feel about Xavier. I mean I'm having his baby. We worked together. We were sleeping together and living together. What did he expect me do, if not fall for him?'

'What are *you* scared of?' Isla whispered, the beats of silence after her question making Lola's pulse throb in her temples.

'I guess I was scared of making another mistake. Of loving him so hard, that I would lose myself. That I'd become nothing more than part of a couple when I've always had bigger dreams.'

'Would that be so bad?' Isla challenged. 'To be a part of a couple with the man you love? To be part of a family with the man you love? You've always wanted what Mamá and Papá have. Ask yourself, which regret would be the biggest?' Isla pushed. 'That you never had your career or that you never knew the kind of love you're in right now?'

Lola gasped softly, certain of the answer, feeling stupid that with a bit of distance and some wisdom from the only other person who knew her so well, everything suddenly made sense. She didn't have to choose because she could have both. She didn't have to be scared she'd become something intolerable because she made good decisions. She didn't have to run away from her fears. She could embrace them and risk everything, knowing the reward was worth it.

'It's not even as if he forced me to choose,' she told Isla. 'He'd never do that, never expect me to be something I'm not. He wants me to be safe and happy…'

'Sounds to me like he is in love with you. Maybe he just hasn't realised it, or maybe he just struggles to talk about his feelings.'

'He does.' Lola nodded, her eyes stinging with tears. 'He's scared that he can't love because his father rejected him and he doesn't belong. But he *does* belong. With *me*.'

'Did you tell him that?' Isla asked.

Lola stood and paced, too restless to sit. 'No…not exactly. I told him I loved him then I said his best wasn't enough for me and ran away.'

An uncomfortable moment of silence passed where hot shame washed over Lola. She'd hurt him too, rejected him out of her own fear. Instead of sitting down with him and calmly confessing her feelings, giving him a chance to assimilate them and respond.

'You asked me what he expected of you,' Isla said, 'but I think you already know the answer to that question.'

'He expected me to reject him,' Lola whispered, scrunching her eyes closed as if she could obliterate the image of Xavier's pain. 'Oh no…' What had she done…? 'I'm sorry. Can I call you later? I have to go.' She jerked to her feet.

'Then stop talking to me and go and get the life you want, the way you always have.'

'I love you,' Lola said. 'Thanks for listening.'

'You're welcome.'

Then Lola ran.

The only place Xavier could think to look for Lola when there was no response at her apartment, was the *Clinico San Carlos*. He reasoned she might have loose ends to tie up. Only no one there had seen her, nor were they expecting her given that she was no longer an employee.

As he drove back towards Casa Colina, his gut churning with impotence, frantic that she might have already gone to Spain while he'd been wallowing, he broke the promise he'd made to her and dialled her number. She'd begged him for space. But he couldn't let her go another second thinking that he was done fighting for her, for them.

After two rings, the call connected. He almost sobbed with relief. 'Lola, where are you? I need to speak to you. I know I said I'd give you space but…' His throat closed, all the feelings he'd repressed fighting to be set free.

'I'm on my way back,' she said. 'I've just pulled through the gates. I'll be with you in two minutes.'

'You're at Casa Colina?' he asked, his brain sluggish but hope choking him.

'Yes,' she said urgently.

'Stay there,' he said, his heart in his throat. 'Don't leave. I'm not at home but I'll be right behind you.'

He tore along the coastal road, impatiently waiting for the gates to his property to open. Then with a final skid of gravel, he sped down the drive, leaving the engine running and the car door open in his haste to get to Lola.

He found her in the kitchen with Tia, who took one look at Xavier and discreetly left the room.

'You came back,' he said, stepping forward, his arms aching to hold her and never let her go again.

She nodded, her eyes wary. 'I should never have left. I'm sorry, Xavier.'

'Why?' He frowned, confused, overwhelmed by his feelings, which were surely too big for any man to survive. 'I'm the one who needs to apologise.'

She shook her head. 'No, *I* do. I told you that you weren't enough when you are. You're everything I want.'

'Lola—'

'No. I should have given you time. I should have told you that it's okay to not have the answers. That I'm scared too.'

'I'm only scared of losing you.' He gripped her shoulders, his hands restlessly caressing them to make sure she was real. 'I don't just want you for the baby. I don't just want you to help me run this estate. I'd live anywhere as long as it's with you.'

Lola placed her hands on top of his, her stare awash with tears. 'Xavier…'

'Please let me speak.' He cupped her face. 'I'm sorry it took me so long to recognise what was going on inside me. I'm sorry that I kept you out and hurt you, because I was so scared that you would see something in me that was unlovable. I was scared that I'd try to love you and it wouldn't be enough. But I know now, what this feeling is.' He pressed his fist to his breastbone. 'I already love you, Lola. I have for weeks. I love you. *You* are where I belong. *You* are my family. You and the baby. I never want to be anywhere else but at your side. Wherever that is.'

Tears spilled over her lashes and he dragged her into his arms. His heart recognising the rhythm of hers, breathing in the scent of her, coming home.

'You don't have to say it back,' she said, looking up at him. 'It's okay to be confused.'

'I'm no longer confused. And it's true. I love you. It's like you said. When you know it's right, you want to fight for it. Give it everything you have. I know this is right. *You* are right. You are the person I'll love for the rest of my life and I don't want to be without you for another second.'

Then he kissed her.

From the courtyard, Lola snuggled closer into Xavier's side as they watched the sun set over the bay. The sky streaked with pink and orange. Her heart finally whole.

'Will you stay?' he asked, one hand holding hers, their fingers entwined, the other stroking her back.

'Of course,' she said, never wanting to be anywhere else but in his arms.

'Not at Casa Colina, but with me,' he looked down at her, his dark eyes gleaming with the feelings she'd waited so long to see. 'For ever?'

'Yes,' she replied, pressing her lips to his. 'I love you. I'll never leave you ever again.'

He cupped her face, his stare intense. 'You know I'd love you even if there was no baby, don't you? You know that I love the woman you are, just as you are and never want you to be anything but yourself?'

She nodded, desperate not to cry again.

'I'm sorry that I protected myself so well,' he went on. 'That I almost ruined the best thing that's ever happened to me. You. The thing I've been searching for my entire life. Belonging.'

'And I'm sorry...' she whispered, '...that I compared what we have with the things of my past. This, us, my love for you. It's everything I want. It's the thing that's been missing from my life. The thing I've felt restless for. *You* are what's been missing and you will always be enough.'

He took her hand, pressed a kiss to the centre of her palm and then pressed her hand over his heart. 'I'm yours. And now that I've found you, now that I've woken up and realised I'm not broken or unlovable, I'm never letting you go.'

She leaned close and kissed him, her love swelling inside her so he was all she saw, all she needed. Their kissing turned heated, the urgency of every touch and caress building until there was only one way to contain the fire—with their passion.

'Hold on,' Xavier said as he gripped her thighs and stood, carrying her.

She wrapped her arms and legs around him as he headed upstairs, laying her down against the cool linens of his bed where he slowly stripped her, caressing every inch of her body with his hands and kisses and flicks of his tongue and they loved each other all night long to seal the promises they'd made.

# EPILOGUE

*Two years later*

HAND IN HAND with Xavier, as the sun set on a stunning late summer's day, Lola trailed behind their dark-haired toddler as they walked between the Casa Colina vines, inspecting the grapes for the upcoming harvest.

'I think it will be a good year,' Xavier said, plucking a fat black grape from the vine and pressing it to Lola's lips for her to taste, his stare, as always, full of love and passion.

In the two years since they'd made Casa Colina their permanent home, Xavier had attended university to learn all about viticulture and loved showing off his new talents.

She parted her lips, smiling as the sweetness of the fruit burst on her tongue. Then, with one eye on Gabriel, who'd they'd named after the storm that had brought them together, she wrapped her arms around Xavier's shoulders and pressed her body as close to him as possible given the constraints of her heavily pregnant belly.

'Every year with you is a good one. A gift.' She brushed her lips over his, smiling when his hands spread over her ribs, clutching her to him as he groaned softly into their kiss.

The baby nestled between them chose that moment to stretch and kick and they laughed together, breaking apart but holding hands.

Xavier dropped his other hand to her belly and rested it over their daughter, who was due any day now. 'She agrees with me about the vintage,' he said with a smile.

'Maybe wine making will be in her blood.' She smiled at him indulgently because they'd made a good life for themselves, supporting each other's dreams and ambitions. Lola had gone back to work part time after Gabriel was born and she planned to squeeze in that master's degree when her current maternity leave came to an end.

'What about Mira?' he asked, expectantly, suggesting another name for the baby because they'd yet to decide on one. 'Mamá said that was what she'd planned to call me, if I'd been a girl.'

'Oh… I like that.' She held his hand and they continued their evening walk, strolling behind Gabriel who toddled ahead, finding joy in every blade of grass, every fluttering insect and simply the sheer act of running.

'Depending on where you're from…' Xavier said, '…it means wonder, or ocean, or a female ruler.' He scooped up a giggling Gabriel into his arms and kissed their son's chubby angelic cheek, holding him out to Lola so she could do the same.

'Now I definitely like it,' she said, loving him harder because, as she'd predicted, he was a wonderful father. His capacity for love and patience seemingly endless.

'One to think about then,' he said. 'Right, young man, time for bed. You have a play date with your cousins tomorrow.'

Gabriel was regularly invited to play with his royal cousins, Princes Rafael and Rodrigo, at the palace. Like

Lola, Queen Phoebe was expecting again and Princess Xiomara was also pregnant with her first child. Their family, the next generation of de la Rosas, was growing and Xavier finally seemed comfortable with his place in it. Although whether they attended the grandest palace ball or a private afternoon tea with the princess, he always had one eye on the security.

Of course, Lola loved that about him, as much as she loved every other part of him and always would.

\* \* \* \* \*

*If you missed the previous story in the
Royally Tempted trilogy, then check out*

Forbidden Fling with the Princess *by Amy Andrews*

*And if you enjoyed this story, check out these other
great reads from JC Harroway*

The Midwife's Secret Fling
Secretly Dating the Baby Doc
Nurse's Secret Royal Fling
Her Secret Valentine's Baby

*All available now!*

# MILLS & BOON®

## Coming next month

### RISKING HIS HEART FOR THE ER DOC
Traci Douglass

'Remember, team. Secure knots mean the difference between a successful rescue and… Well, let's just say we all prefer happy endings here,' he said, earning chuckles from the group. 'All right. Everyone ready to start?'

Andy avoided Jules's gaze as he moved among the team, double-checking their equipment himself to ensure they were all fastened properly. 'Good. Let's start the simulation.'

'Excuse me, Dr MacDonald?' Jules asked from behind him, and Andy closed his eyes, taking a deep breath for fortitude. 'Could you double-check my alpine butterfly loop again, please? It's been a while since I've done one and I want to make sure I have it correct.'

Andy took another breath then stepped back in front of her, his gaze fixed on the knot as his fingers brushed hers and that odd spark that always seemed to happen whenever she was close flared to life inside him again. He snuffed it out fast. He'd put all that behind him a long time ago. He didn't want to bring it into the present now. Especially since she was on the team and also starting in the ER at Teton Memorial, which meant they'd be seeing more of each other there, too. And he knew personally what a bad idea it was to get involved with a colleague in any way beyond strictly professional.

*Continue reading*

**RISKING HIS HEART FOR THE ER DOC**
Traci Douglass

*Available next month*
millsandboon.co.uk

# COMING SOON!

We really hope you enjoyed reading this book.
If you're looking for more romance
be sure to head to the shops when
new books are available on

## Thursday 25th September

To see which titles are coming soon, please visit
**millsandboon.co.uk/nextmonth**

---

# MILLS & BOON

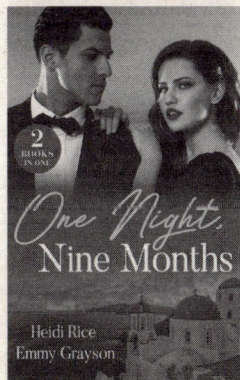

# afterglow BOOKS

Afterglow Books is a trend-led, trope-filled list of books with diverse, authentic and relatable characters, a wide array of voices and representations, plus real world trials and tribulations. Featuring all the tropes you could possibly want (think small-town settings, fake relationships, grumpy vs sunshine, enemies to lovers) and all with a generous dose of spice in every story.

♪ @millsandboonuk
◎ @millsandboonuk
afterglowbooks.co.uk

#AfterglowBooks

**For all the latest book news, exclusive content and giveaways scan the QR code below to sign up to the Afterglow newsletter:**

SCAN ME

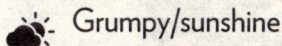

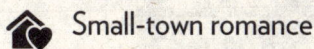

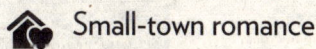

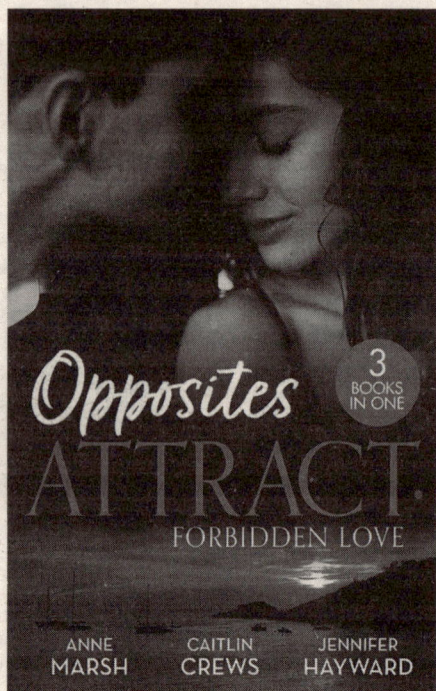

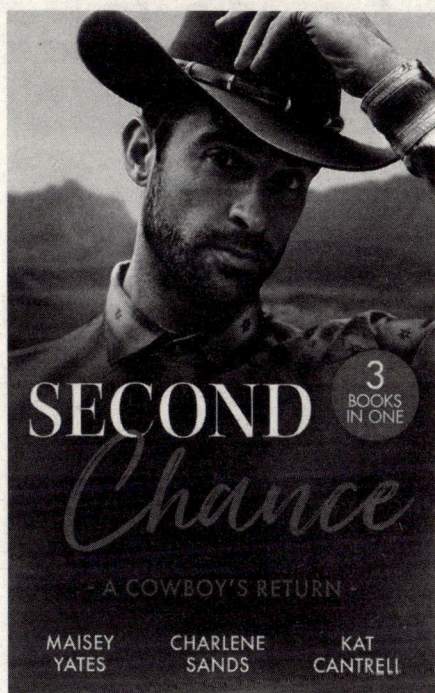

# LET'S TALK

## Romance

For exclusive extracts, competitions and special offers, find us online:

**f**  MillsandBoon

**X**  @MillsandBoon

**⊙**  @MillsandBoonUK

**♪**  @MillsandBoonUK

Get in touch on 01413 063 232